In Ascension

Also by Martin MacInnes

Gathering Evidence
Infinite Ground

In Ascension

Martin MacInnes

Black Cat
New York

First published in 2023 in the United Kingdom by Atlantic Books, an imprint of Atlantic Books Ltd.

Printed in the United States of America

First Grove Atlantic paperback edition: February 2024

Library of Congress Cataloging-in-Publication data is available for this title.

ISBN 978-0-8021-6346-2
eISBN 978-0-8021-6347-9

Black Cat
an imprint of Grove Atlantic
154 West 14th Street
New York, NY 10011

Distributed by Publishers Group West

groveatlantic.com

24 25 26 27 10 9 8 7 6 5 4 3 2 1

CONTENTS

In Ascension

PART ONE

Endeavour

ONE

I was born in the lowest part of the country, 22 feet beneath the sea. When my sister arrived three years later we moved south into the city proper, Rotterdam's northern district. The land was newly excavated, freshly claimed from the seafloor, dredged by ships and reinforced by concrete. Parts of the street came loose, the ground underneath still soft. I remember burning incense, a brackish smell indoors, as if every moment were a spell, a scene that had to be called into being.

The river beach was artificial, and when we walked over it I imagined underneath us was a hollow area, a huge chasm. We went there on weekends and on holidays, my father paying careful attention to the tides, never settling in one place but marching from one direction to another. I poured sand into my plastic bucket, compacted it, upturned it, did it again and again. 'Don't dig too deep,' my father warned, before turning his vigilance back to the water.

In the Second World War, the centre of Rotterdam – the historic old town – was entirely destroyed. My parents' memories, growing up, were of wide spaces, broad avenues, wind that whipped in from the ports. They could see further because so many fixtures had been levelled. They showed me photographs printed on small sheets of white card with large black borders. The scenes were cloudy, dirt filled, and everything – from the remaining buildings to the figures caught walking between them – seemed smaller, lower. This reassured me, indicating that the world was growing, still in a state of creation. Maybe one day it would be finished. Rotterdam's skyline – powered by glowing refineries lining the huge port – now resembled Manhattan, a forest of steel, chrome and glass. One Sunday afternoon when I was five years old my spade sliced through the sand and clanged against the concrete underneath. The impact fizzed across my nerves, leaving me light-headed. It wasn't real. I will never forget the look of horror my father directed at me. I'd ruined something, the look said. I'd pierced the illusion and now I had to pay.

My mother, Fenna, came from the north, the only child of a nurse and a factory worker, both of whom died – her mother of cancer, her father of an unspecified illness shortly after – when she was starting university. It was tempting to see mathematics – her passion, her life's work – as a consolation, an escape from reality that could hide under the guise of a confrontation, but as Erika, Fenna's first cousin, said, that just wasn't true. Fenna had always been interested. Not just interested – captivated, obsessed. She was a shy, withdrawn child, who rarely spoke unprompted and who was so accustomed to positioning herself around a book – hands gripping it, eyes gazing at it, knees raised in support of it –

that she seemed incomplete without one.

She never attempted to describe what she did, an unhelpful habit I'd perhaps picked up myself. Though she spent most of her life at the university, she was never a teacher, an explainer. Mathematics wasn't about communicating, passing something between people; it was purer, closer to music, an act of revelation. The titles I glimpsed on her shelves – *Philosophy of Cusp Forms*; *Projectile Transformations*; *Hyperbolic Motion*; *Ultraparallel Theorem* – were like convex surfaces; I ran my hands over them without getting any closer to the substance underneath. On one spine was an infinity symbol, two loops running into each other endlessly, with no accompanying title. I couldn't see what she did all day, couldn't imagine what she thought of all her life. If Fenna could speak the language that she thought in, the sound would be like nothing in the world.

She frequently suffered migraines, lying in a room of her own, eyes closed, wet white handkerchief spread over her brow. During these episodes, the tension inside her spilled throughout the house. Our father, Geert, patrolled the building, ensuring we never raised our voices, never opened or closed a door, never turned on our computer. He would glare at me for even thinking too loudly. He liked this, taking care of Fenna as a form of discipline. It gave him purpose and occupation. If anything, it was more awkward after she recovered, in those brief periods where, having lost the roles

we were trained in, none of us knew what to do. I'm certain
Fenna exaggerated her symptoms, or at least prolonged them
sometimes. Her episodes put a barrier around her, gave her
space, time alone. No more questions, no explanations
necessary. But mainly it would be for Geert, making him feel
useful, giving him a role, distracting him, and thus protecting
us, from the more volatile parts of his personality.

There were two sources of violence in my childhood, and
one of them was growth itself. My bones lengthened in
sudden, dramatic spurts. Nights could be agony, unbearable
pain throbbing through my legs. I'd go months without a
full sleep. I had nightmares of a miniature industry working
beneath my skin, rebuilding me, leaving me outside as
a stranded and helpless observer. I sweated, sometimes
vomited, from the sheer strangeness of the experience. And
yet through all this Fenna was there for me, able to put aside
her own suffering. I didn't have to call for her, didn't have
to make a sound, she somehow sensed when I needed her,
and she came. She soothed me, pushing the damp hair from
my forehead, pressing her hands onto my thighs and calves,
gripping them, digging into the flesh, then rhythmically
massaging up and down, grappling with the pain and trying
to shape it into something manageable. I remember looking
up and seeing her standing by the foot of the bed, and at
first failing to recognise who she was. There was a wildness
in her as she pushed into my limbs with force. She pushed

again and again, with rhythm and discipline, while I tried to remain quiet, tears appearing not from the pain but in gratitude for the first startling signs of its relief. As she stood above me, in the dark, she almost seemed a part of me. I wonder if she enjoyed this – the fact that I needed her, the sense that we were joined. We had never been this close. We never spoke on these occasions – I wouldn't have been able to, had I tried. She made strange, soft, bird-like fluttering sounds, trying to soothe me, the last sounds I heard before falling asleep.

I measured myself by tape every evening – wary of marking the walls – and noted the discrepancies in the morning. It used to frighten me, the knowledge that this power came from within, that there was something inherent in my body furling out like this. It was like my full adult shape had been prepared, condensed, knotted into a fine ball at birth and left to slowly open out. I was daunted – I wasn't sure I could do this on my own, but with my mother there, in the night, not just overseeing me but directing me as I grew, and changed, I knew I didn't have to, knew I wasn't really alone at all. When I took my first slow and unsteady steps in the morning, setting myself down on the kitchen bench with the table before me and the wall at my back, Fenna looked at me with simple gratitude and pleasure. It meant something to me – the evidence that my appearance had made her happy, the proof that she really wanted me, after everything.

———

Geert had only ever wanted one thing – to be an architect. He was intent on this as a child, and studied towards it. But something went wrong, and his entrance exams were a disaster. His performance in those exams was so woeful, he had forgone the possibility of ever repeating them. He had blown his one chance, and he never got over this. It was only long after I left home that I heard about these ambitions, and how they'd been thwarted; he never said anything to me. It was Erika who filled me in again. She didn't know the full story herself, but hinted that nerves were a problem, that Geert had suffered from crippling anxiety.

And so Geert, who had only ever wanted to be an architect, to build things on the land and to see accumulation, had ended up doing the one thing he expressly didn't want to do, the same work his forebears had done: he went to sea. Initially, like his father and grandfather, he worked on Atlantic trawlers, away for months at a stretch. He made this decision, if I've worked out the timeline correctly, almost as soon as he failed the entrance exams, as if he'd wanted to punish himself, feel the sting of the freezing salt air on skin sliced raw from the thick ropes. He did this for years, lasting longer than many, and saved a considerable amount of money. Somehow, then, inexplicably, he met Fenna.

They collided on the street, at night, falling into one

another. He was intoxicated, he had come from a bar, and he was aghast, mortified at his clumsiness. They spent the next twenty-four hours together. Afterwards, he was changed. He was obsessed, he couldn't think about anything else. Overnight he became a different person. He was filled with purpose, potency. He couldn't bear to be away from Fenna. Going to sea was a desertion, a disaster. Jealousy and paranoia ate at him on the ship. He was as surprised as anyone that Fenna – dark, sophisticated, beautiful – had shown an interest in him, and he taunted himself – it had all been some dream, surely. Coming ashore, he made a rash, emotional decision, something completely unlike him: he vowed never to go back to the ship. Though Fenna was sure to come to her senses soon, and to want nothing more to do with him, he had to leave open the slim possibility they might continue to see each other, might even – he almost couldn't bear to think it – build a future together. That day, he made two phone calls, one to his port agent and the other to the woman he would spend the rest of his life with.

It's all there – the sea, the mysterious woman, the chance encounter that transforms two lives. The fact that cliché is the only way I have found to talk about it is, I think, proof of just how inexplicable and unjustifiable – and how much of a mistake – their union was.

As it turned out, Geert hadn't actually left the sea entirely. He would continue working there, indirectly, for almost four decades, until finally, in some anonymous, sparse water board office, his lungs gave out for good, and he died.

Geert's great-grandfather, on his father's side, had worked for the Dutch East India Company, the VOC, in its dying throes. His father in turn had also worked for the VOC, as had his father – or so the story goes. Johannes, Geert's father, liked to tell stories about the adventures of our forebears. I remember Fenna's blank smile as the old man went on – she didn't believe a word of it. The VOC, Johannes said, was the beginning of the modern age, the invention that made all this – he gestured through the windows at the Rotterdam skyline – possible. Launched in 1602, it was the world's first publicly listed company. It had all the powers of the state. Its fleet of ships travelled the world, signing treaties, making enemies and allies, executing prisoners, colonising whole countries. The VOC even minted its own coins. Johannes told us great adventure stories set in distant Indian Ocean islands, of castaways and buried treasure and amazing discoveries, and my sister and I were captivated. These stories, which were so exciting and dramatic, made our own lives seem dull and unremarkable. But Johannes said none of these adventures would have been possible had the Netherlands been even slightly different. It was precisely because of the lowness of the territory and the difficulty of farming here that the VOC had been created. The Netherlands had had to reinvent itself, and became a country of the imagination.

While the original Netherlands had stayed in one place, its shadow country, the VOC, travelled the world. The original country was in peril, threatened by the water all around it, always at risk of flooding, while the VOC exploited the world's oceans; as if the constant threat of drowning had inspired the country to know the oceans like no one else did.

Geert didn't like these stories; this was one of the reasons Johannes enjoyed telling them. Johannes was big, loud, a red-faced man who seemed to overflow from his armchair. To us, he was nothing like our father – Geert was wiry, exhausted, reluctant and uncommunicative. But I see things differently when I look back now. All his life Geert was afraid of his father, whose attention and approval he craved, even as he hated himself for this weakness. Little things Johannes said – jokes, comments that made us laugh – had an effect on him. You could see Geert biting his tongue, then leaving the room, Fenna's look of mild concern underneath her smile. But the last thing I ever would have suspected, back then, was that Geert feared Johannes in the same way my sister and I feared Geert himself.

It's obvious now that he didn't just suspect he'd disappointed his father, he had it proved to him again and again. First of all, there was his work. In his father's eyes Geert was weak, unable to stomach the sea. For the rest of his working life, right up until he died in one of their city offices, Geert worked for the regional water board, the *Waterschappen*, as a hydraulic engineer and advisor. As I found out later, when in a fit of predictable remorse I began researching his life, trying to piece everything together, the *Waterschappen* went all the way back to the thirteenth century, when it formed a set of semi-autonomous government bodies, holding elections and taking taxes. Johannes never said this in his stories – it would be giving Geert too much credit – but there was a clear link between the innovations of the *Waterschappen* and the establishing of the VOC. The work it did, and continued to do, was vital. I wish I had understood this at the time, when Geert was alive.

Without the *Waterschappen*, the Netherlands couldn't exist. The country would immediately be inundated, overwhelmed by water; more than two-thirds of the land would disappear. The *Waterschappen*, with their armies of engineers, were constantly adapting and designing new ways to dam the rivers, remove excess water, and build up artificial coastlines such as the thin beach we visited regularly in my youth. The work was never finished; water management was an unlimited project. This was what I failed to understand at the time, and what I can see now was the pressure Geert carried on his shoulders every day of his long service. So when he came home in the evenings it was not in relief, but in resignation. It didn't stop. Weekends and vacations were only temporary reprieves from the task of understanding, predicting, negotiating and dispersing the water that would otherwise flood the wider Rotterdam region, an area containing more than 2 million people.

Once he had committed to this life, there was no way he could get out of it. He was angry at us, his daughters, because the financial demands of our existence bound him to it. But his temperament was also affected by what he saw at work, a world that was perilously balanced, an environment hostile to humans, with catastrophe deferred only through the surgical intervention of specialist teams. Not that he wanted gratitude for it, just some recognition of the existence of the threat.

He saw complacency everywhere, and he hated it. Last thing every evening he set our plates out at the table for the next morning's meal, like a summoning, a small prayer, as if this preparation and investment would make the new day more likely to come into being. He rose early, even on days off, insisting that we did too, typically no later than 7 a.m. I remember him standing in the garden at dawn, directly outside my room, feet crunching on the stones, and with excessive, vigorous energy, beginning to loudly clean my window. It was with surprise that, later, I wondered whether his actions, which I had always interpreted as sadistic, were really more about wanting us to enjoy ourselves, to go out and do things and experience the world. Our freedom was an affront to his confinement but work had also taught him that life could not be lived passively, it had to be seized and fought for. If he worked as hard as he did – sometimes he came in so stiff he could barely sit down, preferring to stand in doorways or with his back against the wall – then the least we could do was relish what he had given us, not waste away our days in bed.

As children, my sister and I never tried to understand his formidable temper, we simply feared it, tried as much as possible to hide from it. Perhaps the most frightening thing of all was that it was completely unpredictable. Because we didn't know him, we didn't know what he might do. Anything we said or did, no matter how innocuous, might unleash this torrent inside him. I have never once heard anyone roar like my father did. These great blasts of noise seemed to echo in the chambers of the house for hours, for days afterwards. He would smash objects, flinging them against the wall. His energy, the vigour of his anger, was astonishing. He moved with unbelievable swiftness, bounding across the room to grab me and lift me by the collar of my shirt. These outbursts of course only happened while Fenna was at work. It was as if all throughout her silences his resentment and anger were gathering, and he waited, brooding, for the chance to let it out.

Helena, being three years younger than me, was spared the worst of it. Geert frequently hit both of us, hard slaps that we tried to cower from and palm away, protecting our heads, inadvertently frustrating and so provoking him even more. But worst of all were the sustained beatings that lasted several minutes. As far as I know, Helena was never subjected to these. I don't know why; perhaps Geert satisfied his appetite with the violence he committed on me. Perhaps Helena simply didn't provoke him in the way I did. Or perhaps something in the way that I reacted to my father's beatings inhibited him from carrying out the same attacks on his youngest daughter.

I never spoke about this to Fenna, but she must have been aware of it. The migraines, as well as forcing a general silence in the house, a silence that prohibited all forms of communication, and thus ruling out the possibility of me telling her the story, may also have been a symptom of her own fear and sense of helplessness when faced with Geert's rage. Though he never laid a finger on our mother, the threat was implicit, clear in the bruises on my arms, neck and face. I had been thrown repeatedly against a wall. The worse the beatings got, the more withdrawn Fenna became. She spent less time at home, working longer and longer hours at the university, retreating into a purer world of symbols, logic, timeless truth. Ironically, given what would happen later, I never understood this, and I blamed Fenna for not helping us. For all I know, maybe she did try to intervene, and Geert's response was so explosive that it immediately ruled out further efforts. The long nights where she wordlessly, but not silently, nursed me, soothing my stirring limbs, were her way of caring for me, protecting me, retrieving me.

One of the few things I remember our mother saying about Geert's qualities was the same thing that to Helena and me was a source of such terror: he was impossible to predict. She smiled as she said this, her voice softening, her eyes straining towards some memory from the deep past: 'Whatever he does, it is always a surprise.'

It seemed particularly tragic, though probably not all that unusual, that what had once defined him positively had gone on to be the essence of all that was worst in him. Like all children, I've never been able to convincingly imagine the lives of my parents before me, a period of innocence, with fewer obligations and commitments, and I've certainly never believed that Geert's nature could ever have been a source of delight, of enchantment. Geert forever showering our mother with kindnesses, surprise gifts, impromptu weekends away. Geert, put into a novel situation – meeting Fenna's extended family, say, or her work colleagues; difficult circumstances for anyone, and certainly for a quiet and withdrawn man like him – and surprising her, astonishing her, showing further reserves of his personality, new sides to his character, so that she can fall in love with him all over again. Could that really be true? His total unpredictability, in this early stage, veered close to a kind of endlessness, an unlimited, uncontainable personality. He could do anything at all. The potential for violence may have been there all along, ready to be triggered by a special set of circumstances – fatherhood – but otherwise not only lying dormant, but actually driving the happiness he created and the good things that he did. Maybe that explained why Fenna could never confront him, could never challenge him about the violence: if she condemned him then she also condemned all the happiness they'd enjoyed, and however much she regretted the pain he caused us – a pain she clearly experienced herself, in her migraines – she just couldn't bring herself in all conscience to do this.

One of the harder things, for Geert, in his later decades at the *Waterschappen*, was how much everything had changed, particularly in the level of automation introduced into the work, something he never fully trusted. Prediction was fundamental – forecasting annual water levels, gauging the severity of an upcoming storm, deciding in advance whether to call for the evacuation of an area – but the further we moved into the twenty-first century, the harder this became. Temperature fluctuated abnormally, the seasons overlapped dramatically, and flooding became an issue throughout the year. Months' worth of rain fell in a single day. Enormous breakers hurled themselves against the sea walls and the bulwarks and the artificial coastal barriers that Geert and his colleagues had erected. What had always been a difficult job quickly became impossible. The rising temperatures led to a series of river spills, creating a permanent marshland. Mosquitoes arrived, thriving in the new wetlands and introducing the first strains of malaria in the region in more than seventy years. Geert, at this stage, was close to breaking, completely overwhelmed, at a loss either to explain or to keep up with the changes. Reality had defeated him, completely outstripping the limits of his imagination. When he arrived home in the evening he was slow, ponderous, almost shocked. He had no idea what the next day would bring; he could no longer picture what would happen. It must have terrified him. The whole ecosystem was changing and he couldn't keep up. The smallest detail could effect the wildest change. Mosquitoes would colonise the landscape. Excess salt inland would ruin agriculture. But this was only the beginning. When he looked outside, I thought, he could see only the end of the world.

Against his wishes, new automated storm barriers were installed, an artificially intelligent system that communicated with satellite data and erected defences whenever flooding threatened. The lives of over 2 million people depended on this inscrutable intelligence, and at this, Geert finally broke. He had been left behind. His retirement was coming up and there was no question of him continuing, even before the illness. His whole life was an effort to keep the sea at bay, and when he relapsed, and his lungs gave out, I imagined – or hoped – that there was the tiniest, briefest moment of calm and acceptance at the end, his last conscious moments, as he knew he didn't have to struggle any longer.

As a frustrated architect, he always considered himself and his achievements a disappointment, but the irony – and I wish he could have seen this – was that through his work he constantly built and rebuilt the country, hour after hour, day after day. Without the passion, ingenuity, and courage of people like Geert, our country couldn't have existed. He was architect and archaeologist, planning and excavating, implementing systems to dredge and divert water, digging up the country, bringing it out into the open. There were vast, highly elaborate artificial coastlines, peninsulas built from imported sand, tall embankments that would be naturally dispersed as the water shifted, disseminating the sand evenly across the land edge. There were concrete and steel megastructures embedded in the coast, shifting it and raising it as necessary, new superficial landscapes that were printed from factories.

I expressed none of this while Geert was alive. Perhaps I didn't feel he deserved to hear it from me. But sometimes I still wonder whether I could have said something, maybe not in so many words, but still something, a gesture, a signal of my appreciation for what he'd achieved, telling him, as if he needed to hear it, that it had been worth it, the forty-year battle; that it hadn't been for nothing.

On the morning of the funeral, Fenna dug out a photo of

me aged six or seven, standing with Geert, both of us grinning and wearing waders. She said that when I was young, before I started school, I followed him everywhere, and frequently went with him to work. I had forgotten all about it. I had always been fascinated by islands, and I recalled now Geert telling me how the Netherlands, as a military tactic, when the country was at risk of invasion, would release the gates and barriers, flooding the country and transforming it into an archipelago, the water level too high to wade through but too low to sail in, making it impervious to attack – using the country's vulnerability as defensive strategy, as strength.

At the funeral, I was the only member of our immediate family who helped carry the casket. I was the only one tall enough. I had always been ashamed of my height; I wanted to be more petite, more like my sister, not long and angular like this. I could carry my father because I was more like him than I realised; I had been carrying a part of him all along.

TWO

Our mother wasn't expressive when Geert died. She seemed more surprised than upset, intrigued almost by this changed world, the suddenly more spacious house and garden, the smaller meals, the softer scents and flavours, the new feel of the mattress, the absence of sounds she had become accustomed to, such as the almost permanent flow of folk music from the radio into the kitchen and garden. Helena and I stayed with her for as long as we could, but she neither wanted nor needed us around. The morning after the funeral she appeared in the kitchen with her work things and left on her bicycle just as she would on any other day. We lay around the house redundantly, drinking, sorting through Geert's things, Helena seeing to the practicalities, contacting the lawyers, while I veered from appalling, cheap nostalgia – picking up Geert's boots, seeing if they fitted me, lifting up his sweaters and being drawn to the loop of the neck – and blind fury, remembering the worst of it. Helena didn't engage with my excesses, and after three days, after Fenna insisted she was OK, and only after Erika promised to come round regularly and check on her, we left our mother alone in the house.

Helena left as quickly as she could, first to New York then to Jakarta, while I stayed closer to home, studying marine ecology and microbiology in Rotterdam and at the Max Planck Institute in Bremen. Inheriting our mother's talent for mathematics, Helena ended up in financial law, working for a series of banks and insurance adjustment companies. It was Helena herself who pointed out something I couldn't see: if she followed Fenna, then my work followed Geert. This shocked me – both the evidence of inheritance and the fact I hadn't seen it.

Much of my childhood remains blank, my earliest memories beginning around five or six years old. It always alarms me to hear others recalling details from infancy; I can't imagine a memory and a language so close to non-existence. I learned to speak late, as I neared school age, something that drew concern from Fenna at the time. I've never asked Helena about her first memories, but I wouldn't be surprised if her experience was completely different to mine. Helena and I are very different people, three years and two oceans being the least of what separates us. The first thing that comes to mind when I picture her is the expression: mouth open in a small 'o', stoic yet innocent. I see her like a cartoon fawn – small, meek, in need of protection. It's an idealised picture, typical of my lack of understanding and tendency to substitute sentiment for insight, because she's much stronger than the image allows. When we were young we were pushed together out of necessity; unable to describe what was happening to us, we naturally turned to each other, the only other person who could understand. It's logical that at the first chance of fleeing she should do so. I've never blamed her for that.

Helena managed to avoid the worst of it herself, while remaining terrified of our father. She was very clever, very skilful. Something about her made her less of a target; I don't know exactly what. A talent, a knack. She was quieter, she got on with things, whereas I protested. She didn't complain, but continued looking outwards, seeing everything through those narrow eyes under the awkward, severe fringe of her pre-pubescent years. I don't think I've ever seen her cry; she has a remarkable talent for observing almost anything with apparent equanimity. Geert admired this, and I was envious of it; I wanted to be cold and cool like Helena, who shrugged off the world. But I couldn't.

For all the nights Fenna massaged my limbs, Helena slept soundly. This is a gift she was born with, and which she retains to this day. She loves to sleep; uncharitably, I've sometimes thought that sleeping suited her because it was closer to her passive waking state. But actually, as Helena grew older, and we moved to a new house, still within the Rotterdam limits, and for the first time we had our own rooms, she became increasingly assertive and sure of herself. Her voice changed, becoming lower, louder, less liable to be dismissed. Again, I envied this. Helena had the advantage of youth, of watching and learning from what happened to me, putting forward a personality that could protect itself. I didn't have the luxury. I came first; I didn't know; I could only be myself, feet swinging from chairs, mouth hanging open while I read. Helena was a realist, a fighter, a survivor. Geert's terrorising had ironically carved her into the type of person who could withstand it, just as it meant she was less likely to be a target of it.

When we were younger, and shared a room, in the bunk-beds that I loved, with their sense of enclosure and intimacy and camaraderie, we naturally shared a lot of other things too. Helena had the advantage of the books I read, and the disadvantage of the clothes I too quickly outgrew. We invented games and told elaborate stories where we featured as heroic protagonists facing unnameable nemeses. We had our toys, our shared computer, but what we most enjoyed – and I'm as sure as I am about anything in my life that we were equal in this – was being outdoors, in the field near our first house or in the small wooded area it connected to. We lost hour after hour there, pushing through thick under-growth, creating tunnels with our bodies, new pockets of empty space that hadn't existed until we went there. Many of my memories from our time together are silent; we're busy at something, playing together, but not talking. This was strategy: the lack of speech in our games took away the feeling of time passed, instead making it expand, our determination not to talk about Geert being, among other things, an attempt to make him less substantial. The only time I spoke to Helena about the beatings, I immediately regretted it; her eyes pleaded with me to stop. It was for my sake as much as hers; nothing could be gained from repeating this. After that one occasion, not only was the topic sealed forever, but Helena seemed to amend her understanding of the past, as if willing herself into believing these experiences had never actually taken place.

Our early closeness wasn't helpful – that's obvious. As we aged, we drifted apart. It was precautionary, tactical. Helena was at risk of becoming similar to me, and thus being an equal target for Geert's beatings. Instead, she had to be tough. Only in pushing me away – bewildered and possibly hurt as I was – and assuming her own space could she become her own person. There's no other way to see it than that I had held her back, drawn violence towards her. If she had stayed in the same space as me, continued to be like me, then I am certain the attacks would have repeated.

One of the things I am most grateful for in my life is that Helena never had to be like me. If one single thing justifies my existence, it is this. I was an example in negative. If I lived my life in error, drawing pain helplessly and unconsciously towards me, then it was still worthwhile in repelling that same pain away from my sister. Eventually, having fled, she would lead a happier, more comfortable and more confident life without me.

Beginning from our adolescence – and despite the fact that I'm 4 inches taller – people have always inverted our ages. Whatever I do, however I behave, I'm always taken for the younger sister. It's something fleeting, ineffable. A bearing, an ease of being in the world which you can't just will, and which I've never had. Helena somehow just knows that she belongs, that she has a right to be there, wherever she is. It's wonderful. And so now, when I do see her – when I travel to Indonesia, and she hosts me and we go out on boats together, or when we drink in bars on her visits home – I'm always the junior partner, the one being led. It's not even primarily a financial thing – it's fundamental. My sister has a maturity, a considered sense of perspective, which I find completely alien. In my mind, the world is not reasonable, and can never be made reasonable. It is much more interesting than that.

From age ten I was allowed to swim in the Nieuwe Maas on my own. The cold water shocked me and soothed me and took my mind away. I would enter the water and lie back and close my eyes and drift. Afterwards I came stumbling back along the stony beach, my feet blue and insensate from the cold. I perched with a towel around me, shivering, my head on my knees. As I tipped the water out of my ears the sound of the traffic came back. I didn't want to go home, and it took a long time to persuade myself to get up again. The stones pressed through my thin soles as I put my weight down, and every time I left the beach I told myself all I had to do was put those same stones in my pockets and walk out into the water and I would never have to go home again.

It was an effective fantasy; I was able to carry on because I knew I didn't have to. Every time I swam a little further, the stones cutting deeper into my feet as I clambered back ashore. One afternoon in early autumn I felt particularly hopeless. I saw no realistic escape from the situation with Geert and I lived in constant terror of him. Storm clouds were approaching and the beach was deserted. I felt a dangerous sway, the freedom of disregarding my own safety, and I marched into the water, a grimace on my face. The water burned me, sending a startled energy whipping through my body. It was so cold. As I reached the point where my shoulders became submerged, my chest started to convulse and I swallowed mouthfuls of bitter water, and very faintly, as if from a great distance, I sensed that I was about to give way.

I plunged under the water, eyes open, burrowing and kicking out all the way down. It was only a few metres deep, but I felt as if I was tunnelling further, that I had entered a chasm and was swimming in a new territory, a secret chamber of my own. The water was cloudy from the movement of my limbs, but when I stopped I could suddenly see everything very clearly. The larger rocks on the river-bed studded with worms, sponges, limpets and lichen. Beyond them the tufts of floating green and purple riverweed. Nothing made the slightest sound; no thudding in my ears from the water pressure, no chattering voices competing in my head. I gazed at the scene, hanging horizontally, suspended beneath the surface, no further movement to cloud my vision, and as if from nowhere I realised, suddenly, with appreciation, that absolutely everything around me was alive.

There was no gap separating my body from the living world. I was pressed against a teeming immensity, every cubic millimetre of water densely filled with living stuff. These organisms were so small I couldn't see them, but somehow I felt their presence, their fraternity, all around me. I didn't look through the water *towards* life, I looked directly *into* water-life, a vast patchwork supporting my body, streaming into my nostrils, my ears, the small breaks and crevices in my skin, swirling through my hair and entering the same eyes that observed it. In what felt like minutes, but must have been only seconds, I saw a completely different world, a place of significance and complexity, an almost infinite number of independent organisms among which I floated like a net, scooping up untold creatures with every minor shift and undulation of my body.

With a shock I breached the surface, gasping and heaving, coughing and spluttering as water surged out of me. I ducked involuntarily on each convulsion. Finally I gathered myself, and looked towards shore.

The shore had gone. Thick white wisps of cloud drifted over the water. I turned, and it was the same, the mist covering the horizon. I didn't panic. I sensed a warmth over my shoulders, a feeling of peace. For several moments I drifted. Then I stopped, dug the last of the water out my ears, and listened for traffic. I plunged under the water again and propelled myself forward. In under a minute I had reached shore.

The mist was becoming thicker and I couldn't find my things; I could barely see my arms in front of me. I walked carefully along the pebbles and returned, repeating the process in reverse. When I finally found my own bundle – quick-drying towel; trainers stuffed with woollen socks and house-key; jeans and sweater and T-shirt – I looked down on them as if they belonged to another person, not mine to take. Gathering the objects up, putting on my clothes, I felt I was only now inhabiting a personality, that until I entered these pre-set shapes I was diaphanous, and this form did not necessarily match up with who, or what, I was.

It was only as I began drying and dressing that I became aware again of how cold it was. My hands went a deep red and my knuckles acquired a blue tint, sore as I pressed them, as if air-bruised. My trainers were scuffed and split from the many times I'd gone over the same ground. I gripped the house-key, holding it tighter to break through the dull insensitivity of my freezing palms. I held on to this, shivering from the cold, and I thought of Helena, of how much I had to tell her.

I towelled my hair hurriedly, checked to make sure I had everything, then began running through the stones towards the gap in the long wall. I passed through it, onto the path parallel to the road. I was running as fast as I could, generating heat, wet hair whipping by the sides of my face, watching the rapid exchange of feet on the ground, enjoying the motion and feeling separate from it too, like I was in two places at once. When I saw the house at the end of the road, I stopped to ready myself. I had to make myself familiar, know the right things to say, assume the correct shape again. I had been somewhere wild and dangerous, and now I had to return. And at the thought of this – the absurd rituals of family life – I began convulsing again, but this time in laughter, a deep, heaving force that made me buckle on the roadside, arms planted at my knees, enjoying the bittersweet warmth of every breath.

THREE

The microscope seemed to generate the creatures spontaneously, producing life where there had been none before. They appeared like tiny circular pieces of glass, and if they hadn't been moving independently I might have thought they were reflections of the lens. Having received the gift for my eleventh birthday, I became increasingly interested in microscopy. I got better at looking, expanding the world by diminishing it, peering down into the smallest crevices. Digging deeper and deeper into the micro-scale brought out unimagined receptacles of time and space. These creatures were complex and purposeful and beautiful in their own way – tight knots of DNA circled by drifting flagella propelling themselves through water. I peered in awe at the oval nucleus of an amoeba. Individual bacteria were intelligent and wilful: they had a sensory system, they reacted to stimuli and experienced and acknowledged time. At this same magnification, I could see the composite cells of my own body.

Ordinarily I couldn't see any of this. Only through careful and deliberate study could I witness what had been in front of me all along. And so I did this, at home and at school. I remember this as a great period of visibility, the world bursting into appearance. The air was thick with teeming life, just as the oceans and the rivers were. A spoonful of seawater or a pinch of soil between your fingers held billions of living things. We were blind to this out of necessity, because if we saw what was really there we would never move. It was around us, between us, on the edge of us and inside us. It coated our bodies and we released waves of it when we breathed and spoke. It was in every skin cell and in the eyelashes that fluttered when we dreamed. It adapted to every aspect of our behaviour; if animals were shaded out, and microorganisms illuminated, then our ghosts would be clear in these bright peripheries. My favourite species were those that lay dormant in husk form before reanimating, such as the rotifers discovered in Arctic ice-sheets after 24,000 lifeless years. Able to withstand almost any force, they seemed to challenge the distinction between life and death, annihilating the concept of straight and linear time to suggest something more circular and repetitious instead.

Throughout my school years I worked hard to be as anonymous as possible, something that wasn't aided by my unusual height. Every decision I made was done in service to the larger project of becoming less visible. At home, as I grew taller and taller, I learned to affect my posture to appear smaller than I was. My height was confrontational, too loud, and an affront to my father. Whatever gave me the right to grow out like this, to take up disproportionate room in our house?

By mid-adolescence my height had levelled out, and I

wasn't so conspicuous among my peers. I joined several clubs after school, with others who were similarly interested in laboratory and fieldwork. When I left home, finally, for university, I immersed myself in study, and excelled. I felt at ease and in control of what I was doing for the first time in my life. Though they lived just a few miles away, I saw my parents and sister only irregularly. Our relationship had changed, and we were awkward in each other's company, unsure in which arrangement to sit when we met at a restaurant for lunch. Even Helena looked at me curiously, interestedly, sensing the shift.

At the earliest opportunity I specialised in marine work. I was already learning German in preparation for my master's in Bremen. The culmination of this degree was a six-week placement a third of the distance across the Atlantic, on the Azores islands, collecting phytoplankton in the mountain lakes. The subterranean heat, the mid-ocean remoteness, the relatively clean air from the small number of vehicles combined to make the lakes a promising location for unusual algal strains.

I left early each morning, trying to gain an elevation before the sun came up. I swam and dived, collecting samples which I stored in a fridge in my room back at the guest-house. I got into a routine, and before the first week was out I realised I was relishing it – the clear air, the dramatic geology, the priority of the climate I had to base all my movement around.

I had missed this time alone, outside, far from the mass unconscious contact of the city. I was twenty-three, I worked on my own, my Portuguese limited to the basic vocabulary and rote statements I'd managed to learn so far. I stayed with a young family in a large eighteenth-century villa a twenty-minute drive from the main harbour. The family laid out breakfast and prepared dinner through the week; at first I was mortified, insisting through gesture that I would provide for myself, but by the end I'd learned to accept and even enjoy my position as an overgrown, passive, and largely silent child.

I swam in the small cove near the guest-house last thing in the evenings, diving and playing in the stringy white surf, watching the stars become clearer each night as the moon waned, losing myself and forgetting my compass points – the sky, the sea – floating, tumbling, sinking in the cooler water, coming out breathlessly onto the firmer sand, then sitting on the long flat rocks in reflection. I imagined a life of this, in close contact, as I saw it, with the stuff of the world. I would establish my career, I would push my research, I would be restless, more determined and more committed than any of my peers. This was the objective and the priority of my life, more so than family, than relationships, than any other form of knowledge or attainment at all. I would work ferociously, happy in the contentment that it gave me.

There were few cars, the empty roads spooling out like toy tracks, twisting at wild angles up dramatic climbs from the villages into the mountains. The heat at sea level was oppressive, relieved by the cool winds coming in through the built corridors. I thought of my father and the old Rotterdam he described, the wider avenues created where the medieval town had been destroyed, the wind that was now extinct in the city, forced elsewhere by massive glass and steel offices. The VOC had used the old route to the Indian Ocean, launching on trade winds from Cape Verde and the Azores, sailing west then going south on currents and turning east at the Cape of Good Hope. These were the same winds flowing over me now, striking off the flat white buildings and blasting the surf against the rocks.

The mountain lakes were so remote, and involved such punishment just to reach them, that they remained largely deserted. After reaching altitude, the paths down into the craters were narrow and steep and occasionally required the use of ropes. I arrived sweating, sunburned and out of breath, quickly establishing my base – towel, planted parasol, water bottle, work kit – and waded out into the emerald green water. I collected samples from upper, mid and lower levels, packing the vials into the chilled containers in my bag. I allowed myself to lie down briefly as I dried, soaking up reserves of energy ahead of the long climb out of the crater and across the mountains home.

On the walk back I smelled the sulphur from the geysers, white steam twisting skyward. Farmers baked meats in scald-pits, carcasses infused with the scent and the feel of the burned-up inner rock. They were prize items for cruise-ship passengers shuttled in on yachts from the larger islands. I was fascinated by the sickening smell – rot, flesh – and by the sight of the charred meat slabs being delivered from the vents. I imagined that the flesh had always been there, burning in the lower earth, and was only now being excavated, eaten like the ritual consumption of a god. Water and steam ejected dramatically, implying the original formation of the islands, the chaos of lava and fire, cooling and hardening and creating the terrain.

I was returning late one afternoon to the village when I noticed it – a feeling that something unnameable had changed. At first I mistook it as an extension of the dislocation I already felt, my basic estrangement – lack of language, ignorance of context – from the people around me. I had come down from the lakes, as usual, around 6 p.m., noting the fatigue, the tension in my calves, the automatic motions of my body. With the guest-house in sight, I stopped. The usually shuttered cafés were open; people drifted in twos and threes through what should have been deserted streets; amplified voices and music played out from concealed speakers. If I saw more people than I usually did, if I initially sensed a feeling of excitement and opportunity, then I dismissed it as a mistaken attribution, an effect of my satisfaction after a good, long day's work and a pleasant, even thrilling descent from the mountains. It wasn't the scene around me that was different, as I came back into the village, it was my relationship towards it.

Still, I enjoyed this feeling, and wanted to prolong it. I was tired, and unusually hungry, so I decided to eat an ersatz burger in one of the small cafés opening late. After settling at a table and ordering my food, I looked up from my notes, alerted by something on the television at the bar. A news feature was playing: three officials stood behind a podium, faced by dozens of microphones and cameras. I made out block capitals rolling across the lower segment of the screen: UN, NASA. I flinched, and immediately went to retrieve my phone, then stopped, remembering I had no data left – in fact had purposely let it run out. If the story was important, I would find out soon enough, anyway.

I ate quickly and ravenously and drank three bottles of wheat beer before leaving the café and trailing across the central plaza towards the guest-house. I had the impression, again, of difference, a certainty not only that something had changed, but that this change was being demonstrated, was being lived, all around me. I wondered if I was witnessing the beginning of a festival, the quiet early stages when everything is still being set up. I could see no costumes, no stalls, and while the streets were busier, these were hardly crowds. And yet I could feel it, palpably – something new was taking place right now. Standing there, I tried to pinpoint exactly what it was, but I couldn't see it. Enjoy it, I told myself. It doesn't have to mean anything. Enjoy it for the feeling itself.

The shaded anteroom of the guest-house felt cooler after the warmth of the evening air. The dark shelves and cabinets were made from redwood sourced from the sheltered inner islands. Stepping in, almost immediately I collided with Isabella. Isabella – not much older than me, dark-haired, and petite – smiled as she usually did, and we performed our scripted interactions. But this time, instead of wishing me *boa noite*, she continued smiling, looking at me in expectation. She then said something I didn't understand. I was frustrated with my poor grasp of the language – I felt I should have known the words she was using, that it was important, and yet they meant nothing to me. I did my best to smile warmly and apologetically, and then finally shrugged. Just as I stepped away, turning towards the dark wooden staircase, Isabella called out my name with renewed urgency. She smiled again, gestured to me, then drew a circle with her fingers, pointing upwards. I nodded uncertainly, and ascended the stairs.

Later that night, when my eyelids started to feel heavy and I got up to pull the shutters across the windows and peel back the bedsheet, I recalled the image from the television screen. There was something curious about it. It wasn't the jostling mics or the flashing cameras, but the expressions of the scientists standing before them. They were smiling. The older spokesperson in the centre had a red sheen across his face, hair unkempt. The usual laborious preparations had been foregone. There was an air of spontaneity and excitement, the same excitement I had glimpsed earlier in the village and in the café, and which Isabella had tried to communicate to me at the bottom of the stairs, pointing to me and gesturing at the sky.

On each of my last four days I saw the sperm whales breach. Tourists began appearing, narrow boats with vertebraic rows of sunglasses, phones, and bright orange life-vests. The whirring sound of drone cameras was a constant. I went home exhausted, arms, calves tight from the long steep walks to and from the lakes. I ate large bowls of pasta and drank jugs of water with crushed ice and lime. The winds at night rippled through the shutters on the two- or three-hundred-year-old buildings. The skiffs in the jetty bobbed up and down. There were splashes that might have marked a further breach; it was hard to tell without a moon. The night before my flight I made my way carefully past the rocks one last time and swam out in the oily black water, turning to float on my back and look up at the immensity.

———————

Sitting by the runway-facing window, I heard my phone ping with an alert from the airport Wi-Fi, and I logged in. It was the lead story everywhere. More details would be released later, and the initial announcement was brief: NASA engineers had made a radical breakthrough in propulsion technology. There were rumours that spacecraft could achieve more than 10,000 times their previous velocity. For now, the Scientific Council said it was confident 'major applications' would be found in the coming years. Researchers were setting up larger trials, and it was already being described as one of the most significant engineering advances in history. The details were vague, but it had to be nuclear based, surely. Had they finally produced scalable, safe fusion?

I read email after email, article after article as I waited for my boarding call. Javier said that while he wouldn't go so far as to call it a hoax, the pay-off from the alleged breakthrough was years away, and in that sense nothing substantive had changed. We should be sceptical of the timing; this could all be a glorified PR event, an exaggerated blast of good news after everything that had happened in the past few years.

Other reactions bordered on the ecstatic. It wasn't just the breakthrough itself, but what it might lead to, what other advances and applications it might enable further along the line. There was potential for an exponential creativity explosion, whole new industries driven by this single, pivotal change.

The consensus lay somewhere in the middle, a kind of cautious, wait-and-see optimism. There had been little in the way of concrete details. All of this, the spokesperson said, would be forthcoming. Even so, I found it impossible not to be excited, swept along just a little by the sense of hope, opportunity, revelation. The most exciting thing was that none of us knew what would happen next. And while the sceptics might be proved right – maybe the research would stall, maybe the applications wouldn't turn out to be as widespread as hoped – we didn't know that for sure. What we had, I thought, what they had given us, was exactly what we needed – some hope.

FOUR

At the start of the final year of my doctorate I flew to South America's Caribbean coast. My supervisor had secured me a position as menial help on an expedition ship travelling south-east through the Atlantic. Although the exact purpose of the voyage wasn't clear, I was eager for experience and this was my only route aboard. I waited three days in the walled city for notice of the ship's departure, ahead of a voyage lasting anywhere between one and two months. I walked the interior of the old city again and again, spiralling its centre, observing the huge, impregnable doors and long shadows, the elaborate cathedrals with the stench of rotting plumbing underneath. Confirmation finally came just as I was about to give up; *Endeavour* would leave the following morning from the deep-water harbour 12 miles past the walls.

We departed with clear skies and no wind, the ramparts around the city quickly fading, and after lengthy demonstrations of the evacuation procedures by two of the Russian crew, I was shown to my cabin, a low, narrow box with a set of iron beds stacked either side. We were several feet above the waterline, the porthole sealed shut and painted over. I exchanged brief introductions with my cabin-mates – young researchers like me – slotted my things into the allocated drawers, locked them to prevent spilling and made my way to the kitchen. We'd alternate between kitchen, linen and 'wet' duties – helping prepare and bring in the dives each day – and though a schedule was posted it was provisional and subject to sudden change.

Endeavour was a five-tiered vessel roughly 60 metres in length, painted off-white with the open deck a stark deep green. The inner corridors were long and cramped, the whole interior repetitive and confusing, walls lined by identical cabins, stairs and massive white steel doors that gave out onto the sea air.

The first days were long, dull, difficult. Not just the work, but getting used to the feel of the ship, the unsteady floor and walls, which were a particular problem when you were serving food and drinks. You had to think before you walked, check the floor, gauge the look of the other passengers before setting off. I was always conscious, always sceptical, which was proving quite a stressful way to be. By the time of evening clean-up I was exhausted, desperate to return to my cabin and shut myself away. I had no leisure time. There was the additional stress of not knowing anyone while being in contact with so many people as I served and cleaned. Felix, one of my cabin-mates – 3 inches shorter than me and never seen without his red cap – helped me on our first day in the kitchen, but other than that I'd barely had a conversation stretching further than two lines.

On the fourth day I finally got some time out on deck with the divers, checking oxygen supplies, SD cards, suit-locks, taking registers and confirming launch and retrieval times for multiple descents. Although I was happy to be outside again, it was still frustrating being primed for a dive I'd never take. I crouched while the swell crashed over me, saltwater stinging the back of my throat. Towards the horizon were several uninhabited atolls. But the real interest, the focus of the dives, were the reefs further down.

The divers went 60 to 100 feet, drifting at the edge of the possible. As I ran through checks with each of the surfacing divers they nodded back with a glazed expression. Emerging in their bodysuits, lying on the deck, they were nameless, impersonal, almost unhuman. I never actually heard them speak. It was funny to think I could have nodded to them in the corridor, or passed them their plate in the dining hall, and that the recognition only went one way. Though I concentrated on the divers' eyes, I couldn't match them with the faces I saw in interior levels; they remained mysterious, as if they had crawled out from the water originally, and returned there again every evening.

We spent five long days and nights around the San Andreas reef. I had responsibility for safely extracting SD cards and manually uploading footage onto the server. The divers worked tirelessly, descending after dusk with headlamps and cameras, sleeping a couple of hours and going back out again, suits yet to dry. Basking sharks drifted on the horizon; huge whale sharks spun softly and mournfully below. The best raw footage was put on a wall screen in the theatre after meals, left playing in a loop overnight, more powerful for the lack of sound and narrative, just the scene itself, the intermittent clarity, thick, murky clouds suddenly transforming into a direct confrontation with an animal.

'No one is here to commit to anything,' he was saying. 'We just want to get a little more information. We know there's stuff on the seabed that we want, but if potential damage is judged excessive, we won't drill. Simple as that. We're not the bad guys here. That's what's great about *Endeavour* – we're working together, drinking together. So it's really in your interest to share what you know, otherwise, how do we judge risk? How do we know we're not making a mistake? And if we do go down there, how do we do it in the cleanest way possible?'

I lingered slightly longer than necessary before clearing away the plates. As service staff, we tended to be invisible, which had its advantages. Nick Freeman's broad Australian vowels emerged through his thick moustache, and he didn't give me so much as a glance. Everyone knew him – a consultant with one of the South African firms. He was seated next to a woman probably not much older than myself; she'd glanced up a moment ago, mouthing 'thank you' as I cleared the empties. I had a vague feeling she was a palaeontologist but couldn't remember where I'd got that from.

'Some of the species broadcast on the wall,' the woman was saying drily, matter-of-factly, 'resemble the first motile creatures. The first nervous systems, 570 million years ago. By the time we name them, they may be all but extinct.'

'I agree,' Nick said. 'It would be better if we had never encountered these things. But here we are. We can't go back now. We can't pretend these metals don't exist,' he went on. 'There are six to eight times as many reserves in the seabed as on the land. Green energy relies on this. Come on – be realistic.'

'What's realistic,' she shot back, 'is that time is different down there, life moves slowly. And we can destroy it in an instant. A whole ecosystem, gone; even in ideal circumstances it would take millennia to recover.'

Nick seemed to be readying a shrug.

I walked back towards the kitchen, stopping a moment while the ship leaned. There was an art to this, with the swell gathering, the floor increasingly unsteady. So far, thankfully, I'd neither dropped anything nor been struck by seasickness. After two hours more in the kitchen, running through the conversation I'd overheard and being repeatedly pinned back by the rush of hot air from the dishwasher, I peeled off my gloves, dropped them into the bin and slowly made my way back to the cabin. But before I got there, I paused by the stairs, went up on a whim, and pushed outside for a breath of unfiltered air.

It was surprisingly loud, the top-mast fluttering and shaking in the wind. I felt the relief of the cooler air gusting over my burned and clammy skin. It was almost midnight, and the ship's inner lights dimmed. The water was calm; an edgeless black meeting the vast sky. I took hold of the perimeter rope, shook off my shoes, planted my feet down firmly on the fibreglass composite, and carefully walked out towards the bow.

I was now at the tip of *Endeavour*, holding the rope-edge and leaning forward, eyes shut, enjoying the freedom and feeling of escape, the huge vault of the sky I sensed above me, the stars. And then, from nowhere, a quiet voice sounded; my eyes shot open and I leaned back again, gathering myself in.

'I'm sorry,' he said. 'You probably thought you were alone.'

He stood a few feet to my right, short, slim, fair-haired in loose fitting T-shirt and long shorts. He raised an eyebrow and smiled nervously. 'I didn't mean to startle you. You clearly hadn't seen me there, and I wanted to leave you alone, but then I worried you might hear me coming past and that would be worse.'

I gave a light chuckle. 'Don't worry. I'm almost surprised it's just us out. It's incredible here.'

'I try to come out as often as I can, though sometimes it's

not possible.' His accent was hard to pin down – Scandinavian, I thought, clipped, with a hint of Eastern US. 'I have to admit, I find it easy to lose myself out here. Two whiskies, five minutes sitting by the bow at midnight, I can barely remember my own name.'

'I can imagine.' Now I could see him clearly, I noticed his irises were an unusually vivid blue. And though I'd initially taken him for young – one of the other junior researchers – I saw he was actually quite a bit older than me.

'There's nowhere else I'd rather be right now. Nowhere.' He grinned, shook his sandy hair. 'When I stand here, I feel like I'm slipping away.' He gestured at the water – 'It anticipates us, contains us, outlives us. And we are right here with it.' He stopped, and I could see him breathing, his narrow chest inflating under his baggy shirt. 'Ahead,' he pointed again, 'is the mid-Atlantic Ridge, 28,000 miles around. Cape Verde, the Azores, Iceland, Ascension. I can't tell you how important this journey is to me. You'll see what I mean, I hope, when we get there.'

FIVE

A week in, and I was finally striking up conversations and learning a little more about the trip. *Endeavour* was part-funded by groups who wanted to mine and dredge the seafloor. If this compromised the expedition, it wasn't exactly a shock – corporate sponsorship always seemed to lurk in the small print, and ISA had been authorising seafloor surveys for years. Regardless of what we found, permits were unlikely to be given out for some time yet – or so I hoped.

There was more to this, I learned. It was a shock and a thrill to hear we were sailing towards a newly discovered hydrothermal vent. NASA wanted to trial some new kit there, and had sent an engineer to oversee it. I was scanning the passengers in the dining room, trying to match names with faces. Rumours spread in the kitchen. Obviously reps like Nick wanted any info they could get – vents held all sorts of treasures – but Felix said there was talk the Nuclear Regulatory Commission was scouting for a possible dump site for nuclear waste. This seemed unlikely. It was exciting, and the tempo was changing, the days starting to run together. I barely had time to pause and ask how, in an area as well studied as this, the vent was only being discovered now.

We picked up speed, ploughing south-east, due to continue straight on for the next seven days. There were fewer and fewer birds as we lost sight of the islands and continued on into the blue. In the mornings and evenings I worked in the kitchen. Not trusted with food prep, I served, cleared, cleaned. Felix said I was 'better at destruction than creation'. I protested, but there was some truth in it – despite my sister's claims about how messy I was, I didn't mind cleaning the way some of the others on the ship did, mostly because I appreciated working alone. All of us were researchers – that was what brought us here – but I seemed to enjoy the isolation most. When I cleaned, I knew what I was doing, and I could work to a rhythm that let my thoughts run clear, giving me time and space to speculate about where exactly we were going and what we might find there.

Most people agreed that ocean vents were life's beginning. At their base, archaea – *the ancients* – feasted on methane and sulphur, converting gases into sugars and founding the food chain. The archaea – small, structurally simple, distinct from bacteria – were some of the first living things, appearing 3 or 4 billion years ago in a chaotic era of mass volcanic eruptions. At some point long after this, something even more radical happened, and archaea grouped with bacteria to form a new kind of cell, containing a nucleus. All multi-cellular life – plants, fungi, animals – come from this.

But archaea still exist. They're drawn to inhospitable regions – Antarctic ice-sheets, the salt plains of Chile and

Eritrea – but their most exotic site of all, arguably, is in our stomachs. Presumably they act symbiotically, and help us in some way. No one's really sure. Among other strange characteristics, archaea have the ability to become dormant, and to reanimate after tens of thousands of years.

I first came across them when I was eleven years old, the point at which my interest in the microscopic world began. It was also when Geert's attacks were continuing. I started to get pains in my stomach, and rather than thinking they were caused by my father, a manifestation of fear, I imagined instead I was part of an ancient story, colonised by strange creatures building biosedementary structures on the seafloor. It was an escape, a flight from autobiography. I never believed I would actually go there.

The exploration site we aimed for was so deep, and bore such unbelievable pressure, that just to observe it took a great amount of ingenuity. The submersibles cost more than the ship did. Getting there was the easy part. Seeing it – and, crucially, retrieving footage – was the challenge.

Amy Delacroix, a French-Canadian engineer, had helped design the subs. This only came up some way into our conversation, after I had tried to engage her with some of the speculative ideas about algal agriculture that were occupying me more and more in my doctoral research. I had a rare evening off work, I hadn't been counting my drinks, and I was taking advantage of Amy's generosity. She seemed to remember everyone's name, even ours, and Felix said she'd already questioned him for forty-five minutes on his thesis on the engineering implications of cephalopods. Even if she wasn't especially interested, she'd at least been in a position like ours before, a lowly researcher scrambling for opportunities, and was sympathetic, happy to humour and encourage us. It was just past the golden hour, three days before we were due to hit the coordinates, and a few of us were standing out in the breeze.

Amy had platinum blonde hair and a tough edge built from years of being patronised or worse by male colleagues. She'd worked with NASA at the Jet Propulsion Lab for six years designing exploratory vehicles, so must have been a decade older than she looked. I was a little awe-struck. Amy seemed to lose attention, eyes wandering past me. 'You were saying?' she prompted, holding her wine glass so loosely and casually I was amazed it hadn't fallen.

'It's nothing.'

'I was listening, Leigh.'

'Yeah?'

'Uh-huh. You know, we might have more in common than you think. Space agencies are going to launch more off-world missions in the near future, and some of those are going to be crewed. And people are going to need to eat while they're up there. So I'd say storage and growth of versatile, high-yield, nutrition-heavy crops will be pretty relevant in the coming years.'

This wasn't something I'd ever thought about; my eyes lit up at the suggestion. I blushed, grateful for the sunburn, and quickly brought the conversation back to subs. Each of them cost several million dollars to build and trial. She'd seen the process through from beginning. 'It's Stefan's voyage,' she said. 'I'm not interfering unless he explicitly asks me to. It's more authentic this way – I mean, the people ultimately using the equipment aren't going to be designers. But of course, I'm happy to help.'

The sea, she said, was a sort of intermediate stage for the subs, whose utility was off-world. 'The past few years there's been an explosion of funding. It's changed everything, in terms of what we might do. Every major space agency has essentially torn up its twenty-year forecasts. We can go further now. *Much* further. And it's realistic to think we can start doing so pretty soon. Saturn's moons are a feasible target. If I tell you Europa's seas are 100 miles thick, you'll get an idea of why we're interested in vents.'

The only deep-sea subs I'd seen were large top-loading bubbles. They looked like re-entry capsules in science-fiction films. 'Like a diving bell? Oh god no, those are not what we're using,' Amy laughed, blowing hair strands out of her eyes. 'I've no experience with crewed subs, that's something else entirely, I'm afraid. That's vanity. Why would we limit our designs to something a person can fit inside? You're really cutting back on what you can do. If a person's inside, you can't take risks. A human is a soft part, and has to be protected. The really interesting places can't accommodate a person. So it makes sense to cut out the vulnerable parts from a system.'

'So what I saw didn't come from NASA?'

'No! Definitely not. If you're preparing something for off-world use, you want it to be as small as possible, reducing payload. The first machines to explore Europa or Enceladus will likely be descendants of what we've got wrapped in the deck below us now.'

Scintilla was 3 feet long, largely plexiglass and steel, and could apparently stand greater pressure than any other marine vehicle. New optical equipment – designed by a Serbian astronaut who became obsessed with improving visual systems during a stint on ISS – allowed *Scintilla* to record images at distance even in opaque environments. *Scintilla* could also collect sediment and water samples. This had not, Amy said, been easy to build.

She took a sip from her wine, and seemed to contemplate it. I watched her run her tongue across her lips, feeling the burn on my face again. 'Look, it's fraught with paradoxes. First, you need to decide whether the vehicle should be remote operated or autonomous. Obviously the first's easier, quicker to build, and if there's a visual feed it's an advantage if you can move it around. But there's a limit to what you can do with ROVs, and where you can put them. At extreme depths, they basically shut down – comms fail, and because they're not autonomous, the thing just sits there. Comms are one of the first things to go – another soft part, if you like. So ROVs are great for shallower areas, but not so great on a trip like this. And useless in Europa's 100-mile seafloors.'

'So you built something autonomous?'

'We tried. There are various stages between ROV and automated. The quickest useful thing to build – useful for getting started – is a vehicle with a route programmed into it. So, for example, you direct it to explore the seabed in a zig-zag motion for 150 metres.'

'So it isn't actually autonomous.'

'It's controlled externally, remotely, it's just that the instructions are coded in a bit earlier, so it doesn't have to rely on a volatile feed.'

'But then to code its movements, you'll need a map of where you're going?'

'The paradox! But again, we trialled these vehicles at shallower depths, which helped us batter out improvements. Later, with more autonomous systems, we found similar problems. The core system isn't so different from self-driving cars; you train it using images which it learns to recognise. Paradox again: we can do our best to create conditions that resemble what we *think* is down there, but without going there it's basically a guess. I wouldn't look too worried, Leigh. There are various fail-safes built in. We also have ROVs that we can use as support or retrieval vehicles. But can I let you in on a little secret?'

'Yeah?'

'Nobody really expects *Scintilla* to come back up from the vent – not from ultimate depths, assuming the vent's as deep as people are saying. At least no one at JPL does. I wouldn't be distraught, honestly. The ROVs and other kit will retrieve data. And we'll bring *Scintilla* up from shallower depths – we'll be careful with it. So it should, I imagine, still give us interesting footage and samples. But if we want to push it, push it as far as the vent reaches, then yeah, I wouldn't put money on seeing it again.'

A light cut out in the cabins behind us, and the sky became clearer. I was starting to feel cold, wishing I'd brought my sweater.

'The main issue right now isn't getting to the moons, it's the secondary vehicles we'll use on arrival. That's what we need to get right. It's my understanding the advances in thrust design make medium-range travel pretty straight-forward.'

'When you say medium range—'

'I mean within our solar system. We're not getting out of there for a long time.'

'So all this,' I said, nodding past the railings, 'you're not interested in it, not really? Not interested in what's there? I mean, this is just a trial for you? A rehearsal for space?'

'Oh it can be both, I think. I can be interested in all this – how could I not be? – while still seeing it essentially as a read-through.'

'And Nick,' I nodded towards the Australian, loudly holding court on the opposite side of the deck, 'he's presumably interested in off-world minerals. So he wants to see how *Scintilla* works?'

'I think you know the answer to that.'

SIX

While I made a point of getting to know Amy better, I didn't
feel I was being dishonest, or particularly cynical. I liked
Amy, enjoyed being around her, and if there was a chance
she might help me later in my career that was a bonus. I was
hardly a burden on her, busy as she was; I was careful not to
overdo it, and I knew if she found me irritating she wouldn't
think twice about swatting me away. Felix and I suspected
she liked playing mentor, and it was possible to indulge this
in a way that flattered her and worked for both of us. As
suspected, she had worked a series of service jobs through
most of her study, and she was quick, maybe too quick, to
note perceived slights towards us from the other passengers.

We were in the long stretch between the Caribbean and
the mid-Atlantic, the unbroken blue where the lights of a
large container at night were an event, where we trawled the
horizon for plumes, where dolphins matched our tempo and
rode alongside us, and where dazzling, glassy translucent
fish bounced up and startled us, tracing wide arcs through
the air. More than a week past land now, with only migrating
Arctic terns above us, I felt I was finally settling into the
ship's rhythms. Early morning setting up the dining space
ahead of the buffet. Then clearing tables, washing everything
and making my way through my assigned deck, cleaning the
toilets and the shower rooms and putting out fresh laundry

for the cabins every third day. Afternoons were down time – I dozed, read, snacked, sat out on deck, and took turns on the long-range tripod cameras set up by bow and stern. Prep for dinner began at 5 p.m. for a 7 p.m. start. It was 9.30, 10 p.m. by the time serving staff could eat. Felix and I usually ate together, after clearing away the main meals.

It was funny, in a relatively small ship like this, how you always seemed to see only the same few people. It was an unwritten rule that you kept the same seat at meals, and so I got to know those on the tables I served, and found myself running into them in the corridors and out on deck. I still hadn't spoken to half the people here, and by this stage I didn't imagine that would change. We seemed to have gravitated and settled into small, unofficial bubbles. I didn't actually see Amy all the time, I just remarked on it every time I did, as I didn't with others. It was as if an appreciation of anything greater than eight or nine people at once was too much, and so I only carried the people that I knew, and automatically nodded hellos to strangers I was sure I was seeing for the very first time, marvelling at their ability, at all other times, to remain hidden.

Usually, on introductions, I said I studied algae, but this was not dry land and this was not an ordinary group of people, so I went further, explaining how algae was a false term, how it covered a huge range of organisms, from giant forest kelp to beach-weed to single cyanobacteria cells, some of which were as closely related to us as to each other. Then I said something about algae's enormous agricultural potential, and how this was partly what I was working on in my thesis, and what I wanted to pursue afterwards, funding permitting.

Introduced at last to Stefan, leader of *Endeavour*, I saw to my surprise we had already met, sharing that conversation three nights previously at the bow. He smiled sheepishly, and again I noted the almost unreal blue of his eyes. He asked the question, raising his voice above the engines and the wind: 'Why algae in particular?' And whether encouraged by Stefan's own frankness several nights before, or just freed by the continually dramatic setting on the ship, I found myself actually thinking about this, then listening, in some surprise, as I opened my mouth and said, 'Because it lets us breathe.'

Stefan liked this. He nodded happily, and we spoke about this and about the journey. I quickly found he was very easy to talk to, that I had none of the usual qualms expressing myself around him, maybe even that we'd developed a rapport. He seemed to enjoy my lack of deference – 'A natural consequence of seeing me at my most vulnerable,' he deadpanned, referring to his boyish excitement when we had first met – and we shared an uncommon passion, an obsession really, for marine microbiology. For us, it wasn't work – this was our lives.

They had only got the alert three months ago, meaning everything had been put together very quickly. A measure not so much of excitement as unease, uncertainty. Nobody understood what it *was*. A telecoms company had found it first, rolling fibre-optic along the Atlantic bed back in April; suddenly everything had just stopped. They lost the cable, the programme stalled. Rather than getting divers in – too expensive, too laborious, and anyway the obstruction was likely much too deep – investigators leased an orbiting satellite for a new depth reading. The results came back at 12 kilometres, as deep as any vent in the world. Which of course didn't make sense – the Atlantic was widely charted. Previous surveys had put the area at between 3 and 4 kilometres. There had been tectonic activity here around three years previously, but of nothing like the kind required to gouge out such an enormous depression. The vent must have existed earlier – so why hadn't anyone seen it?

'It's impossible,' I said. 'It's an error, it must be.'

'They did try using more traditional methods,' Stefan said, out on the deck again, 'but all their instruments were lost.'

'They *lost* them?'

I was sure, now, that the irises weren't real, that he was wearing tinted contacts.

'WTO announced a switch in trade routes, put an embargo

around the site. As a precaution. A pretty expensive precaution, you can imagine.'

'So that's why this happened so quickly.'

'Every day the embargo continues is a financial disaster.
They want us to investigate so that trade can revert and
everyone can pretend it never happened.'

'But at the same time it's an opportunity for prospectors
and strip-miners.'

'Yes,' Stefan agreed. 'And for us too.'

We'd been talking more generally about research interests.
I had to constantly remind myself our positions were
diametrically opposed – I was on the very bottom rung,
Stefan expedition leader. But he spoke to me, exceptionally,
as an equal. While being careful not to pry, he was interested
in what drew me to marine work. I tried to speak carefully,
to measure my words and not say anything I later regretted.

'Do you have a theory,' I asked, 'about the 12-kilometre
reading, assuming it's correct?'

He smiled, his bare feet gripping the composite, one arm
clutching the railings. 'Actually I do. I believe an unusually
large mineral layer precipitated when the vent first emerged,
blocking sonar and radar. This would explain earlier the
readings of 3, 4 kilometres.'

'Like a false floor?'

'Yes. It would have to be a massive precipitation, of course,
but it's not impossible.'

'And then the recent earthquakes were strong enough to split this layer?'

'Exactly. The problem then is why other vents are not similarly blocked.'

'Maybe they are.'

'I don't follow?'

'Most of them. And we've only found those where the false floor has broken.'

'It's possible. I hadn't actually considered that. Hopefully, soon, we'll find out.'

There was a pause in conversation, and I suspected Stefan wanted to tell me something, that he was holding back for some reason. We continued looking out onto the nightwater, the sea rushing before us.

'I think,' he said eventually, still looking ahead, 'that life on Earth is already stranger – much stranger – than we credit. It's perhaps difficult to really face this; certainly it's difficult to do the idea justice. I think we might share this frustration.'

'Yes. I think we do. That's why I get up every day and go into the lab – because I want to face it, this strangeness.'

'I know the phrase was mine, but what does it mean to you, to face it? What do you mean by that?'

I thought for a moment, listening to the ship's movement. 'I mean I want to explore this strangeness as rigorously as I can, and to see myself in it too.'

'Yes,' he said quickly.

'I don't want to "other" the strangeness. I want to accept it and recognise it. One of the first things that excited me – really excited me, and I can remember this vividly – about the ocean, was the knowledge that it already contains everything. It's like you said earlier: the stuff of the body – of every body, of every living thing – it's still there.'

'The body before it was cast,' he said.

'I feel like it must be a developmental problem, a preserved childhood state, or something – I just can't accept this fact as trivial, and move on. How can you take this for granted? How can anyone do that?'

'This is why you're interested in cell development?'

'The cell is basically an ocean capsule. A preserved primordial capsule, holding the original marine environment inside. This is . . . this is just beyond incredible, isn't it? I mean, you could describe us as both people, and as mobile assemblages of ocean. I am not ready to get over this.'

Stefan gave a quiet laugh. 'It's what we're hearing now, sloshing beneath us as the ship goes through it. It's a mistake to think of our origins, of all life's origins, as belonging only to the past. It's still there.'

'I want to know what's inside this vent, and how deep it goes.'

Stefan looked ahead, then checked his watch. 'We'll, we're due to approach the embargo zone in twenty-eight hours.'

SEVEN

I couldn't sleep the following night. When the engines stopped, the silence was shocking. Everything clear and stark. The dark water was unusually calm, barely a swell. I went round the deck perimeter, hearing the ship creak and strain. *Endeavour* seemed smaller, more exposed; swaying and drifting in the still water, it was as if we had returned to an earlier age, crossing the ocean with no sense of what we would encounter on the other side.

The silence didn't last. Minutes later the crew were out, stomping past me on the composite, yelling at each other in Russian. I backed off, retreated through the steel door and immediately almost clattered into Stefan. He barely paused, veering away, clutching a bundle of printed sheets. He called out to Karlsson, who barked something back. Dawn was breaking, electric lights dimming in the corridors, and reluctantly I made my way down to the kitchen to prep the buffet. I wanted to be out on deck, where the action was, not stuck in here pouring cereals and fruit juice.

The priority now, according to last night's meeting, was to locate the edge of the vent. The methods they were using were thousands of years old. I heard the heavy clunk of the zodiacs lowered from the ropes, and soon after, the first motors of the teams going out, carrying coils of sounding wire. Slowly, each of the four vessels would unspool the wire, recording the depth where the plummet landed. The coils ran to 4.5 kilometres, judged sufficient to indicate the dropping-off of the seafloor. This would let them determine the vent's edge, and draw its shape. As a technique it was laborious and unwieldy, and there was the risk of the plummet getting stuck before it reached true depth, but for relatively shallow areas it was supposed to be fairly reliable.

While all this was going on, Amy was making last-minute checks on *Scintilla*. I glimpsed her sitting in the corridor in shorts and shirtsleeves, hair up, fingertips flashing over her laptop. She seemed in her element, and I wanted to watch her for longer, but I had to get back downstairs. I still hadn't had a proper look at *Scintilla*, and I made a note to find time to ask Amy if I could do so before its first descent.

Scintilla, later, would measure the deep parts using sonar and radar. Divers were testing water temperature and salinity and acid levels to calibrate the device. Sonar readings were always unreliable, but Amy said you could mitigate errors by programming the device according to the characteristics of the water. What lived there, what composed it, what its character was. 1,500 metres per second as a standard measure of sound velocity isn't helpful, because speed varies in different conditions, and every part of the ocean is unique. So to get a reliable depth, you need to know the area already. The paradox again. As a general rule, you couldn't learn anything radically new, rate of progress capped from the start by inertia, inability to recognise anything past the limits of present imagination. You could only see, essentially, the world as you already knew it.

'If something unprecedented does exist in the vent,' I said to Felix, as we made our way back upstairs, 'there's no guarantee we'd acknowledge it. Even if it moves right past us.'

I dwelled on this as I waited out on deck, watching the activity. I questioned what else I had already missed so far, in my own life, simply through the limits of my character. If we were blind to anything representing a new category, then our individual histories might have amounted to a series of glancing encounters with unspeakable wonders – as a general summation, it felt about right. Life as a repeated failure to apprehend something. Coming close then veering away again, sensing this unnameable category, music heard distantly through a series of doors, a dull, echoing bass, a sound hitting your body.

A distant humming, a smudge of darkness on the otherwise clear horizon – one of the zodiacs was coming in, early. I pushed off from the railings and began to circuit the perimeter, the engine noise of the zodiac louder or quieter according to the objects between us – the life-rafts, the riggings, the emergency supply units.

Voices called from the other side of the ship, over the louder motor of the incoming boat. Karlsson was visible, his wavy, thick blond hair recognisable against the zodiac's black gunwale. He was close now, and shouting something to Stefan I couldn't understand, waving as the boat came in. One of the crew threw a rope towards *Endeavour*. Karlsson was hauling up the sounding equipment, which was odd, given they would be going back out to take further readings soon anyway. I edged closer, and saw it wasn't the wire-coil he was passing up; it was a sonar device. Stefan wore a stern, troubled expression, gathering the rope in. And then I understood. Karlsson wasn't sketching the vent's edge; his team had gone straight for the centre, the projected centre, far out over the horizon. This wasn't authorised, it wasn't the plan. Hence the yelling, Stefan's consternation on deck.

'Thirty-six,' Karlsson kept yelling, calling it louder, just that number, finally barking it out as a question, an interrogation, stress on the third syllable. From his look of astonishment I understood what he was saying. I felt the number thud against me and push through me, leaving a deep hole – I was hollow, brittle at my centre. Thirty-six was a distance, a measurement. 36 kilometres. Three times the depth of the Mariana Trench.

EIGHT

The crews worked slowly and methodically, fixing the line on their respective drop-points, ensuring the descent was consistent, following the line forward 50 metres, retreating and confirming readings, starting the whole process again from the next point. In this way, they gradually drew the shape of the vent, tracing the floor as it fell away. They set up parasols to block the sun but their faces still burned. They came back to *Endeavour* when the sun was at its zenith, filled up on bacon, eggs and black tea, slept and went back out again. They didn't stop when the sun had gone down, preferring to work in the softer temperature, the calm under the stars, sleeping in turns until daybreak. At last the four zodiacs were moving towards each other, suggesting the end, the closing-in of the vent edge, was in sight.

As the data came in, Stefan charted it on the board in the theatre. I switched between the outer deck and the theatre, the sea and its representation, and by the second day a rough picture was beginning to emerge. The shape appeared approximately oval. A Cassini oval, Stefan said. As the teams continued to draw the unusually large perimeter, excitement gradually levelled off, tempered by unease. We were very close to the edge of this, and our vessel, swaying in the calm water, seemed smaller, more vulnerable than it had before. It struck me then that we knew almost nothing about this place, that we might be in some kind of danger, and that our actions were reckless, provocative.

No one could explain Karlsson's depth reading, taken 18 kilometres from the edge and so not actually by the centre, where the vent would be deepest, at all. Clearly it wasn't valid; something unusual was happening in the water, causing a delay in the echo of the sound-waves and rendering sonar useless. I utilised my invisibility during the afternoon meal, flitting between tables and the kitchen, watching the generally muted conversations spiked by bursts of energy and speculation. Nick said his firm expected nickel, cobalt, iron and manganese near the vents. Could chemicals and minerals distort sonar to this extent? he asked. Amy shrugged. It was the beginning of a thesis, anyway, a possible explanation for the failing instruments, but it wasn't doing much to calm nerves.

The shape, and huge extent of the vent-field, was causing a lot of comment. How could this be the result of a natural process? Stefan was particularly excited – I saw him standing next to Amy out on deck after I'd helped clear away the tables, and he gestured to me, his pupils dilated as adrenaline rushed through his body. 'Leigh, this is marvellous!' For an alarming second I thought he was going to hug me. 'What an unbelievable discovery!' he cried, startling others on the far side of the ship.

'Yes, yes!' I called, laughing.

'It changes everything! This could revolutionise cellular theory. I have so many questions! How deep is it really? What is in there? And how rare is the site? Could there even be a whole class of "super-vents" that we are yet to discover, or have we stumbled upon a truly exceptional phenomenon? We know almost nothing about sub-abyssal depths, and I've been thinking: what if this place is the remains of a *truly* ancient site? The legacy, perhaps, of an extraordinary cataclysmic impact millions, even billions of years ago? Could we be in contact, essentially, with a location of singular importance in the history of life on the planet? A cradle, a garden?'

'Jesus, Stefan,' I let out. His theory, emerging in a rush of excitement, left me unsure what to say. There was so much to take in. But while I was broadly carried along on his momentum, Amy stayed grounded.

'This can't be the result of a giant meteor impact, assuming that's what you mean,' she said. 'If it was, you'd expect iridium in the fossil record, and according to records there isn't any.'

Stefan impatiently waved away Amy's scepticism. 'Leigh,' he said. 'What do you think?'

'I agree,' I said, 'it's exciting. But I don't really know what to think, not yet, when we've still to fully chart its depth, and analyse samples.'

'Come on! Where's the harm in a little speculation?'

'Well, I'm sceptical about asteroids and meteors . . .'

He looked surprised, perhaps wounded. 'Can I ask why?'

'In my experience, when people look to astronomy for causes, they're pushing the answer further away; it's a form of giving up.'

'You've seen this happen – where?'

'Well you mentioned first life, so let's take panspermia. It's just . . . unimaginative as a theory, you know?'

'You're saying I'm unimaginative, Leigh?'

'No! I'm saying panspermia is. It's boring. Why do people want to believe life came from somewhere else? Why are they so insistent on that? Like it's supposed to be romantic? Why couldn't life have begun here all along? Like we were saying the other night, Stefan – life is *already* alien, is already rich and strange – we don't need to say it arrived seeded on a meteor to make it more so.'

He smiled. 'So we're ignoring the late heavy bombardment? The potential incubating effect of the pulverised earth? You're as bad as she is,' he said, gesturing at Amy. 'OK, then at least can we agree that exploring potentially the deepest vent in the world is at least exciting?'

Stefan was eager to push on. He strode round the ship, bare feet stepping lightly through the corridors and the sun-warmed outer deck. His eyes, carrying the same vivid blue, linked him to the water in a way I found distracting, so that when the two of us were outside I kept switching my perspective between his features and the sea. He looked younger. Sometimes, overhearing him speak, glimpsing his arms waving, I'd detect a hint of mania in his movements. Perhaps I was wrong. Maybe this was happiness. He was happy to assume full responsibility for decisions – while consulting widely, of course. It was his assertion that, rather than waiting for the zodiacs to complete the perimeter survey before sending them out into the vent, we should restart *Endeavour*'s engines now, cross the edge, navigate towards the centre and run surveys from the ship directly. Others resisted this. There was a surprising amount of pushback on the idea. People didn't want to force *Endeavour* over just yet.

Stefan debated this in the theatre. The AC hummed, our mass of bodies blocked the windows. There were two broad camps. One wanted to push over the line, following Stefan's lead. The other, led by Nick, stressed caution, said with edge-mapping now 85 per cent complete we'd have the zodiacs back in a day or two, and it made sense to use them as a scout mission first. To some of us, this latter position was melodramatic. Felix and I argued for hours, spilling out from the theatre to the bar and outside, where an unusual wind, in the gaining darkness, was whipping the top-sails and making a distracting fluttering sound, like a large bird forcing its wings. I couldn't resist taunting him a little. 'You think we're in danger? Think the ship's going to get sucked down to the bottom of the sea?'

'No, Leigh,' he said calmly. 'I don't think that's going to happen. I don't think anyone in there thinks *that*.'

'I'm not so sure. I think some of them are spooked. They might not endorse Karlsson's 36 kilometres, but they're worried about whatever it is that's creating the distortion. So they want to stand back, send in small teams only. They don't actually want to go there themselves.'

'Or they just realise that where we are now is a good base? We understand it. We know how deep the water is. We've calibrated sonar and the readings match what the zodiacs are getting with rope. We're on firm ground here, so why disrupt that?'

Karlsson, surprisingly, gave his weight to the more cautious approach. Given his trademark gusto, I expected him to be leading the charge onwards, but instead he was calm, withdrawn, quietly stating we should wait. The image of him coming back in the zodiac – dazed, burned, wild-looking – was so incongruous. But the decision, ultimately, was Stefan's, and after all the debate in the theatre, and long consultations with Amy, Karlsson and Nick in the control room, he announced over the intercom that with the perimeter survey almost complete we would move on to the next phase. At midnight tonight we'd restart the engines and cross the line. We'd stop approximately 18 kilometres in, where Karlsson had made his depth reading, and begin a thorough survey of the central zone.

———————

As the floor jolted, the engines clanging into motion again, I grabbed on to the metal bedframe and thought how easy it would be to stay here, and not go forward at all. Movement was what I wanted – I had campaigned for this – but when we began I felt a tightness in my chest, fluttering stabs of uncertainty. We didn't have to do this. It wasn't too late to revoke our decision and go back.

We moved slowly forward. Despite what I had thought, we hadn't actually been stationary at all, the current pushing us steadily backwards over the past few days. Felix and I left our cabin and ascended the stairs, and coming outside we saw it was busier than at any time previously in the voyage. Not only were almost all of the passengers standing out, gathered by the railings, looking forward, they appeared different, more substantial. Something had changed them.

'They've dressed for it,' Felix said, the rest of his words lost under the engines. And he was right – most of the passengers wore formal clothes. I almost didn't recognise Karlsson: long trousers, hair waxed back. They looked like a wedding party, a church congregation. People had been drinking, there was laughter, the lights reflected off flutes and wine glasses. It all seemed a little forced. Felix grabbed two beers from the ice-bucket and we pushed towards the edge, provoking disapproving glances and murmurs from others maybe twice our age.

'How long is it?' I said.

'Four minutes,' the woman next to me replied. As the remaining time ebbed away the clatter and the laughter and the clinking glasses faded, and the only sound was *Endeavour*'s engines and the constant blast of sprayed water as the ship ploughed its way onwards. 23:57. People lifted their heads up high. They were presenting the best of themselves. They were nervous and anxious, just like I was, and rather than waiting it out in their cabins, or taking an Ambien, so that you slept through it and only woke in that same blue, still water and could pretend you hadn't moved at all, that you were still in a safe place, they had come out for it, facing it, finding reassurance in ceremony. And so there had been singing, and drinking, and sentimental conversation, and people dressed as if for a religious event. Reining in the unknown, as if they could protect themselves, ward it off.

'Ten,' a voice called – reedy, high, uncertain. 'Nine,' Stefan continued, sounding more confident. 'Eight.' Together, we joined the chorus.

NINE

It didn't *feel* any different. But no one had gone into the water yet; I hadn't actually realised this until Felix mentioned it in the kitchen while we were preparing breakfast. The longer we left it, the more stigma was attached. It was surprising how quickly a group of experienced professionals could develop something like superstition, and it was fascinating to watch. Whatever reasonable objections people raised – higher aluminium levels, a possible toxic run-off from the minerals – underneath it was a simpler, older, baser fear. It wasn't just that the area below us was unknown, it was that it appeared to be resisting us. Our measurements were blocked. We were repeatedly pulled back. Very early in the process – perhaps from the start, with the original theory of a mineral layer concealing the scope of the vent – people had assigned it agency, will. Whatever it was, overnight it was pushing *Endeavour* away.

Stefan put a call out for volunteers. Technically there was little justification for a dive – Amy lowered camera traps almost as soon as we arrived – so he must have agreed about the need to break the spell. Stefan himself would go down. He asked for others to join him in the initial team. We were packed into the theatre, which had suddenly gone very quiet. I looked around me and saw nobody had raised a hand.

'I'll go,' I said. 'I'll do it.'

Stefan held my gaze, nodded firmly. 'Thank you, Leigh. Anyone else?'

Karlsson hung back by the wall, head lowered. Other voices sounded, including Amy's, and quickly Stefan had his names.

It was still dark when my alarm woke me. I felt my way to the bathroom, and then to the supply room on the deck above, where the wetsuits and equipment were stored. Through the porthole you could see the first signs of light breaking. By the time I joined the others outside it was 05:30 and the air was cluttered with the last of the darkness, a woozy, dreamy indigo colour. The wind had picked up, and the sea waves were high. I had to grab hold of the railings to steady myself. I shivered in the new air. For the first time in many days it wasn't warm.

Amy looked at me. 'You all right?'

I didn't tell her I'd spent half the night awake with repeating, circular thoughts. 'Sure,' I said. 'I just want to be in already.'

The zodiac floated, attached by rope. Stefan thumbed over to me and climbed in first. One by one, we threw him our gear, then took the remaining steps down the ladder, and with Stefan holding out a hand we joined him on the boat.

We were using the zodiac to get closer to Karlsson's point before making the dive. *Endeavour*, overnight, had shifted position again, retreating hundreds of metres back towards the line. This meant the other passengers wouldn't see us go under, would have no proof of us entering the water. Something as trivial as this could make a difference – the point in going out here and doing this, at dawn on our second morning, was to demonstrate lack of fear and lose some of the developing superstition. Doing it off-stage might lessen the effect.

Stefan pulled the motor and increased speed, and we slipped and bounced on the choppy surface. The sky was lit up, and we carried east as if making for the huge red sun on the horizon. In this moment, all my misgivings fled, and I felt utterly happy to be here. Stefan pulled the motor again and we slowed, then Amy checked something on her phone, nodding; we cut the engine.

We confirmed oxygen levels, put on flippers and applied our masks. I pulled the rest of the bodysuit over me, the cap stretching tight at the skull, sleeves snug on my fingertips. The material was thinner than I was used to. It was like being wrapped in a second skin. Amy had brought them from JPL; they were recommended on dives in 'areas of unknown provenance', which made me wonder where they'd tested them.

Stefan went first. He tapped me on my shoulder. 'It's going to be fine. You're going to enjoy this.' He perched on the edge of the gunwale, raised both thumbs, nodded, and tumbled backwards. Brief splash, silence. Amy next, then

Eric and Ursula. I was alone on the boat, rocking in the swell. They had disappeared. Chatter and small talk and four black-suited bodies gone. I moved to the edge, and though I had no audience I still raised my thumbs like the others had and thrust myself backwards over the side.

I sat up gasping, sweating, heart pounding, hands gripping hard onto the metal bedframe. Another nightmare, tilting backwards, free-falling, tumbling faster and faster into heat and light and noise, the fire of the earth's core as I descended. It was either the second or third night of the dreams. The bedsheets were soaked. I stepped onto the floor and put my arm out to stop from falling. My ears hurt; my balance was shot. I made my way slowly to the bathroom.

On the first night after the dive I was delirious. I slept the whole day then Felix saw my bed empty, went out looking for me and found me glassy-eyed by the railings, apparently ready to go back in. Felix couldn't make sense of what I was saying. Dr Anderson looked me over: either sunstroke or food poisoning, possibly both. It didn't look like decompression sickness, but he wanted to keep an eye on me as a precaution. He gave me pills, which I threw back without reading. Gathering myself, I muttered something about being the only green-face on the ship. Anderson frowned at this and when I opened my eyes I was back in my cabin, in bed, in darkness.

I still couldn't remember everything. After falling backwards from the zodiac the water had enveloped me as an oddly neutral medium: no odour, no temperature, and with my bodysuit extending over my fingertips it made no direct impression on my body at all. I was untouched. The moment had a kind of hyper-reality. Because it felt as if I wasn't wearing a suit at all, and yet the sea had no effect on me, my brain made the decision that I wasn't actually in the water, I was watching myself in a film or a dream. Sealed off from the water while immersed in it, I almost had to take it on trust that I was really there. I looked out at it remotely, through a lens. The experience was uncanny, with something of the vivid irreality I'd noted in my childhood during episodes of shock. I was there and not there. I swam through the sunlight layer at the same time as I looked back on myself from some unknown, uncertain future point.

There were maybe seventy seconds between Ursula and me going down, but even in the clear water I couldn't see anyone. Above me was the zodiac's shadow. I imagined I could feel *Endeavour*'s engines a couple of klicks away. It was only then that I started to become aware – really, viscerally aware – of the depth.

I was perhaps an equal distance from the seafloor and the upper sky, the ocean under me as far away as aircrafts above. The realisation hit me in the pit of my stomach. I moved my arms to test and reinforce buoyancy, some precaution against plummeting, and then suddenly I felt like I was moving through the sky. The space beneath seemed to open up, and the sunlight layer became more intense, the whole depth illuminated like a glass medium. I imagined I saw further and further down, right to the core, the crust opening, the exposed mantle bright with fire, widening and drawing more and more down into it, eddying, sucking me down in a corkscrew motion, forced in by the compelling Earth, the pull of the bottom, the attractive force of the archaea, seized by some death instinct towards the place where all this began.

I swallowed oxygen, tested and flexed limbs, told myself relax, you've done this a thousand times before. Then something strange happened, as everything became easy, generous. I was no longer moving myself; I was carried. My voice became quiet, echoing further and further away. A diver's dark silhouette spun slowly down, tumbling until it disappeared. The disappearance calmed me. Everything was perfectly still and quiet. My heart rate dropped, I stopped hearing my breath's repetition. I lost myself into a wide, vast warmth, a wholly enveloping medium. Suddenly the sea was bright with colour, as life surged: a purple and yellow sea lily uncrushed itself, pushing away water in a spray; red-tipped tubeworms undulated successively like the drift of a breeze over a wheat field, a thought unfurling across a bed of neurons; jets of bio-light glowed and pulsed, as outlines of animals burst in rapturous communication then disappeared again into the darkness; transparent cephalopods hung suspended in an immensity; bacterial symbionts draining and nourishing everything; archaea under it, at the heart of it, crawling, synthesising, stretching back, inexpressible return—

Blinding sunlight. Suddenly pulling off the mask, gulping wild oxygen, gasping and crying out. Drifting, hanging as a star on the sea surface. The sky and sea exactly the same ultramarine. A sense of existing at a great height, of exceeding something, of being close to the unlimited. Tears and laughter and saltwater rushing in. This immense, inexpressible happiness, every single memory at once. The zodiac gone. The other divers gone. Calm, peace. Then a shape, *Endeavour* – and ever, and ever – just visible on the horizon. Getting smaller, edging further away. The swell of the water, the play of the light.

I took a breath and swam onwards, limbs tightening on every stroke, the ship holding a single shape, a static distance. I swallowed more water, pushing desperately on, lungs heaving. *Endeavour* came into focus at last. When I reached it I hung on the surface, floating gently in the swell. Even this close, the ship looked different, two-dimensional, as if painted onto water. I couldn't believe we lived in this place. Several figures bobbed around it – Stefan and the other divers. They were lying forward with their faces planted in the water, fascinated, limbs splayed like stars.

The climbing sun burned my crown, seeding the beginnings of a headache. My hands tingled, my stomach turned. I pushed over to the port-side steps, struggling at first to make purchase, then gripped on securely and yanked myself up. I clambered aboard, running my hands through my hair, shivering, ecstatic. It was uncanny to be standing again, to feel the force of my weight on the ground. A world again. My stomach swirled, recalibrating, and a lightness rushed through my head.

'Everything OK?' Felix called, distracted as he hosed down the deck. I nodded, squinted at the ship's clocks – 140 minutes passed since my dive. What happened to me, down there? How far did I go? Feverish and light-headed, I could think only of going back in.

TEN

I still didn't feel right three days after the dive. My fever had subsided to 102, but I was groggy and my head felt airy, vacuous, and my skin itched. I couldn't hold food down. I struggled to tell Anderson exactly what it felt like. I wasn't myself. 'Explain,' Anderson repeated, an edge of tiredness in his voice. Raw, I said. Like a layer has come away. 'Your skin is extra-sensitive?' Yes. Sort of. It's like I can feel it moving. Like it's alive. 'I'd say that's a good thing,' Anderson smiled. No. Alive separately, different from me. Every cell buzzing and spinning.

The general antibiotics would take longer to fully kick in. Anderson expected the cognitive symptoms – mild delirium – to subside with my temperature. I was improving. This wasn't DCS. There was nothing to worry about. Yes, I said, gazing forward, perched on the end of the medical bed.

Felix guided me back to the cabin. 'All this just to get out of kitchen duties,' he muttered, shaking his head. 'I'm kidding,' he said, looking at me oddly.

Something is off; I am not myself. He helps me into my bunk, then tells me to call him if I need anything. I lie back in the bed as the door clips closed, leaving the cabin dark. The mattress and cushions mould me. I feel this through the base of my head, my back, my rear and my legs. I am being re-made in a new position. I want to see this, to watch the creation, but it is dark and I can't make out the line separating me from the rest of the room. Not just my skin but every part of me is shifting and crawling. A cloud of insects, pressed into roughly human form. Each of the insects has its single living purpose, its vitality – I can feel them, their industry – but at the same time they carry me across a wave. Felix helps hold me together, but parts come away in his hand, spilling across the corridor, and now they are spreading through the cabin. I am slipping away, coming back, falling away again. The insect cloud regenerates, keeps me alive. The rough shape of a person. I am grateful to them, and I am them. They carry me across a wave.

When I woke I felt much better, clearer and more familiar, but still with an odd sense of recklessness and exposure, a kind of self-sabotaging urgency. My phone told me I'd slept for fourteen hours. My temperature was down to 101.4. I watched myself through my phone's camera lens, pushed and prodded my face. I got up to the bathroom, feeling supple and loose. I was physically different but not unwell. I relished these first moments of recovery, the fleeting unfamiliarity and gratitude towards ordinary things.

I took a long shower and changed into a new set of clothes. Suddenly I was hungry, eager to get down to the dining room and learn what I'd missed in the previous few days. I moved slowly along the corridor, not so much out of hesitancy as out of an interest in what was around me: the panel fixtures on the walls, the way the carpet felt against my soles. I was animated, and though I'd barely eaten in the past three days I had energy, purpose. I was eager to go on, to continue with the expedition.

Amy checked on me at breakfast. She said she and the others on the dive showed symptoms too – nausea, loss of balance, fever, mild delirium. She'd been worried about DCS as well – she could barely remember ascending – but the symptoms hadn't persisted and she was fine now. The others seemed to be doing better too, just as eager as we were to dive again. She said they were prepping the sub for a fourth descent; this one would go deeper, past twilight and even into Hades, assuming the vent reached that far.

'Did you get samples?' I said, between mouthfuls of hard granola.

'Extracted, stored, labelled, ready for analysis.'

'And you're at what, exactly?'

'5,800 metres at the moment. Like I say, we're looking to drop down later today.'

Lab equipment on *Endeavour* was limited, and protocols for handling deep-water material meant the ship couldn't analyse anything further than the sunlight layer. So when the subs and the sounding lines came up, everything had to be scraped off and put into quarantine. All material was carefully packed and preserved in the cold room. In a sense the ship was already quarantined – we got up, and ate, and continued our work the other side of a vast sea border.

Anderson wanted to give us another medical review. It seemed pretty clear that something in the water was to blame, but he was being cautious and wanted a full list of everything we'd eaten. Before I could do this, however, I got a note from Stefan saying he wanted to see me in the theatre. The last time I'd seen him he was floating in the water.

The theatre was one of the larger rooms on the mid-deck, with rows of chairs, a projector facing the fore-wall, and plenty of standing room at the sides. When I got there I was disappointed to see Amy, Eric and Ursula too. I'd thought Stefan wanted to see me alone, that he had something important to tell me, perhaps he was even going to promote me and give me a more active role. He walked in and closed the door. It was odd to see the room virtually empty. We were standing close to the door, close together.

'We won't have long alone here so let's make this quick,' Stefan began. 'Each of us has been ill since the dive.' He paused, scanning the group for a reaction. 'You're all experienced divers, you know this is not unusual, that the causes can be multiple. I think it's important we don't make too much of what happened.

'I'm not suggesting you lie,' he said, before any of us could react. 'I'm not asking you to do anything you're not comfortable with. I just think there's no reason to keep talking about it. We shouldn't speculate on what happened, certainly not around others. In a worst-case scenario, I could see them petitioning to turn the ship around.'

'No,' I said automatically. 'They're not doing that.'

'We already saw that in the debate about crossing the line,' Amy said. 'People are afraid. They're ready to be irrational.'

'I agree. We have to be careful. If we say too much, say the wrong thing, we could inadvertently end all this right now.'

Eric spoke up. 'And Anderson?' We waited for Stefan to respond.

'Look, we're all feeling better, aren't we? In fact, I feel better than at any time so far. So why would we need to keep talking to Anderson? If symptoms return, then that's different, but as it is I think we need to move on completely. And I think the surest way of dispelling unrest and proving there's nothing in this would be to get back in the water.'

ELEVEN

I looked into imagined depths, the base of the vent broiling with archaea and bacteria, churning through the gases emitted by the opened earth, a cycle of transformation beginning. The possibility of life, mineral into organic, objects creating themselves in a frenzy of feeling, striving not to end, briefly distinct from what surrounds them before coming apart again, back into disparate chemicals. I took a breath, felt a stabbing in my abdomen: anxiety, indigestion, the trailing memory of the illness picked up in the water. I clutched at the pain, grasping myself, and looked back, turning away from the edge and towards the ship, the low roofs of the decks, the clip of the neat doors closing onto snug cabins. I flashed the rest of the dive team an OK sign, kicked backwards from the stern, tumbled into the water.

Something had got inside us, a compulsion, a desire, a need to return. It was automatic and involuntary, a magnetic attraction drawing us in again and again. While the sub continued its descent, all five of us made several dives. This time, and in spite of the earlier symptoms, there was no trepidation, no hesitancy at all.

It was exhilarating. I have no words for what I saw and what I felt as I descended, exploring the upper level of the sub's journey, the sunlight layer above the oval vent. I was not afraid. I pulled the full bodysuit over me, tipped backwards from the stern, and swept through the bright water for as long as my oxygen allowed. Afterwards I lay out on the deck, chest inflating and deflating rapidly, images spinning through my head. Waiting out the period until the next dive I towelled up and went indoors, back to the theatre, which, under Amy's direction, was continuing to beam near-live footage from *Scintilla*'s journey beneath us.

To begin with, we couldn't see anything. The sub kept getting stuck, tangled in free-floating weeds. But it was trained for this, and Amy cheered like a proud parent as it freed itself. Even by mid-range in the sunlight level the water was opaque. *Scintilla* adjusted its lighting, and the whole theatre flickered. I was getting impatient, and decided to go out for some air again, watch the water from the deck, where a little group had formed. Though we couldn't see anything from here – the sub was hundreds of metres down already – it was satisfying to look on. For this – the fourth launch, the one that aimed for Hades – all non-essential ship work was suspended, and the atmosphere on deck was optimistic, collegiate, with just that hint of tension surviving from earlier.

While the water continued to pull me in, I was drawn, equally involuntarily, to my past. I returned to the ocean, as I returned to my childhood in Rotterdam, to Geert's inexplicable beatings and to the nights following when Fenna mended me, kneaded me, and ushered me back as best she could. I looked back on the events as if they'd happened to another person, pitying this character as I would a stranger. But if she was a stranger, she'd still shaped the person I'd become. I didn't want to think about this connection to her, didn't want to admit it, sitting out on my towel in the sunshine.

I resisted being so easily explained, but I couldn't help suspecting there was something in it. I wanted desperately for my life to be my own creation, to not have my present behaviour reduced to things that happened when I was young. My swims in the Nieuwe Maas were a reaction to Geert's beatings and the site where I first discovered hope. Going into the water was in the first instance an escape, and maybe in some sense it still was. Maybe what I thought was an objective and impersonal interest in the origin and development of cellular life was in fact something smaller, an attempt to flee my own history but also an acceptably disguised way of exploring it. Maybe, rather than investigating the origins of life, I was merely and regrettably pursuing my own individual history. While I opened my eyes and with difficulty raised myself on deck, gazing out again into the ultramarine, fierce sunlight bouncing off the blue, I recalled the life forms I studied, further insight into which I believed existed in the vent below us now, the same organisms that populated and substantiated the pain I felt as a child. They were, in a sense, the physical constituents accompanying and embodying that earlier drama, my nine-year-old self hugging her cramping stomach the day after a beating. But they were more than that – their purpose was infinitely variable, they were the source, I thought, of joy and exhilaration as much as they were terror, pain. They were the source of everything, inside us and beyond us, before us and long after we were succeeded. While I studied it, I had to admit I was entangled in it too. It couldn't be otherwise – I came from it. And as part of this honesty I might have to face that my mind – my 'character', as I might call it, which I still willed in some naive way as my own creation, an infinitely regressive loop – was not separate and cut off either. Entangled in its thicket, I looked into the water with eyes that were born there, several billion years before. This challenged me, reduced me and provoked me, but it also instilled in me a desire to keep going, to keep pushing, to continue this exploration just as far as I could take it, across the remainder of my conscious days.

We huddled in the theatre again, watching the spectral, loamy greys and whites of the sub's beam as it crawled through the midnight layer. My mind was full of fractal sponges and long, leaf-like creatures built completely from repetition, self-similar organisms stating themselves again and again, the creatures of the Avalon period, the original radiation of multicellular life. But in reality, I saw little.

Anything we observed here – anything living; and Ursula, an expert on cetaceans, believed large vertebrates may well exist here – fed primarily on extremophile archaea and the filtered organic fog of bodies torn apart at the sunlight heights. The sub swivelled just a little and the white wash of its beam through the outer darkness illuminated an inestimable distance – 2 metres or 200 metres, laterally – and I saw glimpses of tiny particulate matter, microcosms of a formerly coherent whole, the spray of a body, which fed this dark life here and below the midnight layer too, the twilight and the hadal – and even the sub-hadal, the below-underworld, should such a place exist. The generosity of porous life, I thought, watching what I believed was the disintegrated water-torn body of something that had lived, had sensed, had felt, had possessed its own wishes. Death begetting life. I was moved by this, stupidly; the sacrifice of everything that lived, everything that turned to mist. Silica mats descending and giving rise to the same conditions that created the sea vent. Diatoms and coccoliths' skeletons and shells sinking to the last, building up beds of chalk and limestone across billions of years. The silent weather of a body, pushing onto the ocean and the atmosphere, sustaining new life, continued life, bringing—

Everything stopped. Everything went dead. 'Fuck!' Amy shouted. The feed cut to absolute black as the theatre, in turn, was plunged into invisibility. Pockets of blue light shone from phones, people murmuring; someone found a switch. Not an electrical problem – power continued to run through the ship. Not a local problem on the projector either. So it was the sub itself, *Scintilla* – the feed had gone, still only descending through the upper regions of the midnight layer.

We played the recorded images back, as if attempting to pretend it wasn't true. Felix and I went to the kitchen and put out a spread. Food helped. There was a lot of confusion in the hours that followed; rumours, attempts at clarification, conflicting information, all driven by the absence of any clear statement from Stefan, Amy and the team, locked in the control room. The most dramatic rumour was that something had struck the sub, shattering the camera lens – protected behind reinforced plexiglass – and compromised the whole structure. Some said the mission was over, we had no choice but to abort it. This idea, of going back, was devastating; I wasn't prepared for it. Others said it was only visual contact that was lost, and while this was a huge blow, it didn't affect our goal of charting the vent's absolute depth. In the early evening Stefan called us back and announced, in the theatre, that until we had established exactly what had happened, no further dives would be permitted.

Fenna was never maternal in any conventional sense. She was uncomfortable with closeness (I can't, for instance, once remember us even briefly hugging). The clear-cut way I've always seen this is that it was a necessary correlative to her brilliance in mathematics. She was attracted to the infinite, to the glacial calm of a perfect clear reality, beyond organisms, beyond matter. It calmed her, it made sense to her, an appealing alternative to the desperate and disappointing mutability of living stuff.

She never really approved of what I did. I remember her asking me, when I was thirteen or so, if I was really sure of what I wanted to study. Initially seeing it as criticism, more proof of my aloneness, I now wonder if she was actually trying to nudge me closer to her own world, to mathematics or physics, which Helena would later study. We were taking a rare walk. As we left the park we came into a wooded area and stopped by a small stream. We were watching the rush, the white froth over the surface, when she turned to me. 'Do you know about Pacific salmon?'

'Do I *know* about them?'

'Yes. In your study. Or your reading. Have you come across them?'

'Not really.' I crossed my arms defensively. 'Why?'

'They're interesting. You'll hear about them soon enough. They hatch in streams like this, then migrate to the ocean. When they're ready to spawn, they cover huge distances to return to the stream they were born in.'

'The same stream?'

'Yes.'

'That's amazing.' Enthralled by the story, it still felt strange that this was coming from Fenna.

'Yes,' she said. 'But that's not all. Weeks after releasing their spawn, their bodies become soft and they disintegrate. They come apart in the same stream, saturating the water with nutrients so their young can grow fat on them.'

'Like cannibalism?'

'I suppose it is, indirectly.' She smiled. 'It's not easy, you know, being a parent. I hope you know that. But I'm not just talking about families and children; I mean everyone. Everyone is a parent. That's what getting old is: *catastrophic senescence*. That's what dying is. You become a parent. You fall into the stream.'

We walked back the rest of the way in silence.

The worst thing about the violence, maybe, was the suspicion Fenna might have ended it, and didn't. What I've clung to, over the years, as a singular act of devotion – Fenna's hands over my hurt bones in the night – may in reality have inadvertently encouraged him. I tormented myself, picturing the quiet figure of the doctor who aids torturers by ensuring the victim is kept alive and conscious. This is horrible, masochistic, and I can't really believe it. If one of the effects of Fenna retrieving me was that Geert was able, for longer, to continue beating me, then that still doesn't void the love within the act. It can't do. She helped me go on, knowing that one day I would outrun his violence.

'You all right?'

I looked up at Stefan peering down at me.

'Yes. Just thinking. Family, you know.'

'If you ever want to talk . . .'

'Thanks,' I said, pushing out a smile. 'It's OK.'

As the hours continued to pass through the night, and as *Endeavour*'s outer lights were cut, features appeared in the upper sky, thousands, hundreds of thousands, millions of densely packed stars, like pinpricks cut across a vast black veil, affording glimpses into a wall of light beyond. The upper distances implied the gulf open beneath us, and as the stars were like punctures through darkness the vents such as the Atlantic crater and the Mariana Trench were similar holes cut in Earth's crust, the light of distant stars and the light of Earth's furnace, contrasting indications of a generally hidden illumination. Above us and below us this brilliant radiance.

TWELVE

There were only a dozen of us in the room – I checked the
time, 03:28, most were still asleep, the news only just broken.
Felix filled me in. The control team had somehow re-
established contact with the vessel, which had now reached
a depth of 9,000 metres, broaching the border between the
twilight and hadal layers. Whatever had happened to cause
the loss of visuals also seemed to have affected the sub's
progress, as it was now dropping more slowly through the
water. Less than thirty minutes ago a new image had
appeared, and the control team had had to revise their
understanding of what had happened. If *Scintilla* was still
capable of recording, then clearly the lens hadn't shattered.
The new theory was that an electrical error had shorted the
boards and blocked the flow of data back to the ship.

'But what could have ruptured the wiring?' I said.

'I don't know – it hit something, didn't it?'

'But what?'

'You have a better suggestion?'

The images, when we finally saw them, were barren. They
contained no life. Or no visible life; the scene would be
teeming with microscopic clouds. So there was disappointment over lack of visual proof of vertebrates beneath
the hadal zone. But disappointment wasn't what I felt when
I studied the fourth image. The theatre wall showed a series

of drifting white blocks, carbonate lumps broken off from collapsed mineral towers deeper in the vent-field. We kept looking. Silence as one image bled into the next.

'That's it,' Stefan said. 'No further images, I'm afraid. But we have just received a new radar reading. The updated scan – bear in mind this should be more reliable given it's launched from a lower depth, with better local calibration – is estimating another 200.'

'200 metres? So we're effectively there, we've reached the bottom.'

A strange sensation, a fluttering and sinking in my stomach, a tingling in my hands again.

Stefan shook his head. 'Not metres. Kilometres.'

It was too late now, and there was too much going on, to think of sleeping. 200 kilometres was obviously an error, but what had caused it? And how deep did it really go? More people emerged as news spread, footsteps and voices carrying through the walls. A mist had developed overnight, delaying the dawn. Everything outside was silent and grey. The mast began to creak and stretch, and the deck tilted. On all sides it was the same: a short, depthless view onto the near water. With the sun's position blocked I couldn't set my bearings, and it was as if we were encircled by a shroud. Finally, just after 07:00, the sun burned away the haze and opened out the morning by degrees. Detail after detail was added, a gaining creation, the sea extending further until finally it touched the sky at its limit.

I brewed up some coffee, heated up snacks. *Endeavour*'s inner zones glowed with a softer, lambent light. Topping up mugs, doling out hot rolls, I took stock of responses to the news. Stefan and his group were suggesting that a positive light feedback had followed the latest depth scan. Due to the electrical crisis, a disproportionately massive amount of light was emitted, and rather than reading the response time of each light echo, a chain reaction began, each reflection building on the previous one. So what we were reading was an accretion of many light pulses, not a single light returning and indicating true depth.

Working again, I found it easier to think, engaged in repetitive and predictable tasks. Something about the labour of it – and this applied only in short bursts – freed my mind to wander undirected, bringing new impressions and ideas to the surface. Immediately, I began to think of magnetic fields. So the sub was essentially hallucinating, misreporting internally generated depths. Of course the crater wasn't anything like 200 kilometres down. The depth scans, at this point, whether sonar or radar, were a distraction. The sub could judge an infinite depth beneath us, a depth commensurate with the loop of the universe. But the cause of the error was still interesting. Unusual magnetic activity was observed at depths in the Mariana Trench, and though it would take vastly greater activity to affect the sub like this, it didn't in principle seem impossible. Mantle is exposed at the sea-vent, made of molten iron and nickel, creating the planet's magnetic field. Was it so ridiculous to suggest the vent had caused a magnetic disturbance, disorienting the submersible, shorting some of its boards?

I thought about the five of us taken ill after the dive, the strange experience in the water, the fever, loss of appetite and balance, the violent stomach upset and the sense of general incoherence. Stefan spoke about 'hadal fever', something that appears the first time you approach these places; I had assumed he was describing a largely psychological event. I'd noted at the time, clasping my abdomen, grimacing as I turned in my bed, the fact that all of us have extremophile archaea in our lower gut, kin to the species more than 10 kilometres below us. Were these organisms inside us compelled by a magnetic tide, the same tide responsible for sabotaging the submersible? Was our trepidation and excitement partly molten in origin – was that the reason I couldn't stop thinking about going back in?

Sunlight streamed through the portholes. The eastern sky ridged in accumulations of red, pink, and fiery orange. We were drawn outwards to the deck, watching the morning unfold in silence, appreciating the immensity of the new horizon. The sea was calm, the swell low, the moment almost unbearably perfect, unbearably still.

THIRTEEN

The whole period seemed out of time. We hadn't seen land in weeks. We hadn't seen the lights of a single other vessel, nor the tracks of any aircraft in the sky. Even the terns had abandoned us. *Endeavour* lolled in the water, in the intense heat of the day and the damp, smothering blue darkness of the night. It was hard to imagine that around us life was continuing as usual, that if you were to travel far enough in any direction you would find buildings, roads, great washes of noise as people went about their days.

The sub continued to drop, sinking at its slower pace, stating a depth of 10, then 11,000 metres. And at 16:43, on Tuesday 11 July, the twenty-seventh day of our voyage, the submersible reached 36,000 feet, close to the estimated depth of the Mariana Trench, and further than any mission had previously touched. We were skirting the bottom of the world. It was Amy who announced this, to a hushed, packed audience in the theatre, drawing a spontaneous outbreak of applause.

Having reached this depth, control faced a dilemma. As Amy had explained earlier, the sub was pretty much autonomous. But while they couldn't control its exploration, they could still overrule the autonomous command and bring it up. The question was whether to do this now, at 13 kilometres – have the sub slowly ascend and deliver its data troves – or allow it to continue pushing down. Getting to 13 kilometres wasn't straightforward; the sub was withstanding unbelievable pressure, the equivalent of 1,100 atmospheres. Amy winced as she described this, as if physically relating to the massive burden slowly and inevitably crushing *Scintilla*. No one could say for how long exactly it would bear this; this was one of the things the trial was designed to uncover. They had an idea, of course, but it was only a guess. So Amy, and the rest of the control team, and all of us on the ship, were torn between wanting to protect the miniature submersible vessel – our roaming eye, our light, twisting and slowly buckling in the depths; bringing it back up to the surface where we could finally retrieve its samples – and keeping it down there, suffering the ocean on top of it, pushing it further, lower, beyond the base limit of Hades.

I realised, that afternoon, that I hadn't seen Stefan in some time. He was probably locked in his cabin, earplugs in, going over something technical, but for some reason I worried about him, felt protective over him. And I missed him, his manic energy and earnestness. I missed the discussions we'd had earlier in the journey, which already felt like a lifetime ago. With everything that had happened, Stefan was increasingly inaccessible, occupied with the sub's journey. I rarely, if ever, saw him alone, and I regretted this.

When he returned, calling us back to the theatre, he looked different – eyes blazing, breath heavy, his narrow diaphragm visibly overworked beneath the same loose orange T-shirt he'd worn the first time I'd met him. He had two things to tell us: the submersible had reached past 16 kilometres – proving beyond doubt that the crater below us was not just lower than anywhere else on Earth's surface, but lower by 4,500 metres. This time there was no applause, just shocked silence, some tears, finally a burst of staccato cries – 'Oh my god, oh my god.' But Amy was staring intently at Stefan, who was looking away from her, unable to meet her gaze. 'It's over,' he said finally. 'We lost it, it's gone. 17.2. No contact.'

FOURTEEN

Storms moved over us in the dark. You could feel the electricity in the cabins, the tension, the closeness of the air, the silent sheets flickering around us. Shapes appeared in the illuminated water, shadow objects, deceptions wrought by the storm. The lightning continued to track us, surrounding us as we drifted several hundred metres on the current, pushed back on ourselves, back towards the crater's edge.

We had pressure and temperature readings from 16 kilometres, but water and mineral samples only from the sub's last ascension point, at 11 kilometres. This led to an odd combination of feelings: pride, excitement, euphoria at samples representing a survey of a lower area than any contacted before, and a profound and tantalising regret that we hadn't extracted something from even further below. The ultimate base of the crater was beyond our grasp, so close I could sense it inside me – lingering headaches, dreams of deep falling, regular loss of balance on the deck. I didn't know whether we would ever come back, whether the resources allowed that, or if *Endeavour* would be a one-off mission. Maybe we would wait years for the required advances in sub design. We might never know what was down there – how far it reached, and what, if anything, lived in there. It seemed incredible that this might actually be the closest anyone would ever come to finding out. If the likely result of any follow-up mission was the loss of billion-dollar equipment, could we really expect it to be approved?

As we continued documenting the events of the previous weeks, Stefan informed us that within forty-eight hours we would turn *Endeavour* around and begin the long journey back to port. Though this should have been inevitable, the news struck me as a profound shock. I wasn't prepared for this, wasn't ready to let go. I felt this terrible sense of thwarted opportunity and injustice, and already the beginning of a cheap, sentimental nostalgia for the high points earlier in the mission, points where it had seemed there was no end to where this might take us, no end to the revelations we might dig out. Felix tried to console me, as we nursed his gin mixed with juice under the table. He said this wasn't the end, just the beginning of the next stage, the land-based segment of the mission, where, having recovered deep-water samples, high-spec labs would finally read them and find out what was inside.

'But we won't be there to see it, will we?' I protested. 'Everything we've collected will be taken from us. We'll never see any of this again.'

Scrapings from the sub-hadal zone were treated with all the reverence due an alien life form. Each of the sub's deep-water ascents had followed a rigorous security protocol. The entire outer deck was cleared, and the sub was brought in via an

ROV. Again remotely, the samples were fixed in a secure container, and the sub – after a thorough visual survey – was lowered back into the water for its next descent.

Even after the secure containers were towed onto land they would have to be quarantined for an excessive nine months. No one could tell me where this would happen, which lab would host the samples. Felix said I shouldn't take it personally, he doubted even Stefan knew where it was going. There was the question of who actually owned the samples, whatever was in them. It seemed obvious that Stefan, Karlsson and Amy should continue to work closely with the material, but even Amy would have little say in this. 'I'm an engineer,' she said. 'I don't analyse extremophiles. That's what you do.'

I woke early the next day, feeling strong, and with an almost uncontainable urge to re-enter the water. This might be my last chance to dive. Regardless of Stefan's instructions, I felt compelled to go back in. I thought I was being discreet, moving quietly in the dark, but from nowhere I heard Amy's commanding voice asking what I thought I was doing. She grabbed my mask and took it from me. 'Do you realise the risk you're taking?' she demanded. I couldn't stop staring at her eyes. 'You heard Stefan; until we find out exactly what's happened, it's not safe. You're putting yourself in danger. Though to be honest, Leigh, that isn't even my main concern.

If you drain out down there, someone is going to come in looking for you, and in doing so they're risking their own life.'

I returned, chastened, to my cabin. I wished we could continue, I didn't want to go back, labs or no labs. But we had no choice. The forced schedule wasn't simply down to the failure of the submersible: our fuel and food stocks were getting low. After only thirty-four days, this didn't sound right. *Endeavour* was a reasonably large ship; I'd worked in the kitchen and seen the 23-kilogram rice sacks and the walk-in freezer vaults stuffed with hanging carcasses. But some of the food had spoiled; an electrical error interfering with the refrigerator settings. There was also a separate, minor engine fault which had led to fuel loss, something that apparently happened quite regularly; the software that should raise the alarm was easily tripped. There was more than enough fuel to keep us out here for days, even weeks longer, especially as we used minimal amounts when stationary, but the captain was adamant he wouldn't allow this, that as an inviolable industry protocol they had to keep a minimum fuel surplus in reserve at all times.

On our last night, preparing to turn, we stood outside on the deck again, as we had done when we'd prepared to cross the line thirty-five days earlier. The difference this time was that nobody was dressed formally, and there was even more alcohol. We circled the ship under the twilight sky. The time had passed so quickly, etc. – only it really had. What an extraordinary adventure – how lucky we had been to be a part of it. And inevitably, as the wine drained, and even among the younger of us: would we ever be a part of something like this again?

It was dark now, and just as it had as we first entered the vent-field, a wind picked up. A loud blast from the ship's horn startled me, making me spill the contents of my glass. So we were preparing to leave, but doing so – I checked my phone – eighty minutes early. The horn blasted again, three times. I turned back, looked around, but all I saw were similar expressions of bemusement. I started walking round to the far side. As I passed the bow I sensed a flicker of light – someone shining a beam on me? But it felt as if the light had come from the other direction; from inside the water.

A figure leaned over the railings, shouting. Karlsson, gesturing into the black water.

'What is it?' I asked him.

And then I saw it – a faint glow, maybe 100 metres out. A pool of bright water separate from the darkness.

By now others were rushing to join us. 'A boat's been sighted,' someone called.

'It's not a boat,' Karlsson said.

This was it, then, I thought – the hidden thing, at last, the music separated by previously impenetrable doors. Mass electrical activity in the water, a life-based luminescence, the same thing that had wrecked sonar and radar, destroyed the sub, shorted the food storage and the alert system on the fuel gauge. The thing that had made us ill and driven us back into the water again and again. This was it, I thought – and I was wrong.

FIFTEEN

The crew launched an immediate recovery, *Endeavour* fully illuminated while we lowered and readied the zodiacs and worked out which of us were still fit enough to go down. In all the confusion I was able to slip my suit on without protest, and minutes after Karlsson had first spotted the sub, eleven of us were in the water.

The glowing light was inconsistent, coming and going, as if imparting an intelligent message in code. When we came near to it we cut the zodiac's engine, circling the glow. Amy prepared the ROV, while others took out long, metallic instruments. We wore our suits, not just to shield from contamination but as a signal that if it came to it, and despite all the risks, we wouldn't hesitate in going in. After several minutes' wrangling, Amy finally retrieved it and brought it back on deck – a clump of blasted plastic and fibreglass nestling a bulb inside.

So not the whole sub, just the light. A detached light, miraculously still functioning even after the heat levels indicated by the blistered plastic round its frame. We hauled it onto the ship, only loosely adhering to quarantine protocols. The deck landing area was covered in thick tarp – the light was lowered onto this, then it was sealed and the tarp was too, before the deck was treated with bleach. While this clean-up took place, I was back out on one of four zodiacs, scouting the water. Floodlights beamed out from both sides of the ship, casting a harsh, lunar glow over the midnight water, which added to the shock and unreality of everything. It was the strangest night, five hours moving over the water, the loud hum from the generator behind us, the fierce light turning the water almost white. 'Halt!' a voice called. 'Back there, I think I see something.' But it was a false alarm. With the ship now slipping away behind us, the light was almost extinguished, fading out in front of us, visibility flickering close to zero.

The second shift proved more successful than the first. By nine o'clock that morning we'd recovered six further pieces from the sub. The process of gathering each piece in was painfully slow: the team alerted Amy back on the ship, who prepared an ROV which was then ferried over to the site by another zodiac. Then came the careful raising of the parts, sealing and storing them and deep cleaning the decks. With seven pieces recovered by the morning, each one carefully photographed, Amy was able to make some initial comments on what had happened. Each piece showed evidence of extreme temperature, the perimeters burned, blistered, melted away. In Amy's opinion this was not an 'internal event' – the heat source came from outside. And though she counselled against premature conclusions, she admitted it was possible the sub had reached the true base of the vent, that this active furnace had burned up the vehicle. She was excited, poring over photographs of the frayed, blistered edges of the broken parts, as if trying to appreciate that the vehicle they had built had come through such an encounter without being wholly annihilated.

Everything recovered so far belonged to the exterior, with the exception of the bulb. What we wanted to find, really, was one of the sealed components from the inner chamber. They were built to survive these events; in theory, they could still come up at any moment, each containing a further trove – accurate depth readings, temperature and pressure charts, samples of water and even base rock. We could then establish how deep the crater went, and what lived there. But this now seemed unlikely. It was almost a full day since the light had surfaced – and the captain had communicated that, whatever happened, we would be leaving shortly.

I hadn't slept properly since the discovery – no one had. The cabin doors were open, people nestled in corners, dozed for an hour or two, then went back out to resume the search. There was a constant smell of burned coffee, bleach on deck, brine and sweat. I fell asleep with my head against Amy's shoulder, waking up to her amused smile. I had the feeling again of linear time coming free from its tracks, of our experiences broadening out and encompassing more than had ever seemed possible. The dawn light folding over the horizon. The unbelievable reach of the stars. Amy's breathless commentary on the photographs showing blistered fibreglass and metal. I looked at Stefan – who seemed, I thought, genuinely happy – and I knew he was thinking the same thing I was, that somewhere on one of those components might be a record of a new kind of life, an organism that could tell us more about how all of this began.

I didn't want to leave, I wanted to stay out here forever, while there was still hope, searching. A little over five weeks and I'd forgotten what land looked like. We didn't eat at all in daylight, fasting so we could have a single, full meal last thing at night, before the horn sounded. We washed at last, the residue of the search days draining from us, we ate and drank together, and we joined each other out on deck as the horn blasted and the engine ripped. As we pulled away, beginning our journey out of the crater, I couldn't tear my eyes from it, fixated on the water, the churn of our movement through it, waiting and waiting for the crucial piece to finally come into view.

SIXTEEN

There was no one moment when we realised Stefan was missing. One of the things about the ship was that it sucked people in and hid them away for days. For what was really a limited space – five decks, 57 metres long – the opportunities for concealment were surprising, so no one thought anything of Stefan's surely temporary absence as we pulled away from the vent, breaching the perimeter in reverse and beginning our journey back into port.

Amy, a full day after we'd left the vent, asked me when I had last seen him. I didn't know. His scuba gear is gone, she said. She spoke quietly, as if she could trick the world into not hearing, not waking up to the full and awful realisation. We were still moving, at this point – moving away – which made everything stranger. He couldn't really be missing – we couldn't actually have believed that – because then surely we'd have stopped and launched the boats.

Deep down we knew that if Stefan was gone it was already too late, that the idea of retrieving him was a fantasy. He knew what he was doing. Belatedly the horn sounded and *Endeavour*, with agonising slowness, turned itself around once more. Karlsson and Nick organised teams to go through each deck, searching every cabin, every shower room, every tiny gap and shadowed space. In three hours it would be dark. The crew canvassed the engine rooms, prepared the searchlights and dropped the boats. Amy, with two of the control team from *Scintilla*, put three ROVs into the water. As I descended the steps onto the zodiac, I couldn't help thinking we were doing this for the first time, that all of this was just beginning, that Stefan wasn't gone and at any moment he'd reappear by the bow, grinning and looking over the water as we prepared to launch our maiden dive.

As there was no one moment when he disappeared, so there was no one moment when he died. Our remote location meant the usual formalities and rituals – police investigation, forensics and coroner's report, interviews – were absent. The body was lost and would never be retrieved. That was the point of it.

The vent in the seafloor was an opportunity, a resting place but also a beginning, a folding back into the earth. Stefan's death, as much as his life, was an act of creation. He was close to something now; I sensed it. I wanted it too. I remembered the compulsion I felt floating by the surface with my face pressed down into the glass of my mask. The golden light pulling me, a part of me, ecstatically. I couldn't leave this. I knew the desire, and I wanted to return there.

PART TWO

Datura

ONE

I arrived with my bags and found the room already cleared. Fenna had bought new linen and put a small lamp on the cabinet by the bed. The room was narrow, difficult to reconcile with the memory. Neat, welcoming in a formal, impersonal kind of way. I detected a slight air of awkwardness and Fenna, behind me in the doorway, said she would put on some tea. I looked at the space, its hotel emptiness, heard the water running in the kitchen, and wondered if her offhand manner, her irritation at my and my sister's concern, her lack of interest in our visits since our father had died, was a way of maintaining dignity, avoiding scenes, and protecting her two daughters from the burden of any guilt. The room couldn't help declare an absence – muted colours expressing the light – and as I lowered my bags onto the bed I thought this might have been a mistake. In three short weeks Fenna would have to strip the bedding and take away the lamp, keep the window open late to air the furniture, and work especially hard to recover the equanimity she'd earlier achieved. I could now see that the list of conditions for my staying these three weeks, which had made Helena laugh, were a delaying tactic, a way of asking me to really think about what I was doing and decide whether I wanted to commit to this. She'd anticipated my leaving, when I first asked if I could stay. Barely through the door, already I regretted the upheaval. However separate our routines, however determined we both were not to upset the balance, the damage was done.

Late on the third night I woke up hearing a splashing sound coming from the far end of the house. At first I thought it was spillover from a dream, another half-memory of the ship, not of the dive but of preparing to go in, leaning over the railings and listening to the swell, but as I waited, sitting up in the dark, I realised my mother was in the kitchen. It was 03:38. The noise of plates slipping in the sink and in the drying rack. After every sound there was a pause, as if she were waiting out the time in which I might have woken up. Finally I got up, opened the bedroom door. The hall was dark, but an edge of light filtered out from the kitchen. I crept forward and peered through the gap.

She was in her powder blue nightgown at the sink, colander and sponge in her hands. She rinsed, soaked, then rinsed again, carefully studying each item before laying it down to dry. Was she secretly eating lavish meals in the middle of the night? Had someone been over, even? But then I noticed that the spread of dishes on the drying rack exactly matched those we'd used ourselves. I'd already washed and put them away. The same two glasses and plates. The same colander and lemon squeezer.

I crept away, wishing I hadn't seen this. She looked small

and frail in her pale blue nightgown. The slow, careful way she cleaned implied infinite patience, endless reserves of time. I felt I'd intruded, glimpsed an insight she'd never willingly have allowed, and which I couldn't even begin to understand.

The longer I stayed at Fenna's – strange, now, to call it that, and not simply think of it as 'home' – the clearer it was how carefully and deliberately she'd built up her new life there. She was wary of me as a relative stranger in the house, and waited up in her room each night until I had gone to bed, but after the first week, having spent more time together in the evenings, something seemed to shift, and we became a little freer. She'd measured me, and was learning to see me as only a minimal threat to the order she'd established. Perhaps one of her greatest worries, on learning I was to live with her these three weeks before starting my new job, was that I would bring up something uncomfortable or inconvenient from the past. The fact I hadn't done appeared to have calmed her.

On occasions, she started to smile or laugh. I was worried, once, she might even try to hug me. She looked at me – and I only thought about this after – with curious amazement, as if struck by the fact that I had emerged from her. This was too broad and shapeless a thought to do anything with – certainly we couldn't speak about it. But she eyed me fondly, maybe with a kind of pride, realising she had never given herself enough credit for making this person. I enjoyed these little spells, odd grace periods in which I had total immunity. I could do no wrong at all, my mother purely happy that I was there, that I existed. She appeared youthful, as if the perspective had returned her to the person she had been almost thirty years before. This could be a little unsettling, a graphic shift in her identity, the person I had been talking to moments earlier now in the process of falling away. Recovering herself involved, at the same time, losing herself, or at least as these two distinct identities appeared to me. On one occasion, in the kitchen by the sink, I had an insight into a more dramatic and alarming shift, as Fenna appeared to lose sight of where and who she was, a wet uncertainty filling her eyes. It only lasted a moment, but it was awful, and I desperately wanted my acknowledged mother back, the distant, aloof, independent and generally pleasant older woman I was briefly living with.

Though over two years had passed, I still dreamed frequently of *Endeavour*, waking on my descent into the water. Everything was vivid: the briny smell of the corridors, impervious to our attempts at sterilising them; the sound of air tunnels whipping across locked gates; the sudden loss of stability as my centre of gravity shifted. I pictured our ship from above, a single vessel swept in blue wastes. Despite what had ultimately happened, my abiding memory was of excitement, determination, and the promise of something extraordinary soon to be revealed.

I didn't share any of this with Fenna, despite her asking me about this and the new position I was taking up in California. I refrained from speaking about it, fearing that this other, bigger world might undermine the more intimate one we were developing. With several days until I flew, I tried not to be distracted by where I was going, and to enjoy this unusually prolonged spell with my mother.

When she came in in the evening, her cheeks flushed from the 6-kilometre cycle from the university, and I asked her how her day had been, what she had been working on, I recognised the reluctance in her weak smile and dismissal. This was her world, and it wasn't something that could be communicated in the exchange of a few words before our evening meal. It required investment, and we didn't have time for that. So I didn't press for details, and we kept up this light and airy communication, on the weather, the spiciness of the food, the way I'd tied up my hair that morning. This was the language, the register, that Fenna requested when she prepared the guest room and left a wrapped bar of soap and a toothbrush in the bathroom. Expecting so little from language, we could relax, enjoy the silence while we read, take pleasure in food, sit close to one another on the sofa for our nightly appointment with the detective show. I will never forget her pleasure at the inevitable twist in each episode. The fact that this person could still be surprised by little things like this, someone considered to be old, seemed incongruous and unlikely, even absurd. She was still a child. We all were. This never changes, it never leaves us, this sense of beginning, of always beginning, of always being young.

It came as a shock to realise there were fewer than forty-eight hours until I flew. Without stating it – while saying the opposite, in fact, and telling each other that we would do this again soon, the next time I was in the country – we both understood this was likely to be a one-off, something that partly explained our determination to get along and the real enjoyment we were able to take, in the end. In the final two days a slight change came over Fenna, as she stiffened and retreated, closing herself off to better arm herself against my coming absence. This was for both of us. She didn't want to be hurt, and didn't want me to see her hurt. So it actually made sense, and in this way I was glad, that on my final night Fenna came back from the university later than expected. We ate apart. The strange shift in our priorities over the past three weeks had ebbed away. We were closer, once again, to two neighbours in a guest-house, two people making pleasantries over breakfast and nodding as they each disappeared into unimaginable days.

TWO

It was the tiredness, the dawn sky, the airport effect that left me close to tears at any moment, at the slightest provocation – a glimpse of a distressed child's face, clichéd advertising copy – and made the first part of the journey so difficult. Fenna wasn't supposed to get up; we agreed on that. It was too early. A car was booked to take me to the station at 05:20. We said goodbye the evening before, I thanked her for the previous three weeks, we embraced quickly and she pulled back, hummingbird body stiff and small and thrumming with energy, that soapy smell on her skin, buttery scent on her grey-white hair. I went to say something else, something more, but she nodded impatiently, and so I stopped. We looked at each other one last time, then she turned back to her room.

In the airport train Rotterdam rushed away, and I remembered details from the past three weeks, the half-eaten meals clingfilmed in the fridge, the damp bath mat we shared in the morning stamped by Fenna's prints, the laundry hanging by the tall kitchen window, dried by the light. My eyes swept across the carriage, looking for distraction; I buried my head in my folded arms and willed this time to pass.

I submitted to the airport, directed by officials, shepherded through gates, scanned by thermal cameras and temperature gauges, ushered into a row of uncomfortable plastic seats gripping my carry-on as if it were the most precious thing in the world. Two flights: an eleven-hour haul to California and a short hop through the state. Beyond that I didn't know and couldn't picture anything, which only made this worse. Because I had no idea what my apartment would look like or how my bed would feel, my journey was imbalanced, and I felt as if I were leaving somewhere without a destination, travelling further and further without any prospect of arrival. Everything was negative – the risk I had taken in agreeing to a job I knew so little about, the responsibility I had to the people I was leaving behind. I remembered Fenna in her blue nightgown, absently scrubbing the colander at 3 a.m. I worried I had knocked her balance, jarred something in her life irrevocably, and that the legacy of our three weeks was an unending period of loneliness that wouldn't have existed had I never shown up at her door. I knew I was being dramatic, overstating the significance of a still brief period and the effect my company had had; I knew that in a few days, a week at most, she would forget me, that it would be just as if I had never stayed. Still, I worried, questioned whether I was doing the right thing. The tacit agreement between Helena and me was that one of us needed to stay close to our mother; we couldn't both abandon her. Of course we never spoke about it in those terms, if we ever spoke about it at all, but I could tell Helena was unhappy with me moving so far away, first haranguing me with questions I couldn't answer about my new employer, then going silent and refusing to answer my calls. Soon enough, the three of us would be in different time zones, an equal latitude apart, chunks of ocean creating a dissonance in time. There would be only two, three hours each day when we were awake together, an indictment of our family and proof of how dramatically we had drifted.

Still, I should be focusing on where I was going, the new life awaiting me, the work I'd always wanted and that seemed almost too good to be true. With the promise of virtually unlimited backing of my research, this was the easiest decision I'd ever made, even if I knew almost nothing about the organisation funding me. Fenna wouldn't have wanted the alternative, a world where I continued to work at the university, regretting the incredible opportunity that had passed me by. So while I waited in Departures, scanning the listings, gripping my luggage tightly at my knees, I tried to endorse the decision, tried to commit to it and feel the excitement of a new life just beginning. I thought of *Endeavour*, where all this had started, but however hard I concentrated on the submersible rising, carrying its material from the radical depths, Fenna's image intruded, returning me to my childhood and telling me this was all just futile escape, that every time I tried to push my past into insignificance I only committed to it further. My work inevitably returned me to what I fled, my obsession with origins and

life's formation; all that mattered, I supposed, after everything, was that the fruits of this, whatever they were based
on, had independent merit.

We'd undergone the same checks on departure, so either it
was a symbolic gesture or they thought the aircraft itself was
permeable – microfauna slipping through the walls, our skin
and clothes smeared in life we'd torn down from the sky. After
completing physical checks I moved to the border security
booth for my interview. The guard spoke slowly through the
plexiglass, scrutinising the documents on my phone.

'Purpose of visit?'

'Essential work. I'm a contractor for NASA.'

This wasn't quite true, but it was the best way I could
think of putting it. Stating that it wasn't actually NASA, but
a group including staff from several agencies, was more than
was necessary, and possibly an unauthorised information
breach. Amy and I had stayed in touch after *Endeavour*, and
the offer had come indirectly through her. As the ship pulled
into port, a Health Authority vessel had met us and instructed
us to stay on board. Ferried to a hotel, we spent the next
twenty-one days in quarantine – an excess of caution,
following our contact with yet to be determined materials
from the vent. This period, in which we spoke about our
respective research, was the seed of the job offer I was taking
up now.

The second, short flight to Meadows Field was routine, and I passed through security quickly. As soon as I stepped outside a slim figure in jeans and polo shirt came towards me.

'Dr Hasenbosch? Leigh-Ann?'

'Leigh.' I caught the instinct to put out a hand, reminding myself I was still inside the airport zone. The man, older than he first looked, smiled – he must be used to this.

'Alex,' he said. 'Need anything?'

It was early but the light dazzled. I put on sunglasses for the short walk to the car. The windscreen was tinted, the concrete softened in blue. Alex said it was a two-hour drive to Ridgecrest. We took route 178, cutting east into the country. Surprising landscapes, not what I'd expected at all: huge mountain ranges dusted grey and blue above the treeline, giant oak forests that diminished the tracks and the traffic. The rivers gushed a perfect crystal, almost too blue to be real. For the checkpoints either side of the National Park we stayed in our seats – opened the doors, presented our feet – then the back and trunk of the car were searched, the tyres hosed down and the water collected. Invasive species were linked explicitly to the viral outbreaks, and these interruptions were around for the long term. I didn't like offering my feet; I always thought they were too big. Still a preoccupation the first time I undressed with someone, unfamiliar bodies trying to fix on each other. I waited for one of the guards to comment, or at least react with surprise. It irritated me I was even conscious of something so trivial, that I appeared to care when I would have said I didn't. Who was this guard, to me? Alex, inscrutable behind his stubble and wraparounds, had untied his boots, slipped them off to reveal thin, bright blue socks with yellow spots – not what I would have expected. I imagined him pulling them on in the early morning while it was still dark, grasping the socks in the drawer but not identifying them, keeping the light off in the bedroom so as not to wake his partner.

The sun climbed higher; now we were more than halfway there, excitement edged into anxiety. Now I wondered again where I'd sleep, what the place would be like. There wasn't much to go on: an apartment, an orientation, a lab. I'd given up my life – my job, my home, my partner – to come out to a place where I didn't know a single person. In truth, the relationship had been on the verge of ending anyway, and the job offer was an excuse. Dana did her best to disguise her relief when I told her the news. Eighteen months together and still we lived apart. I liked staying at hers, having the option of a separate place to go to. Relationship as vacation, addendum to real life. We hadn't even spoken in the three weeks since I'd left Amsterdam.

'You're going to want to be careful outside,' Alex said. 'Just to warn you. In the heat.'

I nodded, not really listening. For the hundredth time I

checked my phone, refreshed my email. Nothing.

I lived – had lived – on the other side of town from Dana, closer to the university. It was a twenty-four-minute cycle, door to door. Dana still had a key; the new tenant would change the locks. I'd lived there since finishing my doctorate a year previously. I'd really thought I could settle, working at the university, staying over at Dana's in the place I knew so well: faint toothpaste stains on the enamel, wisps of cut fringe on the floor. Maybe I was too hasty with her: her face smiling up at me, the grip of her fingers pushing away my hair, the sound of her voice as she quietly reassured me, making me stronger. I closed my eyes and bit my lower lip. Suddenly this all seemed a terrible idea. I could go back – it wasn't too late. Tell Alex to turn the car around. But even then, I didn't really believe it.

We moved through the filtered blue landscape, a series of scenes I wasn't really committed to and which I processed as virtual, synthetic displays set up on a screen. You're tired, you're hungry, you're taking refuge in self-pity because it's easy and it's comfortable, pleasurable in its own way, and because it's an excuse to avoid thinking more challenging and exciting thoughts, like the opportunity you've been given and what exactly it might mean.

Dana knew when I was flying and she hadn't messaged. No one had. The time at home was 06:00. I wanted her – I wanted someone, anyone – to stay awake and to miss me, having travelled all this way. The small routines I carried with me weren't noted in their absence by anyone, and I regretted this. I moved from place to place – across a room, through a doorway, past a table – and I carried all this with me and it was not acknowledged. Everyone should be acknowledged. Everyone should be missed when they are not right there with you because of what they carry, this very distinct way they have of bearing themselves that is like no one else and that is built by everything they have done and everything they have seen. When that goes – even just a little way, through the doorway, the other side of the wall, even while you can still hear the movement taking place – it should be missed. It should be startling, when we travel, when we are there and then not there. Travelling is a reminder that every thought it is possible to conceive of exists on a material plane and that it is there and then not there and that fact is extraordinary, and unbearable.

'Five minutes,' Alex said.

I sat up with a jolt, looked out.

The roadside was pale, colour bleached out. Suddenly we were in the city, parallel streets dropped onto featureless dusty plains. Rows of commercial areas gave out onto barren, burned-out semi-desert. I didn't know what I was seeing, watched the passing scenes with sensory rather than intellectual attention. Solar panels glinting on inscrutable buildings, steam rising from empty streets.

'Over there,' Alex nodded, 'those fences, the buildings behind them, the runways; that's China Lake.'

'Sorry, what?'

'The weapons station, China Lake. Where you're working.'

'No, I'm at the Institute. It's private, not military.'

'Same base,' he said. 'Anyway, that's not for a few days. I'll take you to your place first.'

The apartment was smaller than anywhere I'd lived before, the ceilings lower by several inches, which lent an outsize perspective, as if I were walking at an oblique angle, and made me conscious of my height. The storage was creative: bed base hollowed out, drawers feeding directly into the walls. Even with the confinement, everything seemed curiously airy and insubstantial, as if atomic structure had been laid bare. The objects in my apartment, the things I would live around, were in this sense not fully there.

There was a desk in the bedroom, an open-plan kitchen with two black wire stools by the countertop. The bathroom had a micro-shower – impossible to turn in, so that you had to back up into it – and a sink raised above the toilet, which felt like it should have been against regulations, promising nothing would ever be clean. But there was no discernible odour, and closing the windows and the sliding door by the shallow balcony created an almost perfect seal, with only a muffled, faraway sound audible from somewhere deep inside the walls.

The block had a central courtyard with stone benches, tables and a decorative water feature working on a loop. The water was captured and repurposed, but the sound of it spilling and sloshing in the otherwise silent, baking heat felt provocative. I stayed awake as long as I could, determined to push through the lag, but couldn't resist lying down on the sofa.

When I woke up, disoriented and groggy, hours had gone. I watched, gripping the blanket against the air-con, as the room gradually come into focus. I couldn't understand what I had done, couldn't imagine the next day, could barely imagine the next moment. I called Helena, who answered at last. It was late where she was. 'Show me,' she said, and I walked her round the place. She calmed me, the familiar sound of her voice, and made me laugh.

'How's Dana?' she asked.

'I've no idea.'

'Right.' Silence for a few seconds. 'Has Mum seemed OK to you?'

'What do you mean?'

'When you stayed with her. I'm curious – how did she seem?'

'Erm – fine, I guess? Nothing to be alarmed about. Why?'

'It's probably nothing. Listen, I've got to go now. Keep me updated, will you? With work, your first days?'

'Sure. I'll speak to you later.'

The silence was suddenly starker. I put my ears to the wall again and made out that distant sound.

I showered and stood out on the balcony, enjoying the soothing, gently stirring breeze and the darkness. The hills unclear in the distance, formless, blacker than the sky.

THREE

Though I'd tried, it wasn't easy to get information on my new employer. ICORS – Institute for Coordinated Research in Space – was set up to exploit the propulsion breakthrough and accelerate progress. Rather than a half-dozen agencies hatching broadly similar plans, a single, unified programme could streamline resources and bypass the usual governmental checks and restraints, and in theory get missions off the ground much quicker. There were three main bases – California, Beijing, Moscow – and though it sounded unlikely, press releases insisted they were in step with one another, working to apply the new technology and launch a new generation of missions.

This had not been a success. Provisional mission plans focused broadly on the same targets as before – Mars, Jupiter and Saturn's moons. And this was not what the public wanted. After the announcement of the breakthrough, people imagined interstellar travel, unknown planets light years away, distant galaxies even. But none of this was possible. Space was just too big, and even an exponential acceleration gain still limited us to our natal solar system. The only way to get out – to achieve crewed interstellar flight – was through multigenerational teams, and these were impossible to fund because the pay-off was too far away. Access to near planets, moons and asteroids was now much easier, but these targets had always been within reach anyway. This was a huge embarrassment for the Scientific Council, who had rushed through the announcement, finding that the public, in step with the breakthrough, had immediately adjusted expectations and were no longer interested in exploring a solar system long established as a desert.

There was the feeling that people had been cheated, sold the contradictory idea of a huge acceleration that wouldn't take you any further. A backlash began, primarily against the vast amounts of money governments were throwing into this. Climate movements lambasted it as a dereliction of duty, a wilful turning-away from an increasingly devastated planet. Militant eco-groups organised and protested, increasingly effectively. There was growing belief that the design breakthrough was a sham, that it had been held in reserve for a generation, its announcement timed to distract from the latest global mean temperature increase.

Everything had gone quiet, five years passing since the original announcement, and not a single mission launched. The feeling was that ICORS would quietly disband. And then they offered me a job.

My expectation, based on what I had read and on the little Amy had told me on the ship and in quarantine two summers ago, was that ICORS were preparing a mining expedition to one of Saturn's moons. They were conducting food experiments en route, some of which included micro-organisms, and I was being brought in as a consultant. My initial contact in Amsterdam was brief and curt: I would be 'given the opportunity to further my research' using 'close to unlimited resources'. My contract was for eighteen months, with the expectation of renewal. The money was substantially better than my university salary, if not quite life-changing.

Given the scepticism and ill-feeling towards the Institute, and to space research in general, I didn't exactly advertise where I was going. I didn't tell my friends, my colleagues, didn't tell Fenna or Helena or even Dana. It was technically true that I was, as I said, joining a California-based research group as a consultant; I was just hazy on the details. This was by far the most reckless thing I had ever done. And it was exciting, both the feeling of irrational abandonment and the intellectual anticipation – the researchers I might meet, the progress I might make in my work.

One odd thing was the lack of detail provided on the breakthrough itself. Reports described three engineering teams arriving at the discovery at more or less the same time, and while there were precedents for simultaneous discoveries, this one seemed particularly unlikely. Either the announce-ment was misleading – it hadn't come out of nowhere at all, but was the result of quietly accumulating research – or something completely inexplicable had occurred. The researchers weren't named in any of the media pieces, 'protecting them while they furthered their work'. One report alleged that they had suffered mild illness during the time of the discovery, that they had spent around a week in high fever, wrestling vivid dreams; the suggestion was that this had contributed to the engineering plans. This last report in particular preoccupied me, as my driver escorted me to the base for my first day.

It was impossible to appreciate just how huge China Lake Station really was. A sprawling complex of buildings, it seemed to go on forever. You glimpsed it in pieces, and these pieces all looked the same: inscrutable metal hangars and concrete blocks set lightly on the desert floor. Below ground had a substantially greater square footage than above. Tens of thousands of employees, hundreds of miles of road-track and runway. Of the total span of buildings – they appeared to be growing, multiplying, the whole place becoming less rather than more familiar as we moved through it – I would have access only to a small number in the south-west region. Our vehicle was checked at three points, and it took twenty-eight minutes to get from the first gate to the lab building.

Uria met me at reception, while the staff sorted my ID and passes and went through my bag. One of the first things she said was that I reminded her of her daughter, but the moment passed and I never found out exactly what she meant, what she had seen in me from the start, whether it was a physical resemblance or something more substantial. She had short, layered dark hair, and almond eyes darting beneath wire-rimmed glasses. Her biography said she was fifty-seven, which initially seemed about right, but after just a few minutes in her company I would have sworn she was younger. She was around 5 foot 5 inches, with a thin, wiry frame, and wore a white shirt with dark vertical lines tucked into black palazzo trousers.

Uria was Projects Director for the US arm of ICORS. She was from the far east of Russia originally, her father a truck driver who ended up designing cages for mine-shafts, her mother a geologist from Michigan. She had a PhD in astro-physics, had worked with Roscosmos in Moscow and Baikonur for a decade, and had experience in liaison work with the US and European agencies. When ICORS formed, Uria's experience, and her knowledge of people and processes in all the major agencies, made her a natural choice to co-lead Projects. It was clear already she had formidable energy and drive, but she wore it lightly. Impatient people aren't typically described as good listeners, but Uria didn't appreciate ambiguity, and her fierce brown eyes shone right at you as you spoke. I was challenged immediately, tasked with being my best self. She was measuring me, making evaluations, predicting the cost of prolonging this conver-sation. I sensed she'd have no qualms about cutting me off abruptly, but that she'd be the same with almost anyone, regardless of position or experience.

She gave a broad, outsize laugh, tilting her head back and closing her eyes. Her voice was commanding, and projected clearly in an accent that was difficult to pin down. I caught a Latin ring, Spanish maybe – I wouldn't have said Russian. Her biography said she spoke eight languages, and the number had possibly grown in the time since.

'Everything OK with your apartment? If you need anything you have to tell us. Don't be quiet or polite. We don't want obstacles. We want you to be able to concentrate on your work, OK?'

'Yes, thank you. Everything's great. I'm slowly getting settled.'

'OK. Good.' Uria was staring at me. She smiled, beaming again. 'I'm so glad you're here, Leigh. I want to get things started immediately. Let me show you the labs.'

Reception handed me back my things, and we walked diagonally through the atrium towards a closed set of double-doors. I presented my face to the small camera and scanned the QR code in my phone; there'd be a fresh code daily. We went through the doors, past room after room. The corridors reminded me of a hospital: the purposeful marching of staff, the glimpses through opaque windows, the routes constantly branching out. I switched attention between the building and the information Uria was giving me, the speed of her delivery seeming to indicate we didn't have much further to go. There was a lot to get through, and I counted on confirming some of it later with my team.

Abruptly, Uria stopped outside a door. 'I'll let Lin take it from here. He'll get you up to speed. I love first days, don't you? So full of promise. I can't wait to see what you're going to do with us.'

FOUR

It's notoriously difficult to grow algae indoors. Light distribution is invariably uneven: as soon as the organism starts growing, it partially shades itself. Growth inhibits growth. The obvious solution is to use a thinner containment material, but then you risk it collapsing. It's this balance – container weak enough to admit light, but strong enough to hold together – that eludes engineers. Experimentation is long and expensive. You can vary three things: species, container, environment, which means an almost infinite number of combinations. So the perfect solution is out there, we just might never find it.

Although I started on the problem years earlier, I only really made progress in the final years of my PhD. Most designers used plastic rather than glass, and the current best model was a long strip-bag which absorbed enough light for optimal growth in over 80 per cent of the crop. To achieve these numbers, the bag had to be replaced almost weekly; it was so thin that it started to degrade right away, and got worse as the algae grew. This was a problem, as the level of waste meant you couldn't scale up.

Not long after the *Endeavour* project, I decided it was impossible: the container couldn't last. I was cleaning up at the lab, about to quit for the day, my mind wandering, thinking about how the early excitement of my research had ebbed away. I'd lost sight of what I loved and was going through the motions. The longer this went on, the greater the pressure, which just made it harder to work – a self-reinforcing negativity. At this, I felt a sudden pang of recognition: self-reinforcing, a circular process. If the material degrades, then rather than replacing it, with all the waste involved, let it correct itself. I'd already been using a plastic that was part-synthesised from algae; the next step was to rebuild it entirely using the same stuff.

The container would maintain itself independently, in the same way the organism does. The container – the incubator – rather than being chemically inert, plastic in its dead state, would be active, a synthetic membrane repeatedly rebuilt from its own contents.

It proved harder in practice. I needed money and I needed greater expertise in biotech. I patented the idea, secured a grant, and while looking for the right collaborator began studying genetic programming. It took around a year to finally start on trials, and the results were disappointing. The container was too thin. I arrived at 95 per cent yield, the remaining 5 per cent subsumed into waste and fed into the barrier. But the material always split before it rebuilt. I got close, and by any measure had made rapid progress, but I couldn't completely regenerate the container from inside. This was the central feature of the idea, and if it didn't work then the whole thing fell down.

I ran out of money, and had no option but to put the project aside and pursue other research. This was when ICORS had approached me.

Earlier, when my contract was being sorted out and I was being vetted, living those quiet weeks in my mother's house in Rotterdam, three researchers set up my labs. One of them – Lin – now walked me around after Uria had introduced us and said her goodbyes. Putting on over-alls, hairnets and shoe-covers, we struggled for common ground.

'So, the Netherlands,' he said. He was short, slim, with thick dark eyebrows and a gleaming face that seemed to have only just been shaved. His hands seemed unnaturally un-occupied – he kept casting them around, as if looking for somewhere to rest.

'You've been?'

'No. Changed planes in Schiphol. Didn't get a chance to go out. Wish I could have seen Amsterdam though.'

'The cafés?' I said a little tiredly; the clichés had followed me several times already.

'No – the painters, the galleries.'

'Ah. Van Gogh. The Old Masters. Not really my thing. My sister could talk about them for hours though. I did have an Escher print on my wall growing up, but you probably think that's tacky.'

'I always liked the one with the staircase going up and down—'

'That's the one.'

Suited up, we went through the doors. The lab's eight rooms were split into 'wet' and 'dry' zones, the former for storing and using cell cultures, the latter for digital work. One of the basic rules was that wet and dry shouldn't mix, a distinction enforced with almost superstitious rigour. If you handled live cultures you had to remove all paraphernalia – gloves, mask, lab coat, hairnet, shoe-covers – and wipe yourself down before entering a dry part. This was time-consuming, and in some labs I'd worked people were lax, but here everyone seemed to follow procedure to the letter. We would spend a significant proportion of our time cleaning – disinfecting, polishing, wiping down benches and storage racks, removing all trace of what we'd previously done. Nothing we handled was explicitly dangerous – we were essentially growing and mating algae cells – but the staff appreciated the ease of biological slippage, the fall and spread of an agent from one category to another, and the devastating results that could ensue.

Lin walked me round the cold rooms. Everything was controlled. Tissue cells and growth media were kept in deep-freeze vial trays. Brightly coloured plastic marked the materials and gave a childlike aspect to the work. However rigorous the lab was, however painstaking and methodical our work, these people loved what they were doing and maintained a justified sense of wonder. These were the elements of life, stripped back.

Lin pulled off his mask. 'Time to return you to Uria,' he said.

I sat in the small windowless office in the wing behind our labs. There were 128 staff in this tiny and insignificant corner of the station, and as I kept reminding myself, almost a third of them technically worked under me. I pushed away the warm appeal of imposter syndrome, chased the loud thoughts demanding what right I had to be there, in my own office.

My research in algae production was original, Uria explained, and the Institute valued this quality above all others. To work with my IP, they had to bring me in too. But they wanted me there anyway; they wanted to see what I could do. This was flattering of course, but at the same time I was realistic – I didn't imagine for a second I was the only algae specialist developing original research for ICORS. The Institute prioritised speed and worked by scaling up; there were probably dozens of labs, not only here but across China, Russia, and anywhere else the Institute had set up. They threw money at us at an early stage in our career, when we couldn't turn it down. Maybe one or two of us would ultimately stay the course and see our work through to application; statistically, I knew this was unlikely to be me.

But I wasn't put off for a second. Knowing there were other teams working on the same problem made me more competitive. I wanted to be noticed, wanted our work, in my labs, to have an effect. Uria, I suspected, knew this; she fed me the information to drive this response in me.

'We liked your trials. They were ambitious.'

I nodded. 'There were problems with the yield, scaling up. I couldn't finish it.'

Uria nodded back. 'We don't think they're insurmountable problems. In the right environment.'

'And that environment is – here?'

'Sort of.' She gave a slight wince, as if disappointed in her ability to communicate.

'Uria, listen, I – I don't mean to contradict you, or to sound ungrateful, but I spent a long time working on the yield problem, and in my opinion it can't be solved, not yet, not with the materials available to us.'

'Are you speaking about Earth?'

'I'm sorry?'

'The system – are you saying it's not viable on Earth?'

'Well, yes.'

'But Earth's environment is atypical. Your system may work in others.'

'Such as?'

'Atmospheres lower than 1g.'

'1g?'

'One gravity.'

'So, other planets?'

She gave a light shrug. 'Or the transport used to reach them. In microgravity, it's a different proposition, isn't it? Your work may be fully functional there.'

'Hypothetically, yes. But in order to find out, we would need to test it properly.'

'Like I was saying, we have resources.'

'You have low-gravity environments?'

'Sure.'

'And you want me to recreate my work and test the algae there?'

'Broadly, yes.'

'What do you mean?'

'We need you to build the right strain first. As you've seen, Lin and the others have already started on this – you'll lead them. The algae must meet certain specifications, targets relating to nutrition, durability, growth.'

'And the application of this? I mean, what's it all for?'

'That's classified – for now anyway. We'll get to that later.'

FIVE

Having been here a few weeks I picked up my routine, leaving for the station before dawn, hitting the basement pool, then an hour in the gym, then the lab until late. I rarely saw my apartment in natural light. There was little time for reflection, little time to process it all, to understand where I was and what was happening around me.

I worked harder in the gym and my diet changed too. Sometimes I didn't recognise myself. Not just the toned arms and abs, not just the burn on my skin from the heatstorms, but the blank expression, a little like Uria's maybe. This isn't you, I said, but a character entering another kind of fiction. This was a completely new start, and I could be anyone I wanted here. I found out more about the Institute's history, sat in on project lectures, spoke to colleagues in the café and asked them about their work. I wanted to appreciate the scope of the place and what it was doing. Some of the projects sounded unrealistic and I didn't know how to react – was this just rhetoric? Simulation? But I was intrigued every day.

I knew I had to go to Uria now and ask for clarification on the programme, but I was loath to interrupt her – I wanted to prove to everyone I was capable, that I could work independently. I couldn't be a drain on the project leaders. But weeks after starting, I needed further specifications on the environment the algae would be grown in. Without knowing more about the kind of missions they had in mind, I couldn't fulfil my role.

Uria was scheduled to visit the lab briefly, and when she arrived, late in the afternoon, three hours after we were expecting her, I asked if we could go outside. A faint flicker of surprise before she resumed her inscrutable expression. While we walked along the hard pale floor, she asked me how the work was going.

'OK,' I said.

'Then why do you need to see me?'

I hesitated, scanned the length of the corridor, unsure whether it was appropriate to be having this conversation. Uria didn't seem concerned. 'Because I need more information,' I said eventually. 'I realise there are security concerns, but I need to know what it's for. I need details.'

'Such as?'

'Length and nature of proposed journey. Number of personnel. Ideally profiles of the individuals and a summary of where they're going and what they're doing. I don't care if it's a real mission or a simulation, I just need to know what I'm working with.'

'Purpose, destination – why is that relevant?'

'Because we want the crop to survive.'

'OK,' she said, then resumed walking. I was beginning to find her mannered, staccato way of talking irritating.

'OK? So what does that mean exactly?'

'I'm sorry. I've been very busy, there are a lot of things on my mind. There has been some surprising activity recently. I can hopefully tell you more about this soon. But of course you ought to know about the specifications of the project.'

'Uria, do we have to keep walking like this?'

'I'm already late for a meeting.' She slowed again, stopped. 'This is what I can tell you: say the material you are working on will be used as food supply in a mission with a predicted duration of thirteen months. 80 per cent of the journey will take place in microgravity, with the remainder somewhere between 1 and 1.4 gs, although there may also be brief episodes of up to 11gs. The algae will be stored in a single module sealed off from the rest of the ship. There will be three crew. That is all I can tell you at this stage, but I promise I will give you more soon.'

Thirteen months at microgravity – what would that do to a body? Above energy and nutrition, meals were important social occasions, a distraction from monotony and a marker of time passing in a place without light. I set up meetings with resident cardiologists, nutritionists and psychologists, and the programme began to take shape.

The first thing to consider was growth span. The algae would enter the ship in cuttings and grow as a live crop, its chain of generations echoing down the voyage. Thirty days would be the ideal harvest time, replicating Earth months.

We could modify the incubators to increase transparency, use the crop's fertility as a source of solace and strength. It was important there was evidence of prior and wider life. Large hospital trials proved the effect of garden views on patient recovery rate, improving immune response and mental resilience, relieving pain and long-term stress. I imagined building a particularly pleasing green through the strain, using colour to illustrate the journey inside the crop.

In addition to primary responsibilities on the vessel, each crew member should be given a clear and distinct agricultural role, caring for and tending to the crop. The partnership should be made explicit, through feeding waste-water into the incubators, the crew's bodily discharge not vented into space but cycled back into another living system. The algae should be a reassuring organic environment against which the challenging events of the journey take place, demonstrating again and again that the crew's actions – their breathing and digestion, every splash of water they use to clean themselves – are not final, not vented outwards or vacuum packed into storage, but go on to contribute to the ecology that sustains them. The journey should be explicitly circular, with the sense that the crew are moving closer to Earth all the time, even as they are nominally travelling away from it.

How far ultimately will the journey go, in thirteen months, at peak speeds? Will Earth remain visible at all times? The outer planets? Consult with Uria. Factor in first yield for time of possible Earth vanishing. Consult with psychologists on potential effects. Links to mirror-stage and child breaking free from bodily environment of mother. Astronauts as children. How can these unprecedented events be anticipated, and their effects controlled?

Source the full list of medications to be brought onto the ship. Investigate possible changes to efficacy of medication due to microgravity and other factors. How will the medication interact with the algae diet? Other symptoms? Conduct exhaustive survey ruling out all possibility of toxic secretions.

Risk of bodily dissociation throughout the long isolation. Increase in self-fascination, in the body as natural object. Prominence of large agricultural display – a garden, or farm, where the algae grows – could mitigate spread of unhelpful thoughts. Consult on likelihood of serious injury, on healing strategies and the role food will play in this. Anticipate various errors that may prove catastrophic to the life of the algae, and the negative repercussions that may ensue. Crew undergoing feelings of grief, shame, culpability in death of the crop, displaced trauma from leaving family behind. How dangerous could the crop's wilting be, if they cherish it? If the crop resists all interventions, dying without reason, the crew must be prepared and equipped to face this. Demonstrative potential of farm/garden should only work positively:

otherwise risk of associated pessimism regarding ultimate mission aims.

Incubators must be strong enough to withstand brief high-g episodes. This may be our biggest challenge in the lab. The crop's vulnerability may however become an advantage, proving the necessity of the crew, encouraging affectionate care-giving as they realise that a highly vulnerable and interconnected life system depends entirely on the way they act.

SIX

Helena was rarely so insistent. Usually she was laid-back, impassive, quietly in control. This time was different: she said we had to call, and no, it couldn't wait.

It was late. I had the glass doors open to the balcony in the front room, cars sweeping by below, the temperature dropping with the light but the room still sticky. Jakarta time was mid-morning; unusual for Helena to be calling on a workday.

I snatched at the call-icon as the tone sounded.

'You're in the dark?' she said. The laptop glowed with the light from where she was, casting it beyond me. Dust particles hung in the air. She was in her kitchen, sitting a couple of feet from her phone. Her hair was in a high knot and she wore a black Lycra vest top. A bottle of water rested between her and the screen. She always exercised when something was bothering her, overcoming a problem through increased productivity. Run faster, heartbeat intenser, trick time into stretching forward and lending its insight before pulling back in again.

'I was. But now it's light from the screen. I like it in the dark, it helps me concentrate.'

'I know you've been working late, I don't mean to interrupt – I had no choice.'

'Helena, what is it?'

'I should have said something earlier, I'm sorry.'

'Just tell me.'

'It's Mum.'

'OK.' I waited, watched my breath.

'First of all, don't worry, she's fine. She's not in hospital or anything, not anymore.'

'Wait, what? When did she go in? What happened to her? Why did no one tell me?'

'I'm telling you now. Let me speak.' Her words were even, quiet, conspicuously slow. Mine were a burst, a babble – I tried to say everything at once. 'She had a fall. That's it, that's all. She must have slipped on something – we don't know exactly how it happened.'

'Outside? Was no one with her?'

'No. It happened at home.' Something shifted over Helena's face. 'In the kitchen. She lost consciousness. When she came round she was groggy; she doesn't know how much time passed.'

'Oh god. Did she hit her head? Did she have a concussion?'

'We don't think so.'

'But she went to the hospital as a precaution?'

'Her hip is sore, but we don't think there's a fracture.'

'How can she be at home? Who's looking after her?'

'Erika has come round, thank god. Mum's a little cranky. She has a crutch, she's insisting on moving around. Erika found her attempting to get on her bicycle; she was trying to get to work.'

'God.'

'You know how she is. If there's something inconvenient she'll ignore it until it goes away. She thinks she can just update reality like that.'

'When did all this happen?'

Helena paused. 'Last Tuesday.'

'What?'

'Leigh, there was nothing you could do out there. And anyway you're busy, you made it clear there's a lot going on, that you needed space.'

'That's not what I meant. I have to be told about these things. Of course I'll be there, I'll listen, I'll do what I can. Why just tell me now? I don't understand.'

'It's what Mum wanted. She didn't want to scare you. I think she was concerned you'd feel you should come back – though she didn't say that, of course.'

'She wanted it to already be over by the time I knew.'

'Essentially, yeah.'

'Jesus.' I exhaled. 'Now I'm wondering what else the two of you have kept from me.'

Again, that brief flux turning over Helena's face.

'What? What is it? What else is there?'

'I – I don't know. Just her behaviour recently. It's probably nothing – small things, incidental things.'

'Like what?'

'Like she missed appointments we had.'

'It'll be work – she's busy, that's all.'

'It's never happened before.'

'Right.' The block of light from the screen, the faint sound of cars swishing past.

'I don't know, this seemed different. It's just a feeling I got.'

'And then she fell?'

'Yeah.'

'And you're sure you had these thoughts earlier, before? That you're not just working backwards and plotting things?'

'I'm pretty sure. Look, when I spoke to her she was perfectly lucid. I don't want to give you the wrong impression. Maybe it's nothing.'

'We'd know, wouldn't we, if we were there.'

'Maybe. I don't know.'

'Jesus.' I looked around the blank room, this alien space I had gathered around me.

'I can't go back.' I watched my jawline, the set of my face.

'I didn't ask you to.' Helena turned round; I thought I heard a car starting. She faced the screen again. 'This isn't about you; it isn't about me either. This is about Mum, what's best for her, and what we do next.'

'Erika can't stay forever.'

'No. We can help; we can watch her too.'

'You know how she is. It's not as if I haven't tried, but she doesn't give me anything. I find her very hard to read. I'll suggest a call and then she'll say she's busy.'

'She's doing that for you, Leigh. She doesn't want to be a burden. She's giving you the option of not being there. But I think she wants you to insist; you need to insist. For both of you. You can't just let her say no.'

Fenna standing in her powder blue nightgown over the sink in early morning, the material hanging from her shoulder blades, a distant, bewildered expression on her face. I should have said something, done something, but I left it, content my mother's unknowability was original and not medical.

I finally got Fenna herself, sound not image. It was early morning in Rotterdam and she had just woken up. She was leaving for work. 'It's Sunday, Mum.'

'I'm busy. I'm going in seven days.'

'You shouldn't be. You're OK? You can move OK?'

'I'm absolutely fine. I've been fine all these years and that's not suddenly going to change.'

She cut the call, insisting she was busy, she had to go. Lin, after, saw I was distracted, asked me what was wrong. I told him I was fine. I didn't want to be unprofessional – that's how it starts, then suddenly the work slides and the months pass and I'm quietly let go, and for all the time I'm pre-occupied, resenting my weakness, my inability to separate family and work, resenting, as well – the really unconscionable part – the presence of my mother and my sister in my life.

I went to the pool again, the only place I could really relax, burned skin soothed in water. It was almost empty, spotlights over the blue, the perimeter dark and opaque. I pushed myself hard, fifty quick lengths, then paused by the pool edge, panting, absorbing the chemical reek while my arms spread out on the tiles to keep me afloat. It was the fact that she had fallen, lost her balance, collapsed and now couldn't walk without support. That the one thing she needed was support, someone to take the weight off. She would never ask for help. She was scared in spite of her control of fear's expression.

Maybe she'd fallen for us, to show us how alone she was, how difficult it had been since Dad died and she came home only to herself each night. The difference, when you get in at the end of the week, close the door behind you, put the keys on the worktop and take your shoes off and realise that the week's completion entails only itself, that there is nothing after it, only yourself and the beginning of the next week and the one after, that all weeks forever are pressed into a seamless block, there is nothing outside of it, no relief in something shared, no brief escape or refuge – you realise that it's gone.

It was obviously much harder for her than I'd allowed, but that didn't mean it was about that. There didn't have to be a reason – maybe she was just getting old. Maybe there was nothing anyone could do. Maybe she is largely unaware of it, or able to push it away but left with these terrifying moments of alienation. Maybe she is more afraid, and helpless, than at any other time in her life. And she knows that her daughters are doing nothing. Maybe she wakes up in darkness, searching through the house for us, knowing only that it's urgent, it's a crisis, and she has to find us. Maybe she's transported back more than twenty years, trying to find us and make things better, aware at the last moment, as she enters the empty rooms, that this time it is she who is in danger.

SEVEN

I worked in the wet-rooms whenever I could, though the office was eating up more of my time. The team were obviously all capable, and I trusted them more each week. My main worry tended to be on the communications side, but everyone had a clear job to do and we seemed to have reached the ideal flow stage where non-verbal cues take over – nods and head shakes, pointing and thumbs up, a binary yes or no, positive or negative.

Eight weeks in, that changed, with an email from Lin headed 'Gene induction date'. Lin's writing was terse, passive and not entirely clear, and it was possible I'd misunderstood him. Direct gene editing shouldn't come until much later in the process, if at all. That was obvious. And introducing an outside gene – something from a non-algal species – was risky, and only justified in specific narrow circumstances.

I went immediately to the lab but he wasn't there. He had gone for a swim. I saw him in the pool occasionally, both of us embarrassed at seeing the other revealed like this. I had to wait forty minutes for him to come sauntering through the corridor, hair lank and wet, smelling of chlorine. In the time elapsed I'd got worked up. I'd rehearsed what I was going to say, but when he approached in the corridor I was impatient and asked him straight out what on earth was going on. He seemed completely taken aback. He said the instructions to transplant the gene had come from Uria and he'd assumed I knew. Why would she bypass me? What would she hope to gain? 'To be clear,' I began, holding on to the bridge of my nose and looking at the floor, 'are you telling me that you and others in the lab are currently prepping Cas9 to begin working directly on the nucleus of a live tissue cell?'

'Yes,' he said, and before he could say any more I put my hand out.

'You need to suspend all work.'

'All Cas9 work?'

'Everything, everything in the lab. Pack up everything and go. Close the lab as early as it's safe to. Tell everyone to go home. Come back tomorrow as usual. Hopefully I'll have this figured out by then.'

I knew this would set off an alarm, which was partly the point. I needed to make some noise. If Uria couldn't give me answers, someone above her would have to.

Within fifteen minutes Uria was calling me. I stepped into my office, closed the door behind me, braced myself as I answered.

'What is the problem?' Uria began right away.

'It's a security issue. I had no option but to shut it down.'

'What security issue?'

'There are materials of unknown provenance.'

'I don't know what that means, Leigh.'

'It means stuff is going on here that I don't know about
– I'm not in control of my lab. That's a security issue. Lin
was prepping external gene induction. I know nothing about
this. I've never discussed this, not once. It's completely
unacceptable.'

'It was my understanding that we *had* discussed this.'

'When?'

'Our initial meeting, when we discussed additional
resources.'

'Are you serious?' I laughed. 'That's not enough. That
could mean anything. If you mean "we will organise external
gene transfer", then you need to explicitly say that.'

'OK. I apologise. Perhaps I wasn't as clear as I could have
been. There is a lot going on just now.'

'Like what? What is going on exactly?'

'Leigh, I can't.'

'Look, you said I'd have full autonomy in my lab; clearly
I don't. I'm not comfortable with this. Unless I'm given a full
explanation and reassurance, I just don't see how I can
reopen it.'

'Um, that wouldn't be a good idea. We can't lose more
time. I think this is a misunderstanding. Gene transfer is just
an additional resource. It was thought that it could assist
you in some elements of your work, given the unique
specifications of the mission.'

'"It was thought"? By whom? I'm sorry, Uria, but who is

making these decisions? Can you at least tell me how exactly this gene is supposed to help?'

'This isn't my area of expertise, but I gather it may play some role in conferring resilience and longevity in rudimentary organisms, and that this might be valuable in a tumultuous mission environment.'

'Tumultuous?'

'Higher radiation levels. Sudden gravity shifts. Nothing like this will ever have been experienced before.'

'And where has it come from, exactly?'

'I'm not sure I follow.'

'Where was the gene identified? Where was it sourced?'

'Do you mean which species?'

'Yes.'

'But surely you know that – you were there?'

'Where? Uria, you're losing me, I don't know what you're talking about.'

'We spoke about it by email, I'm sure we did.'

'Spoke about what?!'

'The expedition. *Endeavour*. The gene was found in an archaea species recovered from *Endeavour*. Leigh?'

'I'm here.'

Amy and I had stayed in contact briefly, but she'd stopped replying to my messages. I hadn't been surprised exactly. She claimed this was a misunderstanding – separate email folders, a new server at work, data problems. I smiled into the tablet placed upright against several unused cookbooks on my kitchen counter. I nodded – I wasn't going to press her; it didn't matter, not now.

'So where are you, Amy?' She appeared to be in a ground-level room, a sparse office, sunlight flooding through tall windows.

'LA County.'

'JPL?'

'Uh-huh.'

'And how's that going? Are you—'

Amy laughed. 'You know we're not supposed to talk about this. I'm amazed Uria even permitted the call. But . . . it's going well. And it's good to be working with you again, even if remotely, Leigh.'

'You did say, back then, my work might have an application here.'

'Hey, don't blame me for this . . . Anyway, I don't have much time. You said there was a problem, it sounded urgent?'

'I almost don't know where to start. It's not so much a problem, as just . . . I mean I'm baffled. I don't know what's happening. I guess it's partly the heatstorms, moving out here suddenly, all the disruption. You know China Lake is listed as a reserve cooling station? You hear about these things, but until you actually arrive there . . . But I mean . . . it's also the lack of information. No one tells me anything! I thought it would be straightforward: recreate my trials, run the lab, produce a crop that meets the mission specs. I thought it would be simple, and I could just put my head down and get on with it. What? Why are you looking at me like that?'

'You're saying you came out here for an easy life? I don't believe it for a second. That's not how you work. You wanted something stimulating, and you got it.'

'It's bigger than that, Amy. There's stuff going on here I know nothing about. And I'm supposed to be leading this. I've lost confidence in the lab.'

'Right, that's obviously not great – but Leigh, why are you telling me? What can I do?'

'Because it comes from *Endeavour*.'

'What does?'

'The gene they want me to splice into the crop. It's from an archaea recovered on *Endeavour*, and to be honest, I don't know what to think about that.'

Amy nodded, lips pursed, eyes looking straight to camera, watching me. 'But you knew they were part-funding *Endeavour*?' she said. 'That's why I was there. I was working with ICORS developing the sub.'

'Which means . . . Any material found there belongs to them.'

Amy didn't need to say anything.

'It's more than two years now, they're still investigating the site, and I've not heard a thing. And I didn't expect to, not ever. And now suddenly I'm working with a novel gene and it turns out it came from *Endeavour*? Can you imagine how that feels?'

'I'm sure they meant to tell you earlier.'

'Do you know what depth it came from?'

Amy shook her head. 'Really, I'm as much in the dark as you are.'

'So it could be 6 kilometres, or it could be 19?'

'We never learned true depth.'

I wished Amy were here with me; everything would be so much easier. We could get a drink, go for a walk, talk it out. It wasn't the same like this; so much was missed out.

'This is important,' I said, 'you do see that? What was recovered from *Endeavour* needs to be made public, the research has to be shared. We need to know about the life there.'

Amy was nodding, a frustrated look on her face. 'I know. I get it. First life is your thing – it's exciting.'

'It's more than that.' I winced – there was so much I wanted to say, and I felt defeated, overwhelmed already at the prospect. Again, I thought how much easier it would be if Amy were here, in person. 'Look, I've been thinking about this a lot. It could teach us something, and the repercussions might be huge. All I know from Uria is that the gene affects resilience. That's why they want to put it in the crop – to help it grow in microgravity and survive radiation bursts.

Uria chooses her words carefully, right? So "resilience" is interesting. She said "longevity" too.'

'So? What are you saying?'

'I'm saying this gene they've isolated, or something like it – what if it played a major role in the past?'

'In the emergence of life?'

'Yes. I know that sounds dramatic, but bear with me.' I stopped a moment, caught Amy's face, and shook my head, smiling. 'Look, organisms can be divided into two categories, right? Those built from cells with a nucleus, and those from cells without one.'

'Eukaryotes and prokaryotes.'

'Right. And prokaryotes – bacteria and archaea – were around for a long time before anything else came along. Like billions of years. Their energy production was limited; they were stuck. All the evolution in all those billions of years could only reach a certain point. There was no way past this. Whatever happened, in all that time, it kept butting against the growth limit. To me, this period is amazing. Cells rising and falling in water, waves frothing and breaking. Looking back at this, the logical thing was that cells should have continued this way forever, never deviating from this basic form. Life as a marginal transition from mineral into biotic, then back again, repeating over billions of years, interrupted by ice ages and by the sun's expansion, until the planet's eventually burned up.'

'OK, I'm with you. Ceaseless frothing.' Amy looked down at her coffee cup. 'So what happened? What changed?'

'That's the miracle. Life itself isn't a miracle – lots of people think it's inevitable, that in a planet with certain chemicals, placed a certain distance from a star a certain size, proto-cells will develop. This is probably the case across the galaxy, across the universe even, quintillions upon quintillions of planets, all of which are generating this frail, rudimentary, soupy kind of life. And it stays this way, for billions of years on every suitable planet, incomprehensible numbers. So life as a microscopically differentiated liquid capsule, defining itself against what's around it only in the loosest possible sense.'

'The miracle?'

'That happened once. Once only, in all the total range of time and space. This limit, this structural constraint, which had so far held as a constant across the universe, somehow it falls away – here, on this planet. And that's the reason we're here.'

Amy was looking askance, head slightly lowered. After a few seconds she surfaced. 'You sound quite certain about this.'

'About what?'

'The part about it happening only once, development beyond the rudimentary.'

'That's the theory. It's the best explanation I'm aware of for the lack of evidence of extraterrestrial life.'

'OK.'

'Amy?'

'No, carry on. I mean I assume you were getting to a point at the end . . .'

'Very generous of you. I'm trying to show how important the transition is, from prokaryote to eukaryote. A fluke event, interrupting what would have been endless repetition. So it makes sense, surely, that we should find out everything we can about it, about what exactly happened back then – right?'

'And you think the archaea from *Endeavour* can help?'

'Why not? So the theory is archaea and bacteria started to help each other.'

'Symbiosis.'

'Exactly. Which is actually much more prominent in evolution than most people admit. Which is interesting politically. Bacteria still sometimes live inside each other; they're really strange. They borrow genes from each other all the time, wildly different species. There's a theory that all bacteria constitute a single, massively distributed organism – a single *individual*, even . . . Anyway, so we think an archaeal cell and a bacterial cell formed a close chemical dependency, and – we can't say how this happened; this is the miracle – the two cells fused, became a single, chimerical identity. An archaea cell with parts of a bacterial cell inside it. And this *thing* endured, because it was useful, it was helpful, it was easier to live this way. So the bacterial parts get repurposed inside the bigger cell, energy production changes, a ferocious, runaway complexity emerges, and eventually you have a nucleus. You still with me?'

'Sure. Go on.'

'So now you get exponential growth. The new cells process oxygen, which means they can survive in novel places, be influenced by new environments, grow even further. So this massive radiation of species happens, which leads to multicellular life – plants, animals, fungi.'

'And us.'

'Yes. Our cells are an adapted version of the synthesis of two earlier types of cell 2 or 3 billion years in the past.'

'Leigh, you're skipping about a bit. It's interesting but I don't see—'

'What is symbiosis? It's resilience through mutual effort.'

'So – what? You're saying the gene from *Endeavour* might encourage symbiosis?'

'Possible, isn't it? Maybe it's *the* crucial gene in the emergence of complex life.'

'I don't know. Look, I have a meeting scheduled, I have to get going.'

'Five minutes?'

'I can't. I'm already late. But Leigh?'

'Yeah?'

'Talk to Uria. Be completely open with her, tell her

everything. She's not the enemy, I swear. That's the only way this will work. You need to get clearance, as well. I'll see if there's anything I can do – it's worth a shot.'

EIGHT

After Uria and I sat down we reopened the lab, agreeing to use gene induction in only one of the strains and to keep parallel strains untouched. Amy's call helped. I picked up rhythm again, the ritual of the pool each morning, then into the lab, newly short hair damp under the netting. I stitched cuttings and oversaw my colleagues' work. The cuttings and the storage bags were delicate and liable to tear, so we had to work carefully and at a frustratingly slow pace. The new strain I was working on was so fine it reacted to heat, noise, even the air pressure outside. It was an inadvertent weather gauge, unusually expressive, sensitive to the boom of aircraft taking off from the nearby runways. Because it was so needy, I was more invested in it. I spent longer on it, proprietary over it, reluctant to delegate any of its upkeep. I set middle-of-the-night alarms so I could feed it, and when I couldn't sleep I watched the video feed, the greys and greens and still whites, until it lulled me under. I liked the musty, mealy odour that remained on my hands from contact even through the gloves. I smelled my fingertips repeatedly, a habit that Helena, when she noted it on the video screen, said was definitive proof I was spending far too much time alone.

Helena had got a call the day before from one of Fenna's colleagues. He was sheepish and awkward and unsure whether he should even say anything. Helena waved away his doubts and asked him to come out with it. Fenna had managed to get lost inside the university grounds, he said. A student had found her and taken her to reception.

Fenna said it was nothing. She had been a little dizzy after her cycle in. She'd taken the wrong corridor and hadn't recognised where she was, that was all. She was fine, there was no need for any doctor. *Have you any idea the kind of work I do, and how demanding it is?*

Later, we asked Erika if she'd drop in unannounced, just to see how she was doing. At first she seemed OK, Erika said. Then one or two things began to feel off. A hesitancy in her movements, a longer pause before speech. There was a sour smell in the kitchen. Fenna offered Erika a cup of tea, but when she reached the kettle, she stopped. She stood silently for more than thirty seconds. 'I'm sorry,' she said eventually. There were no teabags. The cupboards were empty. When Erika opened the fridge she found a carton of milk, curdled. 'I've been meaning to throw it out,' Fenna said. 'I should stop buying milk, it goes off so quickly, there's no point when it's just me here.'

Eventually, after much persuading, and mainly just to quiet us, Fenna agreed to see her GP and take a blood test.

A call woke me late at night. I assumed it was Helena, braced myself. Instead I heard Amy's voice.

'I've spoken to the directors and it's out of my hands – getting you higher clearance, I mean.'

'Well, thanks anyway.'

'Ah you're sleepy, aren't you? I woke you. I forget other people work to different clocks.'

'No, it's uh, it's fine, really.'

'OK.'

'But, uh . . .'

'Yeah?'

'Did you call just for, I mean just about . . .'

'There's something else.'

'Right.'

'OK. It's been nagging at me since we spoke. What you were saying about soupy life reminded me of something. I mentioned it to a colleague – I hope you don't mind? – and she immediately said "great filter". You know this, right?'

'Uh, yeah?' I yawned, hoping I'd turned my head from the mic in time. 'If we're talking about the same thing. Basically a cap on life on all planets. Like I was saying – one planet gets past this filter – that's Earth. That's the miracle.'

'But what if it isn't?'

'Hmm?'

'So you're saying the filter was early, it was cellular, about limited energy production; that was the cap on size and complexity.'

'That's right.'

'But what if it came later?'

'Later when?'

'Much later. What if we've got the scale wrong, and the filter's actually billions of years later? A technological filter, not a biological one.'

I pinched the bridge of my nose, concentrated. 'So we've not necessarily reached it yet? That's what you're saying? That rather than being the single example of post-filter life, Earth could be one of an infinite number of pre-filter planets?'

'Yeah.'

'Then why the silence? If it's common for life to reach space, if billions of planets are doing this in our galaxy, then where is everyone?'

'We've reached space, but we haven't explored it. We're still locked inside our solar system. Maybe other planets are too.'

'So . . . the filter is embedded in an innovation that enables *distant* exploration?'

'You can see where this is going, can't you?'

'Because we just happen to have encountered that exact innovation here on Earth five years ago. So are you saying we shouldn't use the propulsion? That we shouldn't explore at all?'

'I wouldn't take this too seriously – it's the kind of thing you hear at JPL, and you learn to shrug it off. I just thought it was interesting.'

'Interesting enough to call me at midnight.'

'Ah, Leigh, I'm sorry.'

'Don't be.' I was sitting fully upright now. It felt intimate talking to Amy this way, darkness covering the distance. 'I kind of love it. It's so macabre. The reason we haven't seen or heard from anything off-world is that reaching off-world status is a civilisational death knell. Life either gets stuck there or destroyed there. It still doesn't really explain anything though – we can't see anyone because it's impossible to see anyone. It's circular. It doesn't say why becoming space proficient dooms us.'

'I think it's implied. There would be something in the technology that wasn't realised at the time – like a shadow aspect.'

'A shadow aspect? Is that what you guys are doing at JPL all day?'

'Well . . . I guess you can say that if we're able to do this, and we really start to explore space, then we disprove the theory. The filter, if there is one, was early, was cellular. Which would be reassuring, at least.'

'Maybe. It's another reason to go ahead with the mission. Unless it comes even later. The filter, not the technology that lets you explore space, but what you find – what you contact – when you get there.'

NINE

It was a sign of how worried Fenna was that when the GP called her in she let Erika go with her. We then got the details second-hand. Erika gave the good news first: there was no tumour. But the doctor had questions. He asked Fenna to describe a typical day. What time she wakes. What she eats. Who she sees. He asked her about exercise, and when she told him she cycles to and from work he tapped out notes on his screen. At the end of the consultation he asked how she'd feel about coming in for a longer chat with a specialist. This might involve a 'mental acuity test'.

Quietly, evenly, Fenna told him she was insulted. The doctor managed to calm her down. He said he could see she was operating at a high level, but that didn't mean the brain couldn't still be subject, like any other body part, to a degree of wear. One or two little things might start to go wrong. A specialist would be able to advise; there might, for instance, be medication she could take which would help slow down some of the changes. The fact she was still working was obviously a good sign, but didn't necessarily rule out problems to come.

Another late-night call to Jakarta, the bright light of the eastern morning illuminating my otherwise dark front room.

'I don't understand – is she ill or not? Why can't she have an MRI?'

'She's claustrophobic, Leigh; she's not going to crawl into one of those things. Besides, it's not like an MRI is necessarily the answer.' Helena, after three days' reading, had declared herself an expert. 'They're not definitive. You could get dark spots with no symptoms. Or erratic behaviour and a perfectly clear scan. You can't always just say one person is ill and another is healthy, especially at Mum's age.'

'So what should we do?' I took a large sip from the wine glass.

'Well we reassure her, tell her we're there for her. We need to keep her on the call, really get through to her. It just breaks my heart thinking she's not taking care of herself. There's something that came up in virtually every article—'

'Yeah?'

'—about the importance of connections, the danger in spending too much time alone. They all say that loneliness may be a destructive factor. You know this is a problem with Mum, it always was, the way she lives alone in her own world.'

'Surely she sees people at work?'

'Does she, though? Who knows. She could be stuck in her office ten hours. It's not like she'd tell us.'

'I can't believe the timing of this.'

Helena paused. 'You're aware how that sounds, right?'

'Obviously I don't mean it like *that*. I just wish, if something had to happen, that it happened when I was there.'

'You still can be, Leigh.'

'I can't.'

'Why not?'

'I can't leave here for a day, never mind a week. Just because I'm alone it doesn't mean my life is any less full than yours. This might be the biggest opportunity I'll ever get. Helena? Are you crying?'

'No. I'm just thinking of our mother out there on her own.'

'God, Helena. Look, we'll do what we can. I can try to visit later – I don't know when, or how, but I'll try.'

'Me too. Later. If we tell her we're trying, that's a start. But I think the main thing is we share real conversations; we can't let her feel like she's out there on her own.'

'And we stay in the loop with hospital visits.'

'And even if she says no, we insist on video calls. We need to actually *see* her, see how she is.'

'And see around her. See the house, see how she's keeping it. See the kitchen. Hopefully this was just a one-off.'

'Hopefully. This could all be a false alarm – who knows? Things aren't necessarily going to get worse.'

I called Fenna twice a week. I ordered her some potted plants with instructions specifically to house them in the kitchen, where she'd be closer to them, and where I'd see them behind her on our calls. I gave her very clear and simple directions, knowing she wouldn't read any of the pamphlets from the delivery. She didn't seem particularly interested when the plants arrived, but she was happy to discuss them, willing to try them, grateful maybe to have something to talk about that didn't directly involve her health. Fenna asked, with a glint in her eye, if we wanted her to name them; they were so obviously a surrogate for her daughters. As silly as the comparison was, it was important she had presence, company, other life around her, and plants didn't come with the demands and potential upset of an animal. I liked the idea of a quiet and supportive friend, a presence that nourished and needed her too. And I suppose there was the idea that the plants, as they settled and grew, and flowered, would mimic in some way her own recovery, her confirmed good health. So that when we called, and her peace lilies and philodendron greens were flourishing, we'd know that Fenna was OK, that she was remembering them, feeding them, spending time with them and enjoying them.

Another advantage in getting the plants was that it was a way of showing Fenna my work at China Lake. This was new, and I was surprised at how much her apparent interest meant to me. I took cuttings from the lab, held them up to the camera and told her I had made this, it was the result of months of work, and that it might really mean something. She put her glasses on, peered so close to the screen I could see the ridges and pockmarks around her eyes.

TEN

'We're all very impressed with the work you're doing,' Uria told me in her office, which was only a little bigger than mine, though maybe the size was deceptive given how cluttered it was with folders and coffee cups, sandwich wrappers and redacted reports. 'In some ways you've already exceeded expectations.'

I nodded, scanning her shelves, noting the framed photograph – daughter, presumably – tilted towards her. 'But there's still a way to go,' I said. 'Fine-tuning the strains, then starting up trials. Of course we've still to make a recommendation on which strain is best suited to the mission.'

'That's actually what I wanted to talk to you about. I've been thinking about something you said earlier, not long after you arrived here.'

'Really? What did I say?'

'I remember you were frustrated. You grabbed me, practically, and took me out the lab. You said I was making your job impossible because I wasn't giving you any information.'

'I did?'

'It was maybe a little more nuanced. But I can see you were right. I've been reading your reports on the strains, the efficacy based on the mission as I've outlined it.'

'I've tried to do everything I can.'

'I can see that. We're impressed with the thoroughness of the work, and particularly with your imaginative engagement with the mission.'

'Like I say, it's essential if we want a crop that will work in that environment.'

Uria paused, and even stopped twirling her pen. She looked right at me. 'So I was thinking, why don't we take things further? In the interest of truly getting the best possible crop?'

'You mean, by telling me more?'

'Now there are responsibilities that come with that, and I should make this clear before you come to your decision. You don't have to say yes. You've already been vetted, but you'll be subject to a closer level of scrutiny, should you agree.'

'Which would entail what, exactly?'

She shrugged, showing a slightly pained expression. 'I don't think it's excessive. It's just to rule out breaches. The agreement will be tight. It will make it more difficult for you to leave Ridgecrest.'

'Really?'

Uria noted my alarm. 'I'm not saying you can't. Just that you'll have to plan your movements, and keep us informed in advance.'

'So if I wanted to go back home? If I wanted to see my mother?'

'International travel is slightly more tricky. Bear in mind this wouldn't be forever. In extenuating circumstances, if you put in a request, I don't see why you couldn't do that, no.'

'Right.'

'Second thoughts?'

'None at all.'

'I was hoping you'd say that.' She got up from her chair. 'There's something I think you should see.'

The auditorium was empty, and Uria had guards stationed outside the doors. She escorted me past the stage and up into the central aisle. 'Anywhere's fine.'

We stopped halfway, sat down. Uria took her satchel off her shoulder, unzipped it, and brought out a tablet. She swiped a finger across the screen, tapped it a couple of times. There was a loud clicking sound, and the auditorium went dark. I could no longer see her beside me. More tapping on the tablet, and then the front wall screen activated. Uria appeared again in a faint glow, staring at her keypad. When I looked up, I saw a number of faint illuminated points on the wall screen.

'Those are asteroids. They look close together, but each of them is around 600,000 miles apart. Part of our mission here is to watch them. We've mapped the trajectories of around 2 million. Most of the observation is passive, but if there's any kind of deviation or abnormal behaviour, we upgrade the asteroid from Tier 3 to Tier 2. This has a much smaller pool – typically fewer than 20,000 objects. Observation in Tier 2 is still largely dormant, though considerably more alert than Tier 3.

'Sometimes – rarely – Tier 2 surveillance gathers enough anomalies to transfer an asteroid up to Tier 1. There aren't typically more than 100 objects in Tier 1. Our computers watch them very closely. Detailed profiles build up. If there's a problem with Tier 1 observation, it's that it's overly sensitive. It over-reports, and almost all the data it flags is insignificant. In human terms, you might say Tier 1 occupies a state somewhere between vigilance, paranoia and psychosis.'

In the faint glow of the light reflected from the asteroids, I caught a glimmer of a smile.

'It's not a perfect system. In my opinion, it's not even a very good system. Like many of the systems here, it has its roots in the military. Tier software was developed for use on human crowds. One of the more obvious flaws is that it relies too heavily on upward trafficking. Basically, it's guided by what it's already seen. An object acts in an unusual way, it's studied more, further anomalous data comes in, leading to still greater attention; the process feeds back on itself. But as a rule, any object studied in sufficient depth will eventually exhibit anomalous behaviour. Objects will be anomalous largely because they were the ones picked out, when really it should be the reverse. This creates at least two possible categories of error: false attribution, and blindness.'

'Almost all asteroids are not actively watched?'

'That's right. When you've got 2.75 million rocks spinning through medium-range space, it's helpful to have a system that tells you where to prioritise. You have to manage resources in a way that you can convince yourself is responsible.' She breathed in, breathed out. 'OK.' She began tapping her screen again, and suddenly the whole auditorium changed. The dense, fine points disappeared, and in their place a single, enormous globe arrived. It was faint red in colour, circular, hanging in the darkness, surrounded by space. Uria appeared different, cast in its glow. When I looked back up, the object seemed to have jumped forward. With the edges of the screen invisible, it appeared to float untethered in the middle of the auditorium. I felt I could have got up and walked around it.

'This is Datura. It appeared a little over five years ago. It immediately shot to the front of Tier 1. We had never seen anything like it. As an asteroid, it was completely anomalous. And early indications suggested it was on a collision course with Earth.'

I went to speak but my mouth was dry. My lips hung open stupidly, as I failed to ask the question.

'Fortunately, both our assumptions proved to be wrong. It isn't on a course for Earth. And it isn't an asteroid.'

Minutes later, after I'd recovered from the initial shock
and blurted out a flurry of incoherent questions, Uria
explained a little more. She opened a list of statistics and
measurements on the screen. Datura was shorthand, its full
official name $1t/2020/x488\_u$. Diameter was 1.3 kilometres,
height 1.7 kilometres. The object was almost perfectly oval,
its dark red colour suggesting it was old, subject to millions,
possibly billions of years of cosmic radiation. Its ultimate
origin was without question interstellar. Shape, colour and
velocity corresponded to no object previously observed.
Absence of evidence of even minimal heat absorption, even
during perihelion stage, indicated an unknown, highly
reflective material. It was moving quickly – 112 kilometres
per second – but inconsistently. Acceleration was non-
gravitational, but still without evidence of outgassing, solar
radiation, or any other natural thrust source. Weirdly, it
appeared to increase speed as it travelled *away* from the sun.
Current distance was 1.7 billion kilometres from Earth,
passing further away each second. Extreme hyperbolic
trajectory would take it ultimately beyond the solar system.
Assuming it maintained approximately consistent speed, and
wasn't subject to gravitational boosts from the sun or planets,
it should reach Vulpecula Constellation in a little under
900,000 years.

Three telescope-mounted probes had been sent to get better visuals on the object. Uria tapped her screen again, and the enhanced images came up. This was when I saw the carvings. It took a moment to fully appreciate what this meant. My body began to tense and I felt a surge of internal electricity. The lines were huge, monumental; massive parallel ridges cut across the face, the largest, according to the appended notes, more than a kilometre wide. Fainter vertical lines intersected, giving the appearance of a grid. Grids suggest order, intentionality – a schema, a message, a map. On one augmentation a set of ovals was etched onto the surface, sixteen of them, their diameter ranging from 30 metres to 200 metres. The ovals' ratios were similar to the object itself, as if each sketch represented the whole picture, a self-referential writing system. A language. It seemed possible – the digital enhancements couldn't go any further – that each oval contained further grids and ovals, that the process of regression continued almost infinitely.

The careful uniformity of the grid-lines contrasted the varied positions of the ovals. Some were isolated, others set close together. In three cases the shapes were interlocking, links on a chain.

Uria closed down the projection, and as we left the auditorium, I could barely speak. I was still acting under the assumption this wasn't real, deferring my acceptance of what Uria had told me. I would get to this later, I told myself. This was too big. Keep walking, keep breathing. I will process all this another time. 'I'll check in with you again soon,' she said, a hint of amusement in her eyes, watching me carefully, reminding me about the information embargo.

Outside, in the corridor's bright light, it took me a moment or two to recalibrate and get my bearings. I checked my phone; 12:04, still early in the day. I had to get back to the lab, but I was distracted, unsettled, unable to face Datura head-on but incapable of thinking about anything else. The first slow questions began to surface. How old were the markings? How had they been made? What was their purpose? I was in shock; you can't overhaul everything you've ever believed in a single second.

The streets passed in a blur. For once it was still light when I got back home. My driver eyed me suspiciously when he dropped me off, asking again if I was feeling OK. I nodded distractedly, waved him off. I went up the steps to the courtyard and the elevator, drifted towards my door. It seemed notably quiet inside, as if in response to a guest's departure. I held my body still and listened. I went from room to room, going through my things, opening the cupboards, the drawers, looking for signs. I checked the windows, examined the floors, tried to identify a musk in the air. I was searching. I wanted an answer. My world was shaken, everything had changed. Uria's revelation had floored me, left me stunned. I saw new significance in everything around me and I was light-headed, with a pain in my stomach. I drew the blinds and closed the shutters, lay down on the bed in darkness, closed my eyes.

Everything spun, jostled. I tried to impose order. First, I needed more information. I couldn't form conclusions based on the limited amount Uria had given me. But that would have to wait until Monday at the earliest, as she had gone away to her daughter's for the weekend. My fingers swept over my phone, hovered over Amy's name. I'd be allowed to speak to her now, surely. She'd alluded to Datura earlier, in our phone conversation. That's what she had meant, pressing me on the great filter. She was working on the mission, she had pressed for my inclusion, but was she authorised to speak to me herself? What if my call was hacked and I leaked this and ruined everything? I saw Amy's patient, wry expression, and I wanted to hear her thoughts; someone smart, experienced and reliable as she was. 'No,' I said aloud, and placed the phone under a pillow. Uria trusted me, I couldn't share this, couldn't discuss it with anyone, until I was explicitly authorised to.

I was exhausted, I couldn't sleep, I felt the pressure of a huge backlog of unprocessed information. I heard my hysterical, joyous laugh echo off the walls. I showered, ate, paced the apartment. I went back to the station late in the evening, worked out in the gym, swam in the deserted pool, felt the drift of my buoyancy as I lay on my back, the sense of being gathered up, held, contained by something – the closest terrestrial analogue to microgravity. My skin burned. I remembered swimming at night in the small bay under the light of the moon in the Azores, stretching my limbs in a star design. The electric, inarticulate feeling as I sat at the table in the bar then walked slowly through the village square, Isabella calling to me at the foot of the steps. Then the airport – waiting to be carried again – scrolling through headline after headline on the discovery, the acceleration breakthrough. The beginning of this, the single moment that was responsible for taking me out here and transforming my life.

ELEVEN

Uria didn't come in on the Monday, or at all the following week. She wasn't answering emails, and my calls went straight to voicemail. Something had happened, something big, to draw her away from the station.

I was becoming manic. I couldn't stop thinking about the auditorium. I had to use all my restraint to avoid saying anything in the lab. I went in earlier and stayed late each day, keeping busy, doing double sessions in the pool. I searched online, deleted the browser data, searched again, repeated the process. Datura was the genus of a plant growing in the desert around us, visible from the observatory that had discovered the carved object. It bloomed at night, collapsed at dawn, an unusually large lavender-tinted flower with strong hallucinogenic properties. People swore by it, testifying to the transformative effect of ingesting the plant. Others vomited over and over, panicking, believing they were going to lose their essence, that they were evacuating themselves and the process would stop only at death. The plant had been used in religious ceremonies for thousands of years. There were ancient accounts of three-dimensional objects rendered in astonishing detail; objects, I thought, that sounded a little like the red orb that had lit up the auditorium.

It was hard to get to sleep. The object was burned on my retinas, orange orbs interlocking as I closed my eyes. But instead of dreaming about Datura, I was back on *Endeavour*, falling from the zodiac into the crater, waking suddenly in my cabin with no recollection of what had happened, the chirp of the alarm harsh and insistent. Every night I dreamed of the moment we crossed the line into the crater's territory, holding ourselves against the railings. The waves of confusion and alarm and excitement as the depth readings came up and we realised we had no real indication of what was under us. Amy's face as she tolerated my rambling digressions, her rich voice telling me calmly that all of this was just a read-through for space.

Endeavour and Datura surfaced again and again – while I grabbed my cereal, while I swam in the pool, while I inspected the labs each day. *Endeavour* anticipated this – it was the start of all this, the place where ICORS had tested the sub and found a new species of archaea. But there was something else too. When the alarm pulled me from the water each morning I felt the answer right in front of me, suddenly and agonisingly pulled just out of reach.

In the end it was something banal, an object I'd seen a million times before. I was standing in my apartment preparing breakfast, the sky just light enough to see by, holding an egg from the carton. It was the feel of the object as I turned it over in my hand, the touch and shape of the egg. Stefan's words came back, describing the crater as resembling a

Cassini oval. Datura was oval, carved with repeated inscriptions of itself. They were connected. Datura had appeared five years ago, around the same time as the revelations that lead to the propulsion breakthrough. Reports claimed the engineers had had visions of orbs 'spinning in a loop'. Could these have been ovals? There was more. Tectonic activity linked to the crater zone was detected five years ago, the same time as the emergence of Datura and the dreams. Everything was spinning. What did it mean?

Still holding the egg in the hollow of my palm, I thought of the archaea that was instrumental in the food crop we were developing, and which would be used to feed the crew on a mission, surely, to explore Datura. I pictured the symbiosis the archaea contributed to: two cells, two ovals intertwined, folded into each other and creating the potential for multicellular life. Was Datura an egg, a cell? Was the crater its inverse, its mirror image?

I remembered the dreams, fevers, and lost time on the ship. I remembered the words from the old Daturan narratives, looking forward thousands of years to our night sky, an impossible causal loop. And finally I heard Stefan's voice on the ship, describing giant crater impacts fertilising and incubating early Earth, moulding the perfect conditions for animals to be born, to one day sleep, and dream, and build things on the earth.

———

I didn't need to call Uria because there was a message already waiting for me saying she was back at China Lake and could we meet first thing, as early as possible. I thought her voice sounded different as I drove towards the station in the early light. I came towards her in the corridor, moving quickly and urgently. 'There's something we need to talk about,' I told her, almost reaching her; 'I think I've found something.' Uria nodded, swallowed. She didn't look surprised. I was disappointed, I saw suddenly she knew everything; everything I was about to tell her, it didn't mean anything. I'd planned a more reasonable way of broaching this but instead the words came rushing out. Uria was patient with me, she nodded and swallowed, her gaze alternating between ahead of her and the ground.

'It's a Cassini oval, isn't it?'

'How did you—?'

'I think it might all be connected – the vent, the thrust system, Datura, the food source. I think it calls back to the beginning of life.'

Uria looked at me – calm, patient, tolerant. 'So what does it mean?'

'I – I don't know yet. I don't know that it means anything. But the data is there. All the connections, they're there. Look, we have to go there,' I said. 'We have to do it, now, we have to accelerate it, launch as soon as possible. Do you see? Do you see how important this is?'

'I see, I hear what you're saying.'

'And? Does this sound crazy?'

'I don't think you're crazy. I don't think you're crazy at all. But we're not going to send a mission to Datura.'

'Why not? You were already planning to? Don't you see what it could mean?'

'Leigh, it's not possible.'

I lowered my arms in front of her. I almost groaned. 'Then tell me why. It's the greatest opportunity of our lives. We have a responsibility to do this – something like this might never happen again. We have the means to go there, don't we?'

'In theory, we do.'

'Well why wouldn't we? I can't believe we would pass this up. We're looking for a long-range destination, and you're saying we're *not* going to Datura? Give me a good reason for that?'

'Leigh—'

'It's a simple question. Can you or can you not explain why you're turning away from this?'

'Leigh, will you give me a chance to speak?'

'OK. I'm listening. Go ahead.'

'You want to know why we're not going there? I'll give you a reason. We're not going there because Datura has disappeared. It isn't there anymore. I'm sorry, Leigh. It's gone.'

TWELVE

It was quiet when we left a couple of hours later, the sun directly above us, Uria's expression hidden behind her black wraparounds. When I asked her about theories, something that might explain what had happened to Datura, she gave a dismissive shrug, keeping her focus on the road. 'I see no purpose,' she said, 'in descriptive theories which themselves require further explanation.' There were three options, as far as I could see: concealment, combustion and displacement, either temporal or spatial. But Uria wouldn't budge. 'Forget about that, for now,' she told me.

'I don't understand.'

'No one does.'

'No, I mean I don't understand why we're going here, now, if it's not for Datura.'

'It's complicated,' she said.

Goldstone Observatory was less than 50 miles from China Lake, an hour's drive east through the desert. It was put here for the isolation, the nothing all around. Goldstone's five parabolic antennas linked to Canberra and Madrid to form the Deep Space Network, scanning space for trace events and communicating with probes and other spacecraft. The three sites were an equal distance apart, cutting the earth in segments, giving the antennas broad coverage at any stage in the planet's rotation. Immediately after informing me of Datura's disappearance, Uria told me this was where we were going.

I found her silence irritating. She always did this. She couldn't give me information like this and expect me to stay quiet. Everything had changed. Everything I'd been working on – my whole reason for being here – was now redundant. The mission wasn't a simulation, the aim had been to make contact with Datura – my lab would have provided a primary food source for the flight. Now it had gone, would there even be a mission? And if there wasn't a mission, then why, I wanted to know, were we driving to Goldstone, and during the hottest part of the day?

'You'll see when we get there,' she replied.

'You sound like my mum,' I noted, feeling my cheeks blush. 'So you see your daughter a lot; she lives nearby?'

'For the moment, yes. Maria and her husband are 150 miles away.'

'But she's moving.'

'Because of the firestorms. They're worse there. She has asthma. This is serious for her now.'

I kept quiet. Uria looked ahead.

'They always wanted kids,' she said. 'But not here. Not now. Reproduction is quite a lot lower than official figures, you know? Who could blame them. But at the same time it's sad, isn't it; it's awful. To decide, en masse, that we do not want more of this.'

We continued a couple of miles. We'd passed two, maybe three vehicles in the previous twenty minutes.

Uria angled her head towards me. 'What's going on with your mother?'

'Huh?'

'You said the other week you might need to leave and visit your mother. It seemed more than a routine visit.'

'Uh, yeah. We don't know really. Fenna – our mother – she's been acting a little strange.'

'She's alone?'

'Our father died years ago.'

'I'm sorry.'

'It might be nothing. She's still working. Maybe it's just the loneliness. She'd never complain, or reach out or anything. So it's harder to gauge what's happening.'

We turned off from the main road onto a narrower track, and after we'd hit the next bend Goldstone appeared, five massive white dishes, bright against the dun- and ochre-coloured plains and hills. The observatory was placed inside a small depression, a bowl-like valley similar to the scooped shape of the antennas themselves. Each dish was surrounded by a pool of tarmac with a couple of vehicles parked alongside it. There were seven narrow stone buildings in total.

'What's that expression for?' Uria said.

'It's empty. I mean, where is everyone?'

I'd thought the place would be a hive, with hundreds of researchers and engineers. Instead, it was deserted. We passed down into the valley and parked 20 metres from the first antenna. We got out, tied the reflective shields over the windscreen and the rear windows. I fixed my headscarf, leaning into the car, springing back from the heat-soaked metal.

It was quiet, but not silent. Gusts of wind swept the red sand. There was something under this, a low, gentle humming. I didn't know enough to identify it, didn't want to expose my ignorance. The sound of the universe itself, or the sound of our listening to it? Could I be sure of the distinction? From inside the valley, it was difficult to get a sense of the antennas' scale. I squinted, shielded my eyes; they were hundreds of metres apart, and I guessed the largest was about 80 metres across. The dishes were each set on a limber base support, with a fully rotating head. The mesh underside was dazzling, a fine, dense thatchwork of white steel netting, like a spider's web repeated over and over.

It was possible we were interfering with the antennas just by standing here. Uria hadn't said anything. I looked down at my boots, covered in fine red dust. A faint ripple of wind picked up, travelling across the ground, shaking the weeds and the scattered wildflowers.

'You OK with the sun?'

I nodded.

'Come on then,' she said, and started walking across the valley.

The antennas seemed mysterious, impenetrable, though I knew more or less what they did: sweep the skies, receive transmissions from spacecraft. But the reality here on the ground was different. The discs were monolithic, inscrutable, quite beautifully sculpted. They looked devotional, built in praise, which I supposed they were. The soft, curved white parabolas were like a pale opened hand, waiting to catch something, carry something, pass something on. The container, the object of infinite purpose and adaptability, the thing that enabled other things. A cup, a bowl, an opened hand. A vessel can contain almost anything; so can language. There was no limit to the purpose it might serve.

'That's it,' she said, pointing ahead of us. 'The biggest one, Cassegrain. It's harder to tell from in here, but they're all slightly different sizes. Cassegrain is the most powerful.'

'So that's why we came here,' I said after a moment. 'To see this?'

'These reach much further than Datura. They don't discriminate. An automated radio transmission from a distant probe, or spillover data indicating the formation of a star – it reads them both. It's all light. If it happens, it's light. Do you see?'

I squinted, looking towards her in the hard sun.

'These antennas draw a picture of the universe very

different from what we ordinarily see. We are standing around the basis of a huge archive centre, of a scale you cannot imagine.'

I nodded. I wasn't sure if Uria was looking at me through her glasses. Her tone was different, odd. Almost excited? I didn't know what she was getting at. Was it uncertainty in her voice? Was she struggling over whether to tell me something? She continued to walk while she spoke, the red sand blowing around our feet as we approached the vast dish.

'The isolation is important. The clearer the area, the less interference.'

'Interference from what? Phone signals, Wi-Fi?'

'Everything, really. Everything that comes with human habitation. Radios, televisions, electrical activity in any form. Fridges, microwaves, any domestic power source at all, provided there's enough of it. Road traffic too. On a large scale, at high urban density, even footsteps and voices, even neural electricity, can affect the signal.'

'So it's pretty sensitive.'

'It can see further, but it's also prone to picking up meaningless activity.'

'The more powerful it is, the more isolated it has to be.'

'Exactly. It's better to avoid infrastructure too, hence the portable buildings. Nothing runs under the ground here.'

'What about computers? They're all off-site? Because these all have to be controlled, right? The heads, the dishes?'

'Remote steering, yes, they tilt them to the sky. Computers distribute incoming information. They divide the frequency band into several thousand channels.'

'So this is all one giant telescope? It all links up?'

Uria didn't appear to hear me. She was still moving ahead, and though sweat had appeared around her neck she gave no indication of suffering. If anything, she was walking even faster. I found myself out of breath, struggling for sufficient air.

'You OK?' Uria called, looking back at me.

I nodded quickly, pressed on.

Finally we approached Cassegrain. We stopped, stepped into the large shadow of the parabola. It was cooler under the dish's cover, but the hum was louder. I felt exposed, the deep sound rumbling through me.

'What I said earlier, about information security – that still applies, OK?'

I nodded, wiping my forehead free of sweat.

'I need you to say it.'

'Sure. I understand. I agree, of course.'

She looked into me, and a smile flickered across her face. 'So the dish above us, it's called a parabolic reflector. It's made of fibreglass and aluminium. These are robust, strong materials, but they're not perfect. And what we've seen, beginning several years ago, is that temperatures in high summer, as the firestorms near, are getting so extreme they're affecting the integrity of the dishes. They weren't built for this. It's not something you'd notice superficially, it's not dramatic. But it's insidious. Tiny pockets of the surface begin to curve in the heat. On its own, this wouldn't be a major problem. It would still be an issue, temporarily, but the imperfections would tend to resolve themselves according to average changes in temperature.'

'OK,' I said.

'The problem is that where we are, in the desert, the temperature variation can be significant, as you know. 128 degrees at midday, dropping to freezing during the night.'

'So it holds the errors? Makes them stick.'

Uria was nodding. 'Basically, though it's not quite as simple as that. Keep in mind the perfection of the telescope surface is critical. The mildest warping can scatter the waves and they'll lose focus. It's more of an issue somewhere like this, where the information coming in has travelled so far that it's already weak and difficult to detect.'

'So we might lose something,' I said.

'Yes. Or we could register something that isn't there. Have you heard of heat delirium?'

'More familiar with it every second. You're comparing this to the telescopes?'

'Informally, yes. We've been calling them "whispers".'

'Calling what? The errors?'

'False readings. Indications of astral phenomena that

aren't necessarily reliable, or feasible – events and bodies that can't exist.'

'Uria, are you going to tell me Datura was an error? A heat-generated hallucination, a mirage embraced by dehydrated desert techs?'

She smiled. I felt I was seeing just a glimpse of a more playful side. 'Don't worry, Datura is quite real. The data on Datura is reliable, and we've had a reasonable amount of time to study it.'

'Then what was the error that brought us out here?'

'This is the bit that's difficult to explain. There was a signal, about five years ago.'

'Same time as Datura.'

'Approximately, though actually slightly later. The telescopes picked up information that was initially classified as an error. The data wasn't consistent with anything recognisable. But as we always do, we worked backwards, went to source the problem back to the dish.'

'And you couldn't find one.'

'Nothing that explained the data, no.'

'What was the transmission?'

'A string of numbers. The same numbers repeated. A nineteen-digit number repeated 3,042 times. Let's climb up a little, into the hills.' We began walking across the site. When we turned, the humming sound stopped. The breeze retreated, the silence was starker.

'You understand that Datura was unprecedented. Every-one was excited, and focused exclusively on the object. We were distracted. I think that's understandable.' Uria paused. 'But I regret it, certainly. We wasted valuable time. So the signal wasn't created by surface warp. It wasn't environmentally induced at all. And it didn't tally with any unusual local transmission patterns. But it still wasn't treated as significant. It wasn't until later that we fully investigated.' Uria's tone changed as she looked at me. 'It was so faint,' she said. 'A miracle, really. Like a human ear picking up a footstep 16 miles away.'

'What was, Uria? You're not explaining, you're—'

'You are aware of the *Voyager* probes?' She turned towards me again. The hills were scattered with rubble and tufts of low bush. I hadn't yet seen the signature white spread of the Datura flower.

'What? The old ones? From fifty years ago? I guess, yeah.'

'What do you know about them?'

'That they were a success? *Voyager 1* is still travelling, right? It's supposed to continue indefinitely. But it can't record anything now.'

'It was functional longer than anyone expected, but it hasn't sent anything for years. The last photograph was of Earth 3.75 billion miles away. That was a long time ago. It should have reached around four times that distance now.'

'"Should have"? What happened?'

'We don't know. We lost it somewhere around the heliopause. This was expected. *Voyager*'s energy, its isotope generator, was depleted. It was functionally dead.'

'Uria, can we stop?'

'Hmm?'

She was three steps ahead, she looked confused as she turned. Sweat edged her hairline.

'What is this? What are you getting at?'

She exhaled.

'The error message wasn't an error,' she said. 'It was sent from *Voyager*.'

I thought for a moment. 'No. You just said that was impossible.'

'I know.'

'Then how can it be *Voyager*?'

'I don't know.'

'Well, what did it say?'

'I already said, there was nothing in it, just the signature code again and again. The interesting bit is not that it came from *Voyager*, but where *Voyager* was.'

'You said, what, 15 billion miles distant, at its current position?'

'Current estimated position. That's where it should be. But that's not where it is.'

'So it's deviated. It's further, closer, what?'

'Further. Much further.'

'How much further?'

'In the period since we last heard from it, it appears to have travelled around ten light days, and reached close to the inner rim of the Oort cloud.'

'What? Uria?'

'It's getting late. We should go back.'

'We can't. We can't go back yet. Stop. I don't understand this, I don't understand what you're telling me. *Voyager* has accelerated? How is that possible?'

'It isn't possible. Of course it isn't.'

'Then how did it get there? Why did it send a message?'

Uria looked towards the ground.

'Who else knows about this?'

'Probably not as many people as you'd think. I'm telling you because I think it will help you in your work.'

'But how? How does this tie in . . . OK, OK. I'm just trying to organise my thoughts – this is a lot, you know? Just to get this straight: it's completely impossible *Voyager 1* could have travelled that distance, and sent the message?'

'Do you really need me to answer that?'

'OK. So something brought it there. Lifted it, carried it, whatever. And it happened around the same time we found Datura. So we're saying these are connected? The same – *thing* – is responsible? That's what you believe?'

'We believe the two phenomena – Datura and the signal

– are linked. The same identity is most probably responsible for both.'

'OK, so, what do we do now? What's next?'

'We investigate the signal.'

'Right. We interpret it. With the analysts and the software. I get it. Can we contact it? Can we reply to *Voyager*'s message?'

'That was one of the first things we tried. No response. *Voyager* continues to show no further signs of life. No new messages. We keep trying, of course.'

'So what else?'

'Like I said, we're going to investigate. In the most direct way possible.'

'We're going to go there? That's the voyage? The mission? That's what we're preparing?'

'That's right.'

'Fuck. I'm sorry, just . . . Fuck.'

We walked on, past the car and up to an old track leading into the hills. Pockmarks in the ground, traces of prior features, specks of white in the distance obscure in the overheated air.

'What about Datura?' I said. 'What if it comes back?'

'It might. Of course it might. We don't know. Anything could happen. Leigh, if your reaction is anything like mine, you'll eventually find something freeing in this. We do the best we can, and that's OK. But Datura – we can't just wait for it to appear again. I can't just do nothing. We have a duty to respond, we have to do something, now.'

'OK. So when? What's the timeframe?'

'As soon as possible. Realistically two, three years. From an engineering perspective, little has changed – the intention was always to prepare a long-range mission, the first of the *Proscenium* generation. We'd been working towards a mission to Datura, but now we need to go further. The new thrust design can get us there.'

'To where the transmission was sent from?'

'Yes. The near edge of the Oort cloud. That's where we're aiming for. And Leigh?'

'Yes?'

'I took you out here because of the work you're doing. The further we go here, the more critical food is. You're talking about a self-sustaining, high-nutrition, high-yield crop. You've convinced us. This could make or break the mission. You're promising a stress-reliever, immunity booster, an emotional salve. We have to get this right. So I'm telling you you have full clearance, that from now on you'll be privy to top-level meetings. You're essential. We need you, Leigh, if we're going to do this.'

THIRTEEN

As we approached the vehicle I let out a stream of questions, one after another; reasonable questions, the kind I imagined someone in my position might have asked. I maintained this rational veneer, two acceptable actors exchanging information, when really my mind was reeling, my heart was beating faster, my brain running a million different scenarios. Ridiculous thoughts: that the anomalies could exist in the same universe as my father's green wax coat. That I was helping prepare a possible first-contact mission and I had also taken an unusually long time as an infant learning to speak. As Uria responded to my questions in Goldstone's burning heat, as I nodded and followed up with more questions, I wanted to blurt out secret after secret, the most shameful moments of my life. Baseline reality had irreparably changed, and I felt, standing there in that red bowl, that the usual constraints and conversational decorum should no longer hold. It was the most hysterical, the most alive, that I had ever felt. The world was no longer what we thought it was at all. Already I missed that, the innocence and naivety, the regularity and narrowness of our domestic relations. I regretted the fact that my mother – much too old now – would have to relearn the world. That she might feel, also, that the world had betrayed her.

As Uria closed the car door and switched on the engine, I

looked at every detail inside – the upholstery, the cup-holder, the notepad in the backseat, Uria's spare headscarf – and it was as fascinating as the 80-metre-diameter radio telescopes outside. There was a three-quarters-full water barrel in the backseat, next to the silver heat reflectors we'd taken down from the windows and a tube of rehydrating balm, and it was as if someone – some set designer – had set the items there deliberately to imply the sun, the planets, the Oort cloud and the star system beyond it. I fell silent as the tyres skidded off the rubble and Uria extended her left hand to someone unseen behind the tinted glass of the small building we passed, and we went up, out of the bowl, out of the observatory and on into the straight desert road home.

Helena's messages were piling up; she was worried, I hadn't picked up in weeks. I wasn't avoiding her or Fenna deliberately, it's just that everything was passing in a blur. I sent a brief note saying it was work, it was the time difference – which was true, but it was more than that. I was afraid of sitting down with her, afraid of what she might say. Afraid that Fenna's deterioration would make a claim on me, that the resumption of my old life would jeopardise my progression, that the two zones couldn't coexist and the excitement at Ridgecrest would fade into nothing. When I looked up, at night, I didn't see something cold and barren, but a dark space edged by possibility, fertility. Earth had been uncapped, exposed to tremendous aerial uncertainty. Every star centred a system of planets, moons and smaller rocks, any one of which might contain traces of life. Preserved proto-cells; impenetrable languages; the rendered architecture of a vast, long-extinct civilisation. It wasn't a good idea, looking up. How could I sleep, how could I lie down under this? And how could I speak to my sister?

I'd spent too much time outside at the observatory without protection. For days now my ears had rung and light spots danced across my retinas. I rested at home in the dark under a cold compress, my skin burned up, my sleep interrupted, seeing scenes from my childhood, memories of drifting, then switching as something inexplicable moved across the sky. I was restless and running a mild fever from the lingering heat-stroke, and with my hearing and vision impaired I felt there was something I was close to but still missing, a peripheral significance I was unable to access. I swam harder and longer in the pool, renewing myself, trying to outpace the gaining paranoia. It was possible I was being watched, both at the station and at home, my movements monitored, my conversations taped, my communications copied. The new contracts I'd signed explicitly permitted this.

I had greater access at the Institute. My keycard let me through previously undiscovered corridors and I could now get a view of the runways. Aircraft arrived, odd cone shapes moving in rapid jerks, able to gain and lose exceptional speed almost instantly. I glimpsed indecipherable flashes on the gunmetal horizon. I listened for the delayed sound but heard nothing; it was like I was watching a completely closed event, a technical exercise with a rare level of perfection. From the far side of the territory – 16 miles of asphalt from our labs – there were frequent blasts and screeching sounds. The best views were from the windows on the upper floor, but even then all I could make out through my phone's viewfinder were hazy, layered pastel colours – magnolia strips, eggshell blues, bleached-out brickwork and the occasional fireblast.

I was drawn to the activity on the far side, even as I was awed by it. *Any sufficiently advanced technology will appear indistinguishable from magic.* There was now general agreement that the thrust design was an alien technology transmitted through Datura. The dreams that delivered the information to the engineers were connected to the ovals carved onto the object and to the empty-brackets message sent back from the *Voyager* space probe. What it all meant – why we had been given this power, and why now – no one knew. That the experiments were being stepped up was exciting, we were closer to seeing the technology applied, but it was frightening too. To launch the mission, to follow through with our plans, to actually respond to and engage with the anomalies, we relied completely on our ability to harness a volatile system. Even the designers admitted they knew so little about this that it wasn't safe to conduct a full-

scale trial on Earth. The flashes of colour, the alien appearance of the aircraft, the unprecedented take-offs and
landings, were like tantalising hints of a concealed violence.
My presence in the lab, my responsibility for food systems,
my future involvement in mission prep – the training and
the move up the hierarchy it entailed – all gave my tacit
agreement to an inexplicable and wholly unpredictable new
power.

FOURTEEN

Preparations were taking shape. I sat in on launch protocol meetings and briefings for mobile lab building; submitted provisional sketches for the ship's garden; met with mission directors and department heads, and advised on various criteria for crew selection. Uria and I met up regularly, in and out of the station – including, once, a brief visit to her surprisingly small and sparsely decorated apartment – discussing theories, conjecture, anything that might clarify the link between Datura and *Voyager 1*. Time seemed to rush forward, in an almost unbroken atmosphere of elation. I had little opportunity to take stock, caught up in the sheer momentum of mission prep, buoyed by the surprising realisation that people valued and respected my contributions, that I really could do this.

If we couldn't understand what the signal meant, we could at least look at where it had come from. *Voyager 1* had been chosen for a reason – there must, I thought, be something significant about the spacecraft. Uria described it as an exploratory mission, but that wasn't the whole story. While built to observe, *Voyager* had a cargo, too; it was in itself a message. It seemed reasonable to infer that Datura – the intelligence behind the signals – was responding in some sense to this message. But the transmission picked up by Cassegrain was empty, so far as we could tell. Just a frame, a set of brackets. A static repetition of *Voyager*'s signature code. If the transmission wasn't a message, it might still act as a primer, a clue over what was written on the object. The transmission the frame, the interstellar object the image or text inside.

Voyager built on previous missions; *Pioneer 10*, launched in 1972, was the first spacecraft with enough velocity to breach the solar system. *Pioneer* was like a prototype for *Voyager*; it had an inscribed plaque attached to the fuselage showing a map to Earth, a diagram of the solar system, an illustration of the probe and its components. *Voyager 1* came five years later. Instead of a plaque, it had a copper phonograph record with a gold-plated cover attached to the middle ring. There were primary images etched onto the cover, secondary ones pressed in analogue onto the record, and multiple sound recordings.

Pioneer 10 was still travelling, though *Voyager* had passed it long ago. If the same civilisation encountered both crafts, *Pioneer* would appear much later, like a clarification, a condensed version of *Voyager*'s sprawling archive. *Pioneer* travelled at 25,000 mph. Compared to the speeds we were capable of now, it had barely left the ground. In another 13 billion years – the same as the current age of the universe, again – *Pioneer* still wouldn't have hit the nearest star.

Voyager contained its own description, in elaborate and exhaustive detail. It described Earth in images, and described how to read those images. It built itself recursively, through self-description, just like DNA did. DNA's helical loop was wrought onto the record, next to pictures of cells and cell division. There was a fertilised ovum, a foetus, a newborn child. A diagram illustrating continental drift appeared next to a photograph of a young woman in a supermarket. There was a telescope, a microscope, a seashell, a leaf, a house being constructed, a large factory interior, dolphins, larger whales, the Greenland shark. There was a highway, a string quartet, representations of sheet music next to the instruments required to play them and the source forests. There were bonobo chimpanzees, the parameters of the solar system, a description of set theory, an Antarctic expedition record, astronauts orbiting the moon. There were the inner planets, a calibration circle, the *Voyager 1* craft itself, the faces of the 17,000 men and women who had built it; the common fruit fly, the human eye, spindrift over the Mojave, chains of mountains above and below water. There were pictures of recent advances in computing, the metals used to build hardware in pure form, a dam, a windmill, an ant; a Texan oil refinery, a wheel, an octopus in various stages of colour display, a single crystal of sand in extraordinary detail, the craters of the moon, the ridges and creases and lumps of the human tongue; indoor and outdoor food markets, contemporary and traditional clothing from twenty-seven countries, handwriting in 119 languages, binary code, the

Fibonacci sequence, the essential stages in the factory
assembly of a car; organised protest, cemeteries, still images
from sport; the complete skeleton of a pterosaur, crop circles,
the whorls upon a snail shell, the Andromeda galaxy seen
from Earth; a factory farm, the furthest limits of astro-
photography, mushroom clouds over Nevada, a seismic
reading from a scale 9 earthquake, epidemiology curves
reconstructing the progress of the Spanish Flu, Earth's
population charted as a spirograph. The sound recordings
included greetings in fifty-three languages announcing the
new year, water festivals, smouldering funeral pyres, waves
hitting a shore, Gaelic psalm singing, an engine starting and
accelerating, glass smashing, a male and female climaxing,
a fist hitting a wall, a child born, a building demolished, a
dog reunited with its owner, a green apple crunched, two
hands clasping for the first time, the howler monkey's call,
a deserted infant sobbing, the doppler effect in passing
sirens; equatorial thunder, late-stage marathon runners on
tarmac, the swish of a net as an object hits it, Martin Luther
King Jr's address, trees bending but not breaking, clam shells
opening, the single extant recording of Virginia Woolf
speaking, concrete setting, a glacier travelling, ice breaking,
reptilian and mammalian heartbeats from ascending metabolic scales. There was an acoustic rendition of the writer
and consultant Ann Druyan's EEG as she thinks about all of
the above, considers her life next to the history of the planet

she was born on, her impressions from childhood, her worst nightmares and her greatest dreams, over an hour of Ann Druyan's thinking etched in sound as she sits upright in a hospital bed linked up to dozens of electrodes, thinks about the *Voyager* probe and how it was built and where it might go to and if this – all this – would be encountered by another life, a comprehending intelligence, or if it would simply, finally be dismissed, caught by a minor piece of debris, sucked into a vortex, burned up by a star.

FIFTEEN

Moving further into autumn, the landscape changed. The colder evening temperature clashed with the daytime heat to create banks of hanging fog. Coming home in the evenings I could barely see the direction the driver and I were going in. From my apartment window I looked out onto a drifting grey illuminated by headlights. Long, deep horns sounded from bewildered traffic, like ancient, stranded ships. I bought new clothes, woollen sweaters, thicker socks. I ate warmer meals, vegetable soups, food that reminded me of family, of being young and at home and being cared for. We all got colds in the lab, but worked through it. *Rest*, Uria said, sternly. *Look after yourself. You're no good to us sick.* As we entered December, the desert ground froze overnight. I walked out in it, just to see what it was like; the fast wind whipping at me, the frozen ridges cracking underfoot. The buildings were covered in frost, harder to see in the developing obscurity. I breathed into the scarf raised over my lower face until the air felt dank, unhealthy, extinct.

I took a single day at home each week, catching up on sleep in broken moments through the afternoon. I called my mother and flinched as I saw over her shoulder the kitchen windowsill and the empty space where the potted plants had been. There was a moment's silence where I considered saying something, but I quickly changed the subject. I could see her relief; it was easier this way, but I also knew that I was letting her go.

The drastic temperature drop affected the lab. We used centralised heaters and additional plastic insulation over the tanks. I monitored the temperature from home, watched the camera feed, the faint glow of the crop through the night. Coming in from outside, our hands were insensitive and we had to wait forty-five minutes before it was safe to handle instruments. We weren't allowed to use heaters – danger of bruising the crop – but we could hold each other's hands, an efficient loop, and somehow this way our cold dissipated quicker, our body heat spread together in the closeness. We spoke less in the lab, heads down. I had never socialised much – I was effectively their boss – a rare beer with Lin or some of the technicians maybe, but I noticed the others had stopped going out themselves. We were retreating further into our homes, into ourselves. I stopped doing much at all, other than work, pool, gym. I began several emails to Helena, but closed them before sending.

The team was now working with four different algae strains, two of which we had developed and grown to crop stage, and were now processing into foods. We rendered them into powder form, puree, flakes. These were straight-forward processes that the crew should be able to replicate with their equipment on the ship. The other two strains were at an earlier stage – Lin was tweaking the genomes. We were now planning the first of the animal trials.

We wanted a quick yield from the crop, but Uria also wanted longevity. The mission would be a little longer than nineteen months, not the thirteen she'd initially advised. In the small microgravity simulators the strains grew equally virulently in all directions, something that it was tempting to describe as a panic response. The organism was disoriented, with no sense of up or down, and it over-compensated. On the positive side, this meant a quicker yield, but it was also harder to light, which affected integrity and quality, more so as time went on. Rotating the cylinders gave a better light distribution, and we were trialling various ways of doing this. It might even be possible to exploit the ship's water flow to turn as well as feed the crop.

After Datura and *Endeavour*, I saw the algae in a new light. It wasn't just a food source, or something to remind the crew of home: it was an organism rich in genetic heritage. The crew would carry extant examples of early life. I had spent so long researching the cargo on the earlier probes that I had begun to see our mission in the same way – as a craft bearing a suite of cultural documents, delivering a message. The difference this time was that we knew, at least in theory, that a listener – the entity responsible for all this – was waiting, beckoning us.

Everything on the ship would be part of our response, and this included the algae. I was excited about this, but also wary of how it could go wrong, how the significance might spiral out of our control, out of our awareness even.

I prepared a paper summarising the food project for a group of directors and consultants at the Margulis theatre in JPL. I was ambitious. I said algae showed the volatility and durability of life. It expressed biological breakthroughs and cognitive breakthroughs too. One of the reasons it was so attractive as a food in space was its abundance of iodine and Docosahexaenoic. DHA helps brain growth – seafood diets were 'brainy' because of the algae fish ate. Eating algae cut out the medium, delivering gains directly. The effects from prolonged microgravity and possible exposure to irradiated particles were unknown – it was an unprecedented project. A diet rich in DHA made sense, boosting general health, fortifying the brain, helping maintain focus and alertness and offsetting cognitive weariness.

There was speculation about DHA's role in hominin development. I'd watched footage of chimpanzees fishing algae out of ponds after judging the correct size of branch to break off. The more I thought about it, the more resonant and articulate algae became. From our past – first life, first stirrings in the brain – to our future, in its application as a replacement biofuel, a building material, a food staple, algae seemed to imply more about us than we could possibly say ourselves.

It wasn't just food. The Institute was looking into all sorts of potential applications for algae, from air scrubber to replacement ship parts. A lot was going to change in the next twenty years, as knowledge increased and orbital stations expanded. Everyone was talking about 'husks': ship-frames launched from Earth, making savings on payload. The interiors would be fitted in orbit; eventually whole ships would be constructed off-world. Algae farms were earmarked to produce fibres for various parts, and the forthcoming mission would test how well the crop adapted to stresses in space, and thus how viable these ambitious plans really were.

Some of the visions were insane. One paper circulating in China Lake promised that with each new generation, 'auto-ships' would become more complex and self-sustaining, repairing and improving themselves mid-journey, growing and harvesting new parts. This wasn't limited to uncrewed probes, but included large multi-passenger ships. More distantly and speculatively, we'd see whole ships grown entirely from organic materials, with the frame, the shielding, the interior, the air and water and food supply, the fuel, even the computing systems all grown and hewn from algae fundaments. New ships would be birthed, unfolding out of giant algal sacks on orbital farm stations. The recycling capacity – and so the cost savings – would be substantially greater than anything seen before, with each ship harvesting its own interior for fuel, the crew eating and drinking from the walls, taking the craft apart from the mid-part of the mission, corroding it by eating it, reducing weight costs for deceleration periods and re-entry. The crew would be travelling inside something that lived, that breathed out oxygen as if looking over them. On longer journeys, as crew members died in greater numbers, bodies could be recycled into the food supply alongside placentas and waste – mythologies would spring up around these vessels, whose identity drifted somewhere between cities and gods.

SIXTEEN

Uria finally called a station meeting where she announced details of the *Proscenium 1* mission. A press conference would follow soon afterwards. Nominally, the mission was an experiment that would trial the new thrust design, as well as innovations in ship layout and general systems. But it was much more than this. It was the beginning of a new era of exploration, the first of many *Proscenium* flights. The ship would travel approximately 1 million times further than any previous crewed vessel. The potential for gathering new information was incalculable. The primary aim was to intercept *Voyager*, contacting the entity responsible for the anomalies, but we were also interested in extracting samples from ice-rocks inside the near rim of the Oort cloud. From a microbiology perspective, the Oort cloud was enchanting. It was formed through the gravitational effect of the planets and the sun pushing away material left over from their creation. This meant that objects comprising the cloud might emulate early Earth conditions; their drift away from the sun preserved them in this state, making further development impossible. The most dramatic prospect was that the cloud contained fragments from other star systems. This was a real possibility, owing to the size of the cloud and its gravitational effects. It was even proposed that stars had passed through the cloud before imploding.

Uria described the Oort cloud stretching 100,000 times the distance between Earth and the sun. It was an unfathomably vast spherical shell holding trillions of comets and asteroids, mainly ice objects, some as big as Earth mountains. Distant as the Oort cloud was from Earth, this was nothing next to the vast span of the cloud itself. While it should be possible to reach the inner rim of the cloud in under ten months using the new thrust design, travelling to the other side of it, beyond the solar system, would take decades. This was a journey for later *Proscenium* missions, using larger vessels and multigeneration crews.

The cloud was so enormous it was difficult to picture it having a beginning or an end. In my imagination it was like the universe itself. The area of eight planets circling the sun was a tiny marble in the centre of a massive drum. The drum was the cloud. We were effectively inside the cloud, the tiny lacunae at its centre.

ICORS were delaying releasing details of the anomalies for as long as possible, conducting feasibility studies and trying to anticipate the panic resulting when the news broke. Everything Uria had announced was true: *Proscenium 1* was an experimental flight targeting the near edge of the Oort cloud. But it was more than that. We were responding to a message, accepting its terms. The signal relayed back to us came from the cloud, and everything we had learned in all this time studying the anomalies told us the only possible answer was to go there. It was a directive, an instruction, and in accepting the request we were completing the first ever act of two-way extraterrestrial communication.

'I don't see what's changed. You said it was going to be OK. You discussed it with your boss. You were going to get leave to visit her.'

'I know,' I said. 'And I meant it, I did. But there is just too much going on here now, it's crazy. I just can't, I'm sorry.'

Helena stared at me through the lens. In the gap between her lips I saw her tongue scrape her upper teeth.

'Besides,' I went on, 'she's doing better, isn't she? Nothing's happened in months.'

Helena said nothing.

'Come on. You know I'd go back if I could. This is the most demanding and exciting time of my life. I finally feel like I'm in the right place, that I'm doing what I'm supposed to be doing. Do you know how rare that is, how long I've waited for that?'

'I get it, I really do. And I'm pleased for you. All I'm asking is that you visit Mum for a few days. All this will still be waiting for you when you get back.'

'But will it? What if it changes? What if something shifts and when I return I find I've been left behind? That scares me more than anything else.'

'Really? Why would that happen? You're not making much

sense, Leigh. Can you at least give me some idea of what you're doing, what's so exceptional about this work? Why you're so scared of leaving it even for a second? I know you're in aerospace and it's incredibly exciting, but it's still essentially lab work, isn't it? But of course, I forget – you're not allowed to say.'

'I know how it sounds. And I'm sorry, but it's out of my hands. I've signed up to this and I can't back out now. I'm in it for the long haul. You just have to trust me.'

'Well, when *can* you tell me?'

'Soon, I think. They're making a public announcement in the next couple of months.'

Helena's fierceness had gone, her expression softened. She cradled her herbal tea in both hands. She looked pensive, as if she were backing away. I preferred her fierce, attacking me. Not closed off, backing away, giving up on me.

'Helena, I'm sorry.'

'You don't need to say anything. You've made your position clear.'

'Come on. Don't be like that. What about you? Will you go back?'

'Of course. I have a duty to. She needs me.'

'Helena. I'm doing my best here. Maybe in a couple of months things will be different. It might be easier to get some time out then. I'm trying here, I really am.'

She shrugged. 'It's OK. You do what you have to. But you

should maybe ask yourself how you'll feel if something happens, and you can't get there in time.'

'Don't be dramatic.'

'I'm not. I'm just saying it's consistent. If you're thinking of yourself, then this should be a concern. Because I know what you're like. I know how you'll grieve. This time it's not too late; you actually have a chance to do something, to go back. OK?'

'This isn't about him. Don't make it about him. But I'm hearing you, yes. For me nothing's changed. I'll see where I am in a couple of months.'

Helena's left arm reached for the computer, partly blocking the lens. The call cut and the screen went to black.

PART THREE

Kourou

ONE

When we enter the building we undress as instructed. There's no awkwardness now, no curiosity about each other's bodies. I prod and pull at Tyler's bronzed back, the brush of stubble lining the base of the spine. The area seems detached from the person, a neutral stretch of skin, grown independently.

I feel the arc of K's arm reach my underwear: he apologises. He thought he'd found something.

We go on, using the light's glare to see. We have to do this right away, it's been drilled into us. We took every precaution on the short journey – we weren't outside for long, feet swishing through dry exuviae – but nothing can be left to chance. The problem with us is we're alive, we're open to attack. Kin to all other living things, we share the same space as them, breathe the same air as them, eat from them. As K says, from an engineering perspective, this is suboptimal. It's hard to concentrate. Everything's new here: the great humidity, the gust from the cicadas and the mosquitoes' high wail. I know I shouldn't, that I have to stay focused, but I can't help looking out from the lounge across the lawns. Tyler catches me: 'Come on,' he says. 'We're not finished yet.' He gives a tall, simian yawn.

According to Dr Allen, a single encephalitic tic can cause brain damage, coma, death. Maybe it's jet lag, maybe it's shock, but I let out a laugh. K shakes his head. It's the scale of it: a sub-millimetre tic obstructing a journey to the edge of the solar system.

We finish grooming, and quietly put on clothes. K is standing in the lounge, by the glass front, staring out. We join him. It's the edge of night, the fall of darkness quick as a door slammed shut. In the last of the light you can just make out the sprawling architecture of Launch Pad 1.

When Uria first confirmed mission details, almost a year into my stay at China Lake, the plan seemed set in stone. The craft would launch from Xichang spaceport in Sichuan province, and the crew would train and work through simulations on site. Beijing guaranteed full media blackout, total secrecy and security, no interruptions and the elimination of any threat. At the same time, a secondary crew would train in Moscow, with an ostensible launch from Baikonur, Kazakhstan. This was an insurance policy in the unlikely event of anything going wrong in Xichang. The two crews would work in parallel, and though both would be mission-ready, only Xichang would ascend. Then there was the third crew – here, Uria told us, in California. The chances of this crew ascending were negligible, trivial, null. And yet she maintained California still had an important role to play. All three stations would be in constant dialogue, sharing questions, setbacks and discoveries, through the long journey to launch.

California's station was notable for the status of our food programme, far in advance of Moscow's and Beijing's. Though I shared data from my lab with the others, we continued to lead the way. For this reason, Uria said, in what I had assumed was another routine meeting in her office, shortly after my last, upsetting phone call with Helena, she wanted me to be third crew member in the California team. I immediately blanched. 'Don't worry,' she laughed. 'It's for the crop. It'll give you greater insight into the demands of the journey. It's not real, remember. Training is already a simulation. Think of this as a simulation of a simulation.' She tried to convince me, taking me through her thinking; I was the right age, the right weight and height, I was one of a very limited number of people with full clearance, I was without the distractions of family. If I accepted, I'd split time between China Lake and JPL in Pasadena. Physical training would be tough, she said; there's no getting around that. But I'd enjoy it; it would help me in my work. I'd start solo before joining up with my virtual crewmates later on. At the same time I'd continue overseeing the lab, much of which I could do remotely, trusting Lin with the day-to-day running.

It was a lot to take in, and Uria had barely given me a chance. Although my inclusion had been her idea, she insisted there was broad consensus across all three stations. My prospective crewmates – with two years on ISS between them – had given their blessing too. All that remained, at this stage, was my assent. My plans to visit my sister and mother would have to wait. I had no choice; my priority was always the work, the crop, and if undergoing mission training would help this, then so be it. It never crossed my mind, as Uria and I went through the long contracts, that training would be anything other than a technical exercise.

Ten days later I went up in a KC-135. I can remember how nervous I was. Uria called it an 'orientation exercise', but it felt more like initiation. The absence of clouds made the sky feel unlimited. I was so excited I forgot about the hyoscine pills and only remembered to take them as we were stepping up the mobile staircase onto the aircraft. There were eleven of us preparing to fly oval parabolas over the Sea of Cortez. The craft was wider and taller than a commercial liner, the cabin a perfect white rectangle, immaculate and empty; no seats, no windows, the only interruption to the white being the blue from the loose straps dangling off the walls. We taxi, accelerate, then ascend. O'Neill instructs us and we lie on the pristine floor, children at nap-time in our ICORS jumpsuits. Minutes pass. 'OK – you can begin moving now,' he says. I tense my digits, push one arm gently off the floor. Each time I push it's a little easier. There's no visual proof but I can feel we're approaching 45 degrees, arcing slowly to weightlessness. A shift. Around me half a dozen bodies bounce. Others hold on to the canvas supports and let their limbs trail out after them, waving behind.

I push off against a panel and drift to the far side of the cabin. The aircraft reaches the apex of its parabola and imperceptibly begins to turn, relative to the centre of the earth, reducing thrust and aiming towards a downward pitch. O'Neill says, 'And now,' and we lie back down, the substance of our bodies returns. A further minute's pause, enduring silence, and this time I don't need to be told. A twitching of fingers, an arc of the neck. The first stirring of a cell. Ascension: bodies rising and lifting off the ground, all of us airborne, all of us unlimited. We only look like we are rising when really we are falling. I barely recognise the faces around me: I have never seen them as expressive, as exquisite, as this. So much of the face is ordinarily buried, only two or three times in a life falling into expression, into joy, like this. I am floating through the air, and I almost remember something. I am coming back by degrees onto the cabin floor again, the nose of the plane pitching towards 30 degrees. Vomit first (delayed hyoscine) and then my tears, thick liquid running down my face. The total acceptance of my body, everything I am, by the atmosphere.

Two weeks later I met them for the first time. I was very nearly late, changing outfit three times before leaving my apartment. My stomach felt light and I couldn't imagine anything settling. The car dropped me at the gauche seafood restaurant by the bay, and entering the wide doors I spotted Uria seated at a window table on the far side. She got up, greeted me – unusually bright and attentive, all smiles and sunglasses and white fabrics – and escorted me to the table, the blue-tinted glass holding us in over the waves fizzing off the rocks below. Tyler and Karius got up, and I distinctly remember my first impression being how much smaller they were than I expected. They offered me their hands, gripping firmly and showing the perfect white of their teeth, and I wondered was this medically necessitated, does microgravity loosen gums, are fillings a problem in orbit? Could a cracked molar bring down a starship?

As we sat, I tried to get comfortable on my aluminium stool, my eyes switching between the menu and my pro-spective virtual crewmates. They were lean, in good shape in a kind of muted way, both of them a clean 5 foot 10 inches, short dark hair, quiet and expensive shirts, open collars. Sun-creased faces, pockmarked skin. Forty, forty-two, a decade past me. They immediately got into small talk, and I realised, with surprise, that they were nervous too. We spent the first ten minutes on the wine list, and all the while I was trying not to stare. I looked up at the tables around us, the floor just busy enough to create a general murmur, a hubbub holding a ring around us, guarding our privacy. Uria knew what she was doing, picking this place, this table, this hour.

My stomach settled, and I began to relax – the sunset horizon, the first hit of the chardonnay.

'Uria tells us your work is going to transform space travel,' Tyler said, with a playful, sceptical smile.

'I'm not sure about that . . . But I do think the gardener is going to be more prominent with time, with longer-range missions. It's easy to overlook, but the crop is more than food – it could be the only other life for billions of miles.'

'Guess I never thought of it that way,' Tyler said, his southern US drawl becoming thicker by the minute, which I took as a sign of tentative acceptance. Karius looked up thoughtfully from his strings of squid. I pulled my seat out, excused myself and asked for directions to the bathroom. A couple of minutes later, coming back and looking out over the space, I took a moment. I watched them in long shot, the three of them talking earnestly and silently on the far side. From this angle you couldn't see the rocks, or any land at all, just guests in a raised glass box extending over the sea. The magic hour had gone, it was about to get dark, but the air was still blue, the sea clear behind them, and I felt almost protective, crushed as they were under the vast Pacific.

It only became clear long afterwards that this first meeting was a test. Would we get on well together? Would we irritate each other? Could we tolerate each other across three years' close-proximity training? As Dr Allen, the station's chief medical officer, told me, 'Each crew is a unit. What we are building is a psychological and microbial consensus. Otherwise known as getting to know one another.'

It turned out they were a little younger than I'd thought – thirty-eight, thirty-nine. They brought out their phones before the main course even arrived, and their wives and children were in parallel too. They were like mirrors, I thought, and catching a hint of awkwardness I wondered how much this ate at them, the cliché of the identikit astronaut, a blow to your originality, to your previously unlimited sense of self – can this other person do everything I can do? Can he do it better?

Karius was originally from Serbia. He was good with languages, and occasionally Uria and he slipped into French. I had the sense of someone impatient and easily bored, eager for transcendence. It amused me that here, at the Institute, Karius's facility for languages, matching Uria's, could be counted as evidence of cronyism, small-mindedness, and held against him.

We'd been eating for hours. Multiplied through the black glass, there was an edge of excitement in our massed speech. Though I was careful to match every glass of chardonnay with twice the amount in water, I felt intoxicated. This was a last hurrah, alcohol prohibited for the remainder of the programme. And with the height of the space, the blocked land, the seamless joining of the black sky and the sea, it felt like we were spinning, like we were cut off from everyone else, in a small capsule at the very first phase of a long voyage. I felt fraternal towards the other guests, these people around us I had never met. I smiled, carefully picked up the jug of crushed ice and lime, topped up our glasses and signalled to the waiter for more.

Uria seemed content to say little, to make introductions and steer us occasionally, but otherwise sit back and observe. She was good at this – her invisibility wasn't particularly noticeable. We deferred instead to Tyler. Later, I found this was actually contrary to their experience, that Karius, with the greater number of off-world hours, was senior. Tyler, at the start, was hard to dislike. He was solicitous, he spoke with conviction, gestured loudly with his hands. Everything to him was important. He was earnest, he laughed often. At first I thought he was the one at ease, Karius the more tightly wound. Like Karius, Tyler was an engineer and pilot. Tyler's background was instructive: he was interested in how the world made sense, how it fitted together. There were one or two early references to god. His work was in structural systems, which seemed a repeated reassurance: gravity works, buildings hold, the world endures. I noticed a pattern in his questions, his gently interrogative tone, directness softened through charisma. He wants to define me, I thought, and now I'm doing exactly the same with him. There was just a faint suggestion of restlessness when my answers didn't fully satisfy, and he seemed reluctant to let it go. Uria continued to watch carefully, while Karius looked more or less relaxed. One sister, I said. 'Older?' Tyler asked, and I laughed, saying everyone made that mistake. 'Mother's an academic, father deceased. No, there's nothing else I've ever wanted to do, it's always been microbiology. No, we're not particularly close, I rarely see them.' Tyler nodded forcefully, patting down the information, preserving it. It was consistent with his work – personality should be as sensible, as logical, as mechanical structure. He was looking for the detail that would unlock the mystery of a person, the thing that made them get up every day, do what they continued to do.

Suddenly the light and audio changed. People were leaving. The floor was thinning out. And I realised I'd said none of the things I'd wanted to say. But Uria was smiling, and this time it was genuine. Whatever this was, it hadn't been a disaster; I was confident I hadn't failed, that this was a beginning rather than an end, and that I'd see these people again.

TWO

Pasadena was only a couple of hours' drive from Ridgecrest, and in the first months I tended not to stay over, to insist, even after a late evening finish, on making the journey back to my own place. I was offered a driver but I appreciated the time alone on the road, especially on the long open stretch outside the city, the wide banks of sand, the hills golden in the distance. Parts of the journey reminded me of driving out to the observatory with Uria, a memory that still thrilled me. I couldn't help smiling as I went over this – the thrum of the huge, gently rotating antennas; the heat blasting down on us as we stepped out from the discs' shadows – my hands guiding the wheel.

The main reason, of course, for insisting on getting back each night was so I could check on the algae. Technically there was no explicit requirement to do this; the webcam relayed a live feed from each of the rooms, and Lin briefed me at least three times each day. But I wanted to, I needed to, for myself: I felt a personal desire to be back in explicit contact with the strains. When I stayed over in the hotel in Pasadena, spending almost two whole days away from my crops, I felt restless and distracted. I checked the feed, dialled in on Lin or whoever else was running the rooms that day, but it wasn't enough; the experience was virtual, synthetic – I missed, I needed, the smell and touch of the growing green buds beneath my fingertips.

The drives to and from Pasadena were also a time to prepare for and recover from the ordeal of the gym. A team of instructors pushed me harder and further than I'd ever been pushed before. The work was stepped up incrementally, and after several months, working half in the lab, half with the instructors at JPL, I was finally ready to join Karius and Tyler in floor work and free-weights. The instructors repeated that the priority, over everything, was to build up resistance in our hearts. Microgravity over nineteen months could kill you, your aorta snapping off. They would train us for this, as much as was possible: heart and lungs stretching to breaking point, limbs straining and tearing under colossal force.

Everything was done with full fidelity; as far as the instructors were concerned, we were launching from Cape Canaveral in two years' time. 'The hardest steps,' Karl, my coach, told me from above, 'will be the first you take back home.' Earth will be hell, a home you cannot bear. Gravity crushes you, your body is diminished. You spend months in rehab just to relearn how to walk. You look out at people walking through 1-gravity and you cannot believe their ease, their nonchalance, their indifference to living in this place. 'This,' Karl said, 'right here, right now – this is your chance to give a gift to your future self. Remember that. I guarantee you'll look back on this moment at the end.'

Karl took me into a long, empty gymnasium. My crewmates had disappeared. With the other instructors he strapped weights to my shoulders, back and calves. They watched me struggle to remain upright. They were completely neutral, disinterested. 'You have to make it to the far side,' Karl said. 'Take as long as you need. But you can't remove any weights. That's the one condition. If you do, then everything's over.'

They left me alone in the room. The gymnasium lights went out. I couldn't see a thing – not the floor, the ceiling, the walls, not the edge of my own body. I wanted to laugh, wanted to say something, but nobody was there, nobody was listening.

I took three steps, the pain shrill and shocking. I somehow took three more steps and I felt like I was slipping out of myself. Time passed – I had no way of measuring how far I'd gone. I was calling out, screaming again and again I couldn't do this. I wanted to quit, but I couldn't get the weights off, couldn't find the clip knots in the dark. I'd barely left the starting line and already I was beyond pain. I felt hopeless and afraid, convinced the instructors and medics watching on infrared had given up long ago.

Then I heard something – rasping sounds hitting off the wall. Belatedly I understood. These sounds were a means of going on. I was grunting and screaming on every forward step, using the echo to gauge distance, the aural gust propelling me. I couldn't believe it existed – an end to this – but all I had was my voice, and so I used it, I trusted it, I screamed with it and believed it when it returned to me with the promise of an ending.

I hit the far wall with my left knee first and the contact triggered a switch; light flooded the gymnasium and people were running towards me as I collapsed. Two hours sixteen minutes. I had lost 9lbs. The cleaners mopped it off the floor. I was put on a drip, the first days and nights a blur. My legs exploding with the warmth of their own undoing. I saw my mother standing at the foot of my bed, shushing me, laying her hands on me, pushing into me and giving me back a human shape. I'm crying and I miss her and I need her in the dark, and the revelation, as I come through this, is that she needs me too.

Helena went to visit her. 'The house is a mess,' she reported. 'She thinks only of work, she's exactly like you.' Helena cleaned the place and spoke to Erika and read the doctors' notes. She stayed in her childhood room and heard Fenna walking along the corridor at night, found her sitting blankly facing the living-room wall. The migraines had left after Geert died, but they'd come back with such intensity now they sometimes blocked her speech.

And yet this was only part of the time; it wasn't the whole picture. You have to spend longer with her to get any kind of an idea, Helena said; a week, two weeks, is nothing. Most of the time she's tired, withdrawn, but perfectly lucid and alert and in control of her thoughts. This was what made it so hard. She could really convince you, and then, days later, you'd catch something stricken in her eyes, and she's a child again.

We had to do something. Plainly she couldn't cycle to work. We spoke to the university about reducing hours, shifting the balance to remote working. We dreaded these conversations, but they were the relatively easy ones. The bigger worry was longer term. Helena said the house was far too big, no wonder she gets lost in it when she wakes up in the night. I protested. We couldn't displace her from her home, her memories. She stared at the living-room walls, the right angles she and Geert had nestled inside for decades. There had to be another way.

Helena had little time for my 'bursts of sentiment', when she was the one actually doing something and trying to help practically, despite her own work commitments. 'We'll get someone in to help a couple of days a week,' I said. 'Someone to come by, tidy up, bring the groceries, see to the laundry. Wouldn't it make a difference knowing someone was there, at least some of the time?'

'Someone who could see if she's getting worse. It's not really an answer though, is it? We're just postponing it, because however much we try to avoid it, we know what's coming.'

'We'll deal with it when we have to.'

'Why, Leigh? Why not now?'

'Because what else can we do? I can't go back, you know that. She obviously can't come here. Could she come out to stay with you?'

'That's not going to work. We discussed it already.'

'You have the space. I'll help with money, of course.'

'It's not money,' Helena snorted. 'It's a bad idea. Jakarta is one of the worst cities in the world for someone with her symptoms. You know how it is. Read any number of studies: air pollution corrodes the brain.'

THREE

We were about to begin the first of the animal trials, feeding the primary algal strain to rats in China Lake. The plan from there, assuming there were no ill-effects, no abnormal behaviours or signs of diminishing health, was to escalate it, first by applying higher doses, then by moving onto larger mammals: rhesus monkeys, beagles, ultimately chimpanzees. The process couldn't be rushed: experimental foods had to be trialled for at least a year before we could consider human consumption. It was a pivotal moment, one we'd been working towards from my first day at China Lake, and as it happened I wasn't going to be there to oversee it.

In retrospect, this was probably for the best. I would have been a wreck, watching on impatiently as a crucial new phase began, one in which I had absolutely no control. Instead, after signing off on the algae cuttings, securing them in storage and leaving firm instructions to Lin and James, I rushed to make my flight to Texas. A full year into training, I was finally going to work with a replica of the ship, practising and performing programmed manoeuvres with my crewmates.

Given everything I'd experienced so far, everything that had led me indirectly to ICORS and the mission, it should have been no surprise that this new phase of training took place underwater. The neutral buoyancy pool was over

200 feet long, 100 feet wide, 40 feet deep. In Texas, I averaged significantly more time underwater than I ever had on *Endeavour*. I examined my red skin in the hotel bathroom at night, my hands ancient, bloated and insensate. I imagined time was accelerating, that I was ageing prematurely, that as my mother regressed in our childhood home I was possessed of an age and experience I could scarcely conceive of. For this whole unreal period – two blurry months under-water – various prohibitions were in place: we weren't allowed to drive, to handle knives, to drink from glasses. We were ushered carefully out of the pool after sixteen hours straight, checked by the doctors, questioned by our nutritionists, then driven to our rooms exhausted.

At this stage our suits were standard wet-wear, nothing like the full EVAs that Amy's team would later fit us with, descendants of the bodysuits we had worn on *Endeavour*, developed from high-altitude pressure suits and scubas. Wherever I went, whatever I did, it seemed *Endeavour* was pursuing me. It was reassuring to think that Amy guided it, that the suit we'd transition to later in training went back through her to the days we'd spent in the mid-Atlantic.

Gradually the drowned cabin became more elaborate, until we were swimming through a full-scale ship replica. We were given bigger suits with helmets, and for twelve to sixteen hours daily we crawled through the narrow spaces of the simulated spacecraft, spinning and pirouetting and trying to accommodate in our imagination not just the ship, not just the bulky EVAs, but our altered skin and bone. I confounded the engineers by perfecting exits, beating Tyler by seventeen seconds. We exited the airlock again and again, tethered to the outside of the imaginary ship by a length of rope and made to work elaborate repairs. We performed these routines hundreds, thousands of times, the point being that we shouldn't have to think, it should be second nature, molecular instruction, instinct carved into the body. A thought travels 120 metres per second, and it isn't enough.

One of the primary mission goals – and the only one that could actually be rehearsed – was to collect samples from the Oort cloud. Back in Pasadena, Amy explained the difficulty in simulating the cloud when it currently existed as a theoretical entity; no one had seen it, and there were doubts over whether it was even a real phenomenon. I smiled at this allusion to *Endeavour*, and to the paradoxes our mission was built on.

It was clear now that the crew's dominant experience was confinement. This was underlined when we began Sim 1, the basis of our training for the next six months, and even more gruelling that the 12g centrifuge simulator. It was a full-scale replica of the ship's mid-deck, the frame welded together from two shipping containers in a warehouse hangar. The elaborate interior was rendered out of wood, carved by technicians who believed they were building a science-fiction film set. The effect was surprisingly convincing – a starship hewn from a forest.

The interior was a clean white with rows of panels on two sides. We entered through a porthole screwed closed behind us, and hung on wire harnesses attached to the ceiling. We simulated low-gravity movement fourteen hours a day, seven days a week. To start with it was like being constantly seasick. An audio track played oxygen conversion, water capture, temperature control, a wall panel showed unfamiliar stars, a device mimicked the slow whir and clunk of outgassing. We ate from protein-packs while strapped to seats at a circular table in the centre of the floor. Everything was unwieldy and difficult. I was shamed by my lack of grace, unable to move with the ease the others had. I worked hard at it, and gradually improved. Time moved slowly inside, days passed in silence, as we filled out questionnaires and operated VR tutorials on our tablets.

The thought of nineteen months of this was terrifying. But as K quickly pointed out, it wasn't really an accurate rendering of the ship; it was only the central cabin with a chemical toilet grafted on. The instructors were purposely making things more difficult, locking us together, forcing us against each other in isolation. The real ship had private berths, but here there was no escape, no privacy, nowhere else at all. My crewmates admitted they were finding it just as hard as I was. Constant headaches, weight loss, nausea, vomiting. We agreed it was impossible to live like this long term.

We came out of another fourteen-hour stint and left the warehouse into coruscating sunlight. Usually this was when we said our goodbyes – I'd either retreat to the hotel for a couple of hours or else drive straight back to Ridgecrest – and Karius and Tyler would head off home to their families. We'd meet again in the evening for another stint in the sim. But this time I asked them to wait. Just for a bit. Humour me, it won't take long, I said.

They followed in their cars, and I parked by the edge of the botanics. I led them through to the tropical glasshouse, and we stepped inside. The humid air and fetid stench struck us like a blow. The sound of water dropping and the reproduced audio of birds. There was no one else inside and we went slowly round the perimeter, then gravitated towards the central pool, filled with rocks and lilies, with fine stringy ferns – the original plants, survivors from the Carboniferous – dropping down from above. I was still nauseous after the sim, still adjusting to the heavy, viscous tropical air, so I sat down on the long metal bench, where Karius and Tyler joined me.

I could hear them breathing beside me. After a few minutes, their rhythm slowed. I looked up and saw Tyler's eyes closed. I'd brought them here on a hunch, a sense that we needed this. Words weren't necessary. The garden was what was missing from Sim 1. Everything we complained of – the unnatural confinement, the sense of our most basic desires thwarted and frustrated – was eased by time here in the glasshouse. Sim 1 reinforced the garden as an imaginative aid of surpassing importance. Growth, future promise, transformation and new life. I'd had to show them this to introduce hope, to counteract the endless white sterility of Sim 1.

'Imagine,' I said, 'you could bring this with you.'

We returned to the botanics every week. And it might have been my imagination, making a coincidence into something meaningful, but looking back, this really seems like the time we started opening up to each other.

If it was clear K was the thoughtful one, Tyler was at least more interesting than he'd initially appeared. From the first evening in the restaurant I'd wanted to see him as fearless and uncomplicated, but he was starting to reveal his doubts and hang-ups too. In some ways someone as conservative as Tyler was the perfect choice to lead an exploratory mission. Tyler's whole ethic was war-like, imperious: control the world by telling it what it is. Meet challenges through resistance and attrition. It hurt him so much to be in an unpredictable situation precisely because that was where he thrived. He would begin a process of simplification through classification and he would negotiate a corridor through it. He was addicted to it, energised by it, metabolising strangeness and novelty, turning the real world into waste material. Tyler would be the first person you would put in a combat zone or drop on an alien planet, his fear motivated by an inability to experience true wonder, allowing him to act where others might have fallen to their knees. He was like Columbus seeing the outline of the Americas and describing it in a way that suggests the plants of Europe. He hadn't seen what's there at all. Landing in a new world, he rejects it as impossible, denies it, and creates a doubled Spain instead. The attitude would be extremely practically useful. Tyler was someone you wanted up there, next to you. Whatever unimaginable events transpired, Tyler would hold, wouldn't curl into a ball, head buried in his knees, rocking trauma. It didn't matter if the source of his strength was a fear possibly greater than our own; if it allowed him to function and to appear robust, then I was grateful for it.

He was perceptive on social relations, inserting himself only carefully, deliberately. Quiet when the topic turned outside his expertise, brooding, exaggeratedly deferential in a way that seemed designed to tease me, always courteous to me in those first slightly stilted eighteen months, still trying to work out who I was, caught between demanding what I was even doing there and respecting the judgement of Uria and the other mission staff. He had a firm handshake

lacking the concessions in grip I'd unconsciously grown used
to over at the Institute. You usually saw him, when he was
unoccupied, holding, throwing, squeezing this little red
rubber ball, turning it over between his fingers, pressing on
it, an aid to thinking, a nervous tic, a barrier between him
and pure vacancy. Four siblings. Military family. Careful
stubble, big appetite, reads biographies, no apparent interest
in music. Music is a 'cheat', he says. 'You don't need to dress
it up. It's enough as it is, or should be.' I never asked him
what 'it' was.

He came here by accident. He'd never had any interest in
space at all. He was a practical person. But it was obvious
that he was a perfectionist and ultra-competitive and that
he had ended up here because it wasn't possible to go any
higher. There is a baseline arrogance to all of us in the
programme. Arrogance and impatience and, whatever else
we might say, fear of a certain kind of complexity. That is
why we take seriously the notion of transcending the world.
Why understand something, when you can jump over it?
Why put in the effort? I never saw him so engaged as when
he received feedback. He was so thin-skinned underneath
his suit, so desperate to please, and so determined to present
it as a more honourable wish for self-improvement. He took
medical analysis personally, like poor results were a failure
of will. The doctors, the analysts, the nutritionists, the
instructors, they were all wary of being charmed by Tyler

and getting sucked into his orbit and drained of all possible information they might have on him. This desperate need to hear evidence of who he really is.

K was different. He was always reading, always drinking his lemon balm tea. I'd thought he would be the one I turned to, the nearest thing to a friend. A cynic, a fellow geek and linguist, a quiet and unassuming man. K designed optic systems. He had started as a child in Serbia, determined, as he said, to 'see things as they really are'. There was an irony there, a world-renowned lens designer on a spacecraft whose propulsion system remained dark. Unlike Tyler he hadn't just been to ISS – three tours, in fact – he'd been outside it, hanging by it on a wire line, fixing a replacement part. Technically he should have been the captain in our virtual crew, but he would never have agreed to that, it wasn't him at all. He wasn't being modest, he just wouldn't want the burden of responsibility for other people.

He'd lived in Chicago and Paris but retained a noticeable accent. His humour could be surreal, pitch black. He was very careful in his comportment – deliberate, controlled, measured, wary of where he was putting himself, never assuming an in-born right to be there. We spoke in Sim 1 about spectrographs and exoplanet groups and protein distribution. He was careful to put things in terms I would recognise, his intentions probably good but rarely appreciated. Sometimes he surprised me. Some small, thoughtful gesture, proving that he had in fact been listening all along. Just little things. Forwarding a report based on something that I'd said. He didn't have to do that. Tyler didn't.

Just when I'd come round to thinking K was quite a sweet guy, he'd say or do something to irritate me, pushing me away again, wary of me too comfortably naming him. Don't get too close, he was saying; don't think you can actually do this to someone, don't think that's all I am. He'd contradict me with a statement, but without expanding on it to justify why. Or he'd speak to Tyler about something in a way that excluded me, putting Tyler in an awkward position too. He was protecting himself, establishing limits, thinking about the ship from the start.

Leaving the botanics one morning towards the end of Sim 1, Tyler said he had something to ask me. K had gone off to the bathroom. I wasn't used to seeing Tyler like this – nervous, uncertain.

He looked right at me, earnestly and openly. 'What are slime-moulds?' he said.

A rumour had come out that technicians used slime-moulds to modify *Proscenium 1*'s flight path. I knew nothing about this, but it sounded so deliciously absurd it might actually be true. Tyler said they'd scaled down the distance, marked out the most problematic asteroids and debris fields, factored in gravitational boosts from the planets and moons, and put amoeba slime-moulds in this microscopic replica of the solar system. Blindly intelligent, freaking out staff at JPL, the amoebas invariably alighted on the same route – more efficient, conserving greater energy than anything the software simulations alone could come up with.

Tyler didn't want anything to do with it – it scared him. It was sacrilege, indication of a vast intelligence in something we'd ordinarily consider invisible, inconsequential, little more than dirt. This couldn't be explained. It didn't fit his system. For Tyler, life developed in a line, intelligence mushrooming out with complexity, finding its culmination and purpose in ourselves, god's chosen representatives on Earth. The slime-moulds challenged this. They proved formidable intelligence was in the system from the start. There didn't seem a way out of this, short of overhauling everything he believed, and he wasn't about to do that.

Later, during the endorphin rush of gym recovery – a period we'd learned to grow wary of, where we felt pumped and primed and ready for anything, and in which we often said things we later regretted, seduced by a feeling of openness that at the time seemed incapable of negative consequence – he asked me to explain to him, in qualitative terms, how closely slime-moulds resembled the crops in the food programme. 'They're not the same,' I reassured him. 'There are resemblances, sure – some of the strains originated around the same period. But Tyler, there are resemblances in *everything*. That's the point. Surely you see that? That everything is made of the same stuff? I don't think these experiments should necessarily be shocking.'

For three days he barely touched his food. He'd heard the rumours about *Endeavour*. He was superstitious, fearful. So, at the end of Sim 1, I drove him and K to China Lake, and had Lin and James show them round, take them through the process from beginning to end. Soon after, he seemed his usual self again. I empathised, to an extent; the horror he registered, at eating something to sustain you that is itself capable of drawing a route towards the nearest star.

FOUR

I was spending more time in Ridgecrest, driving back from Pasadena most evenings and weekends. A lot had changed in the time I'd been away. Uria was now based full-time at the spaceport in Xichang, working with the crew as they counted down the final year before launch. The firestorms were moving north, and we'd had a couple of scares here: at one stage it had looked like we might even lose power in the labs. After one or two hiccups, which thankfully were straightened out, the algae trials were progressing well; I received assurances from Lin that we could begin testing on human volunteers within the next two months.

With little left to do in the lab, I met with directors at China Lake to finalise the design of the ship's garden. This involved sketching it by hand and building a 3D computer model. We also constructed a simulation in one of the on-site hangars – it felt easier to communicate my ideas if I could walk people around in them. The ship itself was still shrouded in secrecy: Tyler thought it would be a modular design, that several hundred firms were contracted out to build separate systems, each part remaining sterile, packed in isolation and only assembled in the weeks before launch.

At the same time, there was new activity at the station. Security was stepped up, and substantial parts of the site were off limits. We were no longer permitted phones beyond the gates, and our lab computers were auto-checked constantly. The flight surgeons were escalating thrust trials.

Drives to and from the station were a rare chance to take stock. It amused me, the way even the most dramatic events snuck up on you, their true significance only apparent in retrospect. There was no single moment of transition; everything happened by degrees, each step seeming logical and reasonable at the time. This was a lesson I was unable to learn, despite a lifetime's demonstration. The present, regardless of what it entails, almost always comes with an in-built inertia, a resolute, robust banality. When I looked back, I felt an almost overpowering desire to relive certain moments with the recognition they deserved. My father's funeral; my first day at Ridgecrest; my conversations with Helena as it slowly dawned on us our mother was unwell. As difficult as each of these experiences was, none of them at the time seemed remarkable. Driving the three hours between Pasadena and my apartment, I could see that this was a strategy aimed purely at my survival. Real life, present life, was often just too much.

Occasionally I regretted the extra thinking the quieter stretches of the road allowed. So much was going on at JPL and China Lake. Work, for a long time – both training and lab and garden design – was incredibly demanding, and I could see now that this was helpful. I used work to avoid other responsibilities. Helena's calls had got shorter and less frequent. I still tried to speak to Fenna once a fortnight, but it wasn't always possible, especially during the particularly demanding schedule of Sim 1. Generally, guiltily, I trusted that if I didn't hear from or about our mother, then at least nothing had gone seriously wrong. With a child's logic, I reasoned that if a message couldn't reach me, its potential content could never be realised.

I thought again of Goldstone – the burning heat, the shadow of Cassegrain, the satellite cathedral that had received the extraordinary contact from Datura. And in those long drives, several hours there and back almost every day, this odd combination – the arc of the mission, my guilt over my mother and sister – began to converge. When I saw the monumental curved rim of the radio telescope, every hum and rotation of its blank face gesturing to the inconceivable, the barren distances it reached, I thought inevitably, sentimentally, of Fenna. It occurred to me that there was a greater chance of deciphering Datura's alien language than of understanding, at any one moment, what Fenna might be thinking. I had never understood her, and it went both ways. Our only closeness was in the residue of violence, the mute contact of our bodies pressed in the night. Of course we would never find a time to communicate – we were far past that point, assuming it had ever existed. Any attempt to allude to the past would be cruel and unjustified, would only hurt her in her large, empty house and her confusion. But if

I couldn't tell her what I thought, I wondered, as I drove along a stretch of sand-backed motorway so monotonous it was as if I remained completely still, then perhaps I could at least show her what was around me when I thought.

Writing to Fenna never worked. At the most you got two curt, clipped lines back. She just wasn't very comfortable with words. I thought about this during training; maybe this, unconsciously, was one of the things that drew me to Uria. Same age as my mother, comically opposite, fluent in nine languages while Fenna's silence fanned out further all the time. Once, on an endorphin high post-workout, I described the situation to my crewmates. The next morning I woke at dawn, and pursued every single way my words might come back at me.

The three weeks at home, before I first flew out to Ridgecrest, were wonderful, and yet Fenna and I had barely exchanged a word of any consequence. Our proximity was the thing itself; we didn't need to describe it. Talking was only going to become more difficult: her pauses were getting longer, she repeated herself, sometimes struggling to name things, as if the world was getting further out of reach.

So I started sending Fenna audio messages, things that she could play back, digest in her own time, with no pressure to reciprocate. At first these were a little stiff – I asked her how she was, told her I missed her, that I thought about her every day. She seemed to like these, to respond to them. The carer was coming twice a week, Erika more frequently, and both of them mentioned 'the records' – Fenna's term for my audio clips – and urged me to continue. I wasn't sure what to say. I recorded myself talking about things in an improvised way – the gym, the food lab, K and Tyler's more annoying habits, Amy's separation from her husband. (I always passed over Uria.) I described my apartment, the way the light changed with the seasons, the different fruits I could get, the recipes I was trying, recommended by James and Lin in the lab. Soon I was doing this daily, automatically. Erika said Fenna played the records late at night, that she went to sleep to my voice turned down low. I recorded other things – traffic flow from my balcony, the drive to Pasadena, ambient noise wandering the supermarket aisles, the hurl of surf when training took us out there. She heard me washing up in the evening and singing and humming quietly, or scolding myself for something I'd belatedly remembered. I got a better mic, so she could tell how close or far away I was standing, hear my breath, gauge my mood from the recording. She heard me sleeping, claimed she could recognise the periods when I dreamed. She remembered my growing pains, my trouble sleeping when I was young – suddenly her voice stopped, and I couldn't hear her. Mum, I said finally – are you there?

I asked her eventually, gently, if she'd like to send messages back. Anything – the television, the kettle boiling, the sound of Erika coming in through the door. I heard her cough lingering through the cold winter, the doors closing, windows creaking open, footsteps approaching and then receding as she searched for something she couldn't recover, couldn't name.

Eventually her records stopped; perhaps she'd listened, and been confused and upset by what she'd heard. I didn't say anything, but continued sending my own unfiltered audio, the background hum of my own life, my own form of loneliness, the domestic space animated only by the feedback of a single consciousness.

FIVE

We were entering the final phase of training. They measured and part-fitted us dozens of times. The tired puns about 'measuring up', 'fitting the task', being 'suitable' for the role. It was unnerving having so many people observing us, filming us, analysing everything we did. The suit development unit knew us better than we did: our weight fluctuations, our sleep, our breath, the way our metabolism trends. 'One way to describe it,' Amy said, 'is that we're building an artificial reproduction of your body.'

'My body without me. With nothing to animate it.'

'Yes. An inert body, it needs to be worn. But it should fit you perfectly.'

They built it around and on top of us. 'A description of the body in such a way that it won't be annihilated in space,' Amy added, reassuringly. It took time. We were fitted for individual parts irregularly, infrequently, in hotel bathrooms and office corridors. It grew up slowly around us – an arm, a faceplate, a set of knee-convolutes, the helmet entire. Modelling like this makes you alert to your body, to the discrete parts and the fluid, seamless blending of the whole. The first layer, next to the skin, was closest to the dive-suits worn on *Endeavour*. A malleable latex that's supposed to recycle sweat. Black in colour, tight without feeling it, it stretched over the fingers and toes and up at the neck where it would later clasp onto the helmet frame. This was the 'skin analogue', or the epidermis. Manufacturers didn't strictly consider it part of the suit at all. We wore it while we worked, while we slept, while we read and watched movies in our hotel beds.

Later they built up other layers around it, weaves and folds of cloth and rubber. I felt like an actor, a prop in a wider production. We tried the pressure suit, and for the first time breathed its artificial air. A comms piece linked to Control, so we could relay messages and record. There was a temperature and oxygen gauge, a straw-clip which we opened by blowing softly twice, feeding us water and protein paste. One beautiful day, under a ridged sky, Amy took us outside to a field in Pasadena. We practised walking over the uneven ground, through the distorted colours and unfamiliar angles of the faceplate. Bystanders took us for biosecurity, walked straight past. We went slowly, awkwardly, animals newly released in birth; estranged, limbs buckling, shivering, shocked by atmosphere, startled by and unprepared for life.

At some point – I don't know exactly when – things began to lurch forward, veering wildly outside my control. The most obvious example, looking back, was the airdrops, though events had been escalating for some time. When I first agreed to join third reserve crew – a technical exercise, a simulation – I never imagined the level at which I'd be asked to participate. The risks I would take, the journeys I'd go on, the unfeasible sums of money invested in us. The trick, always, was to keep constantly busy, to give yourself little time to reflect or prepare, to learn of the latest exercise only at the last possible moment. We'd been conditioned into passive subjects, unfazed by whatever new routine our instructors devised, but even then, the airdrops were a shock.

We joined an airship over the inner Caribbean. Dressed in full EVAs, we entered a prototype re-entry capsule in the hold, strapped ourselves down, checked settings and activated oxygen release in our helmets. My heart was pounding, more in exhilaration than fear. Through the oval window was the two-tone sky and sea. We nodded to each other, gave the agreed hand signal to Mawson waiting outside in the hold, and he released us. For nineteen seconds we buffeted in the air. Then we fell, the sea hurtling towards us. The pressure was intolerable. I closed my eyes, listened to my saturated breath. At some point the parachute released, breaking our descent with a heavy thud. We drifted slowly, and finally dropped into water.

Mawson commanded a team of divers waiting out in the zodiacs. Even for this first drop, the instructions were not to release us, to fix on our position, observe from a distance, time our escape and only then come in for us and bring us back to shore.

We did this forty-eight times across the next six weeks.

No two drops were the same. We fell by night and in the centre of a storm. We dropped with weights attached and a faulty oxygen supply. We landed in a capsule whose hatch cracked open sending water rushing in – K's body was turned around and with oxygen low there was a chance he might drown. Still they didn't intervene: we had to react to each emergency alone in real time and find our own way out. On the first drop of the final week we couldn't get out – the hatch was jammed shut. We followed procedure, didn't panic, talked it through and approached the problem from every conceivable angle. Still, nothing budged. Oxygen levels critical. Sixteen hours after landing the divers finally released us – opening out my faceplate, I gorged on my first mouthful of pure sea air.

Going up for our final drop we braced ourselves for something big. But the descent was routine, gentle even. The seal was intact, and when Tyler unlocked and pushed open the hatch it gave without resistance. We waited for the first buzz of the zodiacs; they normally appeared in under a minute. After six minutes we decided to swim ashore. Distance was deceptive from the airship's windows; maybe we weren't thinking clearly. We removed helmets, locked them in the capsule, guzzled the last of our water and pushed shoreward in our buoyant EVAs.

The sun was high, and when we finally reached the beach we were badly dehydrated, our lips stinging and eyelids beginning to blister. We lay in fern-shade and slept briefly, taking turns to stay awake. An hour or so later we hoisted ourselves up and surveyed our surroundings. Large rocks, a spray of palm trees, mangroves in the distance. No roads, buildings, no signs of habitation. Aware of how absurd we looked, we approached the rocks, clambering up like mechanical crabs. The sun was setting. We took a fix on our position, headed west. The air was bitter, fetid from marsh gas as we waded through the mangroves, sinking deep in muds full of fermenting bacteria. We conserved our breath – this stench is an oxygen regulator, l told myself – cracked lips balmed by the fallen sun. We paused before it disappeared, listened to the toads, the crickets, the desperate jerking of a rivulus fish propelling itself through the mud, inhaling oxygen through its skin. We removed the outer layer of our suits, slung them over our shoulders like mannequins. K pointed to an artificial light 20 miles off. It hurt to speak. I barely recognised my voice, I didn't know where it was coming from, but I distinctly remember telling them that I wanted to do this. No, really, I said, when Tyler grunted. 'I never thought I'd say this, but I want it. I've given everything. Twenty-six months in training. I feel ready for this. I don't want this to just be simulation. Not anymore. You'll say it's the sun, dehydration, but I mean it, I do. I want to go there.'

We were desperate to get back to our homes, but Mawson insisted on keeping us under observation at the clinic for twenty-four hours. I was wired, I didn't think of sleeping. All this time on endings, practising again and again how to land, how to escape, how to swim, walk, how to breathe even. Our exits like ritual, like ceremonial adherence, knowing that when the time came there would be no end, at least not like this.

SIX

I was asleep in my apartment in Ridgecrest when the call came, two messages at once – my phone buzzing and a fist banging loudly on the door. The blue screen of my phone shone in the dark as I tried to dig myself awake. The fist hit the door again, and a voice I didn't recognise called my name. I placed my phone – still buzzing, *unknown number* – on the cabinet by my bed, and pulled on a long black shirt and jeans. I left my room, went through the kitchen towards the door. 'Who is it?' I said, waiting with my hand against the lock, side-on to the door, as if my body was any kind of resistance.

'You have to leave now, Dr Hasenbosch. Station orders.'

I released the lock, opened the door. The courier was early twenties. Civilian clothes, military bearing. His eyes darted across the kitchen, taking everything in. Closing the door behind him, blocking the exit.

'It won't be necessary to get any of your things.'

'Is this real? You can't tell me, can you? Let me get fully dressed at least.'

'We leave now. My instructions are to bring you in immediately. It isn't safe.'

'Ninety seconds, soldier.'

His eyes measured the windows and the doors, swept the counter, settled on the knives. This wasn't necessarily what it seemed.

'I'm going to need your phone, your tablet, other comms devices.'

I glanced at him, turned away, entered my bedroom and closed the door with both hands. Clothes, medicines, essentials. He's hitting the door. What if it's not rehearsal, what if it's real? What if something's happened? And it's at least possible the courier isn't who he says he is, that this is a fairly elaborate robbery predicated on a breach at China Lake.

I grabbed my phone, called Mawson – nothing. Tone rang out. Then Uria in Xichang, no connection. I was about to call Tyler when the knocking became louder, more insistent. *He knows what I'm doing, he won't let me make a call.* 'Now,' he demands, 'ten seconds, I'm coming in.' I look around the room one last time, thin light spilling from the single lamp. Books splayed on the unused half of the bed. Poor spines. Nobody to water and trim the wisteria – it will either wilt or take over the building.

04:45, the day ascending, blue banks of cirrus cloud piled on the horizon. I'm sitting up front and he isn't saying anything. The swish of the air through the opened window, together with the early-morning delirium, makes me feel exhilarated. We go past the station gates for several miles. I have never been this far before. I am alert to every detail: the sleek aircraft sleeping in the dark, the blue lines painted on the tarmac, the lack of visible entrances along the buildings' facades. He runs the car straight ahead and then we tilt and dip and we are entering a sub-level car park whose opening I can't see. Lights strike up around us, armed fatigues point us to a spot. We get out and I'm ushered by a young woman into position against the wall, where my image is recorded.

I'm fine, I tell myself, more convinced with every moment that this isn't a rehearsal, that something significant has happened and everything's changed. If there's been a leak, it hasn't come from me. So why do I feel guilty? Why do I read hostility in the guards' expressions? Suddenly I imagine a fourth anomaly, Datura looming above us in the sky. Panic, chaos, banks emptied, suicides en masse, industry at a standstill.

We enter an antiseptic corridor, the white light so harsh my eyelids flutter. A door opens ahead and Mawson appears. It looks like Mawson – Mawson's size, Mawson's step, Mawson's familiar plaid-style shirt – but as he turns towards me I don't recognise him at all. The compressed body, rigid and tight. The creases on the brow, the harsh O of the mouth.

'Leigh!' he cries out, transforming in front of me. 'So sorry we had to do it this way. I'll explain shortly. The others are already here.'

I'm ushered into a small room, and I feel a flood of relief as I see K and Tyler perched on two medical cots, eyes darting wildly above their N95s. Dr Allen turns from a monitor and hands me my own mask. 'What's happening?' I manage, a note of pleading in my voice. 'No one's told me anything.'

'They're getting us out of here,' Tyler says in a practised, controlled voice, muffled through his mask. 'We've barely had time to say goodbye.'

'Where? Where are we going? How long?'

Tyler's shoulders rise and descend. Allen runs a line from the monitor and attaches it to K's exposed chest.

'Nothing to worry about here,' Allen says briskly. 'Quick health check and I'm on my way.'

The corridor's now deserted. Mawson collects the three of us, accompanied by two armed guards, and takes us via elevator to a series of sub-level corridors. Eventually we come back up, exit by an exterior door, and stand out on the runway in first light.

Mawson nods to the guards, who approach the aircraft, leaving the four of us alone.

'There's been an incident in Xichang,' Mawson says quietly, hair blowing in the early breeze. 'I don't have the details, I don't know how critical it might be, but it's serious. Result is, we have to get you out. Security's compromised, we need to get you to a safe site.'

'Until when?'

'That is yet to be determined.'

'And Baikonur? The second crew?'

'I don't know. I imagine they're being isolated as well. We can look at all that once we've landed.'

I'm not accustomed to seeing my crewmates in distress. Tyler's eyes glazed in shock, K making short paces up and down the tarmac. I imagine the scenes in their homes – the guard at the door intruding on domesticity, the children wailing, the confusion and tears, the total absence of information, the only certainty the fact that you are leaving.

My assumption is they're taking us to Cape Canaveral, preserving us until the crew safely launches from Baikonur. It's clear that whatever's happened, whatever breach has taken place, the programme's been accelerated, launch now in a matter of months or even weeks.

We step onto the empty aircraft. Everything is sterilised in advance. There are six of us plus the two pilots. The aircraft reeks of antiseptic spray and the seats, even the aisle, are coated in a thin layer of plastic sheeting which rustles and crunches on every step, on even the most minor shifts in position. The whole scene – the aircraft, the six of us in two adjacent rows – is like a museum piece, a moment held in a long state of preservation. I can hear them breathing through their N95s, training kicking in – fix eyes on a position, remain still, hold yourself, endure.

K keeps looking to where his phone would be. Tyler doesn't know what to do with his hands. We can't talk, not really. The guards are here to protect us, but they are a security concern too, and we don't know how much they know, or how much they're allowed to know.

'Did you get a chance to say goodbye?' Tyler mumbles. At first I'm confused, then I realise his assumption. As we taxi and prepare to ascend, I allow myself the indulgence of pitying my isolation. There isn't anyone. I did not even think of family.

The hours pass slowly as we sail through the weatherless sky. Finally I make out the coast, then the bright green swamps, the Everglades, but something is wrong. We are much too high. We are not dropping speed. We are not descending. We are continuing south beyond the border.

In total we fly ten hours. We strap in all the way, wary of slipping on the plastic sheeting: no one wants a smashed nose at altitude. The pressure changes and we prepare to go down. I'm unsure which country we are over. We pierce the clouds. Static breakers of the Caribbean sea, a strip of coastal geometry. A modest town, a vast green forest beyond. And inside it a depression, a hexagonal shape stencilled out of the trees, like the outsize footprint of a mythical beast. Inside this – clear as we descend – the gleaming steel and chrome of the distillation towers and launch pads of the spaceport.

SEVEN

On arrival in French Guiana we're taken directly from the runway to accommodation, with only a brief opportunity to take in the features of Kourou spaceport: a vast area bordering the sea, dozens of miles of asphalt and hundreds of windowless grey buildings spread over bright green lawns. K says it's like a business park. As we get out of the jeep, I look to shore and see the silhouettes of the distillation towers, the pipelines and cooling towers, like the giant refineries lining Rotterdam's ports. Beyond this is a sprawling launch zone, with outsize cranes and nests of scaffolding. We're taken past another row of offices, and even beneath my mask and visor the smell of the forest is clear beyond – burned coffee and shit – the calls of dozens of bird species tantalisingly close.

Mawson talks with site security while we stand outside the accommodation unit. 'We have to leave you here,' he says. 'The unit will be locked. No one comes in or out. I know this isn't what you want, but it's essential. Everything you need is inside. The guards will bring you food daily. We'll brief you on everything by video within the hour, I promise.'

It's evening before Mawson dials in. We check our bodies for tics, pass time studying the unit and picking through supplies. A single dorm room with aluminium bedframes, a bathroom with shower attached, a clean white kitchen giving on to a lounge area fronted by glass. An old unit retrofitted with state-of-the-art insulation and air filters. The windows and glass are three layers of reinforced fibre composite. A tiny dragonfly is caught inside the air seal, the larval grub presumably trapped in the glass during construction.

In one sense the unit's limitations are promising: the directors can't expect isolation to last for any length of time. Two, three weeks at most. K and Tyler are reluctant to commit to a more precise guess; preoccupied and frustrated, they give off a hostile body language I know is not directed at me. We still don't have phones. Tablets were laid out on the lounge table when we arrived, loaded with VR tutorials, data from the nutritionists and instructors, a video and messenger app. To no one's surprise we can't dial out. Tyler hurls a plastic tumbler across the floor – the first time I've seen him lose control. K looks on with surprise, disappointment even. I keep quiet, counting on Mawson's call to lift us.

Over the next two hours Mawson lays out the official version of events. Xichang has been attacked. This much we've already surmised. Not only has the local site been compromised, but Crew I are now 'unable to participate'. He won't tell us how bad it is, refuses even to confirm whether they're alive. No one saw this coming. The Institute had full confidence in Beijing's ability to stifle any attempted breach. The eco-groups protesting since the formation of the

Institute now have military capability, and this changes everything. Contingency plans have been rolled out and the mission will launch from Baikonur; the necessary support staff are already on their way.

'As for you,' Mawson says, staring right down the lens, 'we need you intact until the crew's in orbit. We don't expect any trouble in Kazakhstan – you can imagine the security level – but we do need you ready to fly. I repeat – you must be mission-ready. I know this is a shock. I know this isn't what you wanted. My advice is to take it one day at a time, focus on immediate tasks, and before you know it this will all be over, and we can get you safely back home to California.'

The three of us talked things over in the evening, over the tailored meals left in the narrow airlock between the two exit doors. There was a lot that still didn't make sense. It seemed incredible that Crew 2 were staying on site in Baikonur, given what had happened. Mawson was quiet on this, but we suspected the Russian state had had a say in events. For all the Institute's declared internationalism, there was undeniable prestige attached to the launch host. Perhaps Moscow refused to release the crew to a secondary site. Or they genuinely believed they were safer in Kazakhstan. Whatever the reason, we were proof the US station saw fit to do things differently. Mawson said decoy activity was continuing at Cape Canaveral, ostensibly still the official third launch site. No one knows you're here, he said. You're safe. The implication being that the same couldn't be said for Baikonur.

I'd retreated to a kind of electric, adrenaline-fuelled shock. Every cell firing. The others hadn't experienced anything like this either. 'There's a ritual, every time, before you go,' Tyler said, sounding almost choked. 'It's surpassingly important you get a chance to say goodbye. It's a process you have to go through; it takes time. They can't just yank us out our homes and tell us to be ready. It doesn't work like that. We haven't processed this. How can I think of going, when I haven't said anything to my family?'

Mawson assured us we'd get time, after the security protocols had been worked out, to call in to immediate family. We could do this daily, he said. 'But that doesn't fix anything,' K complained, angry, afraid. 'What do we tell them? We still don't know what's happening; no one does.'

We'd stay busy. Early-morning dial-in with instructors. Physical conditioning, VR sims and daily meetings with lawyers and psychologists conducting ongoing evaluation. I was liaising with Ridgecrest, arranging the crops' safe storage and transfer to both spaceports, even though final trials weren't complete. Mawson shrugged. Did I have faith in the crop, in the garden, or didn't I?

EIGHT

- What do you anticipate will be the hardest part of a nineteen-month voyage?
  The lack of sex. [Not a flicker.] I'm the only woman in my crew.
- This is your greatest fear?
  We don't know what's going to happen. That's the nature of the mission.
- You are afraid of the unknown?
  I didn't say that. Would it be helpful if I was? I don't know why you're focusing on fear. If I was really afraid, do you honestly think I would still be here?
- What is the worst you have felt, in all your life?
  Is that a responsible question? Just going straight there?
- Please answer the question.
  [Both of my arms are set horizontally on the chair rests. They keep rising up by themselves.] I was assaulted as a child.
- By whom?
  My father.
- How old were you?
  Nine, to start with.

– **How do you feel about this?**

Are you serious? Is that the best you can do? It was the worst I have ever felt. That is how it felt.

– **Can you tell me some more about this?**

I don't think it's necessary. It doesn't strike me as a good use of our time. What happened to me wasn't unusual: physical and psychological violence. Maybe I was lucky. Maybe most people have it worse. Do they? I don't know.

– **Are you asking me?**

No. I don't know. It lasted longer than it should have done. There were quite a few attacks.

– **No one intervened?**

I think that's implied in what I said.

– **How do you feel about this? That no one intervened?**

You mean my mother? What happened felt inevitable. We couldn't change it. He couldn't not do what he did.

– **You blame yourself. You believe you provoked him.**

I didn't say that.

– **How do you think the experience affected you?**

I had a difficult relationship with my father for quite a few years after.

– **You forgave him?**

I don't think it's necessarily about forgiveness. It happened. But he was still my father. And he had had a difficult life too.

- Did you ever talk about it?

With him?

- With anyone.

When he was older we got on better. We didn't see each other often. I treated him as a different person. The last thing anyone wants is drama.

- Have you ever been prescribed a course of treatment for anxiety or depression?

[Shaking my head.] You already know all this. All my medical records are available.

- I'm asking you.

A couple of times. Nothing sustained.

- Has anyone in your family suffered from a severe mental illness of any kind?

Define severe? No, not to my knowledge. But again, you know all this. I don't understand the purpose.

- Leigh, these sessions are for your benefit. This is your opportunity to speak about anything that concerns you.

Then why ask redundant questions about something that happened more than twenty years ago?

- Because I am interested in any possible bearing the events may have on your experience on the ship.

What has my father got to do with *Proscenium 1*?

- You tell me.

[Sitting back on the chair, controlling my arms again,

setting them down.] I don't believe it's relevant. I don't believe those things that happened are important, in the scheme of things.

– **What do you mean by that? That specific phrase?**

The scheme of things? I mean my life is bigger than those few moments.

– **You believe that? Or you want to?**

[Wait it out. Five, ten, fifteen seconds.] I don't want to dwell on them.

– **But are you afraid you might? On the ship? Dwell on them?**

You think I'm doing this to get away from myself? The ultimate flight?

– **Is it possible that memories mean *more*, 'in the scheme of things'? That rather than being diminished in space, they instead become bigger?**

Because there's nothing else alive, and you actually see this? You sail through this? And you think I won't be able to cope with that?

– **[Pause.] Why are you interested in participating in this mission?**

Because Uria said I was a good candidate.

– **Can you answer more fully?**

I assume you realise how unusual and exceptional *Proscenium 1* is. It isn't something anyone would turn down, not anyone with a grain of ambition, of curiosity.

- You're a curious person.

  I'm a scientist. I like looking at new things and testing them and trying to learn from them.
- That is why you're interested in the mission?

  Look, what is this, am I interviewing here? I designed the crop. I understand it better than anyone does. How to grow it and how to get the most from it. I've already spoken to your colleagues about this, food and mental health.
- You're volunteering to become a crew member for the good of others?

  Not primarily. But if you're asking if I think I can help, then yes.
- It's my understanding that through various simulated experiences you have become familiar with the dimensions of the ship.

  [Nodding.]
- How do you imagine you might adapt to the environment?

  I will adapt as well as anyone.
- The reason it's important to discuss pre-existing trauma should be apparent by now.

  Because there isn't anywhere else to go to, on the ship. I understand that. And the last thing I would expect of my crewmates is that they act as counsel.
- Limited, secure communication will be made available between crew members and mission therapists.

I can imagine how well that's going to work out on a four-day delay.

- **Does that worry you?**

Not particularly.

- **I understand there are certain issues with your mother?**

Who told you this?

- **I understand she isn't well?**

Was this Uria? Because what I said was in confidence. She shouldn't have said anything.

- **Is it important to you, where it came from?**

Of course it is. If I can't trust the Mission Director, I'd say that's a problem, wouldn't you?

- **You realise emails are routinely scanned? You gave consent.**

So that's it. That's what you do all day.

- **You seem upset.**

I'm fine. Really. Are we over yet? I'm sure we're over.

NINE

Tyler calmed a little, having spoken to his wife and sons. Privacy was difficult so we worked out a room rotation to give us space on personal calls. For everything else we used headsets to block out background chatter. Six days on site, and I still hadn't spoken to Helena. Partly this was because I just didn't know what to say. But more important was the feeling of unreality – I knew this wasn't healthy, that it was contrary to the understanding that we should be mission-ready, but it was helping me get through this. Talking to my sister might break the balance that was keeping me afloat. And so I delayed it, despite the psychologists' concerns.

The instructors kept us occupied and stimulated, wary of vacancy (a policy K and Tyler recognised from ISS), but at meals or at dawn, or in the late evening before exhausted sleep, I felt an increasing anxiety and listlessness. Some nights I lay awake, listening to the birds behind us and the rain, the guards prowling the lawns and sterilising larval pools, a reminder of the measures Control were taking to preserve our integrity, the illusion they maintained that they could seal us off from our surroundings, like an original species, a humanity without precedent. Karius said there was a greater density of psittacines around us here than at any other site in the world. The birds copied the howler monkeys' call, which Tyler mistook for a large cat. The parrots' rictus grins and glassy stares, as they repeated words without comprehension, seemed to expose something terrible in our endeavours, a futility we desperately covered over. The spaceports and the rockets unreal, an extended dream, a reverie spun out from something psychotropic in the trees.

We were locked up here with no idea what would happen. It was still possible we would be attacked. Tyler's voice softened on his calls, indicating that his alarm, at least, was dropping, that he believed the ordeal was almost over. K was harder to read – I would have said he was sceptical, careful, observant. He spoke Serbian on his private calls, a clipped, fast-flowing stream, his whole body shifting and becoming more relaxed. Every morning and evening we stopped to watch the sky through the glass wall. It could be really beautiful. Orange light refracted in the sea haze. A darker smog drifting in from the forest, sometimes blocking out the silhouette of Launch Pad 1. Some nights you couldn't see a single star. Wildfires and illegal logging, rubber trees shuttled out on ships, used among other things for the base layer of our EVAs. When I watched the red glow inside the evening haze I thought of my mother. The smog – in theory capable of delaying any prospective launch – was familiar from the refineries back home. It only occurred to me now that these might have contributed to Fenna's disease and the headaches long preceding it.

Through the afternoons we watched the light and shadow

crawl across the lawns and glimmer against the aluminium of the launch pads' scaffolds. A radio drifted outside with a Dutch refrain – Surinamese station – the unbearable heat near the point of combustion. While we waited for updates I tried to meditate. To focus on the light, on time distilled as a golden thread across the white plaster walls, Earth's rotation expressed through a coffee table, a laptop, the struck eyes of a crewmate.

Further amendments to our contracts came daily, HD camera and ultra-sensitive mics archiving unambiguous footage of each of us saying yes. New terms included the provision of a post-mission quarantine of no fixed length. In theory this could last for years. No reason was given for this. Presumably various contingencies were built into the mission, in the event that something unprecedented happened. The sea landing we'd trained for was a part of this, the plan to drop the re-entry capsule in a zero-population area. But if the crew actually brought something back with them, these measures would be inadequate, to say the least.

A related agreement: next of kin – in my case, Helena – would not seek ownership of the body in the event of death. ICORS retained all rights. Paradoxically, Helena, as my nominated proxy, would absorb legal responsibility for me during the voyage. I was required to confirm her sound health; a condition of off-world travel was that the proxy endured on Earth in lieu of the missing astronaut. Officially, should I go, I'd only be alive through my sister, because no legal accord recognised the places *Proscenium 1* would travel to. Of course, she wouldn't know any of this – it would never come to that – but even as a fiction, a technical exercise, it shamed me. At the same time as I discussed this with the lawyers, Helena was taking responsibility for our mother. She was the true older sibling, with a courage and grit I'd never come close to. She didn't get overwhelmed. She dealt with things, she took responsibility. And I never felt younger, or more inadequate, than when I saw her showing such courage.

'Helena, wait, can I say something?' She was unusually quiet, maybe hearing something different in the way I said her name, or in the fact I kept repeating it. 'Helena, I might be going away for a while. It's just work, and I don't know when, exactly, or even if it's really happening, but . . .'

A pause, a bloated latitude, a delay as she waited for me to go on and I waited for her to break in and instead there was just silence, distance, air. 'It's nothing bad, but I'm not allowed to talk about it yet; I'm sorry.'

'If you can't talk about it then why are you calling me?'

'Wait, are you pissed off? Because that's not how I want to end this. We haven't spoken in a while. That wouldn't be good. Please.'

'End what, Leigh? Are you OK?' I couldn't remember another time she'd asked me that. I was glad there was no video feed.

'Yes, of course – it's just a strange situation, that's all. I don't know if I should say goodbye, how much I should say.'

'You won't be able to contact us when you're away?'

'No, I won't.'

'Why not? What kind of place are you going to? Are you in some kind of trouble?'

'Helena, I don't . . . My employers will contact you directly, should it come to that. This will all be clearer in a few days. But this might be the last chance I'll have to call. Look, nothing's wrong, I promise. I'm OK. In fact I'm good, I'm really good. Just a bit up and down. I wish I could tell you more, I wish I could tell you all about this, and I will, someday.'

'You're sounding very strange. Are you sure nothing bad is happening? You promise it's just work?'

'I promise.'

'If something's wrong, we can look at it together, we can figure something out.'

'Helena, nothing's wrong. I just . . . Listen, can you speak to Mum for me, later?'

'But you can, surely?'

'I know, but if I don't, if I can't, will you, for me? Will you tell her if I go away, tell her I had no choice?'

'Leigh, again, you're sort of scaring me. This doesn't sound like you. I don't like this.'

'Just tell her she shouldn't worry, that everything's fine and that she might not hear from me for a long time.'

'How long, exactly?'

'Helena . . .'

'What?'

'I can't, I don't . . . Tell her I love her, that I understand.'

'Understand what?'

'Just tell her. Please. I remember, and I understand. Listen, I know I should have done more, I know I haven't been there when I should have been. I'm sorry. I know this has been so hard on you. One day I'll explain. I promise. Helena?'

'I don't know what to say – what you want me to say.'

'Just say you're there, you're listening.'

'Of course I'm here. I've always been right here. Right from the start.'

A clatter of pots from the kitchen.

'I remember the fields, the woods.'

'Of course. Me too.' Her tone had changed. She was distracted. Maybe she was signalling to Jack.

'Helena, are you having a drink?'

'Jack has just brought me a rum.'

'Fuck, I would kill for a rum. I haven't had a drink in almost twenty-eight months. I'm going to regret this later, if I don't say what I wanted to say, but I just . . .'

'What?' Long pause. 'Listen' – brisk again, using her work
voice – 'it's fine, you don't need to say anything. I'll speak to
Mum, sure. And I'll get updates from your work, and I'll pass
them on. But can I still communicate with you?'

'What do you mean?'

'If something happens, here? Can I get a message to you?
Presumably I can give something to your employers?'

'Yes. I think so. It might not get to me right away, but . . .
Is it Mum? Is there something else?'

'She's OK.'

'And you, and Jack? You're OK? I never even ask, I just
assume you're always fine.'

'We're OK. We're good.'

'I had this idea – you'll laugh – this idea you and Jack were
trying.'

'Trying?'

'You know, to conceive.'

'God! Maybe one day. But Jesus, Leigh, as long as that?'

'Maybe. I don't know.' I laughed. 'It's good hearing you
again, Helena.'

'You too, Leigh.' Keys tapped, her computer chirped.

'Ugh, I know this is lame . . . don't go yet . . . I know we
never say this, and I promise again nothing's wrong, but I
just wanted to say I love you, and Mum—'

'You're sure you're not drinking?'

'Come on.'

'We do too. Same back.'

'Same back?! Helena, are you listening?'

'I'm listening!'

'OK. I'll let you go. I can't wait to see you again, some day.'

TEN

On a medical review with Allen I asked him what he knew about Xichang.

'Probably related to the birds,' he said.

'The birds?'

'The failed migrations. Tens, hundreds of thousands falling on either side of the Atlantic. It's not being publicised, for obvious reasons, but the incidents broadly seem to coincide with small-scale testing of the power.'

'So we're responsible for this, is what you're saying?'

'Perhaps. It's just a theory. These groups were always going to target the Institute. Perhaps the birds just made the issue more pressing. They seem determined to sabotage launch.'

'What exactly happened?'

'To the birds? With many of them, they weren't just exhausted, they weren't just emaciated to the expected degree. They were actually in the process of consuming and evacuating their own organs – they were eating themselves, Leigh, attempted self-digestion, ouroboros syndrome. Have you ever seen anything like it?'

'You really think this might be us? The power?'

'Oh, that is quite possible, I think,' he said, in his crisp English accent. 'A magnetic effect, a transmission error in the brain; something presents itself, and the bird continually restarts its journey. It's not just the birds.'

'What isn't?'

'Giant green turtles in north-east Brazil a couple of months back, not too far from where you are, actually. Washing up on the shore night after night, inert, lifeless on the spring tide. They show unusual malnutrition, but no direct cause of death. It is believed this is the Ascension population, cast thousands of miles off course and failing its migration for the very first time.

'A second wave appeared three weeks ago. Then a third. Fifty-nine females landed in Pernambuco state and attempted to nest under government buildings and on brackish roadside verges. This has never happened before. The animals display the same malnutrition as the Ascension colony. None of the hatchlings survived. The adult females were inspected and tagged, but they died shortly after.'

'Jesus, Allen, this is terrible, this is . . . And this is us?'

'Not a great omen exactly, is it?'

Later, after finishing the call, I found the others in the kitchen and asked what they knew about the trials. 'Allen says they're playing havoc with flight patterns. Migrating turtles dying off in their thousands.'

'That's not actually established yet,' Tyler said. 'The link. There are any number of potential causes – it's convenient to scapegoat a single source.'

'You must wonder about it, surely? This technology we know so little about?'

'Honestly, I'm more concerned about environmental nuts blowing us up. You realise this whole spaceport can be converted into a bomb?'

These circular journeys had wrapped the earth for as long as animals had existed, and for the first time they were breaking. Maybe Tyler was right. Maybe it was infrastructure, the speed and size of urban development; maybe a tipping point had been reached, coastal transformation blocking the cues animals previously relied on to make their way back to the beginning, the places they'd been born. Maybe there was another reason, something else entirely. But it was increasingly difficult to avoid seeing a connection between these mass die-offs and the small-scale power trials.

After Tyler took his turn in the dorm room calling home, K shared a document with me through the messaging app. I looked over – he was beginning another tutorial on his headset, and wouldn't tell me anything about the document, only that I should read it, that he thought I might find it interesting.

It was a chapter from a book on the Manhattan Project. I recalled the look he'd given me when I'd asked Tyler about the power; it was no coincidence that our captain had just left the room. The chapter detailed a young Hungarian physicist working on the programme, Edward Teller. Teller was there, with the others, in Jornada del Muerto on 16 July

1945. Though all the group were anxious, counting down to the test blast, Teller was on another level. He was terrified. Somewhere in the previous months' research he'd found something. He'd made a calculation, and the results had been astonishing. He'd assumed he'd made an error, so he went over everything, checked every step of the formula. He started from scratch, calculated again and again, close to Einstein's definition of insanity, repeating an identical process in the hope if not expectation of producing a novel result. What Teller's calculation told him, apparently, was that there was a negligible but nevertheless real possibility that initiating Trinity on 16 July would detonate an explosion that would consume the world. A chain reaction, the hydrogen in the atmosphere set alight, spreading instantly, all the hydrogen in all the atmosphere, a vast firestorm incinerating every living thing, burning brightly for thousands of years. At some point, after staring at the numbers, Teller could no longer endure this and he reported his findings to Enrico Fermi. Fermi was more experienced. Fermi looked at him, smiled, and offered him a bet. They agreed the odds were approximately 1 in 3 million. 'Pity there will be nowhere to commit your winnings,' Fermi noted. Fermi himself, months earlier, had first mentioned the possibility of hyper-auto-combustion, the runaway incineration of the hydrogen in the air. But he thought nothing of it. It was unlikely to happen. And if it did – well, no one would ever know. He shook his head at Teller's frenzied calculations, the young Hungarian's pallor even in the desert burn, the gradual loss of mass from his body. How much is an acceptable level of risk?, Teller asked himself. One in 3 million, but not one in 2.5? One in 2.98? How could you possibly assign value and weigh a cost-benefit analysis when one of the possible outcomes was the total incineration of everything? We press go, he thought, and the event could be so significant that every single object in the solar system would spin differently.

K took off his headset, laid his tablet on the table. 'You read the piece?' he said. I nodded.

'Every precaution's been taken,' he said. 'The ship will launch by liquid-fuelled rockets, only activating the thrust once it's cleared orbit. But there is still risk. The rockets over-fire and create a premature detonation, the power's activated and unleashed inside the terrestrial atmosphere. Who knows what will happen. Shorter odds than 3 million, I'd say. Their thinking is, the deaths of three crew should be the end and not the beginning of the destruction.'

'I don't think we're a sacrifice. That's not what this is.'

'Tyler's in denial. He refuses to talk about risk. And yet he knows mean speed of the journey is thousands of times faster than anyone's ever travelled before. Some folk, you know, they say we have a death-wish.'

'Come on. You believe that?'

He shrugged. 'Space travel and dying are the only two ways of leaving the earth.'

'I'd dispute that.'

'What?'

'That death means leaving the earth.'

Tyler re-entered the room, looked at us accusingly. 'What? What is it? You two talking about me again?'

ELEVEN

According to some definitions the power technically does not exist. If it cannot be satisfactorily observed and understood then it remains a theoretical property, invoked as a possible explanation for otherwise inexplicable phenomena, but not, in ordinary terms, real. Not felt, not seen, not incorporated into the imagination. This doubled nature – the reality and unreality of the power – has to be built into the craft. The source of the thrust design, the pattern on the object, the thing that will carry the ship. The whole of the propulsion system will be sealed from the crew. It isn't just advisable, it's essential. If you try to observe it, it disappears. The Institute reports 'irreconcilable discrepancies' during the trials. The power is still fundamentally unknown even to the flight surgeons who harness it. Observation could bring the whole thing down. The engineers are quiet on this. Tyler laughs, jokes about a cat. Have we destroyed Datura just by looking at it? Are our telescopes weapons?

It's the most unbearable time of day. My shirt sticks to my shoulders and I go off for a shower and rare privacy. The ice water unfastens my body in a travelling line, and my thoughts follow it. The power is a form of contact; that's what I said to Uria. We activate it, we build this thing from it, the first step in a sustained encounter. It's volatile because it's sufficiently new to us. It resists containment because it is itself a container. Circles inside circles. A technology that enables other technologies, an unlimited application. A thing that can carry other things, two hands together as a cup, a receptacle for water, a signal of generosity, passing something to another. Protect the precious interior. Language, introspection, technology. Agriculture, medicine, weapons and cities and global heating, spacecraft and the exploration of the outer solar system. But should we do any of this?

The power, as we attempt and fail to observe it, resists us like it is itself alive. Life is not necessarily carried in a body. And what is a body, in the loosest terms, but a set of agreements among matter and energy that endures for a period and exhibits a metabolic response? The alien may be a particular way of calibrating energy, not constituted in any one of the properties that delivers the power, but in the act of delivery itself. A state and not a body, a pattern not a form. I stop the water flow, liquid dripping from the shower head and from the aluminium-wrapped coil and from my body too. Then the alien exists for the length of time the journey endures, the process of realising a journey. Not arriving to meet the alien at the end, but enacting the alien for the duration. The alien could never be as simple as an end.

For a brief period yesterday we believed we were under attack. We thought our moment had come, that the saboteurs had identified our location and penetrated the military perimeter and the boats stationed a few miles offshore and entered the site. The alarm sounded, a deep, mournful wail, blasting through the triple-glass walls. Guards running over the forecourt. Vehicles racing, voices yelling over the alarm.

Activity continued, though the alarm still blared. After almost two hours, it stopped – the first, delicious moment of pure silence, vacancy in the air as the echo falls away, even the birds, even the insects stilled. The guards surrounding our unit broke away, then Mawson appeared, giving us the OK sign from the forecourt. Over video he explained the false call. Everyone knew there was a reasonable risk of attack. The main cooling tower had suddenly stopped functioning; this led to an 'error cascade', and the whole propellant plant failed. Engineers, somehow still working through the alarm blast, had inspected the cooling tower and found the sluice – where the seawater entered – glinting with what looked like a single gelatin mass. They estimated 75,000 jellyfish slipping through the sluice, seizing up the whole tower. And though this sounded like sabotage, the engineers identified it as an unusual but not exceptional natural phenomenon.

'*Karenia*,' I said. Mawson nodded. 'I smelled the fish through the filter.'

'I thought you'd be interested in this one,' he said.

'Did no one notice earlier? Have you notified the islands?

Suspend all fishing. No one should enter the water directly; wear masks near the shore, test water daily—'

'Relax, we're on to it.'

'A toxic algal bloom,' I told the others. 'A red tide. It leaches oxygen and kills off sea life, but draws jellyfish towards it. Lots of them. They're more common in the coasts off power stations because of chemical run-off.'

As a further complication I had to explain, first to my crewmates, then to senior directors over video, that the food in the crew diet plan – our algae supplement – while bearing a certain similarity to the toxic substance dyeing the sea red and potentially acting as an ambient neurotoxin, was substantially different. And this food, as we had proven again and again in animal trials, though not yet through human consumption, was perfectly safe.

TWELVE

We're lying in darkness in parallel, feet pointing to the glass front, headsets strapped in, a cushion placed beneath our necks. Our bodies are angled to the west, facing the launch pads and the direction of ascent. The audio is convincing. Every detail is utterly real. I can smell the stale air, feel the heat inside the ship, sense my crewmates strapped to the cabin floor, their bodies held either side of me. Control are issuing final checks. They're talking beyond us now, we're not here to contribute, we're locked inside a system it's too late to get out of. This is everything we've always wanted, it's thrilling, it's terrifying. The heat increases, the first stage of the rockets burning up. Control continue speaking though their words have lost all meaning. We slip off the ground incrementally, and I don't realise until it's too late, until it's already begun. I feel the force applied to my chest as the g level rises. I work on my breath; I know I should close my eyes but I can't avoid looking through the porthole at the increasingly perfect blue sky. And now the blue is thinner and the force on my chest intenser. The oxygen converter is blasting the air. The thrust is kicking in and we're rising, and as there was no one moment when we left the ground there is no single moment when we're no longer of the earth. The planet is a settled thing, an arc of blue water. There is no movement anywhere in the whole of Earth. It is utterly perfect and still. I put my hand out but I can't, I'm strapped down. I want to reach closer towards it, as it leaves. We're still rising, and now the arc is revealed as a sphere. At the last moment we become static, and Earth, at enormous velocity, retreats, tumbles away from us, exceeds our ability to recognise it. I can't take anymore. This is the furthest I've gone – I cut the feed, wrench the headset off too quickly and as the lounge and kitchen come back through the darkness I'm hit with an intolerable pressure, a dangerous light-headedness like breaching after a bad dive. I have the feeling of my body rising up out of me, evacuating my mouth, and then it calms, it stops, and I see the others lying next to me, either side of me, shuddering, shaking, their heads in their hands, tears rushing down their jawlines. This is the furthest we've ever gone. It never gets easier, the twenty-eighth ascent as intolerable as the first. What am I doing, what are any of us doing here. I climb off the floor, look out through the glass wall west. Something is different. There is a light. Launch Pad 2.

'But it's not as simple as that,' K says, his head in the cupboard above the sink. Tyler looks at me from the freezer, curiously. We're picking through the little food that's left, trying to put something together. Another drop's due tomorrow. 'It never is,' K continues. 'You know there's a whole fleet of astronauts who never even realised they flew?'

'What are you talking about?' I'm holding the bag of frozen carrots, enjoying the cool relief.

'The dead astronauts. Astronauts bred out of the dead.'

Tyler has a wide grin now, and I look on, bewildered.

'Seriously. This is true, Leigh.'

'OK, what?'

'Twenty-three years and almost seven months ago to the day: Bush signs an executive order lowering the height of the country.'

'The president can do that?'

'Well, he did. And one of the consequences was that a fleet of test pilots, who considered themselves naval officers, aeronautical engineers, WWII vets – they're now technically astronauts.'

'Because they flew higher than the vertical limits of their country?'

'And into space.'

Tyler looks up. 'Lieutenant Jack M. McLean's 54-mile flight is a full 4 miles beyond the Kármán line.'

'The US's Kármán line,' Karius points out. 'Which is still a full 100 kilometres off the FAI's definition. Plus, you could argue the thermosphere and exosphere are part of Earth as well, not true space at all, which puts the line at 30,000 klicks.'

'Why lower it?' I'm still clinging to the frozen bag.

'Money. Think about it: if you lower the country, you

instantly take more people into space. It makes sense, doesn't it? Three-day commercial orbital flights cost, what, $4 million per head? How many people can afford that? Sub-orbital's a bargain at a sixth of the price. Bring it lower still, you call it space, you open it up . . .'

THIRTEEN

Uria appears on screen. She looks gaunt, hair shorter; she's pale, distressed, she's lost weight. At first I don't recognise her. It's months since I've seen her, and immediately we know. Somehow we just know. And I realise that I've been waiting all this time for it to happen.

'I'm flying out first thing. I'll be with you in two days. Everything's in place, the infrastructure is intact, I guarantee it. It's going to be OK. We've planned for this. We told you we needed you mission-ready – well, this is why. Congratulations, Crew 3 – you're scheduled to ascend on *Proscenium 1*. The ship has been rerouted. Preparations begin immediately.'

The lawns are lit up artificially, the grass a strange ultra-green under the heavy light. It looks like a sports complex, a synthetic field. Generators rumbling and vehicles pulling up and various sets of lights flashing.

Everyone's on site now. Allen is leading the medical transition out of isolation. Mawson and Uria are finalising the ready-room. There are hundreds of security personnel. Tomorrow we'll do a full walk-through. It's strange because it's not. Everything we do now may be for the last time. I've trained for this so thoroughly it feels unreal, as if the experience has already happened, and this is just repetition.

I suppose that was the point. K notes with approval that my heart rate's a steady eighty-four. Not a flicker. There's a deeper pitch to his and Tyler's voices, a surer way of walking. Switching modes, becoming the kind of people who can do this, for my benefit as much as their own. They don't talk about the calls home. They're happy, I guess, just to have had the chance to say goodbye. I feel fine, I feel the same. There's nothing demanded of us imminently; we have one full sleep ahead. Walk-through begins 05:00, and at 17:00 the escort vehicle will deliver us to the gantry elevator. Strangely, all I can think about, at this point, is walking out of our unit, stepping over the lawn. Feeling the grass under my feet again, breathing one last breath of unfiltered air. The lungs of the forest behind us, all around us. I can't think of anything else. There is only Earth. There was only ever Earth. And now we're leaving it.

Even with experienced Control staff, people like Uria who have seen and done all this before, nobody actually thinks it's going to happen. Historically NASA gets the most photogenic staff out and puts them in the wide glass-fronted offices broadcast live. Something like half the people standing and wiping down their brows and hugging each other in shirtsleeves as the rockets launch are secretaries, junior staff, relatives of directors. The offices are literally a front. The real work goes on behind. The people who built the ship and work with the crew and listen to their quickened breath are in no fit state to be recorded. They are worried about their friends. They are studying in great detail every one of the tens of thousands of malfunctions that could bring the ship down over the Atlantic.

Control are distant during the final stages. Even Mawson withdraws; he can't bear to talk to us. They shouldn't be aware of the softness, the pliability, of a person. It will affect decision-making, hurt general performance. They may lose focus, become emotional, and that is not optimal. They shouldn't smell us or watch us eat or hear us rehearse our nightmares in the grinding of our teeth, knowing that at the climax of the journey we'll be subject to speeds approaching 32 million miles per hour. The sky is clear blue. From the raised gantry I make out the horizon, the curve of the earth, the Îles du Salut under the flight path. It is time to go.

PART FOUR
Nereus

ONE

Nereus is 42 feet long upon a single level, interior varying between 5 and 8 feet tall. The bulk of the craft is comprised of the mid-deck, a circular unit with a circumference of 62 feet. Everything else radiates from this central area. Our berths – the lowest part of the interior, and the only spaces painted black – track the circumference, three private cabins attached to each other on the stern end. Tyler's cabin is first – or last – followed by K's, then mine. Each of our cabins has identical frames. Past my cabin, around a third of the circumference along, is the bathroom. Past this – again by almost a third – is the hatch that opens onto the garden. The garden is a separate unit, with a shallow, inactive airlock separating it from the mid-deck. The garden is 15 feet wide and 11 feet deep, with a display of hanging transparent racks running across its centre. Past this, stretching further from the mid-deck, is a second airlock, giving on to a third detachable unit. This is our re-entry capsule. It's slightly larger than the one we trained in. It's a steel bubble big enough to enclose the three of us in full EVAs, plus limited food and at least one ROV, depending on how many samples we've brought back. At the moment, the ROVs and three secure containers are locked in place in the re-entry capsule. Each of these was oven baked sixty-four hours before launch, then sealed in vacuum wrap. There is a rigorous procedure for getting them out and putting them back in storage; we have to ensure that anything found in whatever we might take back ultimately belongs there, and hasn't entered from outside. No inadvertent slippage of biological material into celestial bodies. They don't say it, but Control are equally concerned that nothing, once packed into storage, gets out.

The design dictates that our bow – the part we lead from – is the module we'll return in. We push our ending to the front so we know it's there, like a promise. The core of *Nereus* is Earth-bound, while our heads, our feet, as we sleep, tilt back to the home planet. Though Uria claimed it was a coincidence, saying the design was functional, it seems likely the ship is modelled in some way on Datura. The two spherical units – the mid-deck and the re-entry capsule – are lined up against each other, not quite overlapping. With the garden as a buffer separating them, either sphere is effectively turned into an oval. Ovals have recurred through the history of our contact with Datura, and modelling our ship on this form seems an implicit way of signalling, at the very least, that we have intercepted the contact, and are attempting to respond.

The interior is heavily fortified. Closest to the centre, our supplies are built into the walls, floor and ceiling. Control has programmed each of the 577 days of the voyage in advance, and everything we'll require is stored in reverse order. The first supplies to be packed in the walls were the high protein meal-packs that will prepare us for separation from the craft's main body and our re-entry into the atmosphere. Using data from ISS and the *Apollo* missions, as well as year-long high-fidelity sims, the food team tried to anticipate the shifting emotional and physical needs of the crew. We looked at the various stages of the journey and identified possible lulls, inserting small 'festival' food bounties to break up the tedium. Back then, when I was still working on the programme, I never imagined for a second I might be subject as well as creator.

The wall panels of the mid-deck contain various representations of our journey, from progress charts to individual bio-rhythms fed from the sensors woven into our clothing. All of this can be switched to blank. We communicate with Control through various media: the headsets in our helmets and the neck of our base-layer jumpsuits; the mics in our laptops and the comms screen on the central wall panel. Video and audio are recorded everywhere, with the exception of video in the bathroom. Until acceleration two, all audio will be auto-transmitted back to Goldstone. Visuals won't be sent at all, the footage stored in data banks in the walls and only intercepted at journey's end. There are cams in our helmets and in the collars of our jumpsuits, and they are always filming. All three of us have access to the footage, and no alerts are raised if any particular footage is accessed.

This was our decision. We have to operate in an atmosphere of total trust.

It's strange looking at the walls and noting that one of the first layers of protection from what, later in the journey, will be dangerously high radiation levels is the data storage illustrating everything that's led us to this point. We are protected by our history. Beyond this, the reinforcements are more substantial. There are sixteen alternate layers of water and steel, each 6 inches thick. We're carrying a lake around us, wearing its protection; a fleeing geological force. The lake embedded in the walls feeds the filter cycle and gives us drinking water. The CO_2 we exhale is scrubbed and repurposed, with only trace amounts of waste methane vented into space. Everything that happens is absorbed and processed in the ship, including the diurnal tides of heat and coolness expressed by the wiring, and the heavy and intenser communication periods, when the antennas transfer messages to and from the ship and home planet. The waste we expunge is filtered and scrubbed, fed back into the walls, into the drinking water, into the oxygen and the solution we'll use to feed the algae in the garden: a perfectly circular system.

The exterior of the ship is a smooth off-white. Three antennas radiate from above the central cabin and our berths. This is what we use to pick up Earth words and send ours back. The antennas also draw pictures of the area around us, feeding the data back into the central system and amending our route fractionally according to any obstacles. Our velocity after acceleration is such that the smallest fleck of dust may destroy us. (The system trained on 50,000 simulated voyages, and only once hit anything.) The propulsion system locks on to the exterior of the craft and runs, like the navigation, completely autonomously. Above all other duties, the antennas cast outwards for anything strange: unusual temperature or radiation levels; debris travelling at inconsistent speeds; objects – at any scale – conforming to the standards of a Cassini oval. The moment an anomaly is picked up, an alarm will sound automatically. Still, whenever I enter the mid-deck, coming out of my shallow berth, the bathroom, or increasingly from the garden, my instinct is to approach the wall panels and tap the comms display, not quite in expectation of a message from an outside source.

I can't immediately tell my crewmates apart. They're both in maroon-coloured base-layer jumpsuits floating at a 45-degree angle and dipping into the storage units embedded in the starboard wall. Karius hasn't shaved in the eleven days since we launched, a red stubble emerging along his jaw, but they're both facing away from me and their hair – short, matted, dark from sweat – looks identical. So they're hungry too – their first thought, above all else, is to eat.

'Can I get a little help here,' says Tyler, swivelling round and making a slow waving motion, 'with the furniture?'

First I remove the shell of my EVA, white with maroon bands at the shoulders. I lean back against the port wall, checking that the panels are locked and I'm not inadvertently setting something off. I loop my arms through the restraints, and slowly unlock, unclip, and free myself from the outer layer. I remove two further layers beneath this, so that I'm in my jumpsuit too. It's very hot. K sees my expression, gestures at the air filter. I nod, free myself from the restraints, pack my suit away, and join Tyler on the starboard side.

We have a single round table and three aluminium chairs stored flat in the cabin floor. We've agreed to eat together for anything more substantial than a protein bar. We're committed to this – no lone-eating except in sickness or critical work. Routine and solidarity. But there are practical reasons too: ensuring all crew fully adhere to the assigned diet; watching for stray flakes at risk of drifting into equipment or our eyes.

Tyler and I click the table into place. K increases the lights just a little, and adjusts the settings on the wall opposite so that it gives a mirrored effect, makes the space appear bigger, and produces an additional table with three uninvited guests. Tyler wears a cross tied to a wire loop around his neck, and on a second loop, worn closer to the skin, a plain silver band. Both of these glimmer from his sweat. Our fingers started to swell on the third day, and it was a matter of time before the ring stuck.

'So how do you feel? How was it?' K asks. 'I feel OK.'

Sitting down, our knees knock gently against the underside of the table.

'I'm really hungry,' I reply. 'Noticeably, unusually hungry. Hungrier than before. Are you getting this?'

Both of them nod.

'Otherwise OK. Haven't vomited. Nauseous, head feels a little loose. Bones still shaking, or at least that's what it feels like.'

K has brought the food packs over; we've got two meals each. Flakes of fibre and dried fruit, orange juice, coffee, heated bread and rehydrated eggs. We guzzle this in minutes.

We lift every trace of food out the foil packs, flatten them, break them down, place them in the Ziploc, put it back into the wall panel. We disinfect the table and the floor, then fold up and pack away the furniture. We're floating again, and as I look around the clear space, it's almost as if the meal's a false memory.

Tyler clears his throat. The two of them are a body apart, laterally – I'm facing them from a slightly greater distance. This seems to be our default: a suspended triangle. 'I didn't want to prepare anything,' he begins. 'I worried it might bring bad luck. And yet here we are. Two hours forty-eight minutes' exposure. Nothing catastrophic. I think it's fair to say acceleration one was a success.'

All three of us raise our arms and lean in. We laugh at the awkwardness, but we know we need ritual, and this is a significant first step. Greater challenges remain – navigating the Kuiper belt; exiting the heliosphere; approaching the Oort cloud at the end – but this is one of the biggest steps in the whole journey, and we've overcome it eleven days into flight.

Tyler pivots and floats to the wall. He swipes a couple of times and the lights go out and there's only the fluorescent blue tones of the control panel. Then these fade too. There is now a single image, a faint, distant blue reflecting the light of the sun. It's a pale sphere, and though we don't notice it, it's getting further away.

You drift out of your berth into the empty mid-deck, you see a faint silvery glow in the dark, you're moving automatically and you approach the porthole and look out into stellar radiance, points of light thousands of light years away. You realise you're hanging in this intermediate darkness, transported in a small vehicle surrounded by the closest thing possible to infinity. But it's dangerous, you can't sustain the thought, you have to function, so you close it down, you ignore the porthole and the wonder, you take water from the filter and strap yourself back in, think about smaller worries, try somehow to sleep in this place, and the last thing you realise is that it's always been this way, that the experience is identical to every night on Earth.

Transmissions are piling up in the comms unit. They're too early. We're nineteen light minutes from Earth and only thirty-two minutes have passed since the end of the first acceleration. So they don't know how we are, or rather, they didn't at the time they composed the messages we're currently scrolling through. Right now, they know we're alive. They've heard from us. But their recognition is still travelling towards us.

We go through the placeholder messages: Dr Allen reminding us to give subjective responses as well as hard data. Mawson, slightly awkwardly, congratulating us on something there's no confirmation we've yet done.

We play the messages back a couple more times. Uria is strangely quiet, hanging back. She doesn't want to say anything until she has proof. More than the rest of them, maybe, she's afraid for us.

The earliest time we can hear Control's acknowledgement is 182 seconds away. I don't know why, but we're riveted, locked in place next to the comms screen. It's as if we need Earth's corroboration that we've really arrived here. Perhaps appetite isn't the only symptom – perhaps our thinking's a little foggy too. We can't fully acknowledge what's happened.

Without Earth's confirmation, we're not really sure we've survived at all.

We all know how vital good and regular sleep is, that it can make the difference between a tolerable and intolerable mission. Control had to get the right balance in stressing this – making their point, without overdoing it – but ultimately it was up to us. The first three days were hard; we were too fired up to think of sleeping, we had to wait for the physical crash. Control programmed the days before acceleration to be as active as possible. I was responsible for corroborating data, performing manual air and water checks and comparing results with what the system already told us. I did the same with various bio-rhythms. No one actually thought there were any problems, it was just important to get additional confirmation, to have more than one reliable data stream up and running. Control wanted us focused and alert, staving off the danger of vacancy, of undirected thoughts. Let us settle, acclimatise to the ship.

K and Tyler conducted more thorough technical checks, but in retrospect these seem to have been rhetorical too. If they had found an anomaly, an error somewhere, there was almost nothing anyone could have done to correct it. Everything was autonomous, from the air and water filters to the gel cooling boxes that clean our suits, to the box-like convector oven, to the antennas, the navigation system and the propulsion system – everything was either programmed in advance or designed to learn and adapt from new data, becoming smarter as the journey progressed. Finding an error at this stage would torment us for no good purpose. Maybe, I thought, the ship would realise that, and withhold any negative reports. Mawson had said that eventually, after it gathers enough data, the ship will 'know you better than you know yourself'. You've been watching too many movies, K said. Mawson amped it up a bit, he thought – in reality the intelligence of the ship's systems was no greater, qualitatively, than what we'd carried in our phones. There was just more of it.

For Tyler especially, *Nereus* was a gift, of a scale and richness beyond anything he'd ever encountered. Several hundred firms had been contracted out to build specific parts, the whole ship coming together only at the very end. He and K investigated it, played with it through the control panels and through their laptops the first couple of days, running tests and finding out how far they could get inside, which turned out to be not very far at all. The system offered a simulation of access, rather than the real thing. Tyler said this with a note of disappointment, even betrayal, but it sounded to me like standard user interface. Despite their excitement, they were in exactly the same position I was: they didn't understand the core systems at all.

This was a problem for Tyler, and it was affecting his sleep.

By the sixth day, K and I were managing to get a regular four or five hours, but Tyler was still struggling, spending anxiety-ridden nights on his gel mattress looking up at the blank panels and listening to the steady hum and occasional click and whir from the mid-deck. These sounds weren't anything to worry about: they were expected. It was their absence that disturbed him.

When all three of us were in the mid-deck, we tended not to notice any sounds from the ship. But it was different at night, when we were strapped down, not generating our own noise, and when the air filter was quieter, adjusting oxygen levels to help us sleep. This was when Tyler was listening out for something.

He was obsessed with finding some kind of proof that the ship was functioning. After strapping himself down for the night, he waited to hear this faint and reassuring rattling before submitting himself to sleep. And if he couldn't, he wouldn't settle. On the fifth night he got up, checked the main panels, checked the filter settings, and adjusted them lower still, reducing both noise and oxygen level. He drifted back to his berth, listening for the rattling sound. Then he awoke, suddenly. Something was different. The filter was up high, despite his manual override. He got up, checked the settings again, and found they'd been reset. He overrode them once more, and spent the next four hours listening.

I slept through all this and woke to a tense silence at

breakfast. K, it transpired, had got up to use the bathroom, noticed unusually low settings, and switched them back to automatic. A full twenty-four hours later and they were still arguing about it. K said Tyler was being reckless, risking our safety for something trivial. Tyler, calmly and slowly, said he was doing no such thing. The oxygen levels weren't even approaching dangerous – the minute that happened, a lock would kick in, and it wasn't possible to override it. So what was the problem?

We were aware this was an interesting moment, the first conflict on the mission, and that more than the immediate was at stake. It was important we worked through it ourselves, without involving Control. It felt like a practice run for bigger problems to come.

One of the things, on a ship this size, was that it was impossible to have a private conversation. Everything had to be shared. When you saw your crewmates having an extended discussion, you felt you were being deliberately excluded, and you speculated on what it was about. Because of this, we made the decision to have all comms, written and audio, open to all. Total transparency. This actually made conflict resolution slightly more difficult. There was no room for subtlety, for indirect approach. You just had to come out with it.

I tried to approach things from Tyler's perspective. His wasn't a position K or I envied. As captain, Tyler had ultimate responsibility for what happened on the ship. His decision went. But to his credit, he wasn't forcing his seniority, and we were still talking. Looking at it one way, it was as if he were playing out the nature and difficulty of his role for us, explicitly showing us what he was dealing with. It's no coincidence that of the three of us the captain was the one having the most trouble sleeping. As he told us, over an extended lunch, his was an impossible position: we were his responsibility, and yet almost nothing was under his control. He was still negotiating this. The air-filter issue might sound trivial, he admitted, but hearing the faintest indication of activity from the ship's core reassured him, and made it easier for him to accept this idea of relinquishing authority. 'If I can hear it, I know it's working. If I can hear it, at least I know something's there.'

Silence was frightening. I understood that. Lack of evidence of the ship's ability to maintain itself. The silence that surrounds us, the un-meaning of deep space. Terrifying, endless directionless plane. It wasn't possible to domesticate and cultivate this non-place. If our commander was really abdicating ultimate authority, travelling in a ship whose mechanics he didn't understand, then he needed something else to believe in. Whatever was doing this, carrying us, bringing us on this journey, at least it made a sound. We could hear it, therefore it was real; we could believe in the promise of one moment slipping into another, time enduring, the world going on. I understood this; I sympathised. But it was still a shock to see such clear evidence of psychology taking precedence over everything else. We were still safe, of course – oxygen levels were tolerable, and the three of us came to a compromise.

K, predictably, found it easiest to adjust. You could see that this infuriated Tyler – this ease, this sense of gliding – and I wondered if it was exaggerated specifically for this purpose. He had the shortest one-to-ones with Control each night – in the lead-up to acceleration one, we remained close enough to Earth to still name these exchanges 'calls' and not transmissions. The audio clarity was good, and not noticeably degrading. We weren't directly addressing the acceleration, but as the eleventh day approached I'm pretty sure it was the only thing any of us thought of. Tyler's insomnia worsened. Blood sugar levels and galvanic skin responses were fluc-tuating quite dramatically. Even K occasionally looked pensive.

Maybe it was prolonged shock, maybe it was naivety, but I seemed to be handling things OK. Tyler said, twice, that it was easier for me, and though he was smiling when he said it there was an element of truth. Both of them were struggling with automation in a way I wasn't. It's the hardest thing in the world to shake your habits. They were always talking about ISS, how things were done on the station. The ability to go EVA on the station. The variety of food available on the station, not just an algal garden but lettuce, sprouts, onions. The variety of people, the fact that folk came and went, the existence of traffic on the station. The genuine portholes. The fact that the station was not hermetically sealed. I was kind of shocked by how much both of them, but particularly Tyler, laboured this.

It was as if it was only dawning on them now that our main task was to keep ourselves alive. Sentient flesh hitting the coordinates – that's why we were here, and why this wasn't a more elegant and streamlined uncrewed craft. We could have lain down attached to two drips – input, output – for the full nineteen months. (There had been some allusion to this at the early part of my involvement in China Lake, but evidently it hadn't gone anywhere.)

I tried to keep in mind they had children and partners. And though Control's selection criteria seemed in thrall to a certain intractable way of doing things, you had to trust at some point that they knew what they were doing. Allen might be odd and not my first choice for conversation, but he couldn't be accused of under-thinking. The same went for Uria. There was also a quieter voice questioning my attitude, asking how authentic this newfound confidence was.

A countdown on the central panel and on our laptop screens told us exactly how much time remained before acceleration one. You couldn't disable this, it was insistent, urgent, following us everywhere we went. For two hours and forty-eight minutes the ship would increase speed at a velocity significantly beyond anything anyone had ever experienced before. The rate of gain would increase during the acceleration, so that by halfway through we would be travelling 300 times faster than our initial speed. We couldn't anticipate how this would feel. There was an estimated peak of 11gs, but nobody really knew. The training was barely relevant, but we held to it. Helmet locked. Each layer of EVA in place. Ankles, knees and shoulders strapped, as you lay back on your gel mattress. Chin tucked in, as far as it was possible in full suit. We hugged awkwardly in suits, before retreating and shutting ourselves away in our berths. If this was the end, I thought, then I'd barely approached it, I stood far back from it. Even if we did make it through, who knew what condition we'd be in. Would we still be ourselves, in any way that we recognised? Would Control still understand us, after our exposure to the power? And if not ourselves, then who, or what, would we have become?

TWO

In some ways Control were the anti-crew, the inversion of *Nereus*. Both of our journeys were about distance: ours pushing the edge of the solar system, theirs bound to a 60-kilometre radius of coastal Florida. The dictate only applied to the core mission team: Uria as director, Allen as chief medical officer, Mawson as crew liaison. Medical and engineering support were constantly available, but in their case individuals were rotated. In the beginning, the core team slept on site, in bunker-like rooms down another featureless grey corridor in the converted academy. As Uria described it, the Control centre was completely unremarkable from outside, multiple two- or three-storey façadeless grey buildings. Control Room 1 was the centrepiece, a large hall filled with row upon row of terminals, huge screens broadcasting core mission data from the front. Parallel to Control Room 1 was Room 2, essentially a rehearsal space for staff to simulate extreme crisis scenarios and develop contingencies in real time. Pretty much all of us were superstitious about Room 2: Tyler, K and I specifically asked not to be told about any of the simulations, from some irrational fear that in learning about them we might bring them closer. For Control, something like the opposite held: they saw it as their duty to go through every possible disaster, almost as a way of banishing them. If they could name it, they could prevent it; certainly they could react to it. It was the unknown, undescribed crises that haunted them, and drove them every day to generate new, ever more elaborate catastrophes.

In the first days after launch Control were right there by our side. They communicated constantly, feeding video and audio, utilising the minimal time delay, saturating us in transmissions. They talked us through everything, this constant voice in our ear. Instructions, requests, check-ups, reassurances. 'Everything looks good from here.' We had team calls every six hours, and the rest of the time an individual walked us through tasks in our headsets. Voices were allocated randomly: I got Uria. I'm not sure about the others, but Uria spoke to me casually, low on technical specs. It sounded like she'd had coaching, her priority being to soothe me, keep me the right side of overwhelmed. She kept telling me how close she was. She described the Room 1 furniture, the blue shirts the staff wore, the food in the cafeterias. Described the heavy tropical rainstorms in the first four days, the flooding which had forced them to evacuate one of the subsidiary rooms, and which occasionally affected the quality of the incoming data tide. She described the motel she'd checked in to but had only set foot in once: a basic unit, the only one within a half-hour drive of the academy.

When I asked her how she felt about the travel prohibition,

she said it wasn't a surprise, it was routine, it was what it was. I didn't fully understand – Why 60 kilometres? Why the severity? – and surmised that, like a surprising amount at Control, its purpose was more symbolic than practical. Tying the Control team to the buildings, fixing a 60-kilometre length of rope around their waists, was a way of limiting the mission, making *Nereus* easier to hold on to, as if we too were reined in by the prohibition. Knowing Uria was 60 kilometres from the centre, and not 200 kilometres, made little difference to me, but they insisted on it as a non-negotiable.

From the first transmission I was absorbed by every detail Uria described. Earth was inexpressibly exotic. I wanted to know every single thing about Florida. I tried interrupting, asking her to tell me more – the sound of raindrops bouncing off the roof, the first folds of colour in the sky, steam rising from the forest verges as the storm begins to fade – but I was still learning to work with the delay, and we clashed, spoke over each other. Silence, confusion, failed attempts to backtrack – we stumbled on.

The others were better at it – they had experience from ISS. K recognised my interest in Uria's commentary, my 'need for the banal'. It helps, he said. They're trained to do this because it helps, this feeling that a part of you's still grounded. 'Be careful, though,' he cautioned. 'It doesn't last.'

Every day it became harder to talk to them. We'd more or less changed form, speaking in longer monologue blocks, uttering in clear diction and basic syntax and trying to anticipate questions. I missed the ease of the early days, when I could sense Uria close by, picture her driving through the Florida storms, the moon glow off her neck and the rain shaken off the leaves.

- Tell us how you feel. Tell us what it's like.
- You've got to see this. There's a red glow in the cabin with lights off, I swear.
- Don't stint on the details, nothing's too small, we want to know everything you're feeling, everything you're seeing - interpret as widely as you want.
- I can't describe this. Both planets are visible at once. I don't know what to say. I'll try to compose something later. Is that enough? It's too soon here.
- Everything you tell us has tremendous value. The more data you send, the bigger the picture we get.
- K, are you sending on the images? OK, I think K is giving you stills from the telescopic feed and from the porthole feed. Aren't you - K?
- He is, Leigh, yes.
- Look, you know they can hear themselves asking questions on the audio we're sending, right? Is there a way to filter that out?
- Any symptoms, any unexpected thoughts? Please don't discriminate. This is a first, Nereus - virgin territory,

and Earth is waiting. I repeat, please tell us what it's like.

- Can't we just turn them off?
- That's the cleanest way, sure.
- And they're only asking the same thing, the one thing over and over.
- I'll convert the feed to text. We can record more later.
- Yeah. Shut it down. Are we still recording? Cut out this last bit, we'll send on the first reports, and K's images. K – you have the images?
- I already said yes, Tyler.
- Good. OK. I'm shutting it down. It's just us again. Good.

The planets appeared static through the porthole, when really Earth was diminishing all the time and Mars growing larger, casting a red glow through the dimmed mid-deck. According to the display, our next scheduled meal would coincide with our first planetary fly-by.

I brought my arm towards the porthole and skimmed its surface with two fingers, trailing them across the planets. Tyler and K had done the same – a primitive compulsion, an inability to acknowledge scale. Allen would like it, the psychologists too – the desire to touch the fibreglass when planets appear.

The engineers constructed the porthole with care, inserting faint moisture impressions the other side of the fibreglass. All this was an illusion – in reality there *was* no porthole;

the whole cabin, the whole ship was sealed under sixteen layers of water and steel. There was concern at this early in the design stage: Allen predicted various ills, from rapidly deteriorating depth vision to catastrophic claustrophobia, psychosis to asphyxiation, loss of hearing, balance, and an inability to digest food. He insisted the crew needed access to the outside, a visual way out, proof of a world bigger than the interior, and Control considered breaking the seal and installing a true observation window. In the end, they settled on this compromise: a false porthole permanently displaying a single live feed from one of the cameras mounted on the outside. The difference was marginal: the camera was the other side of the screen, 8 feet back. The transmission lag was microseconds. We really were seeing what was there. Most of the time you didn't think about it – it was a convincing reproduction, we recognised the porthole unconsciously, and so far at least, the dire problems Allen had predicted hadn't come to pass.

Sometimes, though, you looked at it and told yourself this wasn't a real window, that you were actually staring at a massively fortified barrier. The effect was strange, as you struggled to hold both realities at the same time: the appearance of looking out and the fact of being entirely walled in.

We have seven days to prepare for the next jump. Mars dominates, big as a full moon in Earth's sky. Ceres is ahead, and beyond it Jupiter at 300 million miles, a faint edge of light in the enormity. Earth is still visible, just – a light point, the appearance of a faint blue star, almost engulfed by the adjacent Sun. We're drawn to this morbidly, transfixed by its diminishing. Sometimes it seems like the planet is imploding, like we're a watching a live, slow-moving annihilation. Other times the effect is softer, quieter, and with our apparent stillness it seems Earth is gliding from us, and we feel like we are the ones being abandoned. What is beyond doubt is that the planet is being erased, its colour leaching out, and though we knew this was coming, and started simulating the moment years ago in training, it's still quite hard to accept.

A good enough telescope could in theory pick up Earth for most of the journey – an infinitesimally small star – and K suggested he could reproduce this. He offered to digitally recreate Earth, produce a rendered planet behind us as a faint, static presence. It would be a 'real' image, he said. He could capture it now, while it was still visible, freeze it in place until the moment we returned and the planet started growing again. It wasn't really so different from how we'd set up the porthole anyway, pulling an image a little closer, switching it between places. 'We've all brought photographs with us,' he said, 'family, friends, places that are important to us. And we don't question it. Why should this be any different? We're just using the image as a tribute, a reminder.'

He was right, of course. As well as the library in our respective laptops – photos, videos, audio files: our own personal civilisation, our *Voyager 1* – we'd attached pictures to our berths. And while Tyler and I had brought small luxury items – Tyler's cross and wedding band; the silver dive watch Helena had bought me for my last birthday and the miniature white bowl crafted from the silt of the Nieuwe Maas – K had photographs only. Why add to the load, he said? But he knew we needed an accurate view through the porthole, and put up little resistance to our protests.

We were in the mid-deck, locked on to laptops. They both wore headsets, and as Tyler tapped his settings there was a brief, absurd burst of sound – a child's voice singing happy birthday. Tyler smiled at the screen, pressed play again. I was due to take another round of tests, but it could wait.

Since clearing the first acceleration there'd been a noticeable dip in spirits, and it was good to see Tyler's smile again. Our initial highs contributed to the downturn, and after the process we'd endured and the tension building up to it, we were physically and emotionally spent. Following our outsize breakfast we ate twice the amount set aside for lunch, but we were still hungry. Allen said it was expected, after everything we'd gone through. He was speaking in physical terms – food reviving our decimated energy – but I saw us compensating in other ways too. With the planet disappearing, our meals were one way of renewing contact.

'Hey,' I called, waving at them so they removed headsets. 'I want to show you something. Tie your laptops down – this will only take a few moments.'

Mild protest – 'Nothing about this in the day-notes,' Tyler muttered. K made a groaning sound as he drifted over, one of the many habits persisting despite ease of propulsion through low gravity. Tyler joined us by the bow hatch and we passed into the shallow corridor. The light signalled, the hatch opened, and I followed them into the garden, the hatch closing automatically behind us.

'So this,' K said, 'is what you're doing all day.'

The first thing you noticed after stepping inside was how refreshing it was. The air was cooled. Refrigeration stacks ran along both walls. Then there was the smell, a drift of seaweed. Unlike the rest of the ship, the appearance was changing, developing. The garden was filled with life, and it grew.

Or it would do.

'This is the biography,' I said, approaching the wire-framed structure hanging from the centre of the garden, measuring 3 feet across and 4 feet vertically.

'And you call it that because . . .'

K finished Tyler's sentence: 'Because the dimensions are the same as in traditional portraiture.'

'Yeah, I already told him that,' I said, looking to Tyler. 'So as you can see, I've set up the first row of pouches.'

'Are these plastic, are they—'

'Tyler, please don't touch them – not yet. We're going to seed the first pouch together. I'll show you how to feed it, and later I'll show you how to seed the next one yourself.'

Tyler was still hanging alarmingly close. But his curiosity was good, and I didn't want to dampen it. I'd already factored in losses, hence the thirty-two pouches when technically we only needed five or six.

'How much will this yield?' he said.

'Each pouch?'

Tyler nodded.

'A week's recommended intake.'

'Really? As much as that? From this small pouch?'

'It's just a supplement,' K said. 'That's right, isn't it?'

'Exactly,' I said. Though like Tyler, I found myself thinking how small the pouches looked, and was glad we had numbers in reserve. Tyler was watching me; he seemed to register my surprise.

'I guess it's just we're so hungry. I could eat bowls of the stuff.'

I explained the crops' growth period – an average of thirty-two days each.

'Like a month,' K said. 'Close enough.'

'We wanted that familiarity, linearity. You can see it growing, and every month there's a new yield. We grow more, and time passes.'

'Just like at home.'

'Exactly. But it repeats: seeding, growing, yielding. So it's cyclical too, like the calendar.'

K was nodding, drifting close to the pouches again, looking inside the clear plastic.

'If each crop gives a week's share of food, we'll need to plant them one week apart. So that it keeps coming back to us, when we'll need it.'

'You're really into this, aren't you, Tyler?'

'You know I like to cook. Maybe this is the closest I'll get here.'

I took them to the fridge stacks and explained the settings and how they were displayed. Each drawer was locked by key-codes – not, as Tyler offered, to keep him out, but as a caution against the drawers forcing themselves open during gravity shifts.

'That's why we're only seeding them now,' K said – I was pleased to hear the collective pronoun so soon. 'We've waited out the first jump. With acceleration one behind us, we're free to look at the food.'

I didn't need to spell out the other reason for the delay – that this introduction was timed specifically to coincide with visual loss of Earth. It was a small gesture, but it was important to me, as it had been right from the start at China Lake, when I first conceived of how we might use the crop in the programme, the advantages it might confer above the physical.

'So we're setting this up now, six and, what, three-quarter days before the second jump. You're really that confident?'

I returned Tyler's smile. Perhaps it was the family clips he'd just been watching, but he seemed lighter, less worn down. 'I mean, why wouldn't I be? We've come through this much unscathed. I expect more of the same. And the next jump isn't quite so severe.'

'But it's longer. Hundreds of times longer,' Tyler said.

'Actually, yeah,' K said, 'so the crops will be switching between low and high gravity – they can do that?'

'I certainly hope so. That's the idea, anyway.'

'Look at her. Doesn't doubt it for a second.'

'Everything's gone through trials. I know this stuff inside and out. Whatever else happens, I guarantee you one thing: we will eat from the crop.'

'I can hold you to that?'

'Of course.'

We spent a lot of time with the psychologists over the next few days, or rather we spent time against them, on top of them, clashing with them, at a lag beginning at nineteen minutes each way on day eleven, stretching to twenty-nine minutes on day seventeen. So it was difficult to talk, to have any kind of meaningful dialogue at all. This was frustrating from our perspective. More surprising was how much this appeared to frustrate the team in Florida. Allen came on the line several times urging us to persist with the scheduled sessions, repeating to us that this particular moment – visual loss of Earth – was a 'momentous time', and that it was imperative we discussed it and spoke openly and directly about what exactly the experience was like for us.

As Tyler put it, after signing off from a failed session in irritation, 'Do they want to help us, or do they want something from us?'

I wasn't sure either. Sometimes it did seem like the Control team, and the psychologists in particular, were more interested in labelling than treating symptoms. Given my background in life sciences, and the fact that I was testing and sending back reports, I was the one they came to first. I described our various responses as falling into two categories: conscious and automatic. The former was sentimental: you looked towards the fading planet and felt desperately sad. You regretted the mission, wanted to go back, to step on the ground, breathe unfiltered air and stand under a sky again. Control weren't so interested in this: it was the instinctive, automatic responses they asked about.

All three of us had high temperature, fatigue, and intermittent vomiting. A rash on our skin indicating a possible autoimmune response. Instead of connecting this to the gravity shift, the psychologists seemed to think it was about Earth-loss. At the same time, and quite distinct from the feelings of sadness and regret, there were episodes of brief but overwhelming depression, almost a physiological response, as bad as anything I'd experienced before.

Allen and the psychologists were audibly excited, theorising that Earth's disappearance was being treated by the body like a new and terrible disease. Now that we seemed to be over the worst of it, I could see that this was compelling, and speculated on pharmacological interest in treating Earth-loss. I exchanged messages with Allen: was the illness a natural, in-built response to full planetary erasure? Was it latent in the species – in all organisms even? – a biological measure primed to dissuade us from off-planetary travel and the destruction of the planet? If so, then what did it mean for us now that we had passed beyond this threshold, beginning our adaptation to life on the other side? I questioned our capacity to return, to survive another such transition. We'd be weaker, considerably so, in eighteen months, and the reappearance of the planet, after all that time away, could trigger a response more overwhelming and paralysing than its loss.

I assigned both Tyler and K distinct responsibilities in the garden; it was now quite clear to everyone this was a form of treatment. The second, long acceleration would begin in just under two days' time, and as we seeded the first of the algae – slowly, carefully, with something close to tenderness – I could see already how much they had invested in the crop's survival. We worked together in the garden first and last thing in the day. What we were going through, I suggested to K when he helped me prepare the seeds, was an experience that would soon be shared by everyone. The planet was less habitable every day: imagine seeing Earth retreat, only instead of viewing it from a ship, you're still inside it.

THREE

We strap in for acceleration two. The plan this time is to recline in full EVA only for the transitions, the hours carrying into and out from adjusted gravity. Where the first acceleration lasted two hours forty-eight minutes, this one's planned for seven days. We'll come out of it thousands of times faster than before, still at only a fraction of our ultimate velocity. The rise isn't so steep, programmed to hover more or less around 1g, which means, for the first time so far on the ship, we'll walk across the floor, drop water over our heads in the shower, digest food in the way we used to. Again, this was programmed: an extended period of home-familiarity immediately following loss of Earth.

I lock my helmet, tie my wrists down lying on the mattress, feet pushing to Jupiter. I wait, listen; nothing appears to be happening. Then there is a thud and I'm in darkness, spinning. I feel chaotic, as if my whole body is coming loose. The air rushes out from my lungs. My eyes are forced shut by the pressure. Hold on. Another thud. A smoother flow. And I lose consciousness.

After all this time in microgravity it feels strange to carry weight again. It's difficult to move when you do it by yourself. The upper panels are impossible to reach unaided, a design flaw Tyler's pissed off about. K's vomiting in the bathroom.

We still call it the bathroom, though for most of the journey there's no flow, and we shower using steam and wet wipes while a recording plays a spray. He's vomiting into a white bag which he'll tie and drop into the barrel. We've 6,200 bags, which works out at 4.2 each per day. We have to defecate into these. And they tear easily. It takes me half an hour to get in and out. Sterilising and checking everything over again. K seems to have reached the bathroom in time, at least. I keep bringing my right hand across my abdomen, pressing on it lightly, waiting to feel digestion, food dropping through me, and it's strange, this passage, this life that's running through me, telling me my body's intermediate too.

K gets out, ashen-faced, thumbs an OK sign, closes the hatch behind. Tyler is going through every single panel screen and checking data against his laptop and noting things down. The floor panels feel strange, pressing up against our feet. Tyler – or K, earlier – has already folded out the table and the chairs, and it feels good to be sitting.

Tyler sighs as he lowers himself into the seat beside me. K makes no sound at all.

'OK,' I say, 'anything different this time? Anything specific?'

Tyler looks ahead, arms folded. K yawns wide, releasing a cloud of butyric acid. He moves as if to pull it back. Tyler smiles. 'No, all good,' Tyler says finally. 'I feel good.'

'Yeah,' K says. 'I want to eat. My stomach's empty. You probably heard.'

Even at this distance, Jupiter is incomprehensibly vast. We stare through the porthole at its soft milky hue, the watercolour whirls, repeating our unbelief. K looks at the settings on the screen showing the camera feed. Something in the rendering of Jupiter looks too virtual, too predictable. It's exactly like the images I've seen of it before. This is a senseless thing to say, of course, but I expected the gas giant to appear different when I saw it myself, so close. It looks too perfect, too controlled. It lacks independence, as if conforming to our expectations, which is ironically not what we expected at all. You're in shock, Tyler says. We all are. It isn't the camera, or the screen, K, it's us. We don't know how to see it.

Jupiter's passing marks the midpoint of acceleration two; we acknowledge it with pre-packed vat-grown sirloin and a box of claret. I watch the exposed liquid in the glass, how the volume only appears to be at rest. Tyler, watching K and me laughing, calls over and raises the wine, tipping the box and sloshing it next to his ear. 'Enough for a last top-up, I think.' He joins us, the three of us at the table in the planet's half-light.

'For all we know it could be happening now.'

'What could, Leigh?'

'Contact.'

'Unless you've a radically subjective way of interpreting data, I very much doubt it.'

'Wouldn't necessarily know.'

'That's not contact, that's attempted contact.'

'Consciousness is only one mode of recognition. There are others.'

K nods to my tumbler, smiles.

'Affecting us without our knowledge would still be contact.'

'If we can't notice it, I'd dispute it as contact in any real sense. It seems pretty one way to me.'

'And if we can't notice it, speculating on it is useless.'

'But it's interesting.'

'Oh, it's interesting. But it doesn't go anywhere. Contact as a light frequency we can't see is an interesting prospect, nothing more.'

'I know we never talk about it, but what do you think, what do you *really* think, about all this?'

'Jesus, Leigh,' Tyler moans.

'What?'

'I think it would have been a pity if the anomalies had happened and we didn't do anything,' K says. 'I think we had to respond – I wouldn't have said yes if I didn't. As for what we're going to find? I can't begin to answer.'

'Come on. Try.'

'You're imagining, what, some big, grand rendezvous, contact with Datura as an alien ship?'

K's snigger turns into another cough, and then several more, and he goes a little red. We're all on the lookout for infections.

'You OK?'

He nods, takes a long drink of water, raises his palm to us.

I go on. 'I just want to know what it means. Why contact? Why us, why now? Why is Datura bringing us here? What is the connection to *Voyager*, and what do the carvings mean? For me, a failed mission is preferable to no mission. Even if we don't make it back, I won't regret it. I know it might be different for you – you have families, children, and I understand that, that's OK.'

'Remember those words, K – quote them back at her if shit happens.'

'Why does it have to mean something?' K says. 'Datura is instigating this: sure, OK. But why assume there is a purpose? Or one that we are capable of understanding? It could be completely arbitrary. Maybe it's a game. Maybe Datura itself doesn't understand why it does this; it just has to.'

'Like a reflex,' I said. 'A compulsion.'

'It could be as automatic to Datura as breathing is to us.'

Tyler looks irritated. He goes back. 'I intend to make it

home, Leigh. And I don't appreciate comments to the contrary, even if it's—'

'I didn't say that, Tyler, don't put words in my mouth.'

K coughs again. He looks surprised, as if someone were doing this to him, pulling a string from inside his throat.

FOUR

We move so quickly we don't realise where we are. By the time the light from the screen hits our eyes it's already obsolete. The problem's even worse at Control. Room 1 shows two positions: *Nereus* as transmitted by light, and *Nereus* as anticipated by their model. Neither of these is accurate. The latter is updated constantly by the former, minor discrepancies in the predictions absorbed and put towards future calculations. But neither recorded past nor projected present shows the true position of the ship. *Nereus* exists elsewhere, out of time, beyond two points.

I liked this; it seemed to reveal a truth I already knew. The mystery of the ship applied equally to ourselves, and always had done. Our immersion in the past, our existence, wherever we might technically be, in times and places remote from the present. So many times I had identified errors – in my work and in my relationships – stemming from the original mistake of too many assumptions, of predicting rather than perceiving the world and seeing something that wasn't really there. I noticed this more as I got older. Age was, among so many other things, the realisation that you couldn't correct this, that the pursuit wasn't meaningful, there was no perfect clean reality on the other side. You're flawed, and the world you see corresponds to these flaws. Weaknesses define you, drive new and original strategies to cover them, and they make you who you are. You don't exist without them. Correcting the errors – seeing perfectly and objectively – is neither desirable nor possible. So as I fed the second pouch in the garden, as I stepped cautiously over the floor in the mid-deck, as I gripped Helena's dive watch and as I listened to archived audio clips of my mother's voice, I was moving in a world largely of my own creation, a dream of the future built from an understanding of the past. Exactly like the two points along the display.

Uria continued to send updates from Florida. I think it helped her to talk about ordinary things, the world outside the ship, outside the programme. We'd become reasonably close during training, where we each fulfilled a certain role for the other. One of the first things she'd said to me, back in Ridgecrest, was that I reminded her of her daughter. I gathered they weren't especially close. It was the usual story: overwork, deferral, inability to communicate, a baseless belief that one day you might make things right. I told her a little about Fenna, how she was getting worse; how, if I made it back, she might not even recognise me. Uria never told me what to do. She listened, and I appreciated that.

She told me, now, with a wry laugh: 'I talk to you more than I talk to Maria. You're closer, and you're 400 million miles away.' She was exaggerating, but she was also right; there was a sense in which we enabled each other, supported the other's flaws. When I put the headset down and looked across the cabin, I imagined for a second that all this was the result of a domestic psychodrama I'd somehow got caught up in. I always suspected Uria over-promoted me for essentially personal reasons. But imposter syndrome, I realised early on in training, was tedious, and if I didn't shake it I'd never see this through. So I tried not to dwell on it, and I kept quiet during training. Uria sensed something, and in the first year especially reminded me how remarkable and instrumental the food programme was. Tyler and Karius seemed to have accepted me. But even now, weeks after launch, I felt the pull of anxiety, a voice telling me I didn't deserve this, I wasn't good enough, I shouldn't be here at all.

Uria didn't make decisions alone. The selection process was ratified by the other directors. I'd satisfied stringent criteria across three years' training. If at any stage someone had felt that Uria was making a mistake, that I wasn't up to this, they would have intervened. You don't just let these doubts lie. Not on a standard mission, and not ever on a mission like this. I wondered though whether Uria or I really knew what we were doing here, whether my expertise qualified me for the mission, or whether launching a surrogate daughter past the planets, to the dark edge of the solar system, was some horrible, perverted wish.

The larger moons – Pandora, Prometheus, Rhea, Dione, Enceladus – shepherd the rings so that they hold their form in ice and rock and dust. The outermost ring is 12 million miles from Saturn's body. The planet's ammonia yellow hue lights the mid-deck and strikes our faces. The discs have sublime geometry, the first truly perfect objects I have ever seen. I smell my tears before I feel them moving down my face, the novel saline intensity. The rings appear so close, so deceptively full of body, it's as though we could reach out and touch them. As we pass beyond Saturn, Uria tells me Maria is pregnant. I send Uria my congratulations, bring the others the good news. It feels like an omen, a blessing on the ship; news of life conceived is bigger, and even more extraordinary, from here. But then I remember the travel embargo. Unless Maria travels to see her – and for some reason this doesn't seem permitted – Uria will miss the pregnancy; she'll miss most of the first year of her grandchild's life. I feel a sense of shame, and in that moment *Nereus*'s mission, our nineteen-month voyage, seems insignificant. We should never have left. If it means that only one woman could be there for her daughter, we should never have left the ground.

For us, and for Uria, and maybe for Maria and her partner, the child would be defined by the mission. Ontogeny and flight plan converge: first limb buds unfolding on the pass across the Kuiper belt; neural cells cascading through escape from the heliopause; birth, at the end, as we hit terminus, alighting on *Voyager 1* at the edge of the Oort cloud. Information crossed over, symbiotic. One journey slipped into another, breakthroughs drifting across strata. I feel for Uria, and wonder how she'll cope, unable to be there. So much is at stake, always, but so clearly now. A journey to an unknown presence at the far side of the solar system, and the routine birth of a child. Anxious phone calls to Maria and transmissions to the ship. If there's bad news, will Uria tell us? Will it affect the way her voice sounds, and what will we read into this, not knowing the cause? The transfer works the other way too: a problem on *Nereus*, Uria alerted mid-sleep in the motel, a car brings her to Room 1 but it's too late, it's already happened, all that's left of us is light, and she's distraught as Maria calls her but she can't tell her why, not yet. Maria, in turn, is upset. Her diet changes, she finds it harder to sleep, her stress levels shoot up and increase the chances of premature and low-weight birth. Every single frame in each millisecond is pivotal. How do we go on like this? How do Uria, Maria – how does anyone – go on?

FIVE

We've moved into desert, the dark totality beyond Pluto. This affects us even more than the loss of Earth did. Without planets there is not even the potential for life. We're withdrawing, spending longer in our berths, listening to our libraries and playing sims designed to stimulate depth fields.

I don't remember a conversation about the lighting. The lighting was programmed to simulate tropical Earth, and we'd trained on this. It was essential if we were to maintain diurnal rhythm. And yet almost immediately we shut it down, and I'm not sure why. I'm in my berth now, and when I open the hatch I see the same dim, crepuscular light which is our constant.

We're sleeping differently too. After Saturn, none of us sleeps longer than three hours at a time. The most regular spread of sleep is in three bursts of two to three hours in every Earth-day cycle. Our sensors don't report it as an anomaly, because this still averages out at an acceptable total. But really, looking back, it's a striking departure, and I include the detail in my latest report to Control.

Our test scores are dipping. Speed of response time indicating loss of mental acuity. I think it's just we're not so engaged. We're tired of survey after survey. Communication with Control is difficult, we're talking past each other. It takes more than five hours for a message to reach its destination. Their responses, when they eventually arrive, are beyond obsolete. We knew this would happen, but as an indication of their distance it's shocking, demoralising. It will only increase.

It's harder to make out what we're saying. There's a slight delay after our lips move, as if the words are being dubbed. It was funny at first, like we were on a cheap television show, but I'm tired of it and I just want to feel myself again. Tyler said this happened sometimes on the station – something to do with disrupted body language; in your suit, floating, only half of what you're saying gets expressed. But there are other factors. I never feel clean – dirt is building up inside my ear canals. And my tongue has started to swell. Not much, just enough to make me conscious of it sitting in my mouth. There's a slight lisp when I speak. I have to enunciate very clearly to make myself understood. I choose my words in advance, scanning for impediments. Tyler's noticed it, but hasn't said anything. The feeling is that this is a period that will pass, that we are still in the early stages.

There's fractionally less free space on the ship than when we first stepped onto it. We weren't supposed to gain weight; all space precedents contradict it. That's why you bulk up before a stint on ISS, carrying food reserves, body as transport. We've been surprisingly lax about sticking to the meal plan. It makes sense, overeating when the whole Earth has gone. Distraction, attempts to push grief away, absorbing material grown back on the planet. Tyler called a meeting; he worked out that if we continue like this, we'll run out of food weeks before re-entry. And that's including all the emergency reserves. All of which makes my own work that much harder. We'll need to rely on the garden more than we planned. And the trials, cut short, never tested for this.

Our depth fields are weakening in reaction to the limited space. I've tried everything: the games, the headsets, holding my gaze on the pinpricks of light through the rendered porthole, but nothing works. Everything's flattening out. My hand looks less substantial when I hold it inches from my face; I can't believe what's inside it really exists. I contain nothing. Soon the whole ship will be in two dimensions, like moving through a painting.

We're reaching for the same oxygen, and with every exhalation produce more CO_2. Exercise is an intensifier, and so is speech, which makes me anxious. And when I'm anxious my chest hurts and I take great gulps of oxygen, which generates CO_2 at a quicker rate again. There is no way out of this; it is like being slowly buried alive.

We could approach things differently, our bodies being rare deep objects on *Nereus*. Train our depth fields on each other, explore this inner space. The eyes as windows to the soul; every person a galaxy, a universe. But we don't. We're cynical. Instead of using ourselves to bring depth onto the ship, to furl out the interior of *Nereus*, we hide ourselves away.

This was my idea. Each crew member now has one period daily in which the public parts of the ship are theirs alone. I look forward to floating knowing no one can obstruct me. We're beginning to sleep at separate times. Within the single space available to us, we're moving increasingly further apart.

If failure of perspective is disappointing, it's also inevitable. We need our petty and manageable concerns. I need to grow irritated when, about to leave my berth, I hear Tyler coming out first. I need to resent the sound of K's jaw clicking when he eats, and I blame him for exaggerating his hacking cough. It's something to cleave to, a world I understand. K's lips smacking and Tyler's stale breath before his scheduled visit to the bathroom. Frustration is an energy – I vigorously wipe the panel's surfaces; capture air for manual atmospheric survey; check on the condition of the first pouch of algal seeds, due shortly. And doing this, time becomes less static, begins to take shape, almost to move again.

I was in the garden, cutting a sample of algae for testing, Karius and Tyler behind me in the mid-deck. The airlock was disabled and the hatch open, which meant I could see them. This was unusual, and it turned out to be important. Tyler was unscrewing and cleaning his laptop base. The first thing I saw was Karius spinning away, reflexively moving in the opposite direction from Tyler. I saw this before I heard anything, or saw anything at all from Tyler. I was drawn to Karius because of the odd way he was spinning, the sudden jerk and change in direction. Then I saw Tyler's laptop – or rather bits of it – floating away. And then I saw the blood.

K was close to him, less than 2 metres away. Tyler was strapped to the shoulder restraints. He'd put a large clear bag around his laptop, to stop the pieces floating away. He'd just cleaned out the board, and removed the hard drive. For some reason he'd then taken the long, narrow sheet of aluminium out of the bag. He held the metal sheet in one hand – this is how we reconstructed it later, watching the cam footage – and for a second turned away. As he did this, he spun his right arm – the one holding the metal sheet – and drew it across the reverse side of his lower left arm, which split open at the seam, spurting a large amount of blood.

Tyler dropped the hard drive, which tumbled slowly towards me in the garden. The line of blood started two inches above his hand and extended almost to his elbow. It pooled and billowed. It began to separate, rising in a long, studded arc, red drops held like pearls on a string. Tyler screamed out.

K removed the plain white shirt over his jumpsuit and dived beneath the blood arc, pressing the shirt onto Tyler's arm. I'd finally got myself together, shocked out of suspension by the horrible sound of Tyler's cry. I swung through the hatch and pushed towards them, looking desperately for something to gather the floating blood. In seconds it would be lost in a million different pieces, smeared all over the module. There wasn't time to gather towels. I caught the hard drive, and with the other hand grabbed a sheet of paper Tyler had pinned to the wall. His handwriting – a series of numbers scored through a triangle – reminded me of my father's. I pushed into the blood.

A thick iron smell surfaced. Before anything else I had to get rid of the paper. I spun towards the bathroom, opened the door and took a bag from the top of the drum. I should have taken gloves first. I creased the paper vertically, feeding it into the opened bag. I couldn't see blood on my fingers. I put the bag in the drum, activated the fan, and the vacuum whipped it away with a thud. I breathed out, paused before exiting. I didn't want to do this, find out just how much blood he'd really lost.

Tyler's eyes were closed and his body still. Karius was speaking calmly but increasingly assertively, telling him he wasn't allowed to do that, it was against regulations. Tyler was restrained securely at the shoulders – he wouldn't float away, at least. Karius, without turning, began to address me.

'Activate comms, Leigh.'

'There isn't time.'

'What do you mean there isn't time?'

'We'll do it later. It's not priority. Delay's too long. We

have to seal the wound now. How the fuck did he even do this? Why is there so much blood?' I held on to the restraint next to K, sweeping my head in an arc.

'We need another shirt, or towel – anything, quickly. What are you doing?' K said.

'I'm cutting his body feed, what does it look like? He might have lost too much. We'll say he was irrational, screaming about the monitors, that we had no option but to do this, OK?'

'You really think it's necessary?'

'I went through this with Allen in training.'

I took the largest piece of cloth I could find from Tyler's cabin and we bundled it over the existing knot.

'Tyler!' I shouted. 'Tyler, listen, OK? Open your fucking eyes.'

'His pulse is slowing.'

'He's in shock. We have to seal it now, before he loses any more. We'll use the tissue sealant bandages first.'

'First?'

'They're not going to hold, are they? The fibrin glue? Look at the cloth, how quickly it's coming – we don't have a choice, we're going to have to use the antenna.'

Tyler's eyes flew open. I replaced the tourniquet with the bandages K gave me. K gripped Tyler's arm in two places, twisting hard on the skin. We had ten, fifteen minutes at most, before the bandages burst.

We had everything we needed: the tube of protein paste, the laptop, the microwave generator and the antenna.

K fed images of the wound into the software and it calculated the correct frequency. I set up the m-generator – it looked like a car battery – and the thin antenna pen. Tyler had closed his eyes again, only briefly alerted by the activity around him.

'OK,' I said, trying to sound confident, 'we're going to have to start now, the bandages aren't going to hold much longer. Have you got the frequency? OK. Then start peeling the bandages back – do it slowly, hold the arm down at the same time. I know he seems limp, but he'll start moving shortly, guarantee it. We don't need the programme for this, it's straightforward. Millimetres at a time, right, and I'll follow you with the paste, OK.'

As soon as the cold paste stung the line of his wound, Tyler lurched back and gave a shrill cry. His startled eyes ran across the cabin, trying desperately to understand what was happening.

'Tyler, it's OK,' I said, doing my best to stay calm. 'We're just cleaning and putting a seal on your wound, OK? And it's going to work, so long as you keep your arm as still as you can, OK?'

His eyes settled on the m-generator, which was emitting a high buzzing sound.

As we worked further down his arm we saw the long, clear

slice made by the metal sheet. This wasn't an ordinary injury, it was far too deep. His flesh shouldn't yield as easily as this.

The paste had worked. It had cleaned the wound and temporarily sealed it. Meanwhile, the m-generator continued to hum.

Karius tapped at the computer, and the screen displayed a model. He held this in front of us. At the top of the image, above the disembodied arm, appeared a hand, holding a silver pen. A light activated on the pen, and at the same time the pen I held lit up too. The sound from the m-generator had stopped, and now I felt the frequency, rather than heard it.

'Leigh, you're absolutely sure about this?'

'Not helping, K.'

As I brought the antenna towards the wound, the voice from the programme guiding me, I sucked in my breath and prepared for the sound of Tyler screaming. K was using all his weight to restrain him, contorting his body so that he pushed against the facing panel for resistance. An invisible electromagnetic transmission burned directly into Tyler's arm.

There was a crisp crackling sound and a familiar odour. Suddenly, ludicrously, I was hungry. Tyler looked on wide-eyed, I watched the screen and Tyler's arm, his real arm, and it seemed that I was observing both at the same time, and making no distinction. The antenna remained 4 centimetres from his skin, so that the wound, as it dried and sealed, seemed to be driven from the other side, from something behind it. It took eighteen seconds in total, a number I refused to believe when I watched the footage later. I shut off the m-generator, nodded, and Karius let go of Tyler, who continued to stare at his arm as if it no longer belonged to him.

'It worked?'

It took me a moment to realise why Karius's lips hadn't moved.

'Yes, Tyler, it worked. You can thank us later. Just be more careful next time you decide to re-engineer something, OK?'

'I'm sorry,' he said.

'It's OK,' I said. 'We'll need to keep a close eye on you, but I think you're going to be all right.'

'I'm sorry,' he repeated, pointing with his intact hand towards me. I looked down, and saw that my white vest top was stained all over with his carmine blood.

Tyler rested in his berth while K and I sterilised the ship. Any clothing that had come into contact with blood was destroyed. We scrubbed all surfaces – wall panels, ceiling, floor. We increased ventilation, working from opposite ends of the cabin, too distant to speak over the filter without raising our voices, and we didn't want to disturb Tyler. We checked on him constantly. We re-attached body-monitors so we could check his levels. His colour had drained, and he seemed in a particularly deep sleep. I looked around his berth: a picture of his sons pinned to the wall; a hand-written letter from his wife. I turned away, listened to his shallow breath.

I was more exhausted now than at any other point on the voyage. Karius was going through the motions, a distant, glazed look in his eyes. I composed a message for Allen and we checked it a couple of times before releasing it. Everything they needed was there. We checked on Tyler one last time, ensuring he had enough food and water, then drifted to our berths and closed the hatches.

SIX

He slept for a long time. When he stirred he seemed a little groggy, but basically OK. He kept telling us how hungry he was, that he couldn't wait to eat again. The wound had healed into a black husk. There was something reviving in seeing defences activate so far from home – the arm autonomous and efficient and continuing its recovery almost in spite of us.

Allen reviewed the footage and commended K and I on our quick thinking and our work. But his advice was unhelpful: keep the patient fed and hydrated and let him rest. Watch for sepsis – confusion, fever, shortness of breath, palpitations and tightness in the chest. Every one of these symptoms had been shared by the three of us anyway. Neither Allen nor anyone else at Control could help. And the effect of realising this was that the three of us were pushed closer together. Tyler needed us, depended on us, grateful to us as we checked on him and shared out his workload. Our bonds strengthened. If we were to survive *Nereus*, we had to really trust each other, believe in each other. Control – nine light hours plus behind – were gone.

Where earlier we'd grown apart, our stats now started to converge: sleep length, pulse, temperature and metabolic rate. It was as if we were becoming a unified prototype astronaut, that as no one individual was equipped to survive this, we had amassed ourselves into something greater. We shared the same flora. Our microbiomes were the next substantial life on the ship, more diverse than the crops in the garden. *Nereus* as an arc that carries us, as we are arcs carrying this other life across us and between our bodies. We did not yet know which forms of life were best adapted to surviving this journey.

The garden was thriving. Every day we checked on the crops, fed them, and recorded the latest growth. I had expected setbacks, deviations from Earth trials, but I hadn't expected *this*. Crop A was on course to conclude its growth a full three days earlier than scheduled. This on its own would have been notable, but it was the performance of the following crops that was interesting. Each successive crop grew quicker, the rate of increase stronger every time.

It was still early, and things could change, but it felt significant. My imagination rushed ahead, picturing large-scale orbital farms exploiting low-gravity hypergrowth. If algae adapted this well, other crops might too. One day we might feed Earth at its edges, a green efflorescence exploding above the exosphere. Karius confirmed what I already knew – trials on the space station had never produced anything like this. So either genes we'd spliced in California were responsible, or *Nereus* was an exceptional environment and was driving the change itself. Close observation should be enough to confirm either way, but I couldn't resist speculating. Did this point back to the external gene Uria had ushered in? The gene from the extremophiles dredged up on *Endeavour*?

'We're farming it, but it's farming us too,' Tyler said. 'Feeding on what we recycle. Feeding on us, in a sense. We should remember that.'

K suggested the ship's acceleration drove the growth. There was no reason to believe this, and I was surprised at my crewmate offering something so radical. I told him I would check the daily growth figures and compare these to our jumps; if they coincided, there might be something to it. Most likely a combination of factors was responsible, interacting with each other and creating a growth cascade. As I wrote up these findings in my report, I tried to keep to the restrained, measured language Allen would expect of me, while aware that hypergrowth may turn out to be the most important discovery of the entire *Proscenium* mission. Once word of this reached the mission's investors, further trials would be prepared. Before long they'd begin on manufacture. For this reason, I had to downplay what I saw. I would mark only conservative, early indicators of advanced growth, holding back the full data set until I knew more, and had time to sift through everything more carefully. Maybe then I'd be in a position to state with authority just what was happening, and what exactly was responsible for it.

Tyler was well enough to help bring in the harvest. He

was a natural in the garden, stating it was his favourite place on the ship. Shamefully, I felt a little proprietary about this, as if in spending so much time there he might take something away from me. He didn't seem especially surprised by the hypergrowth; perhaps I hadn't made clear the full significance. He suggested his own recovery had been helped by the algae, and used the word 'symbiotic'. He could feel himself renewing in the garden, he said, more so than when he was lying back in his berth, or sitting down to a snack. He was excited – I was too; Karius, as usual, expressed little interest either way – in the cuttings we took for our first meal, a landmark on the mission and in the history of space flight. Among all the other firsts, this one stood out, because it was something we had actively achieved ourselves. As I took the last of the cuttings, releasing a briny sea smell, it all flooded back to me, the many years of preparation that had led me to this moment. From my awakening as a child in the Nieuwe Maas more than two decades earlier, to the month on *Endeavour* in the mid-Atlantic, my inclusion in the food programme at China Lake, my years in crew training and my launch from Kourou spaceport; everything culminated in this pivotal moment of consumption. Shortly after, with K, Tyler and I sitting attached to the table over our covered pasta trays mixed with ground green algae, I made a toast, and said nothing would be the same again.

———

You couldn't actually see it growing live, of course, but K set up cameras in the garden and in time-lapse you could watch the green life unfurl. Even K found himself watching it back – the simplest thing in the world, a green plant growing, but a miracle too, and we celebrated it against the darkness around us, the limitless, edgeless black, and it carried us. Tyler had a special affinity with the first crop harvested, crop A; he truly believed it had helped him recover. He grew as it did. He was fascinated by each part of the growth process, and especially by the composition of the water and nutrients feeding it. Our water repurposed, the fragments of matter drifting away from our bodies as we slowly come apart, captured in the air-filter and reconstituted, which is just a technical word for transformed.

Tyler was calmer. He'd stopped worrying about the filters. He seemed more at peace with his place here. K muttered something about slicing up his own lower arm, see if it helped him sleep better too. Then, making a scheduled audit of the food stock, K discovered something alarming: we'd consumed a quarter of our total food stock already. This couldn't be right. He checked everything again – a laborious process in low gravity – and then I did too. We had the dubious distinction of being the first astronauts in history to gain significant weight mid-mission. In this sense, the algae's hypergrowth was a boon. Without it, we'd have to ration meals. We'd now experiment with the crop, using it, at least until we'd recovered the shortfall, as a primary food source rather than a supplement. I seeded two additional pouches, G and H. This would give us a surplus. None of us challenged this – it seemed the logical and right thing to do.

* * *

Childhood memories repeated. One day early each summer Fenna took me on a short trip by train to a nearby town, just the two of us. I looked forward to this ritual every year, the casual inevitability of the outing, more special because it fell on no particular date. As soon as the train pulled away I felt the first pangs of regret – already the experience was trailing behind and I hadn't savoured it, hadn't captured it as I should have, as I'd promised myself I would the night before. For the whole journey, the whole of the day, as Fenna and I stepped off the train and walked through the quiet cobbled streets, as we stopped and lunched on our sandwiches and flask on the grass, as we visited the tea-shop in the later afternoon – an exotic and privileged place for me still, as a child – as we entered what I remember as an independent toy store staffed by the same tall, smiling, ancient man, a shop filled improbably with unusual and anachronistic items – hand puppets and ventriloquists' dolls, magic sets, magnifying glasses, telescopes and microscopes (and in which I never saw a single other customer come in or out) – and especially, of course, as we stepped reluctantly back onto the departing early-evening train, I was possessed by an unbearably bittersweet awareness of the preciousness of each moment passing, each moment that would never be retrieved. Even at the peak of it, the two of us quietly eating our sandwiches on the lawn on a plaid blanket, I couldn't lose the sense that this was ending, that the more the experience developed, the more I lost it. The closer it got, the quicker it fled. When I sobbed, later, in the station bathroom, my mother holding my head gently in her arms, shushing me and telling me it would be OK, everything would be OK, what was streaming out of me wasn't, as she might have thought, prompted by a specific fear about returning home to Geert. It was about happiness. The richness of our day had been too much for me. And even now, as I remember the days, the strange, quiet trips to that oddly deserted town, and I picture my mother, her patient, tired smile, the way she carefully adjusted her stride to keep by me, doing this for one reason only – to give me pleasure; to make me feel good; to offer me, for this one day, or this moment, happiness – it's too much, and I burst into tears, holding my breath where I can to gather in the sound so the others don't hear me through the walls separating us. I should have been there for her; I wanted to but couldn't tell her how I felt, and now everything has gone.

———————

Uria said the swelling in our feet was a symptom of pregnancy. Your feet grow bigger and heavier to form a broader base, a foundation for the body that carries the child, a means of staying upright while you transport a new world inside you. It was just the low gravity, but I imagined it was more than that, that we were struggling to contain worlds too. She remembered it – the feet, the hypersmells, the grit beneath her nails, how she had to wear nose clips passing the fish aisle in the supermarket. Maria is doing well, she said vaguely, a little sadly. She told me – her voice artificial-sounding, subject to automated scrubbing and filtering and periodic amplification just so I can make it out – that there was a statistically unusual number of pregnancies among the staff at the academy. More or less, I asked. Two days later her reply came, a single word: more.

There are more of us. More of us all the time.

'Galaxy' comes from the Ancient Greek for milk. People looked at the density of stars and saw birth, maternal sustenance scattered across the sky. A miracle, something over nothing. Fenna says my first word was 'da', that Geert liked to say I'd picked up English. But 'da', in my third language, means 'there' – a gesture, a directive, a hand that's pointing. I prefer this reading. It's there. Like the blank message sent from *Voyager 1*, a bare, empty fact. A world, a thing. It's there. It can't be, but it's there.

SEVEN

We scrub every message, trying to get at the words under the distortion. With transmissions rarer we analyse tone, hunt the buried meaning, the truth beneath what Control are telling us. Everyone's nervous, as we get closer to the most dangerous phase of the journey. Is this when Datura will make contact? Sometimes we catch ephemera – a thunderclap, a cough, the trail of a peripheral conversation – and we study this too. We try to build the scene out, create a world around it. Control as remote as an ancient civilisation, each recorded document given the lavish attention, the sacred significance, of archaeological bounty.

The accelerations are almost routine now; for the last one Tyler even removes his helmet. He says we're adapting, and medical analysis broadly agrees. Every part of us is affected. Hearing, speech, vision, touch, taste and smell. Our thinking is blocked, and this can no longer be put down purely to fatigue. We're reporting consistently low scores. We try to conserve energy, and continue to let our exercise schedule slide. I miss the pool. I miss the ocean more. All I want is to fall into water.

As we come closer to the heliopause we're visibly affected. Simulations fail: our response to the environment is impossible to predict. Training always marked this as a critical mission phase. We try to avoid imagining the worst, stay busy, rehearse for an imagined end long past the heliosphere: our rendezvous with *Voyager 1*. Tyler simulates control of the ROV, releasing it and attaching onto a comet, extracting ice from the cloud, ushering it back in and preparing the airlocks and storage capsules for quarantine. We wear EVAs for the full run-through and rehearse contingencies. The biggest risk is that Tyler inadvertently contacts the ROV directly as he receives it. We'll lock him in the capsule. Food will be delivered and waste extracted autonomously. But this isn't really sustainable; in truth there is no provision to safeguard the ship in the event of contact. The only realistic option, in this case, is to let Tyler go.

K studies *Voyager 1*. How to identify it, how to examine it at distance, how to launch a remote probe to dock and run chemical analysis. After a mere fifty-two years' drifting, the craft's appearance is unlikely to have changed. There is a small possibility it has passed through a dust cloud, affecting the aluminium coat. But the record is encased behind a gold exterior and an additional silver veneer. Reinforced more exhaustively than the other parts of the craft, it's expected to survive indefinitely – after billions, perhaps trillions of years, it will be subsumed within a larger event, and disappear.

Prior to the anomalies, *Voyager*'s last known coordinates were at the outer edge of the heliosphere – the heliopause, where the sun's influence fades entirely. This was the point at which Datura intervened. We expect to reach the location in several Earth-days.

The crops have become lighter, almost pellucid. This never happened in the lab. In some you can see right through them, past ever finer layers of tissue. Perhaps it's because I was so close that I missed something even more obvious. When Karius asked me about their 'change in direction', I assumed he was talking about growth rates. But he meant it literally: the crop has started folding backwards. The limit of the heliosphere, with its steadily higher rates of ionised radiation, is instigating a phase previously absent in the history of the species.

Maybe the explanation is simpler. Maybe the algae, as we approach the heliopause, is expressing a form of regret, nostalgia: arcing backwards, turning itself towards Earth's oceans, hydrotropic at 11 billion miles.

'Solar wind speed continuing to decline.'

'Drop-off not yet sufficiently steep. Still on the approach. It's close. Brace yourselves. Wait it out.'

Finally we reach it: solar wind dips consistently below the speed of sound. And with barely even a shudder from the craft.

K checks again. Tyler ultimately confirms. 'Affirmative. Wind speed maintaining subsonic levels, continuing on the decline. We have hit termination shock. *Nereus* is now officially coasting through the heliosheath.'

We unstrap. We'd kept a little of the wine aside in advance of this moment, but in the event none of us need it. Anxiety and tension leaven out into ecstasy. We embrace. I feel wild, ludicrous, brilliantly happy. K's eyes are glazed with tears. We laugh. K's use of 'coasting' feels provocative, a statement of confidence. We're not just riding this out, we're easing our way through the second major milestone of our voyage.

'But we're still inside it, technically.'

'Technically,' K agrees. 'In the outer edge of the sphere.'

'Everything looks good, Leigh. Relax. Heliopause expected in 2.7 Earth days. After that, we're out.'

We sail through a standing shock wave, spiral-arrayed magnetic bubbles, each 1 AU across, staggered all around us. Wind continues to decline, exhibiting further signs of instability and turbulence. Our elation drops, energy levels evening out. The gathering silence makes me feel uncomfortable. I continue to take unnecessary time readings, against wind decline and high electrons rebuffed by the ship's outer fortifications. Passing beyond the last of the sun's influence, we're coated only by layers of steel and the oval lake threaded between them. We encroach deeper into the furthest extent of the heliosheath, which thins out all the time. Every passing moment launches a greater assault from the interstellar medium. The ship picks up high-energy electrons at a rate ninety-three times greater than just six Earth days earlier. The final boundary – the heliopause – is upon us.

Tyler remains calm. He surveys data streams and assists K on what I know are essentially phatic reviews. They will change nothing. K keeps checking for incoming comms, despite Control languishing days behind us, lost in the temporal gulf. For these truly crucial moments, communication is not possible.

I tell K to stop for a moment. We need to eat, rest. 'Plenty of time for that later,' he replies gruffly. I remind him of our pact, made after launch, to always eat by each other's side. I won't let it go. Eventually he joins us, harnessed to the table.

'You're feeling good about this?' K says, looking up from the green algae towards Tyler.

'The exit is completely outside our control,' Tyler says. 'Anxiety changes nothing, and is therefore counterproductive.'

'Sounding pretty calm,' K says.

'Not calm. Just accepting. It's taken me a long time to get here.'

'Your faith?' I ask, tentatively. Experience has generally taught me not to broach this, but in the glow of the earlier exhilaration I want to push on. I also want to turn our thoughts, even briefly, away from termination shock and the approaching heliopause. And K's right: during training, and at the start of the voyage, Tyler was as anxious as any of us, possibly more so. He always longed for control – he was our captain. But ever since his accident and blood loss he's become a quieter, more passive presence.

'I know you don't share my belief, and I don't expect you to. But I think it's undeniable we are being guided. We are in service to something else, something beyond us, sent here for a reason.'

K puts down his food pack. 'I'm sorry – I can't listen to this. I can't see fatalism as victory. Even if I accepted what you say, I would still be afraid.'

'There's a feeling,' Tyler goes on, unmoved. 'Sometimes you come close, sometimes you veer away. But there are times when I've felt close to something utterly extraordinary. When my sons were born. The weeks after my parents died, when I thought I would be empty, but instead it was the opposite. It's a feeling of calm in the presence of something unnameable, unfathomable, unlimited. When I feel it, it settles me. And I feel it close to me now.'

'You know they can create that in a lab?'

'K,' I come in.

Tyler's smile holds. 'It's OK,' he says.

'Stimulate the brain directly, produce this feeling. Electricity and blood flow, Tyler. It's physiology. It's not god, and it's not meaningful.'

Tyler's nodding, lips pursed. K goes on, steely eyes staring at the wall.

'There were experiments on Tibetan Buddhist monks at Stanford. Twelve of them in long magenta robes, chanting and meditating in a locked room, sitting on the floor with candles and burning incense. You get the picture. The experiments went on for hours. The scientists used an IV tracer to read what was going on at the peak of the experience. Later, they induced the same state artificially: increased blood flow in the frontal cortex, lowered activity in the posterior superior parietal lobe. The monks instantly reached peak transcendence, described by several of them as among the most meaningful events of their lives. And it's demonstrably vacuous, Tyler. It's blood flow and neuronal stimulation; it's revelation on tap; it doesn't mean a thing.'

'Listen, I don't think we should—'

'It's OK, Leigh. I don't mind. It's good to keep ourselves occupied right now, I understand that. And I think these experiments have merit. But they don't prove what Karius thinks they do.'

'It's a cheat code for god, Tyler. Therefore there is no god.'

'I disagree. It's an artificial route to the transcendent, but it doesn't undermine it. The state attained remains meaningful.'

'Then why practise religion at all? Why not use artificial routes – psilocybin, direct brain stimulation?'

'Because it's not sustainable across a lifetime. And because the experience is richer when it's internally derived. Reaching these states artificially is interesting, but the experience is only grafted on. When you have faith, however – when you build your life around it – everything's charged from the inside. I realise I might not sound persuasive, and that's OK. I don't need to argue with you, K – not now. If this is the end, I think it would be a pity to meet it fighting one another.'

K moves his body, appears to concede something.

'Were your family religious?' I say quickly, turning to K. 'When you were growing up?'

K laughs, tilting his head back. 'You realise how predictable this is?'

'What is?' I ask.

'These last-minute confessions. You really think so little of the ship?'

'You've never gone through high turbulence on a commercial liner? Turned to the elderly Greek woman next to you and lost all inhibitions, everything that ever held you back? And that now appears so trivial? Never wanted to speak, while you still can?'

'Nah, never really bothered me,' K says. He looks at me reassuringly. 'I'll concede, however, that this, right now – this is a whole other level.'

'He's stalling,' Tyler says.

'OK,' K says. 'If we're trying to distract ourselves, if it

helps, I'll talk. In answer to your question, Leigh, no, not really. My father might have been, for all I know – he left when I was three. My mother brought up me and my sisters. I was close to her brother, Ivan. A fisherman. When he came back after months out, he brought us these delicious chocolate treats wrapped in fine red tissue. When I was older, he took me out walking – at my mother's request, I think, initially. I didn't have many friends. At first we walked through the valley and by the banks of the lake. I think he was testing me, seeing what I could do. Even on the coldest days, I never complained. I was determined, and I kept up with Ivan, more or less.

'I must have passed whatever test Ivan had set me, because soon he took me to the mountains. I remember my first time on the Carpathians, vast, barren, gleaming under ice. It was a real adventure. Maybe the most exciting thing I have ever done. It's different when you're young, you know? Nothing can equal it. From then on I was addicted, I went whenever could. Soon I was stronger than my uncle, and old enough to regret this. I went out for days at a time, taking just water, bread, a thin tent. When I went away to those places, I entered a new reality. I felt the whole of the mountain underneath me, the ice and wind and the rolling, distant crack of the heavy snow drifts. In the high altitude, I began imagining things. I sensed footsteps behind me, a figure just out of reach.

'Ivan died last year, during Sim 1. They couldn't reach me. And when I did find out, I couldn't get leave to return home.'

'You carried on, you didn't say anything?'

K shrugs.

'I should have gone to see my mother before we left,' I say, after a moment. 'K, are you still checking speeds, are we—?'

'Not yet,' he says. 'It's OK. We're OK, we're good.'

'Before we started training, I let her down. I let my sister down. There was a window where I could have gone, but I focused on work, told myself I didn't have a choice. It wasn't true.'

'How about your father?' Tyler says, breaking the silence. 'Did you get on with him?'

'No. I don't want to overplay it, but it wasn't the life he wanted, and he made things difficult for my sister and me.'

'I'll bet she appreciated having you around.'

'I don't know. There was a limit to how much I could protect her. I've been thinking about this a lot. There was this one time, Helena and I together in our room. I must've been around twelve, which makes Helena nine. Anyway, I started speaking about the violence. She described the things that had happened to her. This was the one time we ever had that conversation. Is everything – look, can you feel that?'

'It's fine,' K says, 'I'm monitoring everything, we're still some time away.'

'I can imagine that was tough,' Tyler says, 'hearing that from your sister.'

'But it's what happened after, I mean. At some point, as we were talking, there was this noise. It sounded like a weight shifting through the door. Helena didn't notice. Later that evening I saw the light on and stepped into my parents' room. My father was prone on the bed, above the sheets, still wearing his long black work boots. His arm was spread over his face, but he wasn't sleeping. He knew I was there. I panicked – he was so small, broken – and I blurted out "What's wrong?"'

'He'd heard you, earlier?'

'I don't know. I don't think the beatings were so bad afterwards – that for Helena, at least, they stopped. They never reached what I experienced. And I wondered. But honestly, I don't know. I never found out.'

I pushed around the remaining pieces of algae. I was aware of my crewmates looking away. I felt strange from having spilled this – light, airy – but also from not having said nearly enough.

'The reason I brought this up, after what you said, is because maybe I wanted him to hear us all along. Maybe I staged the whole thing. Maybe I knew he would walk by, knowing that the only way to show him what he was doing was through a closed door.'

Tyler's nodding, and though I'm not confident I've

communicated anything – perhaps *because* I'm not confident – I continue. I tell myself I'm imagining it, that we aren't there yet and it's too soon anyway for any effects, but I feel a ripple of electricity across the outermost layer of my skin. I feel desperate, energised, vigorously alive. 'I've always been afraid of a lack of volition, of doing things for reasons outside my awareness. He died many years ago, but even now I worry what I might have inherited from my father. I've been trying to prove he has no influence. That's one of the reasons for my work. There's something liberating about the perspective. But in my fieldwork and lab work I'm holding early life; I have in my hands, literally, this material that passes between us. Obviously I can't get away from it.'

I give a bitter laugh, apologise. Neither Tyler nor K says anything. I push around the last stringy pieces in my meal-pack. 'Tyler used the word "guided",' K says. 'You were both talking about influences outside your control. It made me think of the engineers, at the start of this, drawing the plans together to harness the power.'

'The ovals interlocking.'

'They were ill. Something was moving them.'

Tyler's eyes are closed, his hands laid over each other in prayer; he lowers his head and moves his lips silently. 'I can feel it. We're close now.'

————

I close my eyes, breathe in, try to realise it, feel exactly where we are, the edge of the interstellar. I sense it on my skin, the ripple of ionised radiation through the mid-deck. We're drifting out of range of the solar winds, edging into the more dangerous and unstable region of interstellar light. The plasma of another star. We're cruising towards the heliopause at close to maximum velocity, 9,000 miles per second, 4.7 per cent light speed, partly light ourselves. The ship conducts its autonomous adjustments. Radiation levels soar; I imagine my body reacting – skin flayed, soft flesh exposed. I lose this, too, lose even my inner body, nothing surrounding me, nothing to surround.

Our displays illustrate the expanse of the inner solar system. The heliosphere isn't really a sphere at all, more an elongated teardrop shape. The whole inner system – the planets, the sun, the moons, the incalculable asteroids and micro debris – appears as a single curved body drifting through space. Like the juvenile stage of an aquatic life form. Was this all alive, on a completely non-appreciable scale? Was all this – 13 billion years – a brief beginning in a form that was yet to mature?

'Temperature and compression rising rapidly. Approaching formal state transition.'

'Are we there?'

Silence.

'We're there? We're gone?'

Tyler confirms readings. His voice sounds oddly far away. 'Gone. Wind speed and ENA commensurate with formal recognition of extra-helio state.' He checks the screens once more, looks up, turning to us. Clears his throat. 'As of the twenty-seventh day of the third month on Earth's calendar, *Nereus* has debuted in the interstellar medium.'

'What is this? Tyler?'

'What?'

'Comms screen, it's . . .'

The ship shudders, the lights blink. We wait, bodies frozen in place.

K smiles nervously. 'Thought for a second—' he says, before his words cut off, and everything goes dark.

EIGHT

When I regain consciousness I'm floating in darkness. In starlight I see my crewmates drifting beyond me, turning slowly, apparently asleep. Their position reminds me of Stefan and the others surfacing after the first dive. My throat hurts, my mouth is dry, my ears are ringing and my head is dull. Something has struck the ship. I cough, my diaphragm rattles. A movement to my left – Tyler's arm twitching, eyes opening. Confusion, alarm – his pupils dart across the mid-deck. His limbs spasm, and as he goes to speak he dissolves into a coughing fit. Wiping his face, inspecting his hand, he turns to me, and points to the panels, the displays.

Karius wakes, and after reorienting himself he joins us by the comms unit, which is covered in a fine silver dust. We can't initiate it. Everything's down. Everything in darkness. All systems and data streams unresponsive. Navigation chart, body sensors (can't read radiation count), atmospheric readings, comms unit – everything's disabled. We're groggy, slower than we should be, but we don't panic right away. I check my breath. Oxygen levels not noticeably dropping. So bio-support remains functional; only secondary systems disabled. The garden: I swim to the airlock and impatiently hit release. The hatch hisses open. Inside, everything's blue in emergency lighting; there's a strong, thick marine smell.

Crabs and brine. Thick vines hanging in the wet containers, grown exuberantly, abundantly.

'Leigh,' Tyler calls, his voice uneven. 'Check your computer.' I rejoin them. K is tapping quietly on his laptop. He says something in Serbian, then closes the lid with exaggerated care, as if afraid he might lose control and smash up the object. Tyler's face is ashen, staring at the white wall panels.

I enter my berth, my heart beating louder and my mouth drying up. I load up my computer and the screen shows an empty blue. All folders empty. My reports from each day of the voyage, the records from the garden, my VR programmes, my video and audio libraries – everything's gone. I hit the switches lining my wall – lights, power outlets; everything's down.

All my pictures, gone. My family, gone. Fenna is gone. Helena is gone. It's like they never existed, my whole life a dream. And then I see a single photograph of Helena and me as children, printed from a disposable camera and affixed low on my cabin wall. We're standing in the garden in winter sunlight, wearing gloves and scarves and identical sheepish grins. I remember the shutter falling, turning from the garden into the field and running, the warmth gaining in our breath, Helena trailing and laughing, reaching the grassy bank and collapsing together in the frosted turf, coughing, breathing heavily and looking up at the afternoon sky, the perfect moon and the sun about to descend.

I open the hatch. 'Everything's wiped. What could have done this?'

K grunts back, something about irradiated particles and ENAs. He's still attempting to restart comms. Tyler's calm and still, looking over K like a father. Maybe it's the unusual outer silence – the panels no longer release their hum – but I hear something inside. I close my eyes, cup my hands over my ears, isolate the sound, and it amplifies: a roaring, rushing percussion, like waves striking the shore. As I open my eyes I see Tyler attaching to the arm support above the porthole. We're seeing by starlight, which means the camera at least is still working. Tyler's frowning. Whatever he's seeing there, it isn't good.

Eventually we manage to activate emergency lighting throughout the ship, and begin to survey the damage. We're confident now that the air filter is functional. We have our water supply, we have oxygen, we have an excess of algae from the garden. Enough to survive the remaining span of the voyage. Tyler says not to panic, we'll work this out eventually. We have to; with secondary systems disabled, our navigation's down, and a collision is now statistically likely. K refuses to give up on comms. I only manage to wrench him away by offering him fresh, raw cuttings from the garden. We seem to realise, at the same time, that we have an unusual craving for this food.

'Must've been out for a while; I can't get enough of this stuff.'

K nods, scooping up fresh mouthfuls.

'Time settings at zero on my screen.'

'Ours too. Power almost out. Look, we need to decide what to do,' K says, looking in Tyler's direction. 'Now.'

'I'll clean up,' I offer. 'I don't know where this dust is coming from. It's probably nothing, but I doubt it's helping.'

'Something might have shifted in the vents, releasing it. Maybe it went into the wiring. It's not the cause, but it can't hurt to clean it up, I guess. I'll keep trying comms.'

'No.' Tyler looks at him. 'Priority is to establish position manually. We don't know how long we were out. Can you do that, K?'

He nods.

The dust is everywhere. No part of the ship escapes. The bathroom, the berths, the garden. Between the letters on my keypad and in the dead sockets of the comms unit. In the food packs stored in the walls and in the wipes we use to clean ourselves. When we first came to, after the Event, I didn't realise the extent. But in the blue light – and now I'm actively searching for it – it's clear that the fine, dark layer is all around. I can taste it, smell it, I see it embedded in my yellowing fingernails and try to dig it out my ears. But the sound remains – waves striking a shore.

I cough, feeling the dust shaking in my lungs and moving up my throat, and I gag, patting down my diaphragm. Tyler turns to me in alarm.

'You all right? Maybe you should stop, get some rest. You've cleaned up the displays, that should be enough.'

I nod, unable to speak. After I lock the bathroom behind me I struggle for air. The extent of the disaster is dawning on me at last. Whatever has happened, it's more than a glitch. It seems certain we are not going to make it back. If radiation has breached the shield, things are going to get worse. Another stray particle will eventually enter, and instead of passing through us it will bed into a nucleus. Disease will follow, consuming us long before we reach *Voyager* and the cloud.

I barely recognise myself in the cabin mirror. Jumpsuit entirely covered in dirt. Slowly, carefully, I begin to peel it off, starting from the neck. My skin beneath is soft and yielding. When I peel away the upper half, I see the dirt over my chest matted in sweat. I wipe with the moist cloth, and gasp; in the opaque mirror it appears my hand has plunged into a cavity.

Exiting the bathroom, I find my crewmates waiting for me. Harnessed to the table, they look away as I open the door.

'What is it?'

'K's having trouble with our position.'

'What does it say?'

'It's the distant constellations. Must be a distortion somewhere in the feed, because as I see it – and I'm checking and rechecking everything I've written – the constellations are irreconcilable from our present moment.'

'Which means?'

'It means they're younger.'

'Younger, as in . . . ?'

'As in, our location only makes sense if we're looking out from the past.'

'How far in the past?'

'More than 2 billion years. I told you. I can't see where the error is, and I'm going fucking crazy here.'

'One of the theories about Datura, when it disappeared,' Tyler said, 'was that it was temporally displaced.'

'This isn't right. I don't feel right,' I said.

NINE

We get noticeably worse. We have to be careful when we move, our skin is so soft. It takes longer to eat; we bite carefully so we don't chew away a flank of tongue. I try to look ahead: possibly we are still adapting to the diet and the effects will even out later; maybe this is just a brief spell of radiation sickness. All signs, however, indicate the condition is terminal. Our control systems have not revived. We are being bathed in extrasolar light.

After shaving his hair, pre-empting its fallout, Tyler looks like a different person, a fourth crew member. The angles of his face are wrong. The back of his head is abnormally straight, as if the curvature has been planed away. K is talking to his children, making recordings on his draining laptop. Tyler and I alternate in the garden. The growth isn't just accelerating, it's leaping exponentially. Radiation must be contributing. It will be interesting, if we ever return, to study the crops and any relevant mutations. For obvious reasons, this isn't something we discuss.

In the beginning, the harvest helped us track time. We watched the crops growing and blooming, and it took the place of the weather and the seasons, even the light, that we missed. For the first months, it helped. But now, with growth rate continuing to accelerate, the effect is different. Time itself is twisting.

I veer from a sense of levity and apathy, a state in which I am barely conscious, to sudden bursts of extreme clarity and wonder. These latter periods, brief as they are, are expensive. I fall back into sleep, into an exchange of memories and darkness. Occasionally I pass Karius or Tyler as they enter or exit the bathroom, or as they take water from the filter or food from the garden. K has finally given up on comms.

I have to exploit brief periods of lucidity. What is happening to us? How long can we go on? Can we recover, or will our sickness only worsen? There's a flutter of static electricity round my atrophying limbs. I'm drawn repeatedly to the walls of the mid-deck, backed by the arc of water beyond the veneer. I close my eyes, imagine I'm falling. The sensation, when I wake, reminds me of something. I try to focus and pursue the thought. The blackouts are becoming frequent, and they are a part of this too, this thought that's eluding me. I have experienced this before, somewhere. Another ship.

K emerges from his cabin with red eyes and swelling either side of his nose – he's been dreaming again of his children. He discusses with Tyler the moment they became fathers, impressions from the maternity ward, the change that had taken hold in them. Karius, in particular, is affected by these dreams, insisting there's an iron-rich odour in the garden that is reminiscent of afterbirth.

I dream of a water-planet, a sphere covered by a single all-encompassing ocean. Sometimes I'm high enough to detect the planet's curve; other times I veer so close to the surface I can smell it, hear the sway and fall of the surface waves. I will myself to descend, but every time, inevitably, I wake. I sit in my berth and gather myself, trying to remember where I was. The white foamy froth; the alternating eddy and calm; the suggestion of thwarted purpose, of development rescinded again and again, tantalisingly, as the wave breaks.

The crops are still growing, despite the minor light. This shouldn't be possible. It must be the effect of the genes inserted from the archaea. This isn't algae at all, it's a composite, a colony, a fusion of early-life species, suddenly more active in this new phase of the journey. Something in them has been switched on – I don't know what, or how. But I think if we understand this, we might learn more about what's happening to us.

Datura's carvings show cells interwoven, the beginning of a new phase of life, the era of the eukaryotes. *Voyager* shows the same cells 2 billion years later. Here is where you came from, here is where you are. Do you realise this? Are you waking up to this, and is it meaningful to you?

———————

K and Tyler before me, listening, as I go on.

'Almost six years ago, another journey. Amy was there, the mid-Atlantic. We kept diving. I've spoken about this before: it's where we dredged up the archaea. Some of us got sick. I don't know what it was. We lost track of time, and we had this compulsion to go back in, though of course we knew it wasn't safe.'

'This stuff is in the crop?'

'Some of the genetic information has been spliced. The trials showed no ill-effects; we were very careful.'

'That's not what you said in Kourou; you said they were rushed.'

'The human phase, yes. We were pushed for time; there was no option.'

'There's something else, isn't there?'

'We had problems on our ship. Our soundings were way off. The readings didn't make sense.'

'How did you explain it?'

'We never did. An electrical storm, a magnetic event. Who knows.'

'We've passed the magnetic sheath of the heliosphere – you think the same thing's happening to us now?'

'Maybe – I don't know. But something feels similar. Sometimes I'm sure I've been here before.'

TEN

Time passes. Details start to return. I'm in a small cabin. The lights are disabled. I'm bound under restraints. We're sailing somewhere close to the Oort cloud, hundreds of billions of miles from home. Gravity increases – around 0.9 K says, though it feels higher. So we're accelerating, or braking on the approach. Sweat runs down my hairline, the dormant muscles of my arms struggling to bear their own weight. Tyler suffers the most, losing all strength from his body. He falls, wounds himself. He can barely walk. He complains it's cold, spends his time huddled in his cabin. When I bring him food I find him shivering, clutching his bedsheet. I tend to him. I focus on my crewmates to forget about myself. His temperature oscillates, and sometimes he forgets where he is. He calls out for his children. I put bedding in the mid-deck, and K and I haul him out of his berth onto the floor. The three of us camp there, next to one another. Every time Tyler wakes, his eyes try to flee, then he sees Karius and me and it seems to comfort him, and he closes his eyes again and his heart settles. He's still taking food and water. K – whose cough is getting louder, sometimes drawing blood; he thinks I haven't noticed – helps me take cuttings from the garden.

I can tell from the way Tyler winces as he turns that he has sores along his side. Our deterioration seems unusually rapid, but with clocks at zero we have no way to measure time, no clear idea of where and when we are. We don't know when the Event struck, or how long we've been like this. I gather paper and we record messages for our families. This feels important, though almost certainly redundant. No one will find us now. K's throat hurts when he speaks. I'm not sure Tyler really knows what he's saying. The emergency light fails, and then my tablet shuts off and the blue light fades, leaving us in total darkness except for the stars.

My eyes flash open. I try to raise myself but gravity holds me to the floor. Then I realise it's not just gravity – arms are pushing down on me. I see Tyler's face above, I panic, and then I understand; he's trying to wake me.

I sit up eventually. K is still sleeping, the ship silent. 'What is it, Tyler?' I whisper. 'What's wrong?'

Adjusting to the starlight, I see his mouth open and his eyes widen. He is startlingly young. When he speaks, I'm surprised how level and calm he is, how free of pain he sounds.

'We're not going to make it, are we?'

I pause a second. 'You don't know that, Tyler. We can't give up. We've come this far.'

'I know I'm weak, but I don't want to hide from the truth.'

'What do you want me to say?'

'Tell me what's going to happen,' he says, seizing my arm

with surprising force. 'Tell me what will happen when we die.'

K stirs the other side of me, awakened by the unexpected sound of our captain's voice. 'Well, the ship will continue,' I respond. 'Based on our last known position, I'd expect us to approach the Oort cloud in weeks, months maybe.'

'And then?'

'And then we keep going. With our programmed course disabled, we'll continue indefinitely.'

Slowly, I take Tyler's hand away, and ease him back into his bedding. His temperature's stable. His eyes remain open, pleading with me. 'For tens of thousands of years,' I whisper. 'Millions of years. Tens of millions of years. I don't know if the power will ever exhaust itself. We'll pass other stars. Proxima Centauri; Tau Ceti; Lalande 21185. Assuming we maintain high speeds, we may enter, in some distant era, Andromeda.' Tyler's eyes are closed now. K's too. 'After the air filter fails, everything will be preserved. The pictures of your children. The tablets, with your messages home. The data banks, archiving the journey. The crops in the garden. And us. Our bodies will be preserved when we die. We won't be the same, but we'll continue. This is only the beginning of our journey. We'll enter other worlds, other galaxies. Unimaginable, indescribable places.'

I'm no longer sure if the others are awake. Their breath lulls me and I lie down.

'We might still be contacted,' K says, his voice rough and hoarse. He coughs, holds his chest, and spits something into his cupped hands.

Tyler's eyes flash open. 'Do you think they will read us?' he says. 'Will they understand us? Will they look at us, and understand where we've been?'

Tyler's breathing gets louder, his chest lifting and falling. I press his forehead, feel it burning up again. I lie back down, and when I close my eyes I see Helena. She's hiding under the bunk-beds. She's sobbing, hiccupping, she wants to disappear and never be found. Eventually I bring her out. There is a mark on her face. She's fighting back tears, using the heels of her palms to wipe them away, but her upper body shudders as she sobs. 'You have to come with me,' I tell her. 'Can you hear me? It's important, I need you to come with me.' She manages to nod her head, still seizing on each sob. 'Bring your bag. It doesn't matter what's inside. Hurry.' We slip out of the back door unseen, and make our way through the fields. It's light and warm and the fields are deserted. I go quickly, urging her to keep up, telling her it's vital we do this, that we go on. We cross the last of the fields and cut into the forest. Immediately everything is cool and dark. The water flows quickly from the stream. Birds are shifting in the branches above us. 'Come on,' I lead her by the hand. We go on through the forest, climbing the far bank, digging our hands into the muddy clay and earth, gripping on to roots to take our weight. 'We can stop here,' I tell her, and we sit in the earth. Our breathing is heavy, we wait until it settles. I take off my backpack and Helena removes hers. We start digging, breaking into soft clay with our hands. We pull out stones, earthworms, and we keep going, until the hole is almost three feet deep. 'OK, we can stop now. Now open your bag. Look inside. Choose three things and place them into the earth.' She's sceptical, she isn't sure if it's a trick, so I go first, I empty out my bag – a pen, some sweets, the book I'm reading – and she follows. 'Now we need to fill it in. We're burying everything.' It doesn't take long. When we've finished, we step on the surface to level the earth. Helena's jumping, using all her weight to firm up the covering, so that nothing's exposed and no one walking by will ever realise what's there. 'It's gone now.' Helena's eyes are on the ground. 'No one will find this for thousands of years. We'll be long dead. They won't know who we were, but they'll be curious, fascinated by what we left behind. Maybe they'll try to reconstruct us, but they won't know what it's really like to be us, from the inside.' I look at her. 'The same will happen to you. I promise. You'll forget all this. One day, you'll look back, you'll be curious, but you won't feel it from inside anymore – the pain. I promise. You'll leave all this behind.'

Waking, I find Tyler covered in sweat. I prod him. His eyes glow. K and I bring him food and water, which he manages to force down. We lie beside each other, and I listen to their breath.

'I'm afraid to fall asleep,' Tyler says, 'in case I don't come back. I don't want that. I want to keep coming back. Forever. I don't want to go away, everything dark. I want to stay here. All I want is to see . . . that's all. To know something is there. Not nothing.'

'If the air supply lasts longer,' I tell him, 'the algae will continue to grow. It'll spill through everything. Through the containers, across the garden, through the airlock. Drifting through us, inside us, linking us, tangling us up. We'll all be together, Tyler – you won't be alone. I promise you. We'll all be the same. One larger organism. Like we always were.'

K reaches towards Tyler, and whispers, 'Nor at any moment was I not – nor thou, nor these kings.'

One single, original organism, distended enormously through space and time – a 4.5-billion-year migration.

I lie down, turn over, and I must already be dreaming, because I feel a fierce light edging across my eyelids.

Everything turns on this moment. I'm convinced as he enters the room and looks towards me that he doesn't know what he is doing. He has not decided on a course of action; he has arrived at my room for no purpose. He looks down at me, his eyes take in the scene. I'm sitting on the floor, my things spread on the carpet. When he opens his mouth he may do one of two things: breathe, or speak. It's the second option that consumes me, the promise of revelation. The secret behind the universe. He looks round the room, surveys it, his first born, the clutter of her things spread haphazardly on the floor, and it's too much for him – the memory of the first time he held me, how small I was in his arms, his own childhood and the terror induced by his father, my grandfather. As he looks at me, and the bewilderment in his eyes meets recognition in my own – this has happened before, an infinite number of times – the repetition is too much, and rather than speak, his open mouth inhales a quantity of oxygen.

This feeds him. His colour changes. Invigorated, he leans his body fractionally, gaining further purchase before falling forward and bringing his right arm towards me in an arc. Still, at this point, I don't realise what's happening. Still, I think, he is coming forward to tell me something, to bring me a secret, to tell me what it all means, and even as my body is lifted off the ground, and my flight begins, there's a delay. I don't truly understand. I think it's unreal, it's part of a game, there's something else, something more significant, behind it. And as I rise further, inches off the ground, I look into his irises, and see something reflected inside. There's a glow, a light orb inside the darkness, reflecting the sudden, inexplicable appearance of an object tearing through the sky.

PART FIVE

Ascension

ONE

A thick haze drifts over Jakarta bay. Legacy agreements are in place, and four decades into the century the country has 200 active coal plants. Both her sons have asthma. Leendert said his first word at four years old. Chest and throat issues are treatable, neurological ones less so. The problem is general, possibly intractable. Globally, articulation is delayed, in speech and in writing, infancy – defined as an enduring state of helplessness – prolonged.

Mirroring this, her mother's generation is affected too. Senility rises exponentially. In many ways it's a crisis of language, words taking longer to emerge and disappearing quicker. If she believed in such things she might say this was a pathology developed by the species to protect itself, turning away from an increasingly insupportable reality into denial and hallucination. Vision is failing too – everything is, depending how you track it. Depth fields atrophy from lack of stimulation as life is lived increasingly indoors. Sometimes, from her twenty-third-storey apartment, visibility barely reaches 15 feet.

Today isn't quite so bad, the haze thick but penetrable, the air golden, with warm rain washing carbon off the buildings, the roads, the bridges, sweeping it back into the bay. Another vast limestone quarry, material for a country in a state of transformation. She feels a bit of give in her legs, stops to lean against another new building. Weaker bones, softer carbonate. How many vehicles are visible in any one moment? One thousand? Five? Ten? At a certain point, scale is difficult to appreciate, and concrete detail fades into haze.

She is crossing the bridge, dark hair thick with particulate matter, breath shallow under her black filter mask. She drops down off the bridge. It takes eleven minutes to cross the motorway, three separate light systems. She pushes through the crowd and lands at last in the courier depot. As usual – as she has done at eight thirty on the third Monday of every month for the past nine years – she waits a moment before passing through security. She's not sure how much longer she can keep this up. Whether it's worth it. The headaches, the upset, the loss of concentration, the exhaustion and the inability to work for the remainder of the day. Jack has learned she can't be dissuaded and so he gives her space, he puts something in the fridge, he takes the kids out when he can. He notifies her before they return. She hopes the headaches, at least, are an inheritance that will skip her children. Unlike delayed speech, which is just one of the many ways Leendert is coming to resemble the *tante* he never met.

The guard is watching her. Feed must have picked up an unusual movement, the fact she's stopped for no apparent reason. Now he's ambling in her direction. So she pre-empts him and makes for the gates, placing her few possessions in a Ziploc left in a tray. She nods at the second guard, who smiles briefly in recognition, before returning to his tall jar of black tea sweetened by condensed milk.

Few people use these. There are 500 or so at this particular depot, but she never sees anyone come in or out. Most are leased by banks. She approaches, scans her key, enters the code, and opens the box.

It's difficult to pursue a suit against a company if it no longer exists. This proved to be one of the more straightforward issues in a case it seemed would never end. At least you could state this particular problem, conceptualise it, put it in a sentence. At least it had precedent. Company is in trouble. Individuals worry they are liable. Company is shifted into permanent state of slow dissolution with, at last count, twenty-nine reincarnate identities. This was what she was dealing with. She'd figured out long ago that the bulk of the money and infrastructure had been redirected towards one operation in particular, hiding under a name acquired in merger, Cable International Ltd. Proving this wasn't quite so straightforward. Once you showed the direct through-line linking ICORS and CI, you could begin identifying individuals and marking them as responsible. Then, eventually, you might successfully sue for transparency and full release of the records from thirteen years earlier. But, alas, she wasn't there yet. Often she thought she never would be. Nobody at CI denied the through-line outright. Instead the lawyers stalled and just added to the confusion, generating yet more new companies, previously unknown subsidiaries, sister organisations, etc. Sometimes, on a good day, she could believe she was making progress. These days were rare. But the last eighteen months had seen the first tranche released, and though as expected there was nothing really new inside, it was still something.

Their relationship hadn't always been antagonistic. For the first two years, more or less, the Institute had looked after them. It hadn't even entered her thoughts back then that the company wasn't acting in the interests of herself and the other families. After confirmation *Nereus* was gone, they flew them to Houston and bundled them into a large hotel. There was financial compensation, media training, psychological support. Everything bathed in an enduring irreality. Her sister in space, lost to a failed mission, a ship that had gone dark. They would never see Leigh again. There was a cursory presentation in the hotel's lecture hall in which they showed the progress of the journey and where exactly it had gone dark. An 'unpredictable outside event'. Nothing anyone could have done. At this point they'd only asked them not to speak about any of this; they hadn't actually drawn up the contracts yet. She and Jack had a suite, and officials came up every few hours – doctors, lawyers, other support staff. Further along the corridor was a Serbian family with two gorgeous sandy-haired kids who never stopped playing, interrogating each other deep in some private universe. Later, she found out this was the surviving family of Karius Marković, one of the ship's three crew members. She never saw Tyler's family – or wasn't aware of it if she had. She was quite ill during those first days and everyone put it down to trauma, the shock of it all. A woman introduced herself – around Fenna's age, short, completely hairless. She hugged her, looked her straight in the eyes and said sorry. Helena never saw her again.

Months later, with her pregnancy starting to show, they'd held a small memorial in Rotterdam. Officially, still, the line was that her sister had drowned while working at sea. She couldn't bring herself to tell Fenna. Fenna was deteriorating quickly, living in a nursing home, and the doctors were surprised she ultimately lived as long as she did. Leigh's instructions in the event of her own death were for a wild burial in one of the reservations. She remembered her taking pleasure describing the insects, the carrion birds, the wild dogs and boars that would separate her body, leaving only a liquid residue disseminating into the soil and helping the grass grow. As usual, she didn't understand her sister, but she accepted her.

Leigh had drawn up a document and taken Helena's signature as next of kin. She'd wondered if something else was going on – this had been a year or two before Leigh had left for California. She'd recently come back from a long sea trip. She wasn't happy in her work, there were problems with Dana. Maybe the wild burial was there to shock, to interrupt her thoughts, bring her out of a malaise.

As Helena found out, from among the clutch of documents the Institute had asked them to sign, even if there had been a body the company still retained ownership and would only release it at their discretion. This struck her as unusual. She listened to their reasons and nodded, before requesting a full transcript of all legal agreements made between her sister and ICORS. When the lawyers, as expected, told her this wouldn't be possible, she notified them that she was pursuing a case.

All support from the Institute immediately ceased. Their security detail withdrew. A demand was issued for reimbursement of monies paid. She tried to get hold of the other families, but no one would respond. ICORS had latched onto them and given them watertight agreements. She was put under considerable pressure, but she held out. She had the backing of her firm in Jakarta, the support of legal specialists in maritime and extra-territorial law. She worked her contracted job, she gave birth to Leendert, then Alex, all while battling the Institute's increasingly hostile attempts to shut her down.

An unfortunate side effect of the suit was that their names went public, something there was no way around. This happened eleven years ago, two years after Houston. She and

Jack and a one-year-old Leendert moved three times in as many months. Already the legal costs were spiralling. She had to hire her own security people, to protect them from the Institute and from the conspiracists and fanatics who managed to track them down. Leigh – years after her death – had become the face of *Proscenium 1*, and for a while Helena and her family bore the brunt of this lunatic interest.

The Institute's refusal to countenance transparency surprised her, angered her, then finally intrigued her. The organisation disbanded shortly after the legal process began. This just interested her more. Their determination to reveal nothing was striking. Years into the process, with public interest waning, everything caught up in the legal quagmire, she decided, on a whim, to use her firm's site to advertise a holding box in Jakarta bay. Anyone with information pertaining to the Institute in the years leading up to January 2031 was urged to send supporting documents to this address. Jack warned her not to do this. Everyone agreed it was a bad idea. She knew she was inviting in a fresh deluge of conspiracists.

Almost all of it was junk. Maybe 10 per cent of what came in appeared reasonable enough to begin with – anonymous accounts from a sympathetic whistleblower; investigations pursued by a group of professional astronomers – but these either included nothing that she hadn't already uncovered herself, or else ended up veering into absurd and

unsubstantiated speculation. The more interesting corres-
pondences, she noted, never included a return address.

Sometimes she'd sense a pattern, questioning whether two
apparently disparate sources really did converge. One of
these convergences was about lights. Several separate pack-
ages claimed evidence of an unusually fierce light moving
through the sky on the night of 31 January 2031. The authors
based their claims on over a hundred independent reports.
They placed the event within the same three seconds and
over an area of 16 square nautical miles. No one said what
this object was, or what had happened to it. None of the
investigations had got anywhere. But she noted that the
lights fell within range of *Nereus*'s expected re-entry, which
as far as she was aware hadn't been publicly disclosed.

She would have preferred if Jack had laughed. Instead,
when she came home one night clutching meteorological
charts he looked right at her, brushed the hair from her eyes.
'Are you OK?' he said. 'Do you think it might be an idea to
see someone?'

A year later she received information about a cargo ship
in the mid-Atlantic, a Russian vessel registered in Panama
with an unlikely name – the *James and Mary*. The *James and
Mary* transported latex from north-east Brazil to Esbjerg in
Denmark, using only a skeleton crew, the minimum required
for automated sea hauls. It was known as a barren and
uninteresting stretch of water; they never saw anything

noteworthy. But on this particular journey an incident was logged with maritime authorities mid-ocean. It was pure chance the second mate was looking west out of the porthole at just the right moment. There, 50 metres away, flat on a piece of driftwood, was her sister.

She put the package down. She hadn't expected this. She'd become expert at spotting the signs, and everything indicated this one had been sent in earnest. She took a few moments, sitting in the uncovered section of the noodle bar, looking out at the heavily industrialised bay, listening to the clang and screech of the massive port that reminded her a little of home, of the tours Geert had taken them on when they were young. Rotterdam port was so enormous she and Leigh had imagined it a separate country, bringing passports they'd created at home not just for entry into the dazzling territory full of lights, alarms, inscrutable block-based architecture and elegantly choreographed movement, but in case the opportunity came for them to flee, jump on a ship, begin on an adventure that would take them further away than they ever could have dreamed.

The fact this had actually happened to Leigh – that she really had made it aboard such an unlikely adventure – made everything all the more bittersweet. When these absurd claims reached Helena through the holding box, she couldn't help but feel just the faintest frisson of excitement, a desire to cast off on an equally unlikely adventure herself, travelling somewhere unfathomably distant where at last she'd meet her sister at the end.

Helena had no choice. It didn't matter what Jack and the others said. The money wasn't important; she didn't even care, at this point, about her own sanity. Coincidence or not, the timings just about worked, linking the lights and the woman cast away at sea.

She got a recommendation from outside the firm. A one-off fee, payable upfront. Two weeks later the investigator told her no ship existed matching the *James and Mary*'s description. Nothing registered in Panama. Nothing in Russia. The dossier included breakdowns of the latex export trade and video footage of ships unloading at Esbjerg port. The *James and Mary* was a ghost. All trace of it was gone. More likely – the investigator was doing everything in his power to soften the blow – it had never existed.

Someone wrote to her about a fifty-five-year-old mechanic working out of a garage in Buenos Aires. Apparently he lived alone and had long-term memory loss. He spoke with a Serbian accent. He had a protruding crus helix which, in the pictures the media released, were identical to the ears of Karius Marković. She laughed at this one with Jack over dinner.

By now she'd developed a pretty thick hide. Nothing really upset her. She was just tired. Walking through the warm rain and the haze, crossing the bridge, she wondered if maybe enough time hadn't passed. Maybe she should consider dropping the whole thing. It was the first time she'd ever really thought that. She couldn't imagine that, after all this time, something would be waiting for her that would change her life.

TWO

After losing contact with *Nereus*, and after the scheduled return date of the ship passed, the Institute launched several uncrewed scout probes towards the heliopause. None of them returned. Contact broke off in separate stages. The Institute's official line was that something catastrophic had occurred inside the propulsion system; this explained both the loss of *Nereus* and the scout probes. Research on the power was halted, a moratorium put up on all future use of the technology. It seemed pretty clear cut, and the official explanation went generally uncontested. Helena's pursuit through the courts got little backing, and outside of the dwindling number of fanatics continuing to write to her, the *Proscenium 1* mission faded out of view.

The money, personnel, and resources behind the Institute were largely funnelled into Cable International Ltd, a Dutch conglomerate with a long history in communications infrastructure. The bulk of their recent work was in internet provision, and around 2026 they had started looking into low-orbit satellites. This, according to Helena's research, had marked the first discussion with ICORS, and led to everything that followed. CI initially wanted to hire consultants to price out the project, but pretty quickly someone at ICORS saw an opportunity and the companies were effectively, if not legally, merged. After the huge losses incurred by *Proscenium 1*, they redirected their focus onto two areas exclusively: commercial satellite installation and asteroid mining.

Because a lot of the groundwork had already been done, they were able to initiate the asteroid programme pretty quickly. In 2037 – six years after *Proscenium 1*'s failure – the first ore was extracted from Aether, a mid-sized M-type orbiting Mars. After this success, the programme was rolled out on a much bigger scale, and in eighteen months there were over 100 active operations. The profits quickly exceeded *Proscenium*'s losses, and the programme was scaled up once again.

Meanwhile, people were dying. The crews manning the operations were known as *fours*, sometimes spelled *fores*, which led to confusion about the name's origin. Until she actively began researching CI, Helena didn't realise it derived from a statistical curiosity: whatever the scale, and regardless of training levels and health and safety instruction, approximately 4 per cent of all employees working off-world on the asteroid programme never made it back. This seemed high at first, and CI's spokespersons assured the public that as time went on, and knowledge and expertise grew, the number would drift close to zero. But it didn't. It always stayed around 4 per cent. She had to hunt the figures, which were no longer publicly accessible. Pressed on the issue, CI spoke of 'unfortunate collateral losses'. They paid large compensatory sums to the families, and wages originally were so high that attracting employees was never a problem, but maybe their most successful tactic was their hubristic, faux-imperial language. The company were innovators; every single person working on the programme was a pioneer, helping to shape Earth's future, and the people who died off-world were heroes.

This wasn't how the programme had initially been conceived. ICORS had planned on doing everything remotely, autonomously. Machines would dock on the rocks, drill and excavate and bring the riches home. Helena found papers transcribed from a conference in Ridgecrest California, where her sister had trained, and the programme envisaged there had barely resembled the reality. Again it was about money. The research necessary to launch a fully automated programme was expensive and would take years to carry out. They couldn't afford to wait that long. And now that it was up and running and expanding all the time, and – bar the 4 per cent – proving relatively straightforward, there was no indication of methodology changing. CI removed all reference to autonomous missions from their literature. Human labour continued to prove cheaper and easier to manage, and given the current profit level, she imagined CI would be happy to prolong this method for as long as possible.

All missions launched from and landed on 'the wall', a modular quarantine station orbiting Earth. Employees spent forty days there either side of a mission. As the industry developed, and CI's profits escalated, the wall grew bigger. At the moment, capacity neared 10,000, but plans would see this expand significantly. Staff described it as similar to the accommodation zones in offshore oil platforms. They went online and locked into VR while their body adapted to low gravity and guzzled nutrients. She hadn't been able to prove this yet – toxicity records remained the legal property of the company – but she suspected they were fed boosters to condition them for work. Some of the returned *fours* she'd interviewed described feeling more aggressive, more wired, and requiring less sleep after passing through the wall. CI said they would not engage with anecdotal reports, and suggested the reactions described were perfectly natural and consistent with the thrill of working as an off-world pioneer.

The wall was visually breathtaking: a gleaming white Earth border spinning in space, an administrative and medical transit zone taking people off and onto the planet. It wasn't uncommon for people to become lost inside it. CI reserved the right to 'extend employees' residency indefinitely', without any requirement to prove medical grounds. Although the return quarantine period was listed, like the outward stage, as forty days, the reality was often far longer. It wasn't clear why it would be in CI's interest to detain people. She was aware – Jack made sure of this – of her propensity to fall for outlandish conspiracy, but she thought it possible that CI's pharma division used the extra time to conduct research. She knew Leigh's ship had fed data to the Institute and that it was valuable, and she suspected it had been put towards medical innovations; the wall was the perfect place to trial these.

At some point she realised she might be able to help people. She could be useful. It wasn't just about Leigh anymore; it was bigger than one person. After starting out in financial law she'd shifted towards land rights, and now she worked with communities and mediated between them and the state. The physical basis of the country was changing at a quicker rate than before, and she found this interesting, and urgent. She wondered if maybe Leigh had been an influence, nudging her in this more environmentally focused direction, even before *Proscenium*. And what she found, as the case rolled on interminably, was that her experience there was useful preparation towards offering assistance to the families of the 4 per cent.

There were just six of them to begin with, meeting every Sunday evening EST, twelve hours behind where she was. She rarely spoke, and saw her role largely as an administrator, an organiser, an intermediary between families and the organisations that might support them. Though she wanted to help, she was realistic in how much, practically speaking, they could achieve, and cynical and self-aware enough to realise she was doing this partly for her own benefit. Listening helped. Being around these people, even remotely, was good for her. Even the faintest suggestion that another person had gone through something remotely similar made her feel slightly and temporarily less adrift.

It's always 'disappeared', or 'lost'. 'I lost him on *Alpha 7482*, malfunction in depressurisation through re-entry onto host ship. Disappearance somewhere between private quarters and the mid-deck.' Is it still death, in the same way, if it doesn't happen on Earth? As much as the astronauts themselves, they are landmarks too, families of the first humans to disappear in space.

They brought in experts in maritime law who described the pursuit of people missing at sea. In some countries it remained the case that if someone disappeared in 'a body of water with no visible end' then it was legally impossible to declare them dead. The law resisted the disappeared, actively fighting against their almost certain fate. If the smallest sliver of possibility remained that the lost person had been swept onto an island or picked up by a passing ship, then the courts refused to confirm them gone. This actually worked against the families' interests ultimately, as they were unable to inherit property, unable to hold a funeral, blocked from the ritual acceptance of death. Though the description held meaning for each of them, Leigh's case was exceptional, and

Helena in particular recognised the truth of her vanishing in a place without end.

Maybe it's particularly hard for them. It's difficult to compare. Maybe it's that having someone die in space clarifies the original process. It's a miracle we're born and a miracle we die. You see this anew in space. It's happening all over again. The first children will be born there soon, in trials, shuttled back down shortly after. People keep disappearing in space, and they need to counteract that trend, fertilise space, bring birth into space.

There are specific reasons why it might be particularly difficult to accept losing someone this way. Always, the information is minimal. A single line, maybe two. You can't picture it. You've never even seen a photograph of a ship's interior. What does it feel like? How warm is it? What does the food taste like? Do you dream in space? How do you bathe? If you can't relate to it, can't conceive of the person being there, then a gap is created, and the mind exploits the reality chasm. The reason I can't accept it is because it didn't happen. If I can't imagine what that world was like, it never existed. They didn't die there because they didn't live there. There is no basis for the reality. The place can't be imagined, therefore it can't be substantial. This is a difficult position to be in. This is why they have the group.

She knows that the information missing until now will not, should it suddenly appear, fill the lacunae. The chasm is too profound. She will never truly believe her sister is gone. She accepts this, understands this. But she will continue trying anyway. It is no longer really about closure, a coming to terms with things. It is more a question of honour. The story of what happened to Leigh deserves to be known by at least one person who has loved her. That is a minimum. That is the least a life deserves. To not disappear entirely in the dark. She will not stop. She will continue exploring this dark, this infernal bureaucracy, this dead and static air. She will bring it to the light. It's for Leigh and it's for her. Not to bring her sister back, and not to release her, finally, either. Something else. A different kind of closeness, a new kind of sharing.

There is a photograph she keeps, an original stuck to the wall in the kitchen in their apartment. She's had it scanned and copied but the original has gained significance as an object in itself, the slick matte feel of the material passed between hands over the decades. She and Leigh are standing in the garden. It's winter, they're dressed against the cold, and she thinks they're on the cusp of breaking into laughter. You can see the faint cloud of breath between them. It's the one breath, a single cloud. It seems to her a miracle: that the beginning of their laughter has been caught in the atmosphere, held in permanent record. There's a tinge of red in the blue sky; she remembers it was getting late and they were about to be called in, they didn't have long, but as soon as the photo was taken – the single frame following the one captured – they turned and fled, out into the field, abandoned over the grass, pressing into the frost and leaving the ghost of their footsteps as another, shorter record of the fact that they were there.

It's easy to romanticise her now she's gone, particularly given the way it happened, and inevitably this is the version passed down to Alex and Leendert, but it's not authentic, and as tempting as it is she knows she has to fight it, keep the more difficult and complicated and messy reality alive. One of the consequences of Leigh's disappearance is that she's been forced to become more like her, in that she too now holds on to the past in the way her sister did. This hadn't been one of her sister's better traits. Leigh had been nostalgic, determinedly sentimental; she never loved something so much as the moment it was gone. This was a cheaper, more contrived version of emotion, standing in for more difficult truths; amusingly, it had become Leigh's legacy.

That she'd loved her deeply went without saying, but Leigh was also one of the most self-centred people Helena had ever known. For her whole life, Leigh quietly insisted on playing the victim, always thinking first of herself. She pushed away anyone who attempted to get close, and then dramatised and bathed in the bittersweet melancholy of rejection. Helena couldn't get through to her – she wouldn't listen. Sometimes she'd wanted to scream: *This is your doing; you don't have to live this way*, but it was pointless. When she called her, Leigh complaining at her insistence on video, preferring to communicate with an idealised, sentimental version of her younger sister, she'd pick up that tone of suffering and resignation right away. Leigh questioned her, not out of curiosity but just to emphasise the contrast to her own life. Sometimes – on a birthday call, or over Christmas, when they'd had a couple of drinks – Leigh would try to steer the conversation round to Rotterdam and their childhoods, when nothing could have interested Helena less. She never understood what Leigh was driving at, what she wanted to say. She'd allude to things vaguely, swilling drink, tilting her head down shyly. So their father had been harsh and uncommunicative. That wasn't uncommon. They weren't the first family to have a distant father with anger issues. A couple of times she'd sensed that Leigh was alluding to violence. This surprised her. She didn't remember any of this; nothing out of the ordinary, anyway. So Geert occasionally slapped them lightly. This was just what fathers did back then. It certainly hadn't been excessive, not as she remembers it. Leigh's smile suggested she knew something Helena didn't, and these are the only moments she can recall of her sister displaying a superior attitude towards her. As if her experiences privileged her to something Helena could never understand. She wishes she'd told her to just let go. Leigh insisted on letting her childhood define her. The proof of an alternative was right there in front of her – Helena – and Leigh always resented this.

The irony was that it hadn't actually been like that at all. Leigh wasn't the victim. It was she, Helena, who had taken responsibility for their parents in ways Leigh never could. She who had made the effort to be there for Geert over his last difficult years at the *Waterschappen*, when his health was failing and his days were getting darker. She who'd made arrangements for the funeral service and ensured the house was paid off and that Fenna was OK. And more than anything, she who'd acknowledged the reality of their mother's decline and accepted the fact she needed help. She who had visited Rotterdam three times to check on Fenna, to talk to her colleagues and her doctor, and she who had ultimately taken a month's leave to help Fenna move into the nursing home – without question the single hardest thing she's ever had to do.

Leigh had a way of talking about problems that made it seem as though they posed a greater threat to her than anyone else, as if she suffered to a greater extent than other people. When they spoke about the first signs of Fenna's illness, Leigh just tacitly assumed it was less of a burden for Helena to deal with than for her. If it annoyed Leigh, as she claimed it did, that people always assumed she was the younger sister, then it never seemed to have occurred to her to ask why. The mythology of her past – the melancholy she associated inexorably with childhood – seemed, in Leigh's eyes, to give her an out, to free her from all responsibilities pertaining to family. This was recklessly, dangerously, unforgivably immature. Helena always knew this – she'd described it to Jack enough times – but that didn't mean that a single look from Leigh couldn't, in spite of everything she knew to be true, utterly break her. Leigh, in this sense – her ability to manipulate her – was her greatest weakness.

Something Fenna and Helena had often remarked on was how much Leigh resembled her father. The idea would have humiliated her. She was always so unforgiving with him. Helena remembers, distinctly, how proud Geert was when Leigh started university, and how crushed when she said she didn't need his help with moving. Geert had booked two days off work, but he never told her this. She continually pushed him away. Once a month they tried to have a family meal at a restaurant, and Leigh did everything she could to make this awkward, refusing to even look Geert in the eye. If the atmosphere was terrible, it was even worse afterwards, when they'd said goodbyes and seen Leigh off at the tram stop, and the three of them drove home in near silence. She really hurt him. And the remoteness, the scarcity of communication, the determination to push others away, was just as present in him. They repeated identical behaviours such as preparing unnecessarily before going to bed: setting out clothing, taking the cereal box out of the cupboard, laying out a newspaper or magazine by a particular chair. This amused Helena; Leigh and Geert seemed equally awed by the shapeless and limitless expanse of the future, hence these absurd little rituals of anticipatory control, which Fenna often, without thinking, ultimately tidied away, so that all preparations counted for nothing in the end. Both of them got anxious from the sheer scale of what lay beyond them. They reacted to this by trying to become independent, cutting themselves off from other people, strength expressed as attachment to the insignificant. Both of them were scared, but they would never have admitted this.

In the support group, the implication in their reference to their loved ones as lost was that they might find them. Helena became conversant in the legal theory of missing persons, the history of the practice across many territories and millennia. The most interesting aspect was the hinterland occupied by those unrecovered but not yet gone. These people were included in census charts and paid their taxes. They remained in marriages and wanted for crimes. In almost every way – every criterion except the last matter, the physical instantiation of the self – they were active members of society. This was why they called them lost. They walked in the hinterland and they were still there with them. Leigh's awkward, sheepish grin greets them every morning in the kitchen, and Leendert has recently bought a microscope and expressed an interest in the sea. Helena felt, if not at peace, if not close to acceptance, then a quiet belief in her ability to go on. This was new. She pictured the coming years and for once they didn't overwhelm her. She could see how the future would play out, and it was OK.

Then the letter arrived. She almost wishes it hadn't. If it had come earlier, it might have been different. She might have been ready for it then. She can't open all this up again; it will hurt her, destabilise her, expose her. It's not logical. It's the last thing she needs, the last thing she should reasonably do. But it's too late now. She has made her decision. If you could even call it a decision. She has no choice. That's why she's doing this: flying, in three days' time, first to Singapore, then to Cape Town, and finally to Ascension.

THREE

Everything happened quickly. Six weeks between the arrival of the letter and the first leg of their journey out. It was clear immediately that this was different from all the other communications: plain manilla envelope, neat handwriting, single sheet inside. (Some of the documents ran to hundreds of pages: academic articles, reports, letters, strange 'novels', faux 'accounts' of the voyage.) But what really marked it as exceptional was its relatively circumspect claims. There was no vast conspiracy, no plot against the world. The author stated simply that she had a family connection to the mission and believed she could bring Helena closer to Leigh. The phrasing was designed to get a response. She mulled it over before replying, then, one evening, after the kids had gone to bed and Jack was out at work, she poured a scotch and sat down at her desk, set up a burner email and before she could dissuade herself sent a one-line answer. She was about to shut down the screen when a new message alert pinged. They exchanged a series of short and simple messages; she wanted to prove this was a person she could talk to, that someone was actually there.

She'd intended to wait another week but only held out three days. She set up another new email and made contact again – a slightly longer message this time, three lines. A response came an hour later. Helena asked, 'How do I know this is real?'

'You don't. But if we keep talking, you might believe me.'

They wrote regularly and at greater length. She almost shut it down when the author told her, 'I lost someone on the mission too.' So the story has changed. 'It's not like that. Please, let me explain.'

Maria was in her late forties, a couple of years older than Helena. Lived in California with her husband and daughter, worked as a high-school teacher. In another life she'd been in pharma, but after her first child she'd quit and retrained. She scanned documents to verify all this. Driving licence, teacher's registration. Showed proof of address and attached a time-stamped photograph. Helena didn't ask for verification, but Maria insisted. 'It's only fair – you've plenty of reason to doubt me, I appreciate that.'

Maria's mother was an astrophysicist and had been a senior mission director on *Proscenium 1*. She had led the US arm of the whole thing. For almost two years – covering the mission and the months after – Maria hadn't seen her, which had just happened to coincide with one of the most important periods in her life. There had been a ridiculous amount of security attached to the mission, and Uria hadn't been able to tell her where she was. Around nine months in, she stopped calling. This was odd, because Maria had been due to give birth. Her husband Chris said she should contact the police, but what would she say? She didn't even know if her mother was in the country. When Uria eventually did call, something was different. Her voice was less substantial. She sounded groggy, confused, not really herself. Naturally Maria was worried. For the first time she considered her mother as potentially vulnerable. All her life, she'd never seen her ill, but she sounded as if she was recovering from something. Exhaustion, some form of collapse. That would explain the blackout, the two-week disappearance. Uria in a hospital, fluids pumped into her arm. It would be her own fault – she worked too hard. Something like this had been inevitable. But when she heard her mother's frail and distant voice, she softened. When can I see you? Tell me where you are, and I'll come out, anywhere, doesn't matter. It was a ridiculous thing to say, the baby was overdue now and she knew Uria was under strict security, but she asked anyway.

It was a little under a year after this that Maria and her mother finally met up and she at last introduced Uria to her granddaughter. Maria tried to hide her shock: Uria had lost a lot of weight. She wore a headscarf. She didn't say anything at first, the three of them on the beach at Santa Cruz as the sun came up. The delight in her mother's eyes, tears welling but not falling as she lifted Lily for the first time. Moving over the ground like she wasn't there. The waves gently thudding on the sand, the sun, even through the parasols, fiercer every second. She had never seen her mother as purely happy as in that moment.

Uria died sixteen days later. Stage four glioma. This was what she meant when she said she'd lost someone to the mission too. The last two years of her mother's life were a lacuna. She didn't know where she spent them, what her days were like, only that she was working on *Proscenium*. It was pretty clear the mission itself killed her. It took her life, exhausted her, ravaged her. It consumed her unreasonably, unnaturally. Uria gave everything she had to it and when it was over, she just collapsed; she had nothing left.

She had tried to find out everything she could about her mother's last years. 'By this stage you'd gone public with the lawsuit. Some of the info coming out explained certain things: my mother's absence, her distance on the phone, the feeling that part of her had already gone. She was devastated. Nothing like that had happened in her career, losing all crew. Like you, I tried to find out more. If I knew what had happened, even just the broad details, I might understand a little of what my mother went through.

'Obviously, there are a lot of blocks in place. It isn't easy to access this information. I've been pushing at this for more than a decade too. But I have an advantage over you. My mother was a senior figure in the industry for a long time. I know people. And my husband's in the military – that doesn't hurt either. I have some access to Uria's medical and travel records. This is what I've come to tell you, why I finally wrote to you.

'I found three locations that I'm reasonably certain about. I think they correspond to pre-mission, active mission, and post-mission. The ship launched from a port in French Guiana. I don't know how long she was there, or your sister and the other crew. I think weeks at least, possibly months. There's a wall around the port, high security. I've tried to visit but it's not possible. For the duration of the mission itself, I think Mission Control was hosted in a converted military academy in Florida. I drove there but it doesn't exist, there is no land, it's swamp now. Then there's post-mission; this is what I think might be pertinent. The location was just below the equator, an island stuck in the middle of the ocean. A strange place to conduct post-mission, right? Not necessarily. I'm pretty certain this is the land nearest to where the re-entry capsule was due to land. I believe your sister and the other crew were scheduled to return at this latitude, and after the capsule was recovered they were to be brought to the island to recover. Of course, they never got there.'

She hasn't flown in nine years and the airport takes her by surprise. The blaze of sunlight through the glass walls. Airships banking and jet engines accelerating. Every forty-six minutes the soft boom of the sound barrier breaking. Her balance is a little off. She can't make out the announcements. It's like she's underwater – the pressure and turbulence in her ears, the resistance her limbs face on every outward stretch.

It's not that she's afraid of flying; she isn't consciously avoiding airports, and in fact has flown several times in the months following the announcement of Leigh's death. But after so long away, the violence of the accelerations, combined with the casual transfer of blocks of people across large distances, unnerves her. She hasn't flown for nine years largely because there hasn't been any reason to. Travel between the islands is more efficient by water. They use water-taxis in the cities too. There is the argument that in her work, the perspective you get when looking down on the islands from an aircraft is an advantage that no end of satellite feeds can reproduce. She appreciates the theory, but maintains that her priority is the land as experienced by the people who live there. It's too easy to become addicted to the aerial view.

In the last two decades, 7 per cent of the territory has disappeared. This itself is a miracle, a stupendous feat of engineering – it should have been much worse. But the country isn't the same, and not being the same is the new condition. Officially, the state's cartography department produces a new set of images every three months, presenting the latest version of the land. In reality, the total land volume shifts by the minute. Last year was a watershed: for the first time in the historical record more land was created than lost.

Things are changing. Maybe it's part of a trend, though she cautions against complacency. Her work falls broadly into two categories: recognising, reclassifying, duly amending the status of all disappeared land, and ensuring that all newly created land adheres to the formidable, labyrinthine criteria set out by the state. If new land doesn't meet a particular criterion then it can't be lived on. There are 700 islands currently red-taped, due either to state or developer corruption. But this is a relatively small number. Developers are becoming better and more compliant all the time.

This will be the longest continuous period she has ever spent away from her children. When she first told Jack, he didn't seem to believe her, nodding absently while hacking at lines of vegetables. She booked the leave, organised transport; still he didn't believe her. Three nights ago he exploded, telling her she was insane, she doesn't know the first thing about this woman, she might not be who she says she is, identity is easily faked. She watched him, miles across the bed in the dark. So he was afraid too. Afraid of different things, but afraid all the same. 'I'm going,' she told him. 'I have done all the diligence I possibly can, and there is no way I am not taking this journey.'

'What is it you're hoping to achieve?' he said. 'What do you want to get from this island?'

She watched herself particularly closely in the days preceding flight. Leendert noticed it too. *Mum, what is wrong with you?* She held her body tight, and as she prepared food, or dressed, or moved across the room, she did it in a controlled frenzy. She felt as well as saw it. There was panic involved, and it was about time. She was desperate to complete every action in case it was suddenly taken from her. She wasn't rushing to another place, she was completely committed to this one, and she was scared that she would lose it, that it would be pulled away before she could finish it. It was about Leigh in some way, of course. The prospect of getting closer to Leigh, the outrageous idea of travelling somewhere meaningful.

Alex noted another symptom. 'Mum, why won't you watch till the end of things? You've missed out the last episode of almost every single show.'

On the first flight – two hours to Singapore – she went over the documents and reports once more. New information, courtesy of Maria, was that CI had begun buying up territory with a view to laying down mineral rights. As the company experimented with new drilling methods on asteroids, the same systems would come back to open up Earth. And one of those territories, Maria suggested, just happened to be an island in the mid-Atlantic. Assuming everything went smoothly, she and Maria would land there in a little under twenty-two hours.

Cable International had a long history on Ascension.

(Technically, it wasn't actually Cable International, but several smaller companies that would later come under its bracket.) In the early twentieth century they'd used the island as a staging post to spool undersea cables between Rotterdam and Montreal. Later, they'd run lines directly from Ascension to Recife in Brazil. CI were responsible for much of the infrastructure on the island, operating masts, aerials, relay sites and satellite tracking stations. Villages sprung up around camps installed for their workers. There were huge, monolithic radio telescopes lining the coast: listening stations, allegedly, for intelligence services.

The island was one of the last remaining of the UK's 'overseas territories', a colonial relic. First discovered by the Portuguese in 1501, for centuries the only people setting foot there were sailors breaking up journeys from the Cape of Good Hope, feasting on the migrating turtles and the goat stock brought by the early arrivals. Crews left letters in the crevices between rocks in Long Beach, so ships passing the other way could bring them home. In 1815, with Napoleon held in St Helena (the nearest land, at 1,300 kilometres away), the UK set up a garrison on Ascension. They continued to use the island as a strategic territory through WWII and the Falklands War. The RAF occasionally still touched down there. The rumours of significant mineral deposits in the surrounding waters – including allusions to a deep-sea vent – explained the enduring military presence. Everything indicated a lucrative collaboration between the British state and CI.

The more she read about the island, the stranger it seemed. For a relatively unpromising scrap of land – 88 square kilometres of infertile shore and mountain – Ascension attracted a lot of interest. One corner was technically US territory – the air force paraded, performing manoeuvres and selling fast food for dollars not recognised anywhere else on the island. She must have laughed aloud, waking up an elderly passenger two seats along. She mouthed an apology, re-fixed her headphones, and continued reading.

The most remarkable aspect of the island was never stated outright: it was and always had been illegal to live there. Military personnel saw out one-year terms, unable to tolerate the heat, isolation and tedium a minute longer. A handful of researchers visited every year, monitoring – at least until the colony's disappearance – the giant green turtles, and making studies of the unusual forest conditions in the island's peak, Green Mountain, a previously barren rock deliberately and painstakingly fertilised with seedlings from around the world, an effort conceived by Charles Darwin after his visit on the *Beagle* voyage in 1836, and now considered a model of terraforming of particular interest to CI, as the company expanded its asteroid programme and began looking outward at the inner planets.

The population was listed at 800, a rolling roster of

construction workers, soldiers, communication engineers and service staff shuttled in from St Helena ('the Saints') operating the three hotels, the two bars, the single supermarket. As she continued to pore over the literature, everything indicated that not a single person had lived out their life there. Families weren't encouraged. The island accommodated neither the old nor the young: there was only the most basic of clinics, no qualified midwife and no funeral home or cemetery. The more she read, the more convinced she was this couldn't be a real place. It seemed radically incomplete, created in a cursory manner, drawn by a child's hand in primary colours. The names of the island's landmarks just confirmed this: Deception Bay; Comfortless Cove; Green Mountain; Two Boats Village; Dark Crater; Devil's Riding School; Unicorn Point; Sisters Peak. At this point, beginning the descent on the first of her connecting flights, it seemed dazzling that they would land there, set foot on this place, that they were putting their trust in this strange and unfathomable island to support them. Everything about Ascension seemed invented, make-believe, in thrall to a child's sense of wonder and fantasy. Of course *every* territory was invented – Ascension was no different in that sense – but the transparency with which Ascension admitted it was unusual, and provocative. Helena's pulse began to increase, as she thought again about stepping off the plane – and what kind of aircraft could possibly take them there? – onto the island.

The island was the ideal location to host a returning space-crew: the remoteness of the position, the deep ocean setting, the military presence and the absence of a civilian population. But there seemed to be something else, something consonant between the *Proscenium 1* mission and Ascension. Both of them were scarcely credible, outrageous pieces of fiction. That her sister could have trained for and travelled on a deep-space mission was something she would never fully accept. It seemed only right that the place the crew would land on was similarly hard to believe. The thing about Ascension that provoked her, and disturbed her co-passenger with her laughter, was its exposure of how absurd, and unlikely, human settlement was. Ascension showed her, more than anything else, that her sister's inclusion in the *Proscenium* mission was no more unlikely, no more demanding of suspended disbelief, than her birth was. She gave one final smile as the wheels touched down on the tarmac in Singapore, still just the first stage, remarking that the original science-fiction story – the impossible adventure full of wonder and awe – was merely the existence of the species, all the moments she and her sister and their family and every other living person had shared.

Cape Town International is enormous, she thinks, pacing Departures in a state of some anxiety. On three separate occasions she checks prices for an immediate ticket home.

She clutches her satchel, undoes the clasp in her hair, straightens her skirt. What is she doing here? Jack was right, this is ridiculous.

'Helena?'

She turns on her seat, looks up. 5 foot 4 inches, pale-skinned, just a little overweight, with short auburn hair and fierce, glowing grey-green irises. Single shoulder bag, sensible shoes.

'Hello. I didn't recognise you right away; you look younger than you do on screen. I'm Maria.'

She gets up, puts out her hand, and bursts into tears.

FOUR

They land at night in a lightning storm, blue flares over the
runway. The island only comes into view at the last possible
moment before descending. There is no sound, and when
the lightning ceases the whole island is in darkness again.
There is nothing there. The doors open, releasing a wall of
humid air. A bitter, buttery scent she almost recognises. They
stand out on the runway with two dozen passengers and
crew. Nobody is going anywhere. There's a single hangar
parallel to the runway, and only one other aircraft on the
ground. The runway's racked with crevices and potholes,
weeds growing a foot high through the tarmac. With no
perimeter fence, the runway fades into rubble and off into
dry fields.

An overweight and bearded middle-aged man in khaki
shirt and shorts approaches from a hangar. He greets several
of the passengers and hugs them. They are talking quietly
and laughing; she can't make out what they're saying. She
hears a clicking sound, their passports scanned. She fixes a
smile as the official approaches; he grins broadly, showing
all his teeth, and stamps a large seabird across the electronic
page. 'Welcome to Ascension,' he says, before bowing a little.

They walk past the hangar into a small open car park. She
spots two other officials wearing the same khaki gear, sitting
on green plastic chairs and fanning themselves. People

emerge from Land Rovers and greet the other passengers. Soon it's just Maria and her left. 'You have a car?' the official says. 'You have accommodation?' He's still smiling warmly, but maybe his tone has shifted. She looks around the car park. They are hopelessly ill-prepared. She can't get a sense of perspective, can't tell whether they're at sea level or altitude. There are no lights anywhere. Even the runway has gone dark.

Maria is talking to the official, showing him receipts on her phone. He picks up his reading glasses from around his neck, grasping them very precisely and delicately and placing them securely over his eyes. He studies the screen, squints a little. 'Hang on,' he says, 'I'll take you. Five-minute drive.'

The humidity is really something, even compared to home. She sits next to Jerry in the front and leans out of the fully opened window for the feel of their movement through the air. She tilts her head up and can't believe what she sees, the almost purple darkness and the huge, vivid spread of stars. The sky is both immensely distant and close enough to touch.

They take a bend and she sees they are coming down a gentle stretch. There's a white arc ahead and occasionally it moves – the shore, the edge of the island, a row of dark low buildings against it. Jerry doesn't say anything, just drives at a good speed down the black and empty road, every switch of the gearstick making a satisfying clicking sound. She's forgotten what time it is. Her phone must be in her bag. She feels a little drunk, delirious. It's the ridiculousness of the stars, it's the tininess of the island, it's the fact they are there, in a place she still can't quite believe is real.

They slip past a tall, smooth rock, red in the headlights, and at the next bend Jerry takes the speed down and she sees a faded white sign stamped 'Georgetown'. Everything she has seen – the road, the fields, the unclear buildings – is apparent only as an essential form. It's her sleepiness or the darkness or both, but she can't see the details, can't see the features that make things distinct. The small settlement faces a single line of surf. There is a single, massive red rock behind it. The fields they wind through are mute black expanses. She has the same impression she had on seeing the stars – incredulity. It's disorienting, beguiling. She is certain she has never been anywhere even remotely like this. More reasonable questions drift away – how will they spend the next two weeks? What can they realistically hope to achieve here? Something else is happening here, and she has to give herself to it, lose herself in this place.

They roll to a stop outside a long narrow building. The surf is only 20 metres ahead and she can't stop staring at it.

From the firm way Jerry thumps the car door shut she judges they are the only guests. Maria says it's 03:11. They go inside the motel. The rooms have a single bed, desk lamp, chest of drawers, sink, glass wall that slides out onto concrete at the back. Jerry puts them six doors apart from each other, which surprises her. She taps the wall and feels the boards give a little – so that's it. Thin barriers. Toilets at one end, kitchen the other. 'Is there a map of Georgetown?' Maria asks, to which Jerry gives a wry smile and chuckles. Helena smiles too, as if she would never have said such a thing, and as a look of mild hurt passes across Maria's face, she's surprised at how bad this makes her feel – the realisation that she has done something to make this person feel small.

They are exhausted, with still that hint of delirium. She thanks Jerry, who casually waves back as he walks towards his car, says goodnight to Maria and sits on the thin, aged mattress with the door still open. She spots her face in the sink mirror: she's grinning inanely, like a teenager again, returning home drunk. Even the simple room, with its single bed and sink, is like the dorm she stayed in in her first year at university. She recalls that she has a husband, two children, that she is forty-five years old. She gives a loud snort which she only partially conceals; she can hear Maria rattling around outside and she's mortified that she might have heard her too.

She lies down on the bed, looking up at the thin ceiling, the other side of which is a multitude of stars, and they are turning, or rather Earth is turning, everything is spinning, there is a thick odour still in the solid air, the gaining boom of the water, the electric drone of some kind of insect, and she feels herself give way, radiantly a part of this, radiantly happy, spread out on the bed, and she barely even notices Maria peering in at her as she walks across the landing to her own room.

The island has no spaghetti but it's OK because a shipment is due to arrive in seven days from northern Italy via Cape Town and ultimately St Helena. Whatever food was brought over on their own flight apparently didn't include pasta, or else it was immediately snapped up – maybe there is a waiting list, a hierarchy. So Maria has to improvise. She insists. She enjoys cooking. And they have this whole big kitchen to themselves.

There is a haphazard assortment of spices and sauces in the cupboard, leftovers from a thousand lonely contractors. Maria exclaims as she alights on Tabasco. 'In this humidity?' Helena tells her. 'Are you crazy?'

She checks at the store if there is a ratio per person or anything like that, an official register. She really wants eggs. The assistant smiles and says not exactly, just don't go crazy. Somehow Jerry is in the store too, in jeans and shirtsleeves. Lounging against the counter, he's utterly at home here. He smiles at them, toothpick poking out the side of his mouth. Maybe this is just how it is, in the settlement, the same few faces going round and round. Six eggs. Six is reasonable. There is always the bar and the restaurant if they get stuck.

They leave the store, the only people on the whole island wearing shorts. It's not even nine and already the heat is unbelievable. A four-minute walk carrying three bags each almost kills them. Is there a water limit, she thinks, how many showers are permissible per day? Did Jerry tell them?

They are famished. Bread and eggs and fruit and mugs of black coffee. She has to remind herself she has been around this person only a little over twenty-four hours. It doesn't feel like that. Maria is so easy. She was worried on the flight over that they'd try to fill the time with anxious small talk, but it was so natural, the words and silences too. It was a pleasant journey, unlike the previous two flights alone – at least until they hit the storm, the dry lightning, fields of white and blue around them; is this safe, is this critical, her eyes pleading with Maria, who she thought for a second was going to take her hand.

Civilians aren't supposed to come here. Everyone is clear on that. But Maria's connections put them on the monthly shuttle running food supplies and ferrying Cable International employees back from leave. CI are in everything. The pasta shortage is basically the fault of the same people who killed her sister. All Maria said, really, in Cape Town, standing in pre-flight, was not to expect too much, not to expect anything really. It would be naive to imagine they could get answers. It might seem sleepy and deserted but people knew that they were coming and they would be watching them. If they can find people to talk to, great. She doesn't actually think this is likely. She sees the visit as ceremonial. Leigh's body was to have come here. The capsule was to re-enter Earth in these same skies. That means something, that alone is reason enough to be here. And so they will take things slowly over the next two weeks, they will hire a car and explore, and walk, and maybe try to speak to some people, while hopefully not getting thrown off the island.

They go out for a brief shore walk, then they're back drinking at the motel, voices raised because nobody can hear them. The remains of their food are cooling in pots in the open kitchen, while they sit out on deckchairs watching the surf. The moon is down, dimming the stars. I can't remember the last time I did this, she says. Cheap brandy on the porch.

'Were you close to your sister?' Maria says. She doesn't like eye contact, she looks at the water.

'I never really know how to answer this,' she says. 'I know some siblings speak every day, wherever they are; they tell each other things no one else knows. We weren't like that. Sometimes we went months without talking. She was very private, self-sufficient. Kept her feelings to herself. Whereas if I have something to say, I just say it. Leigh could sometimes make things more complicated than they needed to be. That's not to say we didn't get on, though. Our accents came back, we used different words when we were together. She could be surprisingly good company. But there are limits, right? With family? A family is a group of strangers with a destructive desire for common nostalgia. We had privileged access to so much of each other's life, our early life in particular, but I'm not sure we ever really knew what to do with that. I'm not sure we ever really knew each other, in the end. God, I'm getting maudlin – is it the brandy?'

Maria smiles. 'I never had a sister, a brother,' she says. 'It was just me and Mom, growing up. She was always working, and I resented that. I never understood until later that she was doing it all for me.'

'Sounds lonely.'

'It was. But it made me the person I am, so it wouldn't make sense to regret it.'

'Were you close to her? To Uria?'

'I was pretty hard on her. I always told myself she was never there for me – it's like I needed the story, needed to feel I'd done this on my own. When she told me she couldn't see me during the pregnancy I think I enjoyed the confirmation, you know? Which was silly – it's not like it was her fault. You could tell how much it hurt her, how hard it was for her to tell me. She really wanted to be there for me – especially as I miscarried my first child. At four months. Mom was away then too, Kazakhstan. Took her three days to reach me at the hospital.'

'I'm sorry.'

'Yeah. I'm glad I saw her at the end, though. One last time. That she got to meet Lily-Anne. You should have seen her, she was so happy! They both were. And Lily wasn't normally like that with new people. She was a bit frosty, scoping you out. But not with Mom. She just knew. She was comfortable right away, giggling from the first minute. I was envious of your sister, did you know?'

'What?'

'When she was in California. Mom would visit and she would talk about this Dutch scientist, a prodigy, telling me all about her while I chopped vegetables and tried to get the dinner ready. I wished she could have spoken about *me* like that.'

'I bet she did. I bet she was proud.'

'Why?'

'Because they always are! It doesn't matter what we do.'

'I suppose you're right.'

'Did she tell you anything, when you saw her that last time, on the beach?'

'About the mission? Not really. There was an embargo on all that. Still, it's not like she had anything to fear from repercussions. But she was always a professional, always took so much pride in everything she did. She did tell me she spoke to the crew close to the end. It got harder with distance – it would take days for a message to arrive

– but she kept speaking. I'm sorry, this must be hard for you.'

'It's just that I know the messages are there, and I can't reach them. These are the last words Leigh said. Maybe there was something important there, something that was supposed to reach us. They would have known something was wrong, and this was their last chance to say something. I don't understand the secrecy, the denial. I don't blame your mother, I know this isn't her fault, but there's a cache of messages locked away somewhere, held in some data bank in a hollowed mountain, and I'm never going to hear them.'

'You don't know that. They're starting to make concessions; it's working. Seems to me you're getting somewhere – maybe allowing us to come here is the beginning. Maybe they'll finally release the full trove.'

'I guess. I mean, that would be nice. But I don't really think that's going to happen.'

'My mother received her diagnosis while *Proscenium* was mid-flight. So she was talking to the crew in the full knowledge that she didn't have long left. She wouldn't have said anything to them, about her illness. She would have made up something to explain her brief absence, and after treatment she'd have been right back in the control room as if nothing had happened.'

'They got on well, Leigh and Uria?'

'Uh-huh. I wonder if it was because they knew there was

a limit, there was always an end point. Like you got close, but without the responsibilities.'

'So they were using each other? Trying out a particular kind of relationship?'

'Maybe. Or we're overthinking. Perhaps they just enjoyed each other's company. It's not too hard to believe, is it?'

The next time she goes outside, she's better prepared. Light, thin clothing head to toe, with this ridiculous sunhat. Maria stayed in to catch up on sleep, but Helena is determined to get past the settlement and gain some perspective on this place.

As soon as she leaves the shade of the motel, the backs of her hands start to burn. She stretches the long sleeves down to the tips of her fingers. She appears to be the only person outside in the whole settlement, which is probably instructive. Sun breaking through the heat shield over the back of her neck. Keep walking, long clear strides. The motel sits on a field of hard black ash. She comes onto the single road intersecting Georgetown, and notes that every single building, including the Anglican church, has been prefabricated, fitted together like three-dimensional jigsaws from block pieces carried over the sea. The buildings are white, an assertion of confidence against the sterile black and red landscape. It's not convincing. The wood-block prefabs look like they'll barely last the year. They are loosely attached, not committed to the land. She leaves the settlement in minutes, still seeing not a single body. She finds shade behind the last of the buildings and makes an effort to see more widely, to judge what all this is set against. It is a strange sight. Spread around Georgetown is a series of cinder cones. Though it's predominantly red and black, there are blues and greens and yellows in the rock flow, which looks fresh, as if spilled from the earth's core yesterday. She recalls Maria telling her the island is less than a million years old. It's barely there, it's practically still erupting. She can hear the strain of the suspended flow; it's only loosely held together, this moment. It's moving all the time, stretching and creaking, over and underland. She watches the craters, fully expecting them to resume their detonation. The stone beds she stands on are whipped smooth, spectacular. The island is an explosion, and they are living on it, they are counting on it, as if it's nothing.

Ahead is a single road winding the narrow gap between the rock walls and the steep black beach dropping to the sea. The water is fizzing and frothing. She catches her breath, considers turning back, goes on. Hundreds of wire masts and transmission towers point forward to the horizon. There are warning signs stamped to pillars posted on the roadside saying it's not safe to approach. She feels a little dizzy, the air melting the untouched road. Not only has she not seen a single pedestrian, she hasn't seen any vehicles either. She feels they are concealed, they are watching her, pitying her, laughing at her. What does she hope to achieve here? She is only hurting herself.

She smells the opened, uncreated stone, the briny odour of giant crabs scuttling on the shore and the algae skimming the sea surface. She is light-headed, overheated; she feels reckless, without any understanding of her boundaries. She turns back. She's been gone at most an hour. Can't spend the next two weeks in bed with heat-stroke, first-degree burns. It is the fact that the silence feels so unnatural that surprises her. It shouldn't. It's the natural state. And yet she longs so much for something different that she ignores the warnings and steps off-road into the black boulders and goes right up to one of the masts just to hear the hum and crackle of its electricity. It is the most desolate place that she has ever known. No neighbouring land for thousands of miles. No way in or out, no right to reside here, you will not be born and you will not grow old and there is no accommodation of your death here, no structures in place to process the transition. Time on a human level doesn't exist, merely this antic geology, which forces people back inside their homes, their white prefab blocks, drinking sugar-tea and making light conversation and hiding from the terrifying rock as much as from the blinding sun.

———————

There are eleven tracking stations spread across the island, six of them in the east quarter, where the roads are poorer. They are autonomous, though as she peers through the fence she can see this station has two windows. Service staff, maintenance crew, cleaners sweeping up the ochre dust that still gets in despite the perfect seal, as if the building generates its own weather, its own decay. She waits at the fence for forty-five minutes, as if someone might come out and speak to her. They have sent emails, lodged official requests, knocked on doors. They have been on the island six days and she has inspected each of the eleven tracking stations and spent quite a bit of time with the construction crews dynamiting the red rock further inland. They don't know what it's a part of, what they're building. They're just blasting, levelling, laying down foundations. No one knows anything, not about what's happening today, and certainly not about what did or didn't happen thirteen years ago. Nothing endures, there is no organic continuity anywhere on the island.

Maria, driving back in the hire car, tells her this is not necessarily the case. There is a place, she says, in the centre – a mountain, a green mountain.

It isn't actually silent at all, you just need to listen more closely. Once you hear it, it never goes; it stays with you, torments you. It's the breaking water. It heaves onto the shore, beats the rock. There is no point on the island that releases you from the water, it is visible everywhere, slipping into you, setting your thoughts. At first she thought it was her: a reaction to the flight, a problem with her balance, a ringing in her ears. And she was amazed and practically burst out laughing when she found that it came from outside – was not, in fact, herself, but simply the island inside of her.

Maria drags her to Long Beach and they swim in the sea. At first she is embarrassed about her suit, the bald feel of it. She is no longer young. Maria hoots with laughter and rushes in. The cooler water slips all over her and she closes her eyes in pleasure. The body eased, soothed and carried in the upheaval. There is no one else; the car park is empty. The current is strong and the waves are getting higher, and she remembers something about an undertow, something Jerry said. Where is Maria? Suddenly her black swimming-cap reappears and Helena feels a moment of profound relief. Maria smiles. They are further from the shore than they had intended. They come back together, wading in, collapsing on the beach, the rise and fall of their chests, laughter in the baking heat with their bodies cast in sand.

FIVE

It's a miracle the weeds push up. Where is their sustenance, what are they feeding on? They see them only on the roads, by the mast towers, and on the airport runway where they landed. It is as if they thrive on provocation, rising up only when they have something to tear down. They are impish and morbid and embittered and they sort of love them. On the black rubble beaches, on the lower hillsides, they linger; they sit back, wait for the hubris of industry.

It's different when they get higher. They begin at a good pace which is acceptable given the total absence of vehicles. But they slow the hire car soon enough. They almost wish they could go back, do it again, see it all for the first time.

It's impossible to say when it begins. It must be gradual and incremental because you don't see it coming, don't realise until it's on top of you. There is green all around them, green moorside created out of vacuum, and with the windows open they feel the sudden breeze and the coolness, almost the cold of the air – which must be artificial, which can't be real, surely. There is a water-capture system, the micro-forest gathering moisture from passing clouds. There is a trickle-down effect, an exponential cascade, and suddenly there is verdancy. They are driving on hairpin roads barely 200 metres up, and they have been transported to a different country, a different continent, another world. They cannot hide their delight, they are like children. How can this be real? How can this be happening? They go slowly over the tufts of wild grass, the 90 per cent convincing agricultural landscape, but there is a thinness to it. Maybe, despite all the green blooming in a desert, it isn't actually a good thing. They are at the beginnings of the slope on a terraformed mountain, harvested from seedlings transported from five continents. They are still climbing. They have moved from desert to temperate high latitude to something akin to tropical wetland. There are lily pads and giant banana trees and vast tree-ferns drooping over the track and partially blocking the light. They cannot possibly be on the same island, the place of baking red rock.

They get out of the car. They walk for two hours to the summit, which transcends the tropical zone and repeats the lower mid-climate of waving grass and gentle, stirring breeze. They climb higher and higher until they get there, the single point on Ascension from which it's possible to see the ocean on all sides, the waves coming in, the entirety of the island, its masses of heaped, chaotic rock and rigid lines of prefabs. They can see dozens of miles of ocean. A vessel may suddenly appear, falling on the dip of the horizon. It is cold up here and as she shivers Maria comes closer and hugs her, brings her her warmth. This is a very strange place and she is not quite prepared for it. All of the world, all of the continents, all of history and prehistory here on Ascension, on the summit of Green Mountain. The wind stirs the ground and rushes them, and they are quite close to the edge. It is not necessarily safe here; they will have to come down.

Back, past the penultimate tropical zone, into the car again, down into the lower micro-temperature, she tells Maria to stop. Maria doesn't hear, she keeps driving. Stop, she says, louder. Go back. There's something there.

They turn the car around, back. 100 metres. There; there it is. Look.

They get out of the car. There is high grass and it's not quite warm and the wind is softer than at the summit. They get off-road and wade through it till they reach what Helena has seen from the car. A suggestion of a path, a faint break in the grasses. A donkey track, a goat path hundreds of years old, ancient steps still legible in the flowing green.

They walk through it as the path continues further inland. Sometimes they doubt it. Sometimes they are sure this is invention, really there is nothing there and if there is then it's the brief and temporary path they've carved in it themselves. Then, there is a break in the grass ahead; it's easier to make it out from a distance. There, ahead, protected by undergrowth, is a house.

'Come on,' she says.

There is a garden around the house, difficult to make out with the grass so overgrown. A wooden table and two benches looking out over the sea.

'Someone still cuts it,' Maria says. 'The grass level's different. Someone's still here.'

It's a nineteenth-century cottage, a long L with thick stone walls and oak sills. It's set alone here, the only house built on the whole mountain. There's no vehicle, no path made through the garden.

'Should we knock?' Helena says.

They approach the door. She lifts the heavy brass knocker three times. Everything seems still. Her eyes are drawn to the nearest window.

They listen. The windows are sealed shut. No boots on the steps, no obvious indentations in the grass except their own.

'Maybe I was wrong,' Maria says, turning away from the house, descending the first of three stone steps, 'maybe no one comes here. What are you doing?'

Helena presses firmly on the doorknob, twists it clockwise, and isn't in the least surprised when it gives.

'I don't think we should be doing this.'

There is a stale, musty odour on the threshold. It's gloomy inside from the coat of dust pressed up close against the windows. She steps in, covering her mouth with one hand. From behind, she hears Maria's feet on the steps.

The kitchen is long, with an unprotected wood floor and a table pressed against the wall facing the windows. She's getting used to the smell, and takes her hand off her mouth.

Maria is coughing behind her. She approaches the sink, and tries the tap. Nothing happens, but then she feels a pressure running through it and it sputters, emitting interrupted jets of murky brown water.

There's an empty drying rack. Above the sink to the left is an oak cabinet with brass handles. Inside, a collection of white plates and bowls each decorated with a thin maroon band. She takes one of the bowls and runs her finger through the dust. Then she returns it, closes the cupboard and turns towards the table. She's watching the table, imagining a family eating there, returning to it every morning and every evening. Right now, it seems the most remarkable thing in the world.

'Look,' Maria says. She's opened another set of cupboards. These cupboards are deeper, and inside is column after column of tinned soups, tinned mackerel and sardines, preserved meats, pineapples in water. 'There must be hundreds of these,' Maria says. The other cupboards are filled with dry foods too.

Helena pauses before pulling the handle on the tall fridge door, but it's empty, not connected to the supply.

The hall is made of wood too. It's partly this that she's smelling. There's something porous and wet here, as if the oak were still alive, still sap-full. There are five doors, each of which is ajar, and the only source of real light is from the kitchen. Her feet creak loudly on the boards.

The bedrooms are surprisingly large. The beds are made up, the sheets pulled tight across every mattress. In each room she puts her hand against the pillow, presses down. T-shirts and thick sweaters in the cupboards. Boots in three sizes. Identical sets of black trousers, socks, male and female underwear. Nothing appears touched. Maria's saying the place is abandoned. Maybe the family had to leave with little notice. Maybe it's a summer home.

She shakes her head. There are no families. Abandoned isn't the right word.

The living room is the darkest and softest, coated in the thickest dust. Throws over the sofa and the two chairs. Rugs on the floor. A bookcase and a wine rack. The wine looks expensive. The dust comes away on her fingers. 'Is this Cyrillic?' Maria says. It takes a moment to register. Helena stops. 'Let me see,' she says. She opens the books, presses the spines. Illustrations of cameras. A Bible. She opens every single book. Anthropology, astronomy, engineering. She keeps going, Maria watching her in silence. She knows she's looking for something. And she finds it. She breathes out. 'What is it?' Maria says. She steps back, sits on a sofa not intended for her but rather for her sister. A shelf full of marine microbiology.

'You know what this is,' she says, her lips trembling. 'This is for them. This is their house. This is where they were supposed to come back to.'

———————

They've walked through the tall grass and are sitting on the sturdy wooden benches by the table in the garden looking out over the sea. Maria is quiet, circumspect; body tight, chin tucked low. Helena is gesturing with her arms, but her voice is calm, clear, measured.

'You won't believe half the stuff. Crazy, ridiculous theories. There's a whole movement dedicated to proving it never happened, the crew never really left the ground. Others are convinced they crashed in the Atlantic, that Russian cargo picked them up. A church in Texas believes *Nereus*'s course is set for a distant star. The craft will return in 10,000 years, bringing with it the second incarnation of god.'

Maria rolls her eyes. 'I'm surprised you persisted. But I'm glad you did.'

'I am too. For a moment, you know, when I realised it was for them, I really thought she might be inside. That she was waiting for me. I thought we were going to walk into one of the bedrooms and find her there, asleep. I really did. And then I thought, as soon as she woke up, she would recognise me, and she would sit up again. She would talk to me as if she'd never been away.'

SIX

She can't sleep. She goes out, can hear Maria snoring softly as she passes her room. She barely recognises Georgetown by moonlight. The air is warm and thick and she's conscious of her breath. She sounds just like Leigh. She's becoming just like her. God, is that what all this is about, reviving her by becoming her?

She looks up. She has to look up. Breathe, breathe out. Leigh told her, on the deck of a small boat in Jakarta bay, on a night not so different from this, that when whales rise out of the water to gather breath they incidentally collect images – terrestrial and astronomical markers – that become essential in their long migrations. Breath is an opportunity, and whales registering constellations is no more outlandish than the language we carve from air. She smiles – Leigh's earnestness, god, it was relentless. But it was her. And was it a consolation to her, at the end – if she even had a moment to recognise it as the end? Did she see it coming, and did the animal world satisfy her, and not just console her, as she realised it was her last moment?

When they were kids, there was a period lasting about two years when they looked virtually identical. It's impossible to tell them apart in pictures. For those two years they were twinned. And then Leigh shot up, and they grew apart, Leigh very deliberately trying to be a model big sister, trying to protect her. But she didn't need protecting.

In truth, it was she who was the more typical elder sibling in their twenties, she who, whenever she visited Leigh's apartment, always spent time quietly cleaning up: the piled dishes, the grime embedded in the drying rack, the clutter of used packaging, supermarket receipts and old newspaper supplements massed over the circular kitchen table which looked too large, too ill-fitting for one person. When Leigh went out, or went to shower, or lay down in the other room, Helena would seize the opportunity to clean some more. The biggest challenge was the mugs – two, maybe three of them on the worktop, each carrying a desiccated and long-dead teabag. The rim of tannin inside showed how close to the top Leigh poured them. Like anyone who lived alone, a stream of hot drinks served as a kind of company, something to get up for and to sit down next to, something to do with your hands. A warmth. Walking into the room with the kettle boiling, as if someone else was there. Leigh brought out this appalling streak of sentiment in her. She left the place like this because she didn't even consider the possibility of people visiting, and because she naturally believed she didn't deserve any better.

One of the few times, maybe, that she had seen Leigh truly happy was over a dinner reservation in a port-side restaurant one evening, when they were still in their twenties; this would have been two or three years before Leigh moved to

California. Helena was on a short work visit and they only had a couple of hours. Something had happened to Leigh, and she was radiant. She had this easy smile, her arms moved rapidly above the table while she told story after story. She was at ease with herself, so alert and engaged that in comparison her usual demeanour seemed half asleep. Then she told her – she'd started seeing someone. She showed her a photo, coyly and nervously, excited. Leigh and Dana at a beach somewhere, wearing these stupid grins. Maybe this was it, she thought, later, waiting for the airport taxi; maybe all it took was Leigh meeting one person who told her she was good enough, and then that doubt and cynicism and lack of ease would be banished.

When she pictures her sister, she thinks of this face Leigh used to make, a kind of goofy, dorky expression: dropping her jaw, her mouth forming a tall circle, an oval almost. Close to a smile, an awkward look but full of pleasure, the expression of someone who is struggling to contain herself, someone who does not know what to do with delight, and is astonished while she carries it. Helena loves that look, that beautiful and ageless awkwardness, and she sees Leigh inhabiting it through their childhood, their time sharing the same room, their adolescence and their twenties. She wants Leigh to wear that expression always, to recast it through the whole of the past. Somewhere in that look – part of the awkwardness of it – is a recognition of family, the banal intimacy of being and having a sister. Maybe there was even pride in it; pride at being chosen as a sister, given a sister. She remembers Leigh quietly struggling to subdue this pride, this little bit of happiness in knowing they were together, partners in this story.

She's already onto the boulder field past the edge of the road, sloping to the sea. Something scuttles past her and she reels back, suddenly conscious of disturbing a place, a system, that is not for her. The crab is as large as her head, looks like something from a science-fiction movie. Thank god she's not in open-toes.

She goes back up the rocks, onto the soft and springy road, leaves the settlement, faces the cinder cones and the communication masts and moves on towards Long Beach. She walks quickly, and it's helping her, exorcising some of this tension, this horribly overwrought emotion. But she can't help it; passing the bend the settlement disappears and the waves are so much louder, and she wants to just give in, to collapse, to dissolve away into all that surrounds her, to let go.

She slips onto the beach, takes off her boots and socks, feels the first touch of lunar coolness in the damp sands. The waves are massing themselves, and when they finally break, a mile long, the sound is like canons firing. The sheer force of it takes her away. She doesn't know how long she gazes. She is awed and somehow frightened by it. What would happen if she got hurt? Or worse? If she went out into it and never came back?

She is eight, nine years old, sent to collect Leigh from a friend's for dinner, the end of another long summer day. She walks up the angled stone steps, guarded by iron railings, presses on the doorbell and waits. A message passed to Leigh inside, and she appears in the hallway. Patterned shorts and a light green T-shirt, hair tied back in a knot. Tall already, the impression of too-long limbs. Leigh is shocked in this moment – to be sought out, to be called like this. Leigh is almost proud of the attention, bewildered also by the unexpected appearance of her sister in this place. She walks uncertainly towards Helena in the doorway, the square concrete step guarded by the black iron railings over a 10-feet drop. Her surprise is quickly turning to something else – fear maybe, and anger.

'You have to come home,' Helena says. 'Dad wants you for dinner.'

'No,' Leigh says. Leigh is standing 3 feet from her, at least a whole head taller. She steps closer and then suddenly grabs Helena by the collar of her shirt. Helena struggles but can't get away. She's powerless and Leigh senses it. She's almost studying Helena, still holding her tightly by the collar; she looks beyond the railings to the grass below. Gently, softly, she raises Helena off the ground. She can't breathe. The moment stretches on, three, four seconds in suspension.

They are spiralling away together, into a different reality. And then it stops. Leigh releases her, letting go of her collar, and Helena drops back onto the concrete step. Leigh's mouth is hanging open, the pupils in her eyes are huge. She turns away. 'Let's go,' Leigh says quietly.

It's only a short walk back by the edge of the field, and it passes in silence. She is aware of Leigh watching her. She isn't sure what's happened but she wants to go home. When they reach the worn red gate by the hedge, Leigh stops; tries to say something, can't. They unlock the gate and step back into the garden.

She hasn't thought about this moment in more than thirty years. She doesn't recognise her sister at all. Leigh's surprise and pleasure as she realises her adeptness, her capacity for violence, the thrill of power over another who is small.

She can tell by the memory of her sister's expression that this happened once and never again. Leigh had seemed to completely lose control. Did she really think she was going to throw her over the railings?

She tries to think about what she might have done to provoke her, to turn Leigh suddenly into this other person, but all she'd done was pass on a message. There was nothing else, just this one simple message – *you have to come home*. Leigh grabbed her, hands on her collar, lifted her, a faraway look in her eyes. She didn't recognise her at all – she looked just like another person.

Later, when they were grown up, and Leigh, after drinking, alluded to something in their childhood, she was getting close to this – if not this moment exactly, then to its awful power and lack of control, its sense of arbitrary action and abandoned restraint.

She puts her head in her hands, rushes them through her hair. She walks closer to the shoreline, tentative to begin with, springing back when the first froth hits her feet, hurting the burns still lingering from the first day's walking. She hitches up her leggings beyond the knees. Soon the water's at her shins. She stands in a field of white constellations breaking and re-forming every second.

She looks into the sea ahead, and feels brief disorientation because she sees something inside it. Something through it. Something alive.

The first one falls, slaps onto the shallower water. It's black as the water and the sky, its oval shell 5 or 6 feet across. The wave breaks behind it and high water rushes it and for a moment it's gone. Then the water retreats, sucked back on the tide, and the animal resurfaces. It's not affected by what's around it; its progress is slow, inevitable. It's coming towards her; she steps back.

There is another. And another. She sees the whole wide arc of the beach, and the line of turtles slowly, painstakingly, deliberately marching onto it. She edges back through the sand, careful not to startle them. But they are oblivious to her anyway, their world entire. She feels the corners of her mouth stretching, her eyes widening to absorb as much light as possible. There are a dozen – more – fifteen, eighteen, twenty giant turtles slipping out of the water through the sand, held in a perfect parallel line as if connected by invisible tissue. They move with mechanical inevitability, rolling forward like tank treads. Lifting the bulk from below, tipping forward, using the momentum of the minor collapse as a motive force, a means of going on. She sees the tracks they're trailing through the wet sand, and as the falling wave reflects the moonlight sees, for a second, in perfect clarity, the curious, stately, ancient amphibious wisdom of 100-million-year-old eyes.

It's light when she wakes. She feels cold, and rubs her arms instinctively. The sky is pastel coloured, the waves low, distant. There is something moving in the sand 20 metres ahead. The last of the green turtles returning to sea. She gets to her feet, brushes the sand away, and sees the whole long beach studded with perforations, pits dug out by the birthing mothers. She looks out towards the water, shielding her eyes from the sun, and imagines the immense invisible journeys, circles drawn ceaselessly over the globe, the animals returning to the same place they were born.

Oceana

In order to create itself, life already has to exist. Cell theory is circular. Marine chemicals build a membrane that's a prerequisite for synthesising the chemicals needed to build a membrane. The end instigates a beginning. Cells produce the conditions essential for their own creation. Life is circular, atemporal. Every cell an instance of time travel.

We strap on EVAs, affix helmets, check oxygen, internal comms, prepare water and algae supplies. With deceleration levelled we drift in microgravity and prepare to enter Earth orbit. We open faceplates to move Tyler into his suit, talk to him, tell him he's going to be OK. His eyes acknowledge the pretence – he knows he'll never make it. I think of Teller, Jornada del Muerto, the Trinity test. The odds of total destruction then around the same as our own survival now. And is that finally what happened, I ask K, studying the dark expanse of Earth through the porthole, the sun glow over the far side of the inundated planet its only light.

K had seen Earth first as a faint light birthed from the sun. No bigger than a mark, a scuff, an imperfection in the fibreglass, but it's everything, everyone, all of the living and all of the dead. Animalia, Plantae, Protista. I laughed at the catastrophic brilliance of the thought. Somehow, impossibly, we were going home. From Mars onwards, Earth transformed into a blue star, ocean visible at 220 million miles. Blue hanging in outer darkness. Even then, there was something in K's eyes. He knew; he'd seen it in the outer planets. Something wasn't right. But he waited for me to see it for myself, past a moon that hung too close to its parent rock. Our home, our ocean planet, was entirely blue; a drowned globe, continents submerged, everything and everyone under.

'We go now,' he commands, and we carry our captain with us, drifting in low gravity, exiting berths and mid-deck for the final time. We pass through the garden, the crops still growing, where they'll continue to bloom after we're gone, until the ship is hauled into the atmosphere and plummets to the sea.

The re-entry capsule – oval shaped, little bigger than the cockpit of a commercial liner – is ready to go. On-board systems functional. K opens the hatch and we push Tyler gently before us, into the furthest of the high silicone seats modelled on no longer accurate body-casts. We strap the captain into place. He's breathing heavily and his pupils are darting wildly, as if he's trying to escape. K closes the hatch, locks it, reconfirms seal integrity. The space feels too small, helmets brushing the steel ceiling. The observation window shows only the surrounding white of the ship. The three of us seated against each other, strapped tightly at chest, hands, helmet and ankles, bracing for 11g. It's always worse on the way back in. Prepare yourself, think only of what's immediately in front of you. We were warned repeatedly against catastrophic overthinking. The priority is to keep yourself and your crewmates alive. 'Guess we don't have to worry about missing a water landing . . .' K's checking the displays, the fuel gauge, pressure reader, altitude control. 'Everything's good,' he says, through the headset. 'Ready to release?'

'Ready.'

'Ready to descend?'

'Ready.'

Our capsule detaches from the host ship, spins silently away. No sound when we drop into the black. Then the glare from the sun-glow rising on the planet's far rim floods through the observation window – our first direct light since Kourou – and strikes our faceplates, momentarily blinds us. First thing I see is Tyler's gentle smile, then *Nereus* distantly above, turning from us, slowly rotating. K initiates thrust and we lurch forward with violent force. Now Earth is pale blue, we're seeing over the other side, closer. Eyelids shut automatically and mouth creases in a permanent involuntary smile. Skin feels like it's tearing away. Arrowing towards exosphere, bracing for impact, pressure, unbearable heat. Breathing louder, intenser through headset. Earth still rolling, spinning, absence of infrastructure, of all internal light. The white wisps of cloud take greater shape. Don't think, don't grieve, slightest wayward step you'll never make it back. Want to see the others but can't turn neck, bolted in place against headrest. Force is greater, heat is gaining, Earth closer. Spinning wildly as we breach outermost layers of exosphere, altitude control failing. Edge of fire wraps our capsule, a sun around our ship, a torch to light us, burning through the composite heat-shields, metal peeling away, skin coming away, can't scream against this force, several minutes minimum until breaching the other side of thermal catastrophe, a fireball hurtling, a shooting star, a light, oval in my father's eyes, alarms screaming, smell of burning hair, flesh, bone to powder, must be my own or else helmet seal is broken, integrity gone, ocean veering, extinguishing the fire, not yet, veering and turning wildly, atmosphere thicker, torque failing, struggling to direct altitude control, already gone, cannot survive this, what then is this voice, the consciousness delay, slipping out extinguished body in final, prolonged sensitivity, endlessly reverberating thought, eternity of fire and g-force and this single impression. Suddenly there is a drop, a stillness, clarity, slowly dropping, parachute activated, atmosphere breached, and we are falling towards the ocean, so close, tears flooding out, smell of burned keratin, this is our arrival, this is the end

smell of burning but the air is cold. Fused steel and melted composite. Unstrap my hands, helmet still affixed in place. Breath too quick and loud, misting up faceplate. Tyler, K,

are you there? Can you hear me? Try looking out but can't
see through clouded plate. No light in capsule. Comms down,
systems failing. I listen. Something inside, surging, beating,
dying to get out. Slow the rhythm, condensation blocking
visibility. Wait to clear. Significant temperature variation.
Outer darkness not absolute. Observation window opaque,
but a light beyond. And a sound, and a movement in step. A
gentleness, swaying. A light surge, rocking the capsule.
Ocean current, surface waves. Everything returns.

The helmet keeps the head in place, as the suit holds the
body. Lack of feeling under gloves that move by themselves.
Wait it out, focus on the sway, the current. Stabilise heart
rate, temperature falls. Then the gloves lift, hold, find the
helmet lock, twist and lift again. Helmet bounces on the hard
floor. It is so cold. Like moisture on skin. My hair drips, my
breath a silver cloud in the capsule. I still can't see, light
opaque through the warped window composite. A light
beyond, a red haze seeping through. A bright green fuzz
across the floor. The containers opened in the fall, the crop
is everywhere. More of it than I ever imagined, a spread of
grass over the base and the wall panels attaching to the
ceiling even. Breathing in the bitter cold, the enveloping
odour – briny, fetid. The algae, the sea, our bodies. More
than one. I know. I'm not alone. Call out again, a gust of air,
K, Tyler, cloud of breath, are you there? I lift up neck, inhale,
prepare to turn – then stop suddenly, veer away. Close eyes,

push it away. Can't look. Wait it out, surging inside, dying inside, dying to get out. Try again. Opening my eyes, I twist right. Both faceplates are shattered, the blood congealed already. They are gone. There's green inside the blood, webbed lines reaching through. I unclip from the restraints, saying it isn't really them, my friends, my only companions, it's something else, it's more than them, and more than I am. I reach out from the tall seat and fall forward, hitting the facing panel on the other side. I wait, open my eyes, look in again through the smashed faceplates at what remains of my crewmates' sunken faces. The position of the algae is such that it appears to be reaching *out from inside*. Pulse check unnecessary, colour leached, already a hint of putrescence in the capsule air. Touch them. Hold their bodies. Fingers now cold under the gloves. No body warmth. Green shoots over EVAs. Carbs, proteins, fatty acids eaten as the green grows. I am a part of this too. Bodies consumed only by what exists inside the capsule. A body must eat itself. I reach back, pull back.

Air is getting weaker, bodies spilling, ongoing loss of oxygen. Algae should replenish air. Is there enough of the crop, how long till it recycles, exhales, transpires? Eating the same thing eating my friends. There is only so much water inside. The window is so twisted and melted I can see nothing beyond but the light, and the light is fading, the sun is going down over the ocean, over the earth.

———————

I need to get outside, air scrubbing is too slow. The hatch adjacent to the melted window is burned up and twisted and I don't know if I can get it open. Light again drifts past the window. How long have we been here, how many Earth days? The days are shorter, the moon too close. Enormous tides, waves defying credence. If only I could see this. Consume more food, gather energy, metabolism lagging behind earthspin. Green webs tearing through EVAs like lichen on coastal rock. Everything growing, everything spinning. EVA with purple cursive pointing backwards lists the name and birth date of my mother, father, sister. Hold my body. Looped, contradictory syntax. No belonging. No ownership, no body distinct. Suit's seal imperfect, integrity failed. Lift it off. Slough off the outer layer, a significant weight, colossal relief as it falls. Less of me, but I am not smaller. Further layers, base level gone, just skin remaining, exuviae lapping on the capsule floor. The thing surging is wilder and more electric closer to the outside. Straining eyes against the window, still nothing clear. Occasionally the whole capsule lifted by a rising wave. Light seeping through, light from beyond, sun high over the ocean, over the earth. It's time. I grip the hands of the bodies, say goodbye. Good luck, K says. Tyler nods, Godspeed, Leigh. Wrenching onto the hatch, I attach to the lever, fall down on it with all I have, less of me but not smaller, gravity, pressure of my body falling. The lever resists, resists, then gives finally, gently, and the capsule splits, opening onto the edge of outside, the edge of everything, everything beyond, wrenching open a hatch onto the outer world – chemical odour; stunning light; freezing temperature; too thin air – one breath inhaling Earth into boundlessness, openness, infinity. A part of the sea rises, leaps out in an arc and falls back in. A sound in the sky, from the red sun comes a second light, a gaining fireball, *Nereus* streaking through the upper sky at unbelievable speed. And everything is coming away, beginning again, the start of this long journey. One last look and I descend, I dive into ultramarine, everything coming away, falling and dissembling, hair and skin leaving phosphorescent trail, everything blending, merging, fruit opening, a billion seeds, in this last moment the water is no longer lifeless but life-filled, and I'm glad, at the end, to be a part of this, intermediate in this, glad that everything I've seen and done, everything I've felt will be continuous in this, generative and fertile in this flux, cycles of transformation, not ending but beginning, beginning again, as it always was and will be, new worlds in transformation, new eternities, new life, new—